Love and Life

An Old Story in Eighteenth Century Costume

by

Charlotte M. Yonge

Double 9
BOOKS

Love and Life
An Old Story in Eighteenth Century Costume
by Charlotte M. Yonge

Copyright © 2024

ISBN: 978-93-63055-16-2

Published by

DOUBLE 9 BOOKS
2/13-B, Ansari Road
Daryaganj, New Delhi – 110002
info@double9books.com
www.double9books.com
Tel. 011-40042856

This book is under public domain

ABOUT THE AUTHOR

Charlotte M. Yonge was an English novelist and historian, born on August 11, 1823, in Otterbourne, Hampshire, England. She is best known for her prolific writing career, which spanned over 60 years and produced more than 160 works, including novels, children's books, and historical studies. Yonge's writing was strongly influenced by her deep religious beliefs and her interest in history and education. Many of her novels, such as "The Heir of Redclyffe" and "Heartsease," explore moral and religious themes and are known for their wholesome and uplifting tone. She also wrote numerous works for children, including the popular "Book of Golden Deeds," which features stories of heroism and selflessness. In addition to her writing, Yonge was a prominent figure in the Church of England and was involved in various philanthropic and educational endeavours. She founded a school for girls in her hometown and was a supporter of the National Society for Promoting Religious Education. Yonge died on May 24, 1901, in Otterbourne, Hampshire, England. Her legacy as a writer and educator continues to be celebrated, and her works remain popular with readers today.

CONTENTS

PREFACE TO THE SECOND EDITION

The first edition of this tale was put forth without explaining the old fable on which it was founded—a fable recurring again and again in fairy myths, though not traceable in the classic world till a very late period, when it appeared among the tales of Apuleius, of the province of Africa, sometimes called the earliest novelist. There are, however, fragments of the same story in the popular tales of all countries, so that it is probable that Apuleius availed himself of an early form of one of these. They are to be found from India to Scandinavia, adapted to the manners and fancy of every country in turn, *Beauty and the Beast* and the *Black Bull of Norroway* are the most familiar forms of the tale, and it seemed to me one of those legends of such universal property that it was quite fair to put it into 18th century English costume.

Some have seen in it a remnant of the custom of some barbarous tribes, that the wife should not behold her husband for a year after marriage, and to this the Indian versions lend themselves; but Apuleius himself either found it, or adapted it to the idea of the Soul (the Life) awakened by Love, grasping too soon and impatiently, then losing it, and, unable to rest, struggling on through severe toils and labours till her hopes are crowned even at the gates of death. Psyche, the soul or life, whose emblem is the butterfly, thus even in heathen philosophy strained towards the higher Love, just glimpsed at for a while.

Christians gave a higher meaning to the fable, and saw in it the Soul, or the Church, to whom her Bridegroom has been for a while made known, striving after Him through many trials, to be made one with Him after passing through Death. The Spanish poet Calderon made it the theme of two sacred dramas, in which the lesson of Faith, not Sight, was taught, with special reference to the Holy Eucharist.

English poetry has, however, only taken up its simple classical aspect. In the early part of the century, Mrs. Tighe wrote a poem in Spenserian stanza, called *Psyche*, which was much admired at the time; and Mr. Morris has more lately sung the story in his *Earthly Paradise*. This must be my excuse for supposing the outline of the tale to be familiar to most readers.

The fable is briefly thus:—

Venus was jealous of the beauty of a maiden named Psyche, the youngest of three daughters of a king. She sent misery on the land and family, and caused an oracle to declare that the only remedy was to deck his youngest daughter as a bride, and leave her in a lonely place to become the prey of a monster. Cupid was commissioned by his mother to destroy her. He is here represented not as a child, but as a youth, who on seeing Psyche's charms, became enamoured of her, and resolved to save her from his mother and make her his own. He therefore caused Zephyr to transport her to a palace where everything delightful and valuable was at her service, feasts spread, music playing, all her wishes fulfilled, but all by invisible hands. At night in the dark, she was conscious of a presence who called himself her husband, showed the fondest affection for her, and promised her all sorts of glory and bliss, if she would be patient and obedient for a time.

This lasted till yearnings awoke to see her family. She obtained consent with much difficulty and many warnings. Then the splendour in which she lived excited the jealousy of her sisters, and they persuaded her that her visitor was really the monster who would deceive her and devour her. They thus induced her to accept a lamp with which to gaze on him when asleep. She obeyed them, then beholding the exquisite beauty of the sleeping god of love, she hung over him in rapture till a drop of the hot oil fell on his shoulder and awoke him. He sprang up, sorrowfully reproached her with having ruined herself and him, and flew away, letting her fall as she clung to him.

The palace was broken up, the wrath of Venus pursued her; Ceres and all the other deities chased her from their temples; even when she would have drowned herself, the river god took her in his arms, and laid her on the bank. Only Pan had pity on her, and counselled her to submit to Venus, and do her bidding implicitly as the only hope of regaining her lost husband.

Venus spurned her at first, and then made her a slave, setting her first to sort a huge heap of every kind of grain in a single day. The ants, secretly commanded by Cupid, did this for her. Next, she was to get a lock of golden wool from a ram feeding in a valley closed in by inaccessible rocks; but this was procured for her by an eagle; and lastly, Venus, declaring that her own beauty had been impaired by attendance on her injured son, commanded Psyche to visit the Infernal Regions and obtain from Proserpine a closed box of cosmetic which was on no account to be opened. Psyche thought death alone could bring her to these realms, and was about to throw herself from a tower, when a voice instructed her how to enter a cavern, and propitiate Cerberus with cakes after the approved fashion.

She thus reached Proserpine's throne, and obtained the casket, but when she had again reached the earth, she reflected that if Venus's beauty were impaired by anxiety, her own must have suffered far more; and the prohibition having of course been only intended to stimulate her curiosity, she opened the casket, out of which came the baneful fumes of Death! Just, however, as she fell down overpowered, her husband, who had been shut up by Venus, came to the rescue, and finding himself unable to restore her, cried aloud to Jupiter, who heard his prayer, reanimated Psyche, and gave her a place among the gods.

CHAPTER I
A SYLLABUB PARTY

Oft had I shadowed such a group
Of beauties that were born
In teacup times of hood and hoop,
And when the patch was worn;
And legs and arms with love-knots gay.
About me leaped and laughed
The modish Cupid of the day,
And shrilled his tinselled shaft. — *Tennyson.*

If times differ, human nature and national character vary but little; and thus, in looking back on former times, we are by turns startled by what is curiously like, and curiously unlike, our own sayings and doings.

The feelings of a retired officer of the nineteenth century expecting the return of his daughters from the first gaiety of the youngest darling, are probably not dissimilar to those of Major Delavie, in the earlier half of the seventeen hundreds, as he sat in the deep bay window of his bed-room; though he wore a green velvet nightcap; and his whole provision of mental food consisted of half a dozen worn numbers of the *Tatler*, and a *Gazette* a fortnight old. The chair on which he sat was elbowed, and made easy with cushions and pillows, but that on which his lame foot rested was stiff and angular. The cushion was exquisitely worked in chain-stich, as were the quilt and curtains of the great four-post bed, and the only carpeting consisted of three or four narrow strips of wool-work. The walls were plain plaster, white-washed, and wholly undecorated, except that the mantelpiece was carved with the hideous caryatides of the early Stewart days, and over it were suspended a long cavalry sabre, and the accompanying spurs and pistols; above them the miniature of an exquisitely lovely woman, with a white rose in her hair and a white favour on her breast.

The window was a deep one projecting far into the narrow garden below, for in truth the place was one of those old manor houses which their wealthy owners were fast deserting in favour of new specimens of classical architecture as understood by Louis XIV., and the room in which the Major sat was one of the few kept in habitable repair. The garden was rich with white pinks, peonies, lilies of the valley, and early roses, and there was a flagged path down the centre, between the front door and a wicket-gate into a long lane bordered with hawthorn hedges, the blossoms beginning to blush with the advance of the season. Beyond, rose dimly the spires and towers of a cathedral town, one of those county capitals to which the provincial magnates were wont to resort during the winter, keeping a mansion there for the purpose, and providing entertainment for the gentry of the place and neighbourhood.

Twilight was setting in when the Major began to catch glimpses of the laced hats of coachman and footmen over the hedges, a lumbering made itself heard, and by and by the vehicle halted at the gate. Such a coach! It was only the second best, and the glories of its landscape—painted sides were somewhat dimmed, the green and silver of the fittings a little tarnished to a critical eye; yet it was a splendid article, commodious and capacious, though ill-provided with air and light. However, nobody cared for stuffiness, certainly not the three young ladies, who, fan in hand, came tripping down the steps that were unrolled for them. The eldest paused to administer a fee to their entertainer's servants who had brought them home, and the coach rolled on to dispose of the remainder of the freight.

The father waved greetings from one window, a rosy little audacious figure in a night-dress peeped out furtively from another, and the house-door was opened by a tall old soldier-servant, stiff as a ramrod, with hair tightly tied and plastered up into a queue, and a blue and brown livery which sat like a uniform.

"Well, young ladies," he said, "I hope you enjoyed yourselves."

"Vastly, thank you, Corporal Palmer. And how has it been with my father in our absence?"

"Purely, Miss Harriet. He relished the Friar's chicken that Miss Delavie left for him, and he amused himself for an hour with Master Eugene, after which he did me the honour to play two plays at backgammon."

"I hope," said the eldest sister, coming up, "that the little rogue whom I saw peeping from the window has not been troublesome."

"He has been as good as gold, madam. He played in master's room till Nannerl called him to his bed, when he went at once, 'true to his orders,' says the master. 'A fine soldier he will make,' says I to my master."

Therewith the sisters mounted the uncarpeted but well-polished oak stair, knocked at the father's door, and entered one by one, each dropping her curtsey, and, though the eldest was five-and-twenty, neither speaking nor sitting till they were greeted with a hearty, "Come, my young maids, sit you down and tell your old father your gay doings."

The eldest took the only unoccupied chair, while the other two placed themselves on the window-seat, all bolt upright, with both little high heels on the floor, in none of the easy attitudes of damsels of later date, talking over a party. All three were complete gentlewomen in air and manners, though Betty had high cheek-bones, a large nose, rough complexion, and red hair, and her countenance was more loveable and trustworthy than symmetrical. The dainty decorations of youth looked grotesque upon her, and she was so well aware of the fact as to put on no more than was absolutely essential to a lady of birth and breeding. Harriet (pronounced Hawyot), the next in age, had a small well-set head, a pretty neck, and fine dark eyes, but the small-pox had made havoc of her bloom, and left its traces on cheek and brow. The wreck of her beauty had given her a discontented, fretful expression, which rendered her far less pleasing than honest, homely Betty, though she employed all the devices of the toilette to conceal the ravages of the malady and enhance her remaining advantages of shape and carriage.

There was an air of vexation about her as her father asked, "Well, how many conquests has my little Aurelia made?" She could not but recollect how triumphantly she had listened to the same inquiry after her own first appearance, scarcely three short years ago. Yet she grudged nothing to Aurelia, her junior by five years, who was for the first time arrayed as a full-grown belle, in a pale blue, tight-sleeved, long-waisted silk, open and looped up over a primrose skirt, embroidered by her own hands with tiny blue butterflies hovering over harebells. There were blue silk shoes, likewise home-made, with silver buckles, and the long mittens and deep lace ruffles were of Betty's fabrication. Even the dress itself had been cut by Harriet from old wedding hoards of their mother's, and made up after the last mode imported by Madam Churchill at the Deanery.

The only part of the equipment not of domestic handiwork was the structure on the head. The Carminster hairdresser had been making his rounds since daylight, taking his most distinguished customers last; and as the Misses Delavie were not high on the roll, Harriet and Aurelia had been under his hands at nine A.M. From that time till three, when the coach called for them, they had sat captive on low stools under a tent of table-cloth over tall chair-backs to keep the dust out of the frosted edifice constructed out of their rich dark hair, of the peculiar tint then called mouse-colour. Betty had refused to submit to this durance. "What sort of dinner would be on my father's table-cloth if I were to sit under one all day?" said she in answer to Harriet's representation of the fitness of things. "La, my dear, what matters it what an old scarecrow like me puts on?"

Old maidenhood set in much earlier in those days than at present; the sisters acquiesced, and Betty had run about as usual all the morning in her mob-cap, and chintz gown tucked through her pocket-holes, and only at the last submitted her head to the manipulations of Corporal Palmer, who daily powdered his master's wig.

Strange and unnatural as was the whitening of the hair, it was effective in enhancing the beauty of Aurelia's dark arched brows, the soft brilliance of her large velvety brown eyes, and the exquisite carnation and white of her colouring. Her features were delicately chiselled, and her face had that peculiar fresh, innocent, soft, untouched bloom and undisturbed repose which form the special charm and glory of the first dawn of womanhood. Her little head was well poised on a slender neck, just now curving a little to one side with the fatigue of the hours during which it had sustained her headgear. This consisted of a tiny flat hat, fastened on by long pins, and adorned by a cluster of campanulas like those on her dress, with a similar blue butterfly on an invisible wire above them, the dainty handiwork of Harriet.

The inquiry about conquests was a matter of course after a young lady's first party, but Aurelia looked too childish for it, and Betty made haste to reply.

"Aurelia was a very good girl. No one could have curtsied or bridled more prettily when we paid our respects to my Lady Herries and Mrs. Churchill, and the Dean highly commended her dancing."

"You danced? Fine doings! I thought you were merely invited to look on at the game at bowls. Who had the best of the match?"

"The first game was won by Canon Boltby, the second by the Dean," said Betty; "but when they would have played the conqueror, Lady Herries interfered and said the gentlemen had kept the field long enough, and now it was our turn. So a cow was driven on the bowling-green, with a bell round her neck and pink ribbons on her horns."

"A cow! What will they have next?"

"They say 'tis all the mode in London," interposed Harriet.

"Pray was the cow to instruct you in dancing?" continued the Major.

"No, sir," said Aurelia, whom he had addressed; "she was to be milked into the bowl of syllabub."

This was received with a great "Ho! ho!" and a demand who was to act as milker.

"That was the best of it," said Aurelia. "Soon came Miss Herries in a straw hat, and the prettiest green petticoat under a white gown and apron, as a dairy-maid, but the cow would not stand still, for all the man who led her kept scolding her and saying 'Coop! coop!' No sooner had Miss Herries seated herself on the stool than Moolly swerved away, and it was a mercy that the fine china bowl escaped. Every one was laughing, and poor Miss Herries was ready to cry, when forth steps my sister, coaxes the cow, bids the man lend his apron, sits down on the stool, and has the bowl frothing in a moment."

"I would not have done so for worlds," said Harriet; "I dreaded every moment to be asked where Miss Delavie learnt to be a milk-maid."

"You were welcome to reply, in her own yard," said Betty. "You may thank me for your syllabub."

"Which, after all, you forbade poor Aura to taste!"

"Assuredly. I was not going to have her turn sick on my hands. She may think herself beholden to me for her dance with that fine young beau. Who was he, Aura?"

"How now!" said the Major, in a tone of banter, while Harriet indulged in a suppressed giggle. "You let Aura dance with a stranger! Where was your circumspection, Mrs. Betty?" Aurelia coloured to the roots of her hair and faltered, "It was Lady Herries who presented him."

"Yes, the child is not to blame," said Betty; "I left her in charge of Mrs. Churchill while I went to wash my hands after milking the cow, which these fine folk seemed to suppose could be done without soiling a finger."

"That's the way with Chloe and Phyllida in Arcadia," said her father.

"But not here," said Betty. "In the house, I was detained a little while, for the housekeeper wanted me to explain my recipe for taking out the grease spots."

"A little while, sister?" said Harriet. "It was through the dancing of three minuets, and the country dance had long been begun."

"I was too busy to heed the time," said Betty, "for I obtained the recipe for those delicious almond-cakes, and showed Mrs. Waldron the Vienna mode of clearing coffee. When I came back the fiddles were playing, and Aurelia going down the middle with a young gentleman in a scarlet coat. Poor little Robert Rowe was too bashful to find a partner, though he longed to dance; so I made another couple with him, and thus missed further speech, save that as we took our leave, both Sir George and the Dean complimented me, and said what there is no occasion to repeat just now, sir, when I ought to be fetching your supper."

"Ha! Is it too flattering for little Aura?" asked her father. "Come, never spare. She will hear worse than that in her day, I'll warrant."

"It was merely," said Betty, reluctantly, "that the Dean called her the star of the evening, and declared that her dancing equalled her face."

"Well said of his reverence! And his honour the baronet, what said he?"

"He said, sir, that so comely and debonnaire a couple had not been seen in these parts since you came home from Flanders and led off the assize ball with Mistress Urania Delavie."

"There, Aura, 'tis my turn to blush!" cried the Major, comically hiding his face behind Betty's fan. "But all this time you have never told me who was this young spark."

"That I cannot tell, sir," returned Betty. "We were sent home in the coach with Mistress Duckworth and her daughters, who talked so incessantly that we could not open our lips. Who was he, Aura?"

"My Lady Herries only presented him as Sir Amyas, sister," replied Aurelia.

"Sir Amyas!" cried her auditors, all together.

"Nothing more," said Aurelia. "Indeed she made as though he and I must be acquainted, and I suppose that she took me for Harriet, but I knew not how to explain."

"No doubt," said Harriet. "I was sick of the music and folly, and had retired to the summerhouse with Peggy Duckworth, who had brought a sweet sonnet of Mr. Ambrose Phillips, 'Defying Cupid.'"

Her father burst into a chuckling laugh, much to her mortification, though she would not seem to understand it, and Betty took up the moral.

"Sir Amyas! Are you positive that you caught the name, child?"

"I thought so, sister," said Aurelia, with the insecurity produced by such cross-questioning; "but I may have been mistaken, since, of course, the true Sir Amyas Belamour would never be here without my father's knowledge."

"Nor is there any other of the name," said her father, "except that melancholic uncle of his who never leaves his dark chamber."

"Depend upon it," said Harriet, "Lady Herries said Sir Ambrose. No doubt it was Sir Ambrose Watford."

"Nay, Harriet, I demur to that," said her father drolly. "I flatter myself I was a more personable youth than to be likened to Watford with his swollen nose. What like was your cavalier, Aura?"

"Indeed, sir, I cannot describe him. I was so much terrified lest he should speak to me that I had much ado to mind my steps. I know he had white gloves and diamond shoe-buckles, and that his feet moved by no means like those of Sir Ambrose."

"Aura is a modest child, and does credit to her breeding," said Betty. "Thus much I saw, that the young gentleman was tall and personable enough to bear comparison even to you, sir, not more than nineteen or twenty years of age, in a laced scarlet uniform, as I think, of the Dragoon Guards, and with a little powder, but not enough to disguise that his hair was entire gold."

"That all points to his being indeed young Belamour," said her father; "age, military appearance, and all—I wonder what this portends!"

"What a disaster!" exclaimed Harriet, "that my sister and I should have been out of the way, and only a chit like Aura be there to be presented to him."

"If young ladies *will* defy Cupid," began her father;—but at that moment Corporal Palmer knocked at the door, bringing a basin of soup for his master, and announcing "Supper is served, young ladies."

Each of the three bent her knee to receive her father's blessing and kiss, then curtseying at the door, departed, Betty lingering behind her two juniors to see her father taste his soup and to make sure that he relished it.

CHAPTER II
THE HOUSE OF DELAVIE

All his Paphian mother fear;
Empress! all thy sway revere!
EURIPEDES (Anstice).

The parlour where the supper was laid was oak panelled, but painted white. Like a little island in the vast polished slippery floor lay a square much-worn carpet, just big enough to accommodate a moderate-sized table and the surrounding high-backed chairs. There was a tent-stitch rug before the Dutch-tiled fireplace, and on the walls hung two framed prints,—one representing the stately and graceful Duke of Marlborough; the other, the small, dark, pinched, but fiery Prince Eugene. On the spotless white cloth was spread a frugal meal of bread, butter, cheese, and lettuce; a jug of milk, another of water, and a bottle of cowslip wine; for the habits of the family were more than usually frugal and abstemious.

Frugality and health alike obliged Major Delavie to observe a careful regimen. He had served in all Marlborough's campaigns, and had afterwards entered the Austrian army, and fought in the Turkish war, until he had been disabled before Belgrade by a terrible wound, of which he still felt the effects. Returning home with his wife, the daughter of a Jacobite exile, he had become a kind of agent in managing the family estate for his cousin the heiress, Lady Belamour, who allowed him to live rent-free in this ruinous old Manor-house, the cradle of the family.

This was all that Harriet and Aurelia knew. The latter had been born at the Manor, and young girls, if not brought extremely forward, were treated like children; but Elizabeth, the eldest of the family, who could remember Vienna, was so much the companion and confidante of her father, that she was more on the level of a mother than a sister to her juniors.

"Then you think Aurelia's beau was really Sir Amyas Belamour," said Harriet, as they sat down to supper.

"So it appears," said Betty, gravely.

"Do you think he will come hither, sister? I would give the world to see him," continued Harriet.

"He said something of hoping for better acquaintance," softly put in Aurelia.

"Oh, did he so?" cried Harriet. "For demure as you are, Miss Aura, I fancy you looked a little above the diamond shoe-buckles!"

"Fie, Harriet!" exclaimed Betty; "I will not have the child tormented. He ought to come and pay his respects to my father."

"Have you ever seen my Lady?" asked Aurelia.

"That have I, Miss Aurelia," interposed Corporal Palmer, "and a rare piece of beauty she would be, if one could forget the saying 'handsome is as handsome does.'"

"I never knew what she has done," said Aurelia.

"'Tis a long story," hastily said Betty, "too long to tell at table. I must make haste to prepare the poultice for my father."

She quickly broke up the supper party, and the two younger sisters repaired to their chamber, both conscious of having been repressed; the one feeling injured, the other rebuked for forwardness and curiosity. The three sisters shared one long low room with a large light closet at each end. One of these was sacred to powder, the other was Betty's private property. Harriet had a little white bed to herself, Betty and Aurelia nightly climbed into a lofty and solemn structure curtained with ancient figured damask. Each had her own toilette-table and a press for her clothes, where she contrived to stow them in a wonderfully small space.

Harriet and Aurelia had divested themselves of their finery before Betty came in, and they assisted her operations, Harriet preferring a complaint that she never would tell them anything.

"I have no objection to tell you at fitting times," said Betty, "but not with Palmer putting in his word. You should have discretion, Harriet."

"The Dean's servants never speak when they are waiting at table," said Harriet with a pout.

"But I'll warrant them to hear!" retorted Betty.

"And I had rather have our dear old honest corporal than a dozen of those fine lackeys," said Aurelia. "But you will tell us the story like a good sister, while we brush the powder out of our hair."

They put on powdering gowns, after releasing themselves from the armour of their stays, and were at last at ease, each seated on a wooden chair in the powdering closet, brush in hand, with a cloud of white dust flying round, and the true colour of the hair beginning to appear.

"Then it is indeed true that My Lady is one of the greatest beauties of Queen Caroline's Court, if not the greatest?" said Harriet.

"Truly she is," said Betty, "and though in full maturity, she preserves the splendour of her prime."

"Tell us more particularly," said Aurelia; "can she be more lovely than our dear mamma?"

"No, indeed! lovely was never the word for her, to my mind," said Betty; "her face always seemed to me more like that of one of the marble statues I remember at Vienna; perfect, but clear, cold, and hard. But I am no judge, for I did not love her, and in a child, admiration accompanies affection."

"What did Palmer mean by 'handsome is that handsome does'? Surely my father never was ill-treated by Lady Belamour?"

"Let me explain," said the elder sister. "The ancient custom and precedent of our family have always transmitted the estates to the male heir. But when Charles II. granted the patent of nobility to the first Baron Delavie, the barony was limited to the heirs male of his body, and out grandfather was only his brother. The last Lord had three sons, and one daughter, Urania, who alone survived him."

"I know all that from the monument," said Aurelia; "one was drowned while bathing, one died of spotted fever, and one was killed at the battle of Ramillies. How dreadful for the poor old father!"

"And there is no Lord Delavie now," said Harriet. "Why, since my Lady could not have the title, did it not come to our papa?"

"Because his father was not in the patent," said Betty. "However, it was thought that if he were married to Mistress Urania, there would be a fresh creation in their favour. So as soon as the last campaign was over, our father, who had always been a favourite at the great house, was sent for from the army, and given to understand that he was to conduct his courtship, with the cousin he had petted as a little child, as speedily as was decorous. However, in winter quarters at Tournai he had already pledged his faith to the daughter of a Scottish gentleman in the Austrian service. This engagement was viewed by the old Lord as a trifling folly, which might be set aside by the head of the family. He hinted that the proposed match was by no means disagreeable to his daughter, and scarcely credited his ears when his young kinsman declared his honour forbade him to break with Miss Murray."

"Dear father," ejaculated Aurelia, "so he gave up everything for her sake?"

"And never repented it!" said Betty.

"Now," said Harriet, "I understand why he entered the army."

"It was all he had to depend on," said Betty, "and he had been favourably noticed by Prince Eugene at the siege of Lisle, so that he easily obtained a commission. He believed that though it was in the power of the old Lord to dispose of part of his estates by will, yet that some of the land was entailed in the male line, so that there need not be many years of campaigning or poverty for his bride, even if her father never were restored to his Scottish property. As you know, our grandfather, Sir Archibald Murray, died for his loyalty in the rising of '15, and two years later our father received at Belgrade that terrible wound which closed his military career. Meantime, Urania had married Sir Jovian Belamour, and Lord Delavie seemed to have forgotten my father's offence, and gave him the management of the estate, with this old house to live in, showing himself glad of the neighbourhood of a kinsman whom he could thoroughly trust. All went well till my Lady came to visit her father. Then all old offences were renewed. Lady Belamour treated my mother as a poor dependant. She, daughter to a noble line of pedigree far higher than that of the Delavies, might well return her haughty looks, and would not yield an inch, nor join in the general adulation. There were disputes about us children. Poor Archie was a most beautiful boy, and though you might not suppose it, I was a very pretty little girl, this nose of mine being then much more shapely than the little buttons which grow to fair proportions. On the other hand, the little Belamours were puny and sickly; indeed, as you know, this young Sir Amyas, who was not then born, is the only one of the whole family who has been reared. Then we had been carefully bred, could chatter French, recite poetry, make our bow and curtsey, bridle, and said Sir and Madam, while the poor little cousins who had been put out to nurse had no more manners than the calves and pigs. People were the more flattering to us because they expected soon to see my father in his Lordship's place; and on the other hand, officious tongues were not wanting to tell my Lady how Mrs. Delavie contrasted the two sets of children. Very bitter offence was taken; nor has my Lady ever truly forgiven, whatever our dear good father may believe. When the old Lord died, a will was found, bequeathing all his unentailed estates to his daughter, and this was of course strong presumption that he believed in the existence of a deed of entail; but none could ever be found, and the precedents were not held to establish the right."

"Did he leave my father nothing?" asked Harriet.

"He left him three hundred pounds and made him joint executor with Sir Jovian. There was no mention of this house, which was the original house of the family, the first Lord having built the Great House; and both my father and Sir Jovian were sure the Lord Delavie believed it would come to him; but no proofs were extant, and my Lady would only consent to his occupying it, as before, as her agent."

"I always knew we were victims to an injustice," said Harriet, "though I never understood the matter exactly."

"You were a mere child, and my father does not love to talk of it. He ceased to care much about the loss after our dear Archie died."

"Not for Eugene's sake?"

"Eugene was not born for two years after Archie's death. My dear mother had drooped from the time of the disappointment, blaming herself for having ruined my father, and scarce accepting comfort when he vowed that all was well lost for her sake. She reproached herself with having been proud and unconciliatory, though I doubt whether it made much difference. Then her spirit was altogether crushed by the loss of Archie, she never had another day's health. Eugene came to her like Ichabod to Phinehas' wife, and she was soon gone from us," said Betty, wiping away a tear.

"Leaving us a dear sister to be a mother to us," said Aurelia, raising her sweet face for a kiss.

Harriet pondered a little, and said, "My Lady is not at enmity with us, since my father keeps the house and agency."

"We should be reduced to poverty indeed without them," said Betty; "and Sir Jovian, an upright honourable man, the only person whom my Lady truly respected, insisted on his continuance. As long as my Lady regards his memory we are safe, but no one can trust to her caprice."

"She never comes here, nor disturbs my father."

"No, but she makes heavy calls on the estate, and is displeased if he refuses to overpress the tenants or hesitates to cut the timber."

"I have heard say," added Harriet, "that her debts in town and her losses at play drove her to accept her present husband, Mr. Wayland, a hideous old fellow, who had become vastly rich through some discovery about cannon."

"He is an honourable and upright man," said Betty. "I should have fewer anxieties if he had not been sent out to Gibraltar and Minorca to superintend the fortifications."

"Meantime my Lady makes the money fly, by the help of the gallant Colonel Mar," said Harriet lightly.

"Fie! Harriet!" returned the elder sister; "I have allowed you too far. My father calls Lady Belamour his commanding officer, and permits no scandal to be spoken of her."

"Any more than of Prince Eugene?" said Harriet, laughing.

"But oh! sister!" cried Aurelia, "let us stay a little longer. I have not half braided my hair, and I long to hear who is the gentleman of whom my father spoke as living in the dark."

"Mr. Amyas Belamour! Sir Jovian's brother! Ah! that is a sad story," replied Betty, "though I am not certain that I have it correctly, having only heard it discussed between my father and mother when I was a growing girl, sitting at my sampler. I think he was a barrister; I know he was a very fine gentleman and a man of parts, who had made the Grand Tour; for when he was staying at the Great House, he said my mother was the only person he met who could converse with him on the Old Masters, or any other subject of *virtu*, and that, being reported to my Lady, increased her bitterness all the more because Mr. Belamour was a friend of Mr. Addison and Sir Richard Steele, and had contributed some papers to the *Spectator*. He was making a good fortune in his profession, and had formed an engagement with a young lady in Hertfordshire, of a good old family, but one which had always been disliked by Lady Belamour. It is said, too, that Miss Sedhurst had been thought to have attracted one of my Lady's many admirers, and that the latter was determined not to see her rival become her sister-in-law, and probably with the same title, since Mr. Belamour was on the verge of obtaining knighthood. So, if she be not greatly belied, Lady Belamour plied all parties with her confidences, till she contrived to breed suspicion and jealousy on all sides, until finally Miss Sedhurst's brother, a crack-brained youth, offered such an insult to Mr. Belamour, that honour required a challenge. It was thought that as Mr. Belamour was the superior in age and position, the matter might have been composed, but the young man was fiery and hot tempered, and would neither retract nor apologise; and Mr. Belamour had been stung in his tenderest feeling. They fought with pistols, an innovation that, as you know, my father hates, as far more deadly and unskilful than the noble practice of fencing; and the result was that Mr. Sedhurst was shot dead, and Mr. Belamour received a severe wound in the head. The poor young lady, being always of a delicate constitution, fell into fits on hearing the news, an died in a few weeks. The unfortunate Mr. Belamour survives, but whether from injury to the brain, or from grief and remorse, he has never been able to endure either light or company, but has remained ever since in utter darkness and seclusion."

"Utter darkness! How dreadful!" cried Aurelia, shuddering.

"How long has this been, sister?" inquired Harriet.

"About nine years," said Betty. "The lamentable affair took place just before Sir Jovian's death, and the shock may have hastened it, for he had long been in a languishing state. It was the more unfortunate, since he had made Mr. Belamour sole personal guardian to his only surviving son, and appointed him, together with my father and another gentleman, trustee for the Belamour property; and there has been much difficulty in consequence of his being unable to act, or to do more than give his signature."

"Ah! sister, I wish you had not told me," said Aurelia. "I shall dream of the unfortunate gentleman all night. Nine years of utter darkness!"

"We know who is still child enough to hate darkness," said Harriet.

"Take care," said Betty. "You must make haste, or I shall leave you to it."

CHAPTER III
AMONG THE COWSLIPS

The insect youth are on the wing,
Eager to taste the honeyed spring,
And float amid the liquid noon,
Some lightly on the torrent skim,
Some show their gaily gilded trim,
Quick glancing to the sun. —GRAY

Though hours were early, the morning meal was not served till so late as really to deserve the title of breakfast.

When the three sisters sat down at nine-o'clock, in mob caps, and the two younger in white dresses, all had been up at least two hours. Aurelia led forward little Eugene in a tailed red coat, long-breasted buff waistcoat, buff tights and knitted stockings, with a deep frilled collar under the flowing locks on his shoulders, in curls which emulated a wig. She had been helping him to prepare "his tasks" from the well-thumbed but strongly-bound books which had served poor Archie before him. They were deposited on the window-seat to wait till the bowls of bread and milk were discussed, since tea and coffee were only a special afternoon treat not considered as wholesome for children; so that Aurelia had only just been promoted to them, along with powder and fan.

Harriet wore her favourite pistachio ribbon round her cap and as a breast-knot, and her cheeks bore token of one of the various washes with which she was always striving to regain the smoothness of her complexion. Knowing what this betokened, an elder-sisterly instinct of caution actuated Betty to remind her juniors of an engagement made with Dame Jewel of the upland farm for the exchange of a setting of white duck's eggs for one of five-toed fowls, and to request them to carry the basket.

Eugene danced on his chair and begged to be of the party; but Harriet pouted, and asked why the "odd boy" could not be sent.

"Because, as you very well know, if he did not break, he would addle, every egg in the basket.

"There can be no need to go to-day."

"The speckled hen is clocking to brood, and she is the best mother in the yard. Besides, it is time that the cowslip wine were made, and I will give you some bread and cheese and gingerbread for noonchin, so that you may fill your baskets in the meadows before they are laid up for grass. Mrs. Jewel will give you a drink of milk."

"O let me go, sister!" pleaded Eugene. "She gives us bread and honey! And I want to hear the lapwings in the meadows cry pee-wit."

"We shall have you falling into the river," said Harriet, rather fretfully.

"No, indeed! If you fall in, I will pull you out. Young maids should not run about the country without a gentleman to take care of them. Should they, sister?" cried the doughty seven years' old champion.

"Who taught you that, sir?" asked Betty, trying to keep her countenance.

"I heard Mrs. Churchill say so to my papa," returned the boy. "So now, there's a good sister. Do pray let me go!"

"If you say your tasks well, and will promise to be obedient to Harriet and to keep away from the river, and not touch the basket of eggs."

Eugene was ready for any number of promises; and Harriet, seeing there was no escape for her, went off with Aurelia to put on their little three-cornered muslin handkerchiefs and broad-brimmed straw hats, while Eugene repeated his tasks, namely, a fragment of the catechism, half a column of spelling from the *Universal Spelling-Book*, and (Betty's special pride) his portion of the *Orbis Sensualium Pictus* of Johannes Amos Comenius, the wonderful vocabulary, with still more wonderful "cuts," that was then the small boys path to Latinity.

The Eagle, *Aquila*, the King of Birds, *Rex Avium*, looketh at the Sun, *intuetur Solem*, as indeed he could hardly avoid doing, since in the "cut" the sun was within a hairsbreath of his beak, while his claws were almost touching a crow (*Corvus*) perched on a dead horse, to exemplify how *Aves Raptores* fed on carrion.

Thanks to Aurelia's private assistance, Eugene knew his lessons well enough for his excitement not to make him stumble so often as to prevent Betty's pronouncing him a good boy, and dispensing with his copy, sum, piece, and reading, until the evening. These last were very tough affairs, the recitation being from Shakespeare, and the reading from the *Spectator*. There were no children's books, properly so called, except the ballads, chap-books brought round by pedlers, often far from edifying, and the plunge from the horn-book into general literature was, to say the least of it, bracing.

The Delavie family was cultivated for the time. French had been brought home as a familiar tongue, though *Telemaque*, Racine, and *Le Grand Cyrus* were the whole library in that language; and there was not another within thirty miles. On two days in the week the sisters became Mesdemoiselles Elisabeth, Henriette, and Aurelie, and conversed in French over their spinning, seams, lace, or embroidery; nor was Aurelia yet emancipated from reciting Racine on alternate days with Milton and Shakespeare.

Betty could likewise talk German with the old Austrian maid, Nannerl, who had followed the family from Vienna; but the accomplishment was not esteemed, and the dialect was barbarous. From the time of her mother's death, Betty had been a strict and careful, though kind, ruler to her sisters; and the long walk was a greater holiday to Aurelia than to Eugene, releasing her from her book and work, whereas he would soon have been trundling his hoop, and haunting the steps of Palmer, who was gardener as well as valet, butler, and a good deal besides, and moreover drilled his young master. Thus Eugene carried his head as erect as any Grenadier in the service, and was a thorough little gentleman in miniature; a perfect little beau, as his sisters loved to call the darling of their hearts and hopes.

Even Harriet could not be cross to him, though she made Aurelia carry the eggs, and indulged in sundry petulant whisks of the fan which she carried by way of parasol. "Now, why does Betty do this?" she exclaimed, as soon as they were out of hearing. "Is it to secure to herself the whole enjoyment of your beau?"

"You forget," said Aurelia. "You promised to fetch the eggs, when we met Mrs. Jewel jogging home from market on her old blind white horse last Saturday, because you said no eggs so shaken could ever be hatched."

"You demure chit!" exclaimed Harriet; "would you make me believe that you have no regrets for so charming a young gentleman, my Lady's son and our kinsman."

"If he spoke to me I should not know how to answer. And then you would blame my rudeness. Besides," she added, with childish sagacity, "he can be nothing but a fine London macaroni. Only think of the cowslips! A whole morning to make cowslip balls," she added with a little frisk. "I would not give one for all the macaronies in England, with their powder and their snuff-boxes. Faugh!"

"Ah, child, you will sing another note perhaps when it is too late," said her sister, with a sigh between envy and compassion.

It floated past Aurelia unheeded, as she danced up one side of a stile, and sprang clear down into a green park, jumped Eugene down after her by both hands, and exclaimed, "Harriet is in her vapours; come, let us have a race!"

She was instantly careering along like a white butterfly in the sunshine, flitting on as the child tried to catch her, among the snowy hawthorn bushes, or sinking down for very joy and delight among the bank of wild hyacinths. Life and free motion were joy and delight enough for that happy being with her childish heart, and the serious business of the day was all delight. There lay the rich meadows basking in the sun, and covered with short grass just beginning its summer growth, but with the cowslips standing high above it; hanging down their rich clusters of soft, pure, delicately-scented bells, from their pinky stems over their pale crinkled leaves, interspersed here and there with the deep purple of the fool's orchis, and the pale brown quiver-grass shaking out its trembling awns on their invisible stems. No flower is more delightful to gather than the cowslip, fragrant as the breath of a cow. And Aurelia darted about, piling the golden heap in her basket with untiring enjoyment; then, producing a tape, called on Harriet, who had been working in a more leisurely fashion, to join her in making a cowslip ball, and charged Eugene not to nip off the heads too short.

The sweet, soft, golden globe was made, and even Harriet felt the delicious intoxication. The young things tossed it aloft, flung from one to the other, caught it, caressed it, buried their faces in it, and threw it back with shrieks of glee.

Suddenly Harriet checked her sister with a peremptory sign. She heard horse-hoofs in the lane, divided from the field by a hedge of pollard willows, so high that she had never thought of being overlooked, till the cessation of the trotting sound struck her; and looking round she saw that a horseman had halted at the gate, and was gazing at their sports. It was from the distance of a field, but this was enough to fill Harriet with dismay. She drew herself up in a moment, signing peremptorily to Aurelia, who was flying about, her hat off, her one long curl streaming behind as she darted hither and thither, evading Eugene who was pursuing her.

As she paused, and Eugene clutched her dress with a shout of ecstasy, Harriet came up, glancing severely toward the gate, and saying, as she handed her sister the hat, "This comes of childishness! That we should be seen thus! What a hoyden he will think you!" as the hoofs went on and the red coat vanished.

"He! Who? Not the farmer?" said Aurelia. "This is not laid up for hay."

"No indeed. I believe it is he," said Harriet, mysteriously.

"He?" repeated Aurelia. "Not Mr. Arden, for he would be in black," and at Harriet's disgusted gesture, "I beg your pardon, but I did not know you had a new *he*. Oh! surely you are not thinking of the young baronet?"

"I am sure it was his figure."

"You did not see him yesterday?"

"No, but his air had too much distinction for any one from these parts."

"Could you see what his air was from this distance? I should never have guessed it, but you have more experience, being older. Come, Eugene, another race!"

"No, I will have no more folly. I was too good-natured to allow it. I am vexed beyond measure that he should have seen such rusticity."

"Never mind, dear Harriet. Most likely it was no such person, for it was not well-bred to sit staring at us; and if it were he, you were not known to him."

"You were."

"Then he must have eyes as sharp as yours are for an air of distinction. Having only seen me in my blue and primrose suit, how should he know me in my present trim? Besides, I believe it was only young Dick Jewel in a cast coat of Squire Humphrey's."

The charm of the cowslip gathering was broken. Eugene found himself very hungry, and the noonchin was produced, after which the walk was continued to the farm-house, where the young people were made very welcome.

Farmers were, as a rule, more rustic than the present labourer, but they lived a life of far less care, if of more toil, than their successors, having ample means for their simple needs, and enjoying jocund plenty. The clean kitchen, with the stone floor, the beaupot of maythorn on the empty hearth, the shining walnut-wood table, the spinning-wheel, wooden chairs, and forms, all looked cool and inviting, and the visitors were regaled with home-made brown bread, delicious butter and honey, and a choice of new milk, mead, and currant wine.

Dame Jewel, in a white frill under a black silken hood, a buff turnover kerchief, stout stuff gown and white apron, was delighted to wait on them; and Eugene's bliss was complete among the young kittens and puppies in baskets on opposite sides of the window, the chickens before their coops, the ducklings like yellow balls on the grass, and the huge family of little spotted piglings which, to the scandal of his sisters, he declared the most delightful of all.

Their hostess knew nothing of the young baronet being in the neighbourhood, and was by no means gratified by the intelligence.

"Lack-a-day! Miss Harriet, you don't mean that the family is coming down here! I don't want none of them. 'Tis bad times for the farmer when any of that sort is nigh. They make nothing of galloping their horses a hunting right through the crops, ay, and horsewhipping the farmer if he do but say a word for the sweat of his brow."

"O Mrs. Jewel!" cried Aurelia, in whose ear lingered the courteous accents of her partner, "they would never behave themselves so."

"Bless you, Miss Orreely, I'll tell you what I've seen with my own eyes. My own good man, the master here, with the horsewhip laid about his shoulders at that very thornbush, by one of the fine gentlefolks, just because he had mended the gap in the hedge they was used to ride through, and my Lady sitting by in her laced scarlet habit on her fine horse, smiling like a painted picture, and saying, 'Thank you, sir, the rascals need to learn not to interfere with our sport,' all in that gentle sounding low voice of hers, enough to drive one mad."

"I thought Sir Jovian had been a kind master," said Harriet.

"This was not Sir Jovian. Poor gentleman, he was not often out a-hunting. This was one of the fine young rakish fellows from Lunnun as were always swarming about my Lady, like bees over that maybush. Sir Thomas Donne, I think they called him. They said he got killed by a wild boar, hunting in foreign parts, afterwards, and serve him right! But there! They would all do her bidding, whether for bad or good, so maybe it was less his fault than hers. She is a bitter one, is my Lady, for all she looks so sweet. And this her young barrowknight will be his own mother's son, and I don't want none of 'em down here. 'Tis a good job we have your good papa, the Major, to stand between her and us; I only wish he had his own, for a rare good landlord he would be."

The Dame's vain wishes were cut short by shrieks from the poultry-yard, where Eugene was discovered up to his ankles in the black ooze of the horse-pond, waving a little stick in defiance of an angry gander, who with white outspread wings, snake-like neck, bent and protruded, and frightful screams and hisses, was no bad representation of his namesake the dragon, especially to a child not much exceeding him in height.

The monster was put to rout, the champion dragged out of the pond, breathlessly explaining that he only wanted to look at the goslings when the stupid geese cackled and the gander wanted to fly at his eyes. "And I didn't see where I was going, for I had to keep him off, so I got into the mud. Will sister be angry?" he concluded, ruefully surveying the dainty little stockings and shoes coated with black mud.

But before the buckled shoon had been scraped, or the hosen washed and dried, the cheerful memory of boyhood had convinced itself that the enemy had been put to flight by his manful resistance; and he turned a deaf ear to Aurelia's suggestion that the affair had been retribution for his constant oblivion of Comenius' assertion that *auser gingrit*, "the goose gagleth."

They went home more soberly, having been directed by Mrs. Jewel to a field bordered by a copse, where grew the most magnificent of Titania's pensioners tall, wearing splendid rubies in their coats; and in due time the trio presented themselves at home, weary, but glowing with the innocent excitement of their adventures. Harriet was the first to proclaim that they had seen a horseman who must be Sir Amyas. "Had sister seen him?"

"Only through the window of the kitchen where I was making puff paste."

"He called then! Did my papa see him?"

"My father was in no condition to see any one, being under the hands and razor of Palmer."

"La! what a sad pity. Did he leave no message?"

"He left his compliments, and hoped his late partner was not fatigued."

"Is he at the Great House? Will he call again?"

"He is on his way to make a visit in Monmouthshire, together with a brother office, who is related to my Lady Herries, and finding that their road led them within twenty miles of our town, the decided on making a diversion to see her. It was only from her that Sir Amyas understood how close he was to his mother's property, for my Lady is extremely jealous of her prerogative."

"How did you hear all this, sister?"

"Sir George Herries rode over this afternoon and sat an hour with my father, delighting him by averring that the young gentleman has his mother's charms of person, together with his father's solidity of principle and character, and that he will do honour to his name."

"O, I hope he will come back by this route!" cried Harriet.

"Of that there is small likelihood," said Betty. "His mother is nearly certain to prevent it since she is sure to take umbrage at his having visited the Great House without her permission."

CHAPTER IV
MY LADY'S MISSIVE

To the next coffee-house he speeds,

Takes up the news, some scraps he reads.—GAY.

Though Carminster was a cathedral city, the Special General Post only came in once a week, and was liable to delay through storms, snows, mire and highwaymen, so that its arrival was as great an event as is now the coming in of a mail steamer to a colonial harbour. The "post" was a stout countryman, with a red coat, tall jackboots and a huge hat. He rode a strong horse, which carried, *en croupe*, an immense pack, covered with oiled canvas, rising high enough to support his back, while he blew a long horn to announce his arrival.

Letters were rare and very expensive articles unless franked by a Member of Parliament, but gazettes and newsletters formed a large portion of his freight. No private gentleman except the Dean and Sir George Herries went to the extravagance of taking in a newspaper on his own account, but there was a club who subscribed for the *Daily Gazetteer*, the *Tatler*, and one or two other infant forms of periodical literature. These were hastily skimmed on their first arrival at the club-room at the White Dragon, lay on the table to be more deliberately conned for a week, and finally were divided among the members to be handed about among the families and dependants as long as they would hold together.

Major Delavie never willingly missed the coming of the mail, for his foreign experiences gave him keen interest in the war between France and Austria, and he watched the campaigns of his beloved Prince Eugene with untiring enthusiasm, being, moreover, in the flattering position of general interpreter and guide to his neighbours through the scanty articles on foreign intelligence.

It was about ten days after the syllabub party, when he had quite recovered his ordinary health, that he mounted his stout pony in his military undress, his cocked hat perched on his well-powdered bob-wig, with a queue half-way down his dark green gold-laced coat, and with his long jack-boots carefully settle by Palmer over the knee that would never cease to give him trouble.

Thus he slowly ambled into the town, catching on his way distant toots of the postman's horn. In due time he made his way into the High Street, broad and unpaved, with rows of lime or poplar trees before the principal houses, the most modern of which were of red brick, with heavy sash-windows, large stone quoins, and steps up to the doors.

The White Dragon, dating from the times of the Mortimer badge, was built of creamy stone, and had an archway conducting the traveller into a courtyard worthy of Chaucer, with ranges of galleries running round it, the balustrades of dark carved oak suiting with the timbers of the latticed window and gables, and with the noble outside stair at one angle, by which they communicated with one another. To these beauties the good Major was entirely insensible. He only sighed at the trouble it gave his lame knee to mount the stair to the first storey, and desired the execution of the landlord's barbarous design of knocking down the street front to replace it with a plain, oblong assembly room, red brick outside, and within, blue plaster, adorned with wreaths and bullocks' faces in stucco.

Such were the sentiments of most of the burly squires who had ridden in on the same errand, and throwing the reins to their grooms, likewise climbed the stair to the club-room with its oriel looking over the street. There too were several of the cathedral clergy, the rubicund double-chinned face of the Canon in residence set off by a white, cauliflower wig under a shovel hat, while the humbler minor canons (who served likewise as curates to all the country round) only powdered their own hair, and wore gowns and cassocks of quality very inferior to that which adorned the portly person of their superior. His white bands were of fine cambric, theirs of coarser linen; his stockings were of ribbed silk, theirs of black worsted; his buckles of silver, theirs of steel; and the line of demarcation was as strongly marked as that between the neat, deferential tradesman, and the lawyer in his spruce snuff-coloured coat, or the doctor, as black in hue as the clergy, though with a secular cut, a smaller wig, and a gold-headed cane. Each had, as in duty bound, ordered his pint of port or claret for the good of the house, and it was well if these were not in the end greatly exceeded; and some had lighted long clay pipes; but these were mostly of the secondary rank, who sat at the table farthest from the window, and whose drink was a measure of ale.

The letters had not yet been sorted, but the newspaper had been brought in, and the Canon Boltby had possessed himself of it, and was proclaiming scraps of intelligence about the King, Queen, and Sir Robert Walpole, the character of Marshal Berwick, recently slain at Philipsburg, an account of Spanish outrages at sea, or mayhap the story of a marvelous beast, half-tiger, half-wolf, reported to be running wild in France. The other gentlemen, waiting till the mail-bags were opened, listened and commented; while one or two of the squires, and a shabby, disreputable-looking minor canon made each notable name the occasion of a toast, whether of health to his majesty's friends or confusion to his foes. A squabble, as to whether the gallant Berwick should be reckoned as an honest Frenchman or as a traitor Englishman, was interrupted by the Major's entrance, and the congratulations on his recovery.

One of the squires inquired after his daughters, and pronounced the little one with the outlandish name was becoming a belle, and would be the toast of the neighbourhood, a hint of which the topers were not slow to take advantage, while one of the guests at the recent party observed, "Young Belamour seemed to be of that opinion."

"May it be so," said the Canon, "that were a step to the undoing of a great wrong."

"Mr. Scrivener will tell you, sir, that there was no justice in the eye of the law," said the Major.

"*Summum jus, summa injuria,*" quoted, *sotto voce*, Mr. Arden, a minor canon who, being well born, scholarly, scientific and gentlemanly, occupied a middle place between his colleagues and the grandees. He was not listened to. Each knot of speakers was becoming louder in debate, and Dr. Boltby's voice was hardly heard when he announced that a rain of blood had fallen on the Macgillicuddy mountains in Ireland, testified to by numerous respectable Protestant witnesses, and attributable, either to the late comet, or to the Pretender.

At that moment the letters were brought in by the postman, and each recipient had—not without murmurs—to produce his purse and pay heavily for them. There were not many. The Doctor had two, Mr. Arden one, Mr. Scrivener no less than five, but of them two were franked, and a franked letter was likewise handed over to Major DeLavie, with the word "Aresfield" written in the corner.

"From my Lady," said an unoccupied neighbour.

"Aye, aye," said the Major, putting it into his pocket, being by no means inclined to submit the letter to the general gaze.

"A good omen," said Canon Boltby, looking up from his paper. And the Major smiled in return, put a word or two into the discussion on affairs, and then, as soon as he thought he could take leave without betraying anxiety, he limped down stairs, and called for his horse. Lady Belamour's letters were wont to be calls for money, not easily answered, and were never welcome sights, and this hung heavy in the laced pocket of his coat.

Palmer met him at the back gate, and took his horse, but judged it advisable to put no questions about the news, while his master made his way in by the kitchen entrance of the rambling old manor house, and entered a stone-paved low room, a sort of office or study, where he received, and paid, money for my Lady, and smoked his pipe. Here he sat down in his wooden armchair, spread forth his legs, and took out the letter, opening it with careful avoidance of defacing the large red seal, covered with many quarterings, and the Delavie escutcheon of pretence reigning over all.

It opened, as he expected, with replies to some matters about leases and repairs; and then followed:—

"I am informed that you have a large Family, and Daughters growing up whom it is desirable to put in the way of making a good Match, or else an honourable Livelihood; I am therefore willing, for the Sake of our Family Connection, to charge myself with your youngest Girl, whose Name I understand to be Aurelia. I will cause her to be trained in useful Works in my Household, expecting her, in Return, to assist in the Care and Instruction of my young Children; and if she please me and prove herself worthy and attentive, I will bestow her Marriage upon some suitable Person. This is the more proper and convenient for you, because your Age and Health are such that I may not long be able to retain you in the Charge of my Estate—in which indeed you are continued only out of Consideration of an extremely distant Relationship, although a younger and more active Man, bred to the Profession, would serve me far more profitably."

When Betty came into the room a few minutes later to pull off her father's boots she found him sitting like one transfixed. He held out the letter, saying, "Read that, child."

Betty stood by the window and read, only giving one start, and muttering between her teeth, "Insolent woman!" but not speaking the words aloud, for she knew her father would treat them as treason. He always had a certain tender deference for his cousin Urania, mixed with something akin to compunction, as if his loyalty to his betrothed had been disloyalty to his family. Thus, he exceeded the rest of his sex in blindness to the defects that had been so evident to his wife and daughter; and whatever provocation might make him say of my Lady himself, he never permitted a word against her from any one else. He looked wistfully at Betty and said, "My little Aura! It is a kindly thought. Her son must have writ of the child. But I had liefer she had asked me for the sight of my old eyes."

"The question is," said Betty, in clear, incisive tones, "whether we surrender Aurelia or your situation?"

"Nay, nay, Betty, you always do my cousin less than justice. She means well by the child and by us all. Come, come say what is in your mind," he add testily.

"Am I at liberty to express myself, sir?"

"Of course you are. I had rather hear the whole discharge of your battery than see you looking constrained and satirical."

"Then, sir, my conclusion is this. The young baronet has shown himself smitten with out pretty Aurelia, and has spoken of tarrying on his return to make farther acquaintance. My Lady is afraid of his going to greater lengths, and therefore wishes to have her at her disposal."

"She proposes to take her into her own family; that is not taking her out of his way."

"I am sure of that."

"You are prejudiced, like your poor dear mother—the best of women, if only she could ever have done justice to her Ladyship! Don't you see, child, Aurelia would not be gone before his return, supposing he should come this way."

"His visit was to be for six weeks. Did you not see the postscript?"

"No, the letter was enough for one while."

"Here it is: 'I shall send Dove in the Space of about a Fortnight or three Weeks to bring to Town the young Coach Horses you mentioned. His Wife is to return with him, as I have Occasion for her in Town, and your Daughter must be ready to come up with them.'"

"Bless me! That is prompt! But it is thoughtful. Mrs. Dove is a good soul. It seems to me as if my Lady, though she may not choose to say so, wishes to see the child, and if she approve of her, breed her up in the accomplishments needed for such an elevation."

"If you hold that opinion, dear sir, it is well."

"If I thought she meant other than kindness toward the dear maid, I had rather we all pinched together than risk the little one in her hands. I had rather-if it comes to that—live on a crust a day than part with my sweet child; but if it were for good, Betty! It is hard for you all three to be cooped up together here, with no means of improving your condition; and this may be an opening that I ought not to reject. What say you, Betty?"

"If I were to send her out into the world, I had rather bind her apprentice to the Misses Rigby to learn mantua-making."

"Nay, nay, my dear; so long as I live there is no need for my children to come to such straits."

"As long as you retain your situation, sir; but you perceive how my Lady concludes her letter."

"An old song, Betty, which she sings whenever the coin does not come in fast enough to content her. She does not mean what she says; I know Urania of old. No; I will write back to her, thanking her for her good offices, but telling her my little girl is too young to be launched into the world as yet. Though if it were Harriet, she might not be unwilling."

"Harriet would be transported at the idea; but it is not she whom the Lady wants. And indeed I had rather trust little Aurelia to take care of herself than poor Harriet."

"We shall see! We shall see! Meantime, do not broach the subject to your sisters."

Betty assented, and departed with a heavy heart, feeling that, whatever her father might believe, the choice would be between the sacrifice of Aurelia or of her father's agency, which would involve the loss of home, of competence, and of the power of breeding up her darling Eugene according to his birth. She did not even know what her father had written, and could only go about her daily occupations like one under a weight, listening to her sisters' prattle about their little plans with a strange sense that everything was coming to an end, and constantly weighing the comparative evils of yielding or refusing Aurelia.

No one would have more valiantly faced poverty than Elizabeth Delavie, had she alone been concerned. Cavalier and Jacobite blood was in her veins, and her unselfish character had been trained by a staunch and self-devoted mother. But her father's age and Eugene's youth made her waver. She might work her fingers to the bone, and live on oatmeal, to give her father the comforts he required; but to have Eugene brought down from his natural station was more than she could endure. His welfare must be secured at the cost not only of Aurelia's sweet presence, but of her happiness; and Betty durst not ask herself what more she dreaded, knowing too that she would probably be quite incapable of altering her father's determination whatever it might be, and that he was inclined to trust Lady Belamour. The only chance of his refusal was that he should take alarm at the manner of requiring his daughter from him.

CHAPTER V
THE SUMMONS

But when the King knew that the thing must be,
And that no help there was in this distress,
He bade them have all things in readiness
To take the maiden out. —*MORRIS.*

The second Sunday of suspense had come. The Sundays of good young ladies little resembled those of a century later, though they were not devoid of a calm peacefulness, worthy of the "sweet day, so cool, so calm, so bright." The inhabited rooms of the old house looked bright and festal; there were fresh flowers in the pots, honey as well as butter on the breakfast table. The Major and Palmer were both in full uniform, wonderfully preserved. Eugene, a marvel of prettiness, with his curled hair and little velvet coat, contrived by his sisters out of some ancestral hoard. Betty wore thick silk brocade from the same store; Harriet a fresh gay chintz over a crimson skirt, and Aurelia was in spotless white, with a broad blue sash and blue ribbons in her hat, for her father liked to see her still a child; so her hair was only tied with blue, while that of her sisters was rolled over a cushion, and slightly powdered.

The church was so near that the Major could walk thither, leaning on his stout crutch-handled stick, and aided by his daughter's arm, as he proceeded down the hawthorn lane, sweet with the breath of May, exchanging greetings with whole families of the poor, the fathers in smock frocks wrought with curious needlework on the breast and back, the mothers in high-crowned hats and stout dark blue woollen gowns, the children, either patched or ragged, and generally barefooted, but by no means ill-fed.

No Sunday school had been invented. The dame who hobbled along in spectacles, dropping a low curtsey to the "quality," taught the hornbook and the primer to a select few of the progeny of the farmers and artisans, and the young ladies would no more have thought of assisting her labours than the blacksmith's. They only clubbed their pocket money to clothe and pay the schooling of one little orphan, who acknowledged them by a succession of the lowest bobs as she trotted past, proud as Margery Twoshoes herself of the distinction of being substantially shod.

The church was small, and with few pretensions to architecture at the best. It had been nearly a ruin, when, stirred by the Major, the churchwardens had taken it in hand, so that, owing to Richard Stokes and John Ball, as they permanently declared in yellow letters on a blue ground, the congregation were no longer in danger of the roof admitting the rain or coming down on the congregation. They had further beautified the place with a huge board of the royal arms, and with Moses and Aaron in white cauliflower wigs presiding over the tables of the Commandments. Four long dark, timber pews and numerous benches, ruthlessly constructed out of old carvings, occupied the aisle, and the chancel was more than half filled with the lofty "closet" of the Great House family. Hither the Delavie family betook themselves, and on her way Betty was startled by the recognition, in the seat reserved for the servants, of a broad back and curled wig that could belong to no one but Jonah Dove. She did her utmost to keep her mind from dwelling on what this might portend, though she followed the universal custom by exchanging nods and curtsies with the Duckworth family as she sailed up the aisle at the head of the little procession.

There was always a little doubt as to who would serve the church. One of the Canons was the incumbent, and the curate was Mr. Arden, the scientific minor canon, but when his services were required at the cathedral, one of his colleagues would supply his place, usually in a sadly perfunctory manner. However, he was there in person, as his voice, a clear and pleasant one, showed the denizens of the "closet," for they could not see out of it, except where Eugene had furtively enlarged a moth-eaten hole in the curtain, through which, when standing on the seat, he could enjoy an oblique view of the back of an iron-moulded surplice and a very ill-powdered wig. This was a comfort to him. It would have been more satisfactory to have been able to make out whence came the stentorian A-men, that responded to the parson, totally unaccompanied save by the good Major, who always read his part almost as loud as the clerk, from a great octavo prayer-book, bearing on the lid the Delavie arms with coronet, supporters, and motto, "*Ma Vie et ma Mie.*" It would have been thought unladylike, if not unscriptural, to open the lips in church; yet, for all her silence, good Betty was striving to be devout and attentive, praying earnestly for her little sister's safety, and hailing as a kind of hopeful augury this verse from the singers—

> "*At home, abroad, in peace, in war*
> *Thy God shall thee defend,*

Conduct thee through life's pilgrimage
Safe to the journey's end."

Much cannot be said for the five voices that sang, nor for the two fiddles that accompanied them. Eugene had scarcely outgrown his terror at the strains, and still required Aurelia to hold his hand, under pretext of helping him to follow the words, not an easy thing, since the last lines were always repeated three or four times.

Somehow the repetition brought them the more home to Betty's heart, and they rang consolingly in her ears, all through the sermon, of which she took in so little that she never found out that it was an elaborate exposition of the Newtonian philosophy, including Mr. Arden's views of the miracle at the battle Beth-horon, in the Lesson for the day.

The red face and Belamour livery looked doubly ominous when she came out of church, but she had to give her arm to her father till they were overtaken by Mr. Arden, who always shared the Sunday roast beef and plum pudding. Betty feared it was the best meal he had in the week, for he lived in lodgings, and his landlady was not too careful of his comforts, while he was wrapped up in his books and experiments. There was a hole singed in the corner of his black gown, which Eugene pointed out with great awe to Aurelia as they walked behind him.

"See there, Aura. Don't you think he has been raising spirits, like Friar Bacon?"

"What do you know about Friar Bacon?" asked Harriet.

"He is in a little book that I bought of the pedlar. He had a brazen head that said—

'Time is,
Time was,
Time will be.'

I wonder if Mr. Arden would show me one like it."

"You ridiculous little fellow to believe such trash!" said Harriet.

"But, Hatty, he can really light a candle without a tinder-box," said Eugene. "His landlady told Palmer so; and Palmer says the Devil flew away with Friar Bacon; but my book says he burnt all his books and gave himself to the study of divinity, and dug his grave with his own nails."

"Little boys should not talk of such things on Sundays," said Harriet, severely.

"One does talk of the Devil on Sunday, for he is in the catechism," returned Eugene. "If he carries Mr. Arden off, do you think there will be a great smoke, and that folk will see it?"

Aurelia's silvery peal of laughter fell sadly upon Betty's ears in front, and her father and Mr. Arden turned to ask what made them so merry. Aurelia blushed in embarrassment, but Harriet was ready.

"You will think us very rude, Sir, but my little brother has been reading the life of Friar Bacon, and he thinks you an equally great philosopher."

"Indeed, my little master, you do me too much honour. You will soon be a philosopher yourself. I did not expect so much attention in so young an auditor," said mr. Arden, thinking this the effect of his sermon on the solar system.

Whereupon Eugene begged to inspect the grave he was digging with his own nails.

They were at home by this time, and Betty was aware that they had been followed at a respectful distance by Palmer and the coachman. Anxious as she was, she could not bear that her father's dinner should be spoilt, or that he, in his open-hearted way, should broach the matter with Mr. Arden; so she repaired to the garden gate, and on being told that Mr. Dove had a packet from my Lady for the Major, she politely invited him to dinner with the servants, and promised that her father should see him afterwards.

This gave a long respite, since the servants had the reversion of the beef, so the Mr. Arden had taken leave, and gone to see a bedridden pauper, and the Major had time for his forty winks, while Betty, though her heart throbbed hard beneath her tightly-laced boddice, composed herself to hear Eugene's catechism, and the two sisters, each with a good book, slipped out to the honeysuckle arbour in the garden behind the house. Harriet had *Sherlock in Death*, her regular Sunday study, though she never got any further than the apparition of Mrs. Veal, over which she gloated in a dreamy state; Aurelia's study was a dark-covered, pale-lettered copy of the *Ikon Basilike*, with the strange attraction that youth has to pain and sorrow, and sat musing over the resigned outpourings of the perplexed and persecuted king, with her bright eyes fixed on the deep blue sky, and the honeysuckle blossoms gently waving against it, now and then visited by bee or butterfly, while through the silence came the throbbing notes of the nightingale, followed by its jubilant burst of glee, and the sweet distant chime of the cathedral bells rose and fell upon the wind. What peace and repose there was in all the air, even in the gentle breeze, and the floating motions of the swallows skimming past.

The stillness was first broken by the jangle of their own little church bell, for Mr. Arden was a more than usually diligent minister, and always gave two services when he was not in course at the cathedral. The young ladies always attended both, but as Harriet and Aurelia crossed the lawn, their brother ran to meet them, saying, "We are not to wait for sister."

"I hope my papa is well," said Aurelia.

"Oh yes," said Eugene, "but the man in the gold-laced hat has been speaking with him. Palmer says it is Mrs. Dove's husband, and he is going to take Lively Tom and Brown Bet and the two other colts to London. He asked if I should like to ride a-cockhorse there with him. 'Dearly,' I said, and then he laughed and said it was not my turn, but he should take Miss Aurelia instead."

Aurelia laughed, and Harriet said, "Extremely impudent."

Little she guessed what Betty was at that moment reading.

"I am astonished," wrote Lady Belamour to her cousin, "that you should decline so highly advantageous an Offer for your Daughter. I can only understand it as a Token that you desire no further Connection with, nor Favour from me; and I shall therefore require of you to give up the Accounts, and vacate the House by Michaelmas next ensuing. However, as I am willing to allow some excuse for the Weakness of parental Affection, if you change your Mind within the next Week and send up your Daughter with Dove and his Wife, I will overlook your first hasty and foolish Refusal, ungrateful as it was, and will receive your Daughter and give her all the Advantages I promised. Otherwise your Employment is at an end, and you had better prepare your Accounts for Hargrave's Inspection."

"There is no help for it then," said Betty.

"And if it be for the child's advantage, we need not make our moan," said her father. "'Tis like losing the daylight out of our house, but we must not stand in the way of her good."

"If I were only sure it is for her good!"

"Why, child, there's scarce a wench in the county who would not go down on her knees for such a chance. See what Madam Duckworth would say to it for Miss Peggy!"

Betty said no more. The result of her cogitations had been that since Aurelia must be yielded for the sake of her father and Eugene, it was better not to disturb him with fears, which would only anger him at the moment and disquiet him afterwards. She was likewise reassured by Mrs. Dove's going with her, since that good woman had been nurse to the little Belamour cousins now deceased, and was well known as an excellent and trustworthy person, so that, if she were going to act in the same capacity to my Lady's second family, Aurelia would have a friend at hand. So the Major cheated his grief by greeting the church-goers with the hilarious announcement—

"Here's great news! What says my little Aura to going London to my Lady's house."

"O Sir! are you about to take us."

"Not I! My Lady wants pretty young maidens, not battered old soldiers."

"Nor my sisters? O then, if you please, Sir, I would rather not go!"

"Silly children cannot choose! No, no, Aura, you must go out and see the world, and come back to us such a belle that your poor old father will scarce know you."

"I do not wish to be a belle," said the girl. "O Sir, let me stay with you and sister."

"Do not be so foolish, Aura," put in Harriet. "It will be the making of you. I wish I had the offer."

"O Harriet, could not you go instead?"

"No, Aurelia," said Betty. "There is no choice, and you must be a good girl and not vex my father."

The gravity of her eldest sister convinced Aurelia that entreaties would be vain, and there was soon a general outburst of assurances that she would see all that was delightful in London, the lions in the Tower, the new St. Paul's, the monuments, Ranelagh, the court ladies, may be, the King and Queen themselves; until she began to feel exhilarated and pleased at the prospect and the distinction.

Then came Monday and the bustle of preparing her wardrobe. The main body of it was to be sent in the carrier's waggon, for she was to ride on a pillion behind Mr. Dove, and could only take a valise upon a groom's horse. There was no small excitement in the arrangement, and in the farewells to the neighbours, who all agreed with Harriet in congratulating the girl on her promotion. Betty did her part with all her might, washed lace, and trimmed sleeves, and made tuckers, giving little toilette counsels, while her heart ached sorely all the time.

When she could speak to Mrs. Dove alone, she earnestly besought that old friend to look after the child, her health, her dress, and above all to supply here lack of experience and give her kind counsel and advice.

"I will indeed, ma'am, as though she were my own," promised Mrs. Dove.

"O nurse, I give my sweet jewel to your care; you know what a great house in London is better than I do. You will warn her of any danger."

"I will do my endeavour, ma'am. We servants see and hear much, and if any harm should come nigh the sweet young miss, I'll do my best for her."

"Thank you, nurse, I shall never, never see her more in her free artless childishness," said Betty, sobbing as if her heart would break; "but oh, nurse, I can bear the thought better since I have known that you would be near her."

And at night, when her darling nestled for the last time in her arms, the elder sister whispered her warnings. Her knowledge of the great world was limited, but she believed it to be a very wicked place, and she profoundly distrusted her brilliant kinswoman; yet her warnings took no shape more definite than—"My dearest sister will never forget her prayers nor her Bible." There was a soft response and fresh embrace at each pause. "Nor play cards of a Sunday, nor ever play high. And my Aura must be deaf to rakish young beaux and their compliments. They never mean well by poor pretty maids. If you believe them, they will only mock, flout, and jeer you in the end. And if the young baronet should seek converse with you, promise me, oh, promise me, Aurelia, to grant him no favour, no, not so much as to hand him a flower, or stand chatting with him unknown to his mother. Promise me again, child, for naught save evil can come of any trifling between you. And, Aurelia, go to Nurse Dove in all your difficulties. She can advise you where your poor sister cannot. It will ease my heart if I know that my child will attend to her. You will not let yourself be puffed up with flattery, nor be offended if she be open and round with you. Think that your poor sister Betty speaks in her. Pray our old prayers, go to church, and read your Psalms and Lessons daily, and oh! never, never cheat your conscience. O may God, in His mercy, keep my darling!"

So Aurelia cried herself to sleep, while Betty lay awake till the early hour in the morning when all had to be prepared for the start. There was to be a ride of an hour and a half before breakfast so as to give the horses a rest. It was a terrible separation, in many respects more complete than if Aurelia had been going, in these days, to America; for communication by letter was almost as slow, and infinitely more expensive.

No doubt the full import of what he had done had dawned even on Major Delavie during the watches of that last sorrowful night, for he came out a pale, haggard man, looking as if his age had doubled since he went to bed, wrapped in his dressing gown, his head covered with his nightcap, and leaning heavily on his staff. He came charged with one of the long solemn discourses which parents were wont to bestow on their children as valedictions, but when Aurelia, in her camlet riding cloak and hood, brought her tear-stained face to crave his blessing, he could only utter broken fragments. "Bless thee my child! Take heed to yourself and your ways. It is a bad world, beset with temptations. Oh! heaven forgive me for sending my innocent lamb out into it. Oh! what would your blessed mother say?"

"Dear sir," said Betty, who had wept out her tears, and was steadily composed now, "this is no time to think of that. We must only cheer up our darling, and give her good counsel. If she keep to what her Bible, her catechism and her conscience tell her, she will be a good girl, and God will protect her."

"True, true, your sister is right; Aura, my little sweetheart, I had much to say to you, but it is all driven out of my poor old head."

"Aura! Aura! the horses are coming! Ten of them!" shouted Eugene. "Come along! Oh! if I were but going! How silly of you to cry; *I* don't."

"There! there! Go my child, and God in His mercy protect you!"

Aurelia in speechless grief passed from the arms of one sister to the embrace of the other, hugged Eugene, was kissed by Nannerl, who forced a great piece of cake into her little bag, and finally was lifted to her pillion cushion by Palmer, who stole a kiss of her hand before Dove put his horse in motion, while Betty was still commending her sister to his wife's care, and receiving reiterated promises of care.

CHAPTER VI
DISAPPOINTED LOVE

I know thee well, thy songs and sighs,
A wicked god thou art;
And yet, most pleasing to the eyes,
And witching to the heart.
W. MACKWORTH PRAED.

The house was dull when Aurelia was gone. Her father was ill at ease and therefore testy, Betty too sore at heart to endure as cheerfully as usual his unwonted ill-humour. Harriet was petulant, and Eugene troublesome, and the two were constantly jarring against one another, since the one missed her companion, the other his playmate; and they were all more sensible than ever how precious and charming an element was lost to the family circle.

On the next ensuing Sunday, Eugene had made himself extremely obnoxious to Harriet, by persisting in kicking up the dust, and Betty, who had gone on before with her father, was availing herself of the shelter of the great pew to brush with a sharp hand the dust from the little legs, when, even in the depths of their seclusion, the whole party were conscious of a sort of breathless sound of surprise and admiration, a sweep of bows and curtsies, and the measured tread of boots and clank of sword and spurs coming nearer—yes, to the very chancel. Their very door was opened by the old clerk with the most obsequious of reverences, and there entered a gorgeous vision of scarlet and gold, bowing gracefully with a wave of a cocked and plumed hat!

The Major started, and was moving out of his corner—the seat of honour—but the stranger forbade this by another gesture, and took his place, after standing for a moment with his face hidden in his hat. Then he took an anxious survey, not without an almost imperceptible elevation of eyebrow and shoulder, as if disappointed, and accepted the Prayer-book, which the Major offered him.

Betty kept her eyes glued to her book, and when that was not in use, upon the mittened hands crossed before her, resolute against distraction, and every prayer turning into a petition for her sister's welfare; but Eugene gazed, open-eyed and open-mouthed, oblivious of his beloved hole, and Harriet, though keeping her lids down, and her book open, contrived to make a full inspection of the splendid apparition.

It was tall and slight, youthfully undeveloped, yet with the grace of personal symmetry, high breeding, and military training, upright without stiffness, with a command and dexterity of movement which prevented the sword and spurs from being the annoyance to his pew-mates that country awkwardness usually made these appendages. The spurs were on cavalry boots, guarding the knee, and met by white buckskins, both so little dusty that there could have been no journey that morning. The bright gold-laced scarlet coat of the Household troops entirely effaced the Major's old Austrian uniform; and over it, the hair, of a light golden brown, was brushed back, tied with black ribbon, and hung down far behind in a queue, only leaving little gold rings curling on the brow and temples. The face was modelled like a cameo, faultless in the outlines, with a round peach-like fresh contour and bloom on the fair cheek, which had much of the child, though with a firmness in the lip, and strength in the brow, that promised manliness. Indeed there was a wonderful blending of the beauty of manhood and childhood about the youth; and his demeanour was perfectly decorous and reverent, no small merit in a young officer and London beau. Indeed Betty could almost have forgotten his presence, if gleams from his glittering equipments had not kept glancing before her eyes, turn them where she would, and if Mr. Arden's sermon had not been of Solomon's extent of natural philosophy, and so full of Hebrew, Greek, and Latin that she could not follow it at all.

After the blessing, the young gentleman, with a bow, the pink of courtesy, offered a hand to lead her out, nor could she refuse, though, to use her own expression, she hated the absurdity of mincing down the aisle with a fine young spark looking like her grandson; while her poor father had to put up with Harriet's arm. Outside came the greetings, the flourish of the hat, the "I may venture to introduce myself, and to beg of you, sir, and of my fair cousins to excuse my sudden intrusion."

"No apology can be needed for your appearance in your own pew, Sir Amyas," said the Major with outstretched hand; "it did my heart good to see you there!"

"I would not have taken you thus by surprise," continued the youth, "but one of my horses lost a shoe yesterday, and we were constrained to halt at Portkiln for the night, and ride on this morning. Herries went on to the Deanery, and I hoped to have seen you before church, but found you had already entered."

Portkiln was so near, that this Sabbath day's journey did not scandalise Betty, and her father eagerly welcomed his kinsman, and insisted that he should go no farther. Sir Amyas accepted the invitation, nothing loth, only asking, with a little courtly diffidence, if it might not be convenient for him to sleep at the Great House, and begging the ladies to excuse his riding dress.

His eyes wandered anxiously as though in search of something in the midst of all his civility, and while the Major was sending Eugene to bring Mr. Arden—who was hanging back at the churchyard gate, unwilling to thrust himself forward—the faltering question was put, while the cheeks coloured like a girl's, "I hope my fair partner, my youngest cousin, Miss Aurelia Delavie, is in good health?"

"We hope so, sir, thank you," returned Betty; "but she left us six days ago."

"Left you!" he repeated, in consternation that overpowered his courtliness.

"Yes, sir," said Harriet, "my Lady, your mother, has been good enough to send for her to London."

"My Lady!" he murmured to himself; "I never thought of that! How and when did she go?"

The answer was interrupted by the Major coming up "Sir Amyas Belamour, permit me to present to you the Reverend Richard Arden, the admirable divine to whom we are beholden for the excellent and learned discourse of this morning. You'll not find such another scholar in all Carminster."

"I am highly honoured," returned the baronet, with a bow in return for Mr. Arden's best obeisance, such as it was; and Harriet, seeing Peggy Duckworth in the distance, plumed herself on her probable envy.

Before dinner was served Sir Amyas had obtained the information as to Aurelia's departure, and even as to the road she had taken, and he had confessed that, "Of course he had write to his mother that he had danced with the most exquisitely beautiful creature he had ever seen, and that he longed to know his cousins better." No doubt his mother, having been thus reminded of her connections, had taken the opportunity of summoning Aurelia to London to give her the advantages of living in her household and acquiring accomplishments. The lad was so much delighted at the prospect of enjoying her society that he was almost consoled for not finding her at the Manor House; and his elaborate courtesy became every moment less artificial and more affectionate, as the friendly atmosphere revealed that the frankness and simplicity of the boy had not been lost, captain in the dragoon guards as he was, thanks to interest, though he had scarcely yet joined his troop. He had been with a tutor in the country, until two years ago, when his stepfather, Mr. Wayland, had taken him, still with his tutor, on the expedition to the Mediterranean. He had come home from Gibraltar, and joined his regiment only a few weeks before setting out with his friend Captain Herries, to visit Battlefield, Lady Aresfield's estate in Monmouthshire. He was quartered in the Whitehall barracks, but could spend as much time as he pleased at his mother's house in Hanover Square.

Betty's mind misgave her as she saw the brightening eye with which he said it; but she could not but like the youth himself, he was so bright, unspoilt, and engaging that she could not think him capable of doing wilful wrong to her darling. Yet how soon would the young soldier, plunged into the midst of fashionable society, learn to look on the fair girl with the dissipated eyes of his associates? There was some comfort in finding that Mr. Wayland was expected to return in less than a year, and that his stepson seemed to regard him with unbounded respect, as a good, just, and wise man, capable of everything! Indeed Sir Amyas enlightened Mr. Arden on the scientific construction of some of Mr. Wayland's inventions so as to convince both the clergyman and the soldier that the lad himself was no fool, and had profited by his opportunities.

Major Delavie produced his choice Tokay, a present from an old Hungarian brother-officer, and looked happier than since Aurelia's departure. He was no match-maker, and speculated on no improbable contingencies for his daughter, but he beheld good hopes for the Delavie property and tenants in an heir such as this, and made over his simple loyal heart to the young man. Presently he inquired whether the unfortunate Mr. Belamour still maintained his seclusion.

"Yes, sir," was the reply. "He still lives in two dark rooms with shutters and curtains excluding every ray of light. He keeps his bed for the greater part of the day, but sometimes, on a very dark night, will take a turn on the terrace."

"Poor gentleman!" said Betty. "Has he no employment or occupation?"

"Mr. Wayland contrived a raised chess and draught board, and persuaded him to try a few games before we went abroad, but I do not know whether he has since continued it."

"Does he admit any visits?"

"Oh no. He has been entirely shut up, except from the lawyer, Hargrave, on business. Mr. Wayland, indeed, strove to rouse him from his despondency, but without success, except that latterly he became willing to receive him."

"Have you ever conversed with him?"

There was an ingenuous blush as the young man replied. "I fear I must confess myself remiss. Mr. Wayland has sometimes carried me with him to see my uncle, but not with my good will, and my mother objected lest it should break my spirits. However, when I left Gibraltar, my good father charged me to endeavour from time to time to enliven my uncle's solitude, but there were impediments to my going to him, and I take shame to myself for not having striven to overcome them."

"Rightly spoken, my young kinsman," cried the Major. "There are no such impediments as a man's own distaste."

"And pity will remove that," said Betty.

Soon after the removal of the cloth the ladies withdrew, and Eugene was called to his catechism, but he was soon released, for the Tokay had made her father sleepy, while it seemed to have emboldened Mr. Arden, since he came forth with direct intent to engross Harriet; and Sir Amyas wandered towards Betty, apologising for the interruption.

"It is a rare occasion," said she as her pupil scampered away.

"Happy child, to be taught by so good a sister," said the young baronet, regretfully.

"Your young half-brothers and sisters must be of about the same age," said Betty.

"My little brother, Archer, is somewhat younger. He is with my mother in London, the darling of the ladies, who think him a perfect beauty, and laugh at all his mischievous pranks. As to my little sisters, you will be surprised to hear that I have only seen them once, when I rode with their father to see them at the farm houses at which they are nursed."

"No doubt they are to be fetched home, since Mrs. Dove is gone to wait on them, and my Lady said something of intending my sister to be with her young children."

"Nay, she must have no such troublesome charge. My mother cannot intend anything of the kind. I shall see that she is treated as—-"

Betty, beginning to perceive that he knew as little of his own mother as did the rest of his sex, here interrupted him. "Excuse me, sir, I doubt not of your kind intentions, but let me speak, for Aurelia is a very precious child to me, and I am afraid that any such attempt on your part might do her harm rather than good. She must be content with the lot of a poor dependant."

"Never!" he exclaimed. "She is a Delavie; and besides, no other ever shall be my wife."

"Hush, hush!" Betty had been saying before the words were out of his "You are but a silly boy, begging your Honour's pardon, though you speak, I know, with all your heart. What would your Lady mother say or do to my poor little sister if she heard you?"

"She could but send her home, and then flood and fire could not hold me from her."

"I wish that were the worst she could do. No, Sir Amyas Belamour, if you have any kindness for the poor helpless girl under your mother's roof, you will make no advance to excite alarm or anger against her. Remember it is she who will be the sufferer and not yourself. The woman, however guiltless, is sure to fall under suspicion and bear the whole penalty. And oh! what would become of her, defenceless, simple, unprotected as she is?"

"Yet you sent her!" said he.

"Yes," said Betty, sadly, "because there was no other choice between breaking with my Lady altogether."

He made an ejaculation under his breath, half sad, half violent, and exclaimed, "Would that I were of age, or my father were returned."

"But now you know all, you will leave my child in peace," said Betty.

"What, you would give me no hope!"

"Only such as you yourself have held out," said Betty. "When you are your own master, if you keep in the same mind till then, and remain truly worthy, I cannot tell what my father would answer."

"I am going to speak to him this very day. I came with that intent."

"Do no such thing, I entreat," cried Betty. "He would immediately think it his duty to inform my Lady. Then no protestation would persuade her that we had not entrapped your youth and innocence. His grey head would be driven out without shelter, and what might not be the consequence to my sister? You could not help us, and could only make it worse. No, do nothing rash, incautious, or above all, disobedient. It would be self-love, not true love that would risk bringing her into peril and trouble when she is far out of reach of all protection."

"Trust me, trust me, Cousin Betty," cried the youth. "Only let me hope, and I'll be caution itself; but oh! what an endless eternity is two years to wait without a sign!"

But here appeared the Major, accompanied by Captain Herries and Dean Churchill, who had ordered out his coach, Sunday though it were, to pay his respects to my Lady's son, and carry him and his hosts back to sup at the Deanery. It was an age of adulation, but Betty was thankful that perilous conversations were staved off.

CHAPTER VII
ALL ALONE

By the simplicity of Venus' doves.
Merchant of Venice.

That Sunday was spent by Aurelia at the Bear Inn, at Reading. Her journey had been made by very short stages, one before breakfast, another lasting till noon, when there was a long halt for dinner and rest for horse and rider, and then another ride, never even in these longest summer days prolonged beyond six or seven o'clock at latest, such was the danger of highwaymen being attracted by the valuable horses, although the grooms in charge were so well armed that they might almost as well have been troopers.

The roads, at that time of year, were at their best, and Aurelia and Mrs. Dove were mounted on steady old nags, accustomed to pillions. Aurelia could have ridden single, but this would not have been thought fitting on a journey with no escort of her own rank, and when she mounted she was far too miserable to care for anything but hiding her tearful face behind Mr. Dove's broad shoulders. Mrs. Dove was perched behind a wiry, light-weighted old groom, whom she kept in great order, much to his disgust.

After the first wretchedness, Aurelia's youthful spirits had begun to revive, and the novel scenes to awaken interest. The Glastonbury thorn was the first thing she really looked at. The Abbey was to her only an old Gothic melancholy ruin, not worthy of a glance, but the breezy air of the Cheddar Hills, the lovely cliffs, and the charm of the open country, with its strange islands of hills dotted about, raised her spirits, as she rode through the meadows where hay was being tossed, and the scent came fragrant on the breeze. Mr. Dove would tell her over his shoulder the names of places and their owners when they came to parks bordering the road, and castles "bosomed high in the tufted trees." Or he would regale her with legends of robberies and point to the frightful gibbets, one so near to the road that she shut her eyes and crouched low behind him to avoid seeing the terrible burthen. She had noted the White Horse, and shuddered at the monument at Devizes commemorating the judgment on the lying woman, and a night had been spent at Marlborough that "Miss" might see a strolling company of actors perform in a barn; but as the piece was the *Yorksire Tragedy*, the ghastly performance overcame her so completely that Mrs. Dove had to take her away, declaring that no inducement should ever take her to a theatre again.

Mr. Dove was too experienced a traveller not to choose well his quarters for the night, and Aurelia slept in the guest chambers shining with cleanliness and scented with lavender, Mrs. Dove always sharing her room. "Miss" was treated with no small regard, as a lady of the good old blood, and though the coachman and his wife talked freely with her, they paid her all observance, never ate at the same table, and provided assiduously for her comfort and pleasure. Once they halted a whole day because even Mr. Dove was not proof against the allurements of a bull-baiting, though he carefully explained that he only made a concession to the grooms to prevent them from getting discontented, and went himself to the spectacle to hinder them from getting drunk, in which, be it observed, he did not succeed.

So much time was spent on thus creeping from stage to stage that Aurelia had begun to feel as if the journey had been going on for ages, and as if worlds divided her from her home, when on Sunday she timidly preceded Mrs. Dove into Reading Abbey Church, and afterwards was shown where rolled Father Thames. The travellers took early morning with them for Maidenhead Thicket, and breakfasted on broiled trout at the King's Arms at Maidenhead Bridge, while Aurelia felt her eye filled with the beauty of the broad glassy river, and the wooded banks, and then rose onwards, looking with loyal awe at majestic Windsor, where the flag was flying. They slept at a poor little inn a Longford, rather than cross Hounslow Heath in the evening, and there heard all the last achievements of the thieves, so that Aurelia, in crossing the next day, looked to sēe a masked highwayman start out of every bush; but they came safely to the broad archway of the inn at Knightsbridge, their last stage. Mrs. Dove took her charge up stairs at once to refresh her toilette, before entering London and being presented to my Lady.

But a clattering and stamping were heard in the yard, and Aurelia, looking from the window, called Mrs. Dove to see four horses being harnessed to a coach that was standing there.

"Lawk-a-day?" cried the good woman, "if it be not our own old coach, as was the best in poor Sir Jovian's time! Ay, there be our colours, you see, blue and gold, and my Lady's quartering. Why, 'twas atop of that very blue hammercloth that I first set eyes on my Dove! So my Lady has sent to meet you, Missie. Well, I do take it kind of her. Now you will not come in your riding hood, all frowsed and dusty, but can put on your pretty striped sacque and blue hood that you wore on Sunday, and look the sweet pretty lady you are."

Mrs. Dove's intentions were frustrated, for the maid of the inn knocked at the door with a message that the coach had orders not to wait, but that Miss was to come down immediately.

"Dear, dear!" sighed Mrs. DOve. "Tell the jackanapes not to be so hasty. He must give the young lady time to change her dress, and eat a mouthful."

This brought Dove up to the door. "Never mind dressing and fallals," he said; "this is a strange fellow that says he is hired for the job, and his orders are precise. Miss must take a bit of cake in her hand. Come, dame, you have not lived so long in my Lady's service as to forget what it is to cross her will, or keep her waiting."

Therewith he hurried Aurelia down stairs, his wife being in such a state of *deshabille* that she could not follow. He handed the young lady into the carriage, gave her a parcel of slices of bread and meat, with a piece of cake, shut the door, and said, "Be of good heart, Missie, we'll catch you up by the time you are in the square. All right!"

Off went Aurelia in solitude, within a large carriage, once gaily fitted though now somewhat faded and tarnished. She was sorry to be parted from the Doves, whom she wanted to give her courage for the introduction to my Lady, and to explain to her the wonders of the streets of London, which she did not *quite* expect to see paved with gold! She ate her extemporised meal, gazing from the window, and expecting to see houses and churches thicken on her, and hurrying to brush away her crumbs, and put on her gloves lest she should arrive unawares, for she had counted half-a-dozen houses close together. No! here was another field! More fields and houses. The signs of habitation were, so far from increasing, growing more scanty, and looked strangely like what she had before passed. Could this be the right road! How foolish to doubt, when this was my Lady's own coach. But oh, that it had waited for Mrs. Dove! She would beg her to get in when the riders overtook her. When would they? No sign of them could be seen from the windows, and here were more houses. Surely this was Turnham Green again, or there must be another village green exactly like it in the heart of London. How many times did not poor Aurelia go through all these impressions in the course of the drive. She was absolutely certain that she was taken through Brentford again, this time without a halt; but after this the country became unknown to her, and the road much worse. It was in fact for the most part a mere ditch or cart track, so rough that the four horses came to a walk. Aurelia had read no novels but *Telemaque* and *Le Grand Cyrus*, so her imagination was not terrified by tales of abduction, but alarm began to grow upon her. She much longed to ask the coachman whither he was taking her, but the check string had been either worn out or removed; she could not open the door from within, nor make him hear, and indeed she was a little afraid of him.

Twilight began to come on; it was much later than Mr. Dove had ever ventured to be out, but here at last there was a pause, and the swing of a gate, the road was smoother and she seemed to be in a wood, probably private ground. On and on, for an apparently interminable time, went the coach with the wearied and affrighted girl, through the dark thicket, until at last she emerged, into a park, where she could again see the pale after-glow of the sunset, and presently she found herself before a tall house, perfectly dark, with strange fantastic gables and chimneys, ascending far above against the sky.

All was still as death, except the murmuring caws of the rooks in their nests, and the chattering shriek of a startled blackbird. The servant from behind ran up the steps and thundered at the door; it was opened, a broad line of light shone out, some figures appeared, and a man in livery came forward to open the carriage door, but to Aurelia's inexpressible horror, his face was perfectly black, with negro features, rolling eyes, and great white teeth!

She hardly knew what she did, the dark carriage was formidable on one side, the apparition on the other! The only ray of comfort was in the face of a stout, comely, rosy maid-servant, who was holding the candle on the threshold, and with one bound the poor traveller dashed past the black hand held out to help her, and rushing up to the girl, caught hold of her, and gasped out, "Oh! What is that? Where am I? Where have they taken me?"

"Lawk, ma'am," said the girl, with a broad grin, "that 'ere bees only Mr. Jumbo. A' won't hurt'ee. See, here's Mistress Aylward."

A tall, white-capped, black-gowned elderly woman turned on the new-comer a pale, grave, unsmiling face, saying, "Your servant—Miss Aurelia Delavie, as I understand."

Bending her head, and scarcely able to steady herself, for she was shaking from head to foot, Aurelia managed to utter the query,

"Where am I?"

"At Bowstead Park, madam, by order of my Lady."

Much relieved, and knowing this was the Belamour estate, Aurelia said, "Please let me wait till Mrs. Dove comes before I am presented to my Lady."

"My Lady is not here, madam," said Mrs. Aylward. "Allow me—" and she led the way across a great empty hall, that seemed the vaster for its obscurity, then along a matted passage, and down some steps into a room surrounded with presses and cupboards, evidently belonging to the to the housekeeper. She set a chair for the trembling girl, saying, "You will excuse the having supper here to-night, madam; the south parlour will be ready for you to-morrow."

"Is not Mrs. Dove coming?" faintly asked Aurelia.

"Mrs. Dove is gone to London to attend on little Master Wayland. You are to be here with the young ladies, ma'am."

"What young ladies?" asked the bewildered maiden.

"My Lady's little daughters—the Misses Wayland. I thought she had sent you her instructions; but I see you are over wearied and daunted," she added, more kindly; "you will be better when you have taken some food. Molly, I say, you sluggard of a wench, bring the lady's supper, and don't stand gaping there."

Mrs. Aylward hurried away to hasten operations, and Aurelia began somewhat to recover her senses, though she was still so much dismayed that she dreaded to look up lest she should see something frightful, and started at the first approach of steps.

A dainty little supper was placed before her, but she was too faint and sick at heart for appetite, and would have excused herself. However, Mrs. Aylward severely said she would have no such folly, filled a glass of wine, and sternly administered it; then setting her down in a large chair, helped her to a delicate cutlet. She ate for very fright, but her cheeks and eyes were brightened, the mists of terror and exhaustion began to clear away, and when she accepted a second help, she had felt herself reassured that she had not fallen into unkindly hands. If she could only have met a smile she would have been easier, but Mrs. Aylward was a woman of sedate countenance and few words, and the straight set line of lips encouraged no questioning, so she merely uttered thanks for each act of hospitality.

"There! You will take no more roll? You are better, now, but you will not be sorry to go to your bed," said Mrs. Aylward, taking up a candle, and guiding her along the passage up a long stair to a pretty room wainscoted and curtained with fresh white dimity, and the window showing the young moon pale in the light of the western sky.

Bedrooms were little furnished, and this was more luxurious than the dear old chamber at home, but the girl had never before slept alone, and she felt unspeakably lonely in the dreariness, longing more than ever for

Betty's kiss—even for Betty's blame—or for a whine from Harriet; and she positively hungered for a hug from Eugene, as she gazed timidly at the corners beyond the influence of her candle; and instead of unpacking the little riding mail she kissed it, and laid her cheek on it as the only thing that came from home, and burst into a flood of despairing tears.

In the midst, there fell on her ears a low strain of melancholy music rising and falling like the wailing of mournful spirits. She sprang to her feet and stood listening with dilated eyes; then, as a louder note reached her, in terror uncontrollable, she caught up her candle, rushed down the stairs like a wild bird, and stood panting before Mrs. Aylward, who had a big Bible open on the table before her.

"Oh, ma'am," she cried, between her panting sobs, "I can't stay there! I shall die!"

"What means this, madam?" said Mrs. Aylward, stiffly, making the word sound much like "foolish child."

"The—the music!" she managed faintly to utter, falling again into the friendly chair.

"The music?" said Mrs. Aylward, considering; then with a shade of polite contempt, "O! Jumbo's fiddle! I did not know it could be heard in your room, but no doubt the windows below are open."

"Is Jumbo that black man?" asked Aurelia, shuddering; for negro servants, though the fashion in town, had not penetrated into the west.

"Mr. Belamour's blackamoor. He often plays to him half the night."

"Oh!" with another quivering sound of alarm; "is Mr. Belamour the gentleman in the dark?"

"Even so, madam, but you need have no fears. He keeps his room and admits no one, though he sometimes walks out by night. You will only have to keep the children from a noise making near his apartments. Good night, madam."

"Oh, pray, if I do not disturb you, would you be pleased to let me stay till you have finished your chapter; I might not be so frightened then."

In common humanity Mrs. Aylward could not refuse, and Aurelia sat silently grasping the arms of her chair, and trying to derive all the comfort she could from the presence of a Bible and a good woman. Her nerves were, in fact, calmed by the interval, and when Mrs. Aylward took off her spectacles and shut up her book, it had become possible to endure the terrors of the lonely chamber.

CHAPTER VIII
THE ENCHANTED CASTLE

A little she began to lose her fear. —*MORRIS.*

Aurelia slept till she was wakened by a bounce at the door, and the rattling of the lock, but it was a little child's voice that was crying, "I will! I will! I will go in and seem by cousin!"

Then came Mrs. Aylward's severe voice: "No, miss, you are not to waken your cousin. Come away. Where is that slut, Jenny?"

Then there was a scuffle and a howl, as if the child were being forcibly carried away. Aurelia sprang out of bed, for sunshine was flooding the room, and she felt accountable for tardiness. She had made some progress in dressing, when again little hands were on the lock, little feet kicking the door, and little voices calling, "Let me in."

She opened the door, and white nightgowns, all tumbled back one over the other.

"My little cousins," she said, "come and kiss me."

One came forward and lifted up a sweet little pale face, but the other two stood, each with a finger in the mouth, right across the threshold, in a manner highly inconvenient to Aurelia, who was only in her stiff stays and dimity petticoat, with a mass of hair hanging down below her waist. She turned to them with arms out-stretched, but this put them instantly to the rout, and they ran off as fast as their bare pink feet could carry them, till one stumbled, and lay with her face down and her plump legs kicking in the air. Aurelia caught her up, but the capture produced a powerful yell, and out, all at once hurried into the corridor, Mrs. Aylward, a tidy maid servant, a stout, buxom countrywoman, and a rough girl, scarcely out of bed, but awake enough to snatch the child out of the young lady's arms, and carry her off. The housekeeper began scolding vigorously all round, and Aurelia escaped into her room, where she completed her toilette, looking out into a garden below, laid out in the formal Dutch fashion, with walks and beds centring in a fountain, the grass plats as sharply defined as possible, and stiff yews and cypresses dotted at regular intervals or forming straight alleys. She felt strange and shy, but the sunshine, the cheerfulness, and the sight of the children, had reassured her, and when she had said her morning prayer, she had lost the last night's sense of hopeless dreariness and unprotectedness. When another knock came, she opened the door cheerfully, but there was a chill in meeting Mrs. Aylward's grave, cold face, and stiff salutation. "If you are ready, madam," she said, "I will show you to the south parlour, where the children will eat with you."

Aurelia ventured to ask about her baggage, and was told that it would be forwarded from Brentford. Mrs. Aylward then led the way to a wide stone staircase, with handsome carved balusters, leading down into the great hall, with doors opening from all sides. All was perfectly empty, and so still, that the sweep of the dresses, and the tap of the heels made an echo; and the sunshine, streaming in at the large window, marked out every one upon the floor, in light and shadow, and exactly repeated the brown-shaded, yellow-framed medallions of painted glass upon the pavement. There was something awful and oppressive in the entire absence of all tokens of habitation, among those many closed doors.

One, however, at the foot of the stairs was opened by Mrs. Aylward. It led to a sort of narrow lobby, with a sashed window above a low door, opening on stone steps down to the terrace and garden. To the right was an open door, giving admittance to a room hung with tapestry, with a small carpet in the centre of the floor, and a table prepared for the morning meal. There was a certain cheerfulness about it, though it was bare of furniture; but there was an easy chair, a settee, a long couch, a spinnet, and an embroidery frame, so that altogether it had capabilities of being lived in.

"Here you will sit, madam, with the young ladies," said Mrs. Aylward. "They have a maid-servant who will wait on you, and if you require anything, you will be pleased to speak to me. My Lady wishes you to take charge of them, and likewise to execute the piece of embroidery you will find in that frame, with the materials. This will be your apartment, and you can take the young ladies into the garden and park, wherever you please, except that they must not make a noise before the windows of the other wing, which you will see closed with shutters, for those are Mr. Belamour's rooms."

With these words Mrs. Aylward curtsied as if about to retire, Aurelia held out her hand in entreaty. "Oh, cannot you stay with me?"

"No, madam, my office is the housekeeper's," was the stiff response. "Molly will call me if you require my services. I think you said you preferred bread and milk for breakfast. Dinner will be served at one."

Mrs. Aylward retreated, leaving a chill on the heart of the lonely girl.

She was a clergyman's widow, though with no pretensions to gentility, and was a plain, conscientious, godly woman, but with the narrow self-concentrated piety of the time, which seemed to ignore all the active part of the duty to our neighbour. She had lived many years as a faithful retainer to the Belamour family, and avoided perplexity by minding no one's business but her own, and that thoroughly. Naturally reserved, and disapproving much that she saw around her, she had never held it to be needful to do more than preserve her own integrity, and the interests of her employers, and she made it a principle to be in no wise concerned in family affairs, and to hold aloof from perilous confidences.

Thus Aurelia was left to herself, till three bowls of milk were borne in by Molly, who was by no means loth to speak.

"The little misses will be down directly, ma'am," she said, "that is, two on 'em. The little one, she won't leave Jenny Bowles, but Dame Wheatfield, she'll bring down the other two. You see, ma'am, they be only just taken home from being out at nurse, and don't know one another, nor the place, and a pretty handful we shall have of 'em."

Here came a call for Molly, and the girl with a petulant exclamation, sped away, leaving Aurelia to the society of the tapestry. It was of that set of Gobelin work which represents the four elements personified by their goddesses, and Aurelia's mythology, founded on Fenelon, was just sufficient to enable her to recognise the forge of Vulcan and the car [chariot—D.L.] of Venus. Then she looked at the work prepared for her, a creamy piece of white satin, and a most elaborate pattern of knots of roses, lilacs, hyacinths, and laburnums, at which her heart sank within her. However, at that moment the stout woman she had seen in the morning appeared at the open door with a little girl in each hand, both in little round muslin caps, long white frocks, and blue sashes.

One went up readily to Aurelia and allowed herself to be kissed, and lifted to a chair; the other clung to Dame Wheatfield, in spite of coaxing entreaties. "Speak pretty, my dear; speak to the pretty lady. Don't ye see how good your sister is? It won't do, miss," to Aurelia; "she's daunted, is my pretty lamb. If I might just give her her breakwist—for it is the last time I shall do it—then she might get used to you before my good man comes for me."

Aurelia was only too glad to instal Dame Wheatfield in a chair with her charge in her lap. The other child was feeding herself very tidily and independently, and Aurelia asked her if she were the eldest.

"Yes," she said.

"And what shall I call you, my dear?"

"I'm Missy."

"No, Missy, me—me eldest," cried the other.

"Bless the poor children!" exclaimed Mrs. Wheatfield, laughing, "they be both of 'em eldest, as one may say."

"They are twins, then?" said Aurelia.

"More than that—all three of them came together! I've heard tell of such a thing once or twice, but never of all living and thriving. Folk said it was a judgment on my Lady that she spoke sharp and hard to a poor beggar woman with a child on each arm. It was not a week out before my Lady herself was down, quite unexpected, as I may say, for she was staying here for a week, with a lot of company, when these three was born. They do say she was nigh beside herself that the like of that should have happened to her. Mr. Wayland, he was not so ill pleased, but the poor little things had to be got out of the house any way, for she could not abear to hear of them. Mrs. Rolfe, as was an old servant of the family, took that one, and I was right glad to have you, my pretty one, for I had just lost my babe at a fortnight old, and the third was sent to Goody Bowles, for want of a better. They says as how my Lady means to bring them out one by one, and to make as this here is bigger, and the other up stairs is lesser, and never let on that they are all of an age."

The good gossip must have presumed greatly on the children's want of comprehension if she did not suppose that they understood her at least as well as the young lady to whom her dialect was strange.

"And has she not seen them?"

"Never till last Monday, if you'll believe me miss, when she drove down in her coach, and the children were all brought home. I thought she might have said something handsome, considering the poor little babe as my Missy here was when I had her—not so long as my hand—and scarce able to cry enough to show she was alive. The work I and my good man had with her! He would walk up and down half the night with her. Not as we grudged it. He is as fond of the child as myself; and Mr. Wayland, he knew it. 'She has a good nurse, dame,' says he to me, with the water in his eyes, before he went to foreign parts. But my Lady! When the little one as had been with Goody Bowles—an ignorant woman, you see—cried and clung to her, and kicked, 'Little savages all,' says my Lady. There was thanks to them that had had more work to rear her children than ever with one of her own! 'Perfect little rustics!' she said, even when you made your curtsey as pretty as could be, didn't you, my little lammie?"

"Mammy Rolfe taught me to make my curtsey like a London lady," said the other child, the most advanced in manners.

"Aha! little pitchers have long ears; but, bless you, they don't know what it means," said Dame Wheatfield, too glad to talk to check herself on any account; "Not so much as a kiss for them, poor little darlings! Folks say she does not let even Master Wayland kiss aught but her hands for fear of her fine colours. A plague on such colours, I say."

"Poor little things!" whispered Aurelia.

"You'll be good to them, won't you miss?"

"Indeed I hope so! I am only just come from home, and they will be all I have to care for here."

"Ay, you must be lonesome in this big place; but I'm right glad to have seen you, miss; I can part with the little dear with a better heart, for Mrs. Aylward don't care for children, and Jenny Bowles is a rough wench, wrapped up in her own child, and won't be no good to the others. Go to the lady, my precious," she added, trying to put the little girl into her cousin's lap, but this was met with struggles, and vehement cries of—

"No; stay with mammy!"

The little sister, who had not brought her nurse, was, however, well contented to be lifted to Aurelia's knee, and returned her caresses.

"And have you not a name, my dear? We can't call you all missie."

"Fay," the child lisped; "Fayfiddly Wayland."

"Lawk-a-daisy!" and Mrs. Wheatfield fell back laughing. "I'll tell you how it was, ma'am. When no one thought they would live an hour, Squire Wayland he sent for parson and had 'em half baptised Faith, Hope, and Charity. They says his own mother's was called Faith, and the other two came natural after it, and would do as well to be buried by as aught. So that's what she means by Fay, and this here is Miss Charity."

"She said something besides Faith."

"Well, when my lady got about again, they say if she was mad at their coming all on a heap, she was madder still at their name. Bible wasn't grand enough for her! I did hear tell that she throwed her slipper at her husband's head, and was like to go into fits. So to content her he came down, and took each one to Church, and had a fine London name of my Lady's choosing tacked on in parson's register for them to go by; but to my mind it ain't like their christened name. Mine here got called for her share Amoretta."

"A little Love," cried Aurelia. "Oh, that is pretty. And what can your name be, my dear little Fay? Will you tell me again?"

When repeated, it was plainly Fidelia, and it appeared that Hope had been also called Letitia. As to age, Mrs. Wheatfield knew it was five years last Michaelmas since the child had been brought to her from whom she was so loth to part that she knew not how to go when her husband came for her in his cart. He was a farmer, comfortably off, though very homely, and there were plenty of children at home, so that she had been ill spared to remain at the Park till Aurelia's arrival. Thus she took the opportunity of going away while the little one was asleep.

Aurelia asked where she lived now. At Sedhurst, in the next parish, she was told; but she would not accept a promise that her charge should soon be brought to visit her. "Better not, ma'am, thank you all the same, not till she's broke in. She'll pine the less if she don't see nor hear nothing about the old place, nor Daddy and Sally and Davie. If you bring her soon, you'll never get her away again. That's the worst of a nurse-child. I was warned. It just breaks your heart!"

So away went the good foster-mother sobbing; and Aurelia's charge began. Fay claimed her instantly to explore the garden and house. The child had been sent home alone on the sudden illness of her nurse, and had been very forlorn, so that her cousin's attention was a great boon to her. Hope was incited to come out; but Jenny Bowles kept a jealous watch over her, and treated every one else as an enemy; and before Aurelia's hat was on, came the terrible woe of Amoret's awakening. Her sobs and wailings for her mammy were entirely beyond the reach of Aurelia's soothings and caresses, and were only silenced by Molly's asseveration that the black man was at the door ready to take her into the dark room. That this was no phantom was known to the poor child, and was a lurking horror to Aurelia herself. No wonder that the little thing clung to her convulsively, and would not let her hand go for the rest of the day, every now and then moaning out entreaties to go home to mammy.

With the sad little being hanging to her hand, Aurelia was led by Fay round their new abiding place. The house was of brick, shaped like the letter H, Dutch, and with a tall wing, at each end of the main body, projecting, and finishing in fantastic gables edged with stone. One of these square wings was appropriated to Aurelia and her charges, the other to the recluse Mr. Belamour. The space that lay between the two wings, on the garden front, was roofed over, and paved with stone, descending in several broad shallow steps at the centre and ends, guarded at each angle by huge carved eagles, the crest of the builder, of the most regular patchwork, and kept, in spite of the owner's non-residence, in perfect order. The strange thing was that this fair and stately place, basking in the sunshine of early June, should be left in complete solitude save for the hermit in the opposite wing, the three children, and the girl, who felt as though in a kind of prison.

The sun was too hot for Aurelia to go out of doors till late in the day, when the shadow of the house came over the steps. She was sitting on one, with Amoret nestled in her lap, and was crooning an old German lullaby of Nannerl's, which seemed to have a wonderful effect in calming the child, who at last fell into a doze. Aurelia had let her voice die away, and had begun to think over her strange situation, when she was startled by a laugh behind her, and looking round, hardly repressed a start or scream, at the sight of Fay enjoying a game at bo-peep, with—yes—it actually was—the negro—over the low-sashed door.

"I beg pardon, ma'am," said Jumbo, twitching his somewhat grizzled wool; "I heard singing, and little missy—"

Unfortunately Amoret here awoke, and with a shriek of horror cowered in her arms.

"I am so sorry," said Aurelia, anxious not to hurt his feelings. "She knows no better."

Jumbo grinned, bowed, and withdrew, Fay running after him, for she had made friends with him during her days of solitude, being a fearless child, and not having been taught to make a bugbear of him. "The soot won't come off," she said.

Aurelia had not a moment to herself till Fay had said the Lord's prayer at her knee, and Amoret, with much persuasion, had been induced to lisp out—

> "Matthew, Mark, Luke, and John,
> Bless the bed I sleep upon;
> Four corners to by bed,
> Four angles round my head,
> One to read and one to write,
> And two to guard my soul at night."

Another agony for mammy ensued, nor could Aurelia leave the child till sleep had hushed the wailings. Then only could she take her little writing-case to begin her letter to Betty. It would be an expensive luxury to her family, but she knew how it would be longed for; and though she cried a good deal over her writing, she felt as if she ought to make the best of her position, for had not Betty said it was for her father's sake? No, her tears must not blot the paper, to distress those loving hearts. Yet how the drops *would* come, gathering fast and blinding her! Presently, through the window, came the sweet mysterious strains of the violin, not terrifying her as before, but filling her with an inexpressible sense of peace and calmness. She sat listening almost as one in a dream, with her pen suspended, and when the spell was broken by Molly's entrance with her supper, she went on in a much more cheerful strain than she had begun. It was dull, and it was a pity that her grand wardrobe, to say nothing of Betty's good advice, should be wasted, but her sister would rejoice in her seclusion from the grand, fashionable world, and her heart went out to the poor little neglected children, whose mother could not bear the sight of them.

CHAPTER IX
THE TRIAD

"I know sisters, sisters three."

Ere many days had passed Aurelia had drifted into what would now be regarded as the duties of a nursery governess to her little companions.

Fay and Amoret were always with her, and depended on her for everything. Jenny Bowles, with a sort of animal jealousy, tried to monopolise her charge, Letitia. The child was attracted by the sounds of her sister's sports, and there was no keeping her from them, or from their cousin. Then the rude untaught Jenny became cross, moped, showed spite to the other children, and insolence to the young lady, and was fortunately overheard by Mrs. Aylward, and dismissed. Letty did not seem to mind the loss as Amoret had felt that of her foster-mother, for indeed Jenny had been almost as disagreeable to her as to the others during these days of jealousy.

The triad were not much alike: Amoret was the largest of the three, plump, blue-eyed, golden-haired, rosy-cheeked, a picture of the cherub-type of child; Letitia had the delicate Delavie features and complexion; and Fidelia, the least pretty, was pale, and rather sallow, with deep blue eyes set under a broad forehead and dark brows, with hair also dark. Though the smallest, she was the most advanced, and showed signs of good training. She had some notion of good manners, and knew as much of her hornbook [a child's primer consisting of a sheet of parchment or paper protected by a sheet of transparent horn—D.L.] and catechism as little girls of five were wont to know. The other two were perfectly ignorant, but Mrs. Aylward procured hornbooks, primers, and slates, and Aurelia began their education in a small way.

It was a curious life. There was the great empty house, through whose long corridors and vacant rooms the children might wander at will, peeping at the swathed curtains of velvet pile, the rolls of carpet, and the tapestry pictures on the walls, running and shouting in the empty passages, or sometimes, in a fit of nameless fright, taking refuge in Aurelia's arms. Or they might play in the stately garden, provided they trod on no borders, and meddled with neither flower nor fruit. The old gardener began by viewing them as his natural enemies, but soon relaxed in amusement at their pretty sportive ways, gave them many precious spoils, and forgave more than one naughty little inroad, which greatly alarmed their guardian.

Or if the little party felt enterprising, there lay beyond, the park, its slopes covered with wild strawberries, and with woods where they could gather flowers unchecked. Further, there was no going, except on alternate Sundays, when there was service in the tumble-down Church at the park gate. It was in far worse condition than the Church at home, and was served by a poor forlorn-looking curate, who lived at Brentford, and divided his services between four parishes, each of which was content to put up with a fortnightly alternate morning and evening service. The Belamour seat was a square one, without the comfortable appliances of the Delavie closet, and thus permitting a much fuller view, but there was nothing to be seen except a row of extremely gaudy Belamour hatchments, displaying to the full, the saltir-wise sheafs of arrows on the shields or lozenges, supported by grinning skulls. The men's shields preserved their eagle crest, the women had only lozenges, and the family motto, *Amo et Amabo*, was exchanged for the more pious "*Resurgam*."

Aurelia found that the family seat, whither she was marshalled by Mrs. Aylward, was already occupied by two ladies, who rose up, and made her stately curtsies with a decidedly disgusted air, although there was ample space for her and Fidelia, the only one of her charges whom she had ventured to take with her. They wore the black hoods, laced boddices, long rolls of towering curl and open upper skirts, of Queen Anne's day, and in the eyes of thirty years' later, looked so ridiculous that Fay could not but stare at them the whole time, and whenever Aurelia turned her glances from her book to see whether her little companion was behaving herself, the big blue considering eyes were always levelled full upon the two forms before her.

The ladies were in keeping with their dress, thin, stiff and angular, with worn and lined faces, highly rouged, and enormous long-handled fans, and Aurelia was almost as much astonished as the child.

There was a low curtseying again, and much ceremony before it was possible to get out of the pew, and the two ladies mounted at the door on lofty pattens which added considerably to their height, and, attended by a loutish-looking man in livery, who carried their books, stalked of into the village.

Aurelia found from the communicative Molly that they were Mistress Phoebe and Mistress Delia Treforth, kinswomen of the Belamour family, who had in consequence a life residence rent-free in a tall thin red square house near the churchyard, where a very gay parrot was always to be seen in the windows. They no doubt regarded Miss Delavie and the little Waylands as interlopers at Bowstead, and their withering glances made Church-going a trying affair—indeed the first time that Aurelia took little Amoret, they actually drove the sensitive child into a sobbing fit, so that she had to be carried out, begging to know why those ladies looked so cross at her.

The life, on the whole, was not unhappy, except for fits of homesickness and longing for letters. The arrival of the boxes from the carrier was the first comfort, and then at last came a thick letter from home, franked by Sir George Herries, and containing letters from everybody—even a few roundhand lines from Eugene.

Her father wrote at length all the excellent moral and religious essay which had stuck in his throat at the parting; neither was Betty's letter deficient in good advice, though she let it appear that the family were much amused at Lady Belamour's affliction in her triad of daughters, the secret having been hitherto so carefully kept that they supposed her to have only one.

"It will be your Charge," wrote Betty, "so far as in you lies, to render them not merely the Graces, as my Father terms them, but the true and faithful Guardian to these Infant Spirits. Though their Mother has shown no Care or heed in entrusting them to you, yet remember that it is truly the good Providence of their Heavenly Father that has put these little Children of His in your Charge, to receive from you the first Principles of Religion and Morals which may mould their whole Lives; and I trust that you will do the Work faithfully and successfully. It may be dull and tedious at Bowstead, but I had much rather hear of you thus than exposed to the Glare of My Lady's Saloon in London. No doubt Harriet has write to you of the Visit of young Sir Amyas, the Sunday after your departure. We have since heard that his expedition to Monmouthshire was with a View to his marriage to Lady Aresfield's Daughter, and this may well be, so that if he fall in your way, you will be warned against putting any misconstruction on any Civil Attentions he may pay to you. Ever since your Departure Mr. Arden has redoubled his Assiduities in a certain Quarter, and as it is thought the Dean and Chapter are not unlikely to present him to a good Vicarage in Buckinghamshire, it is not unlikely that ere long you may hear of a Wedding in the Family, although Harriet would be extremely angry with me for daring to give such a Hint."

Certainly Aurelia would not have gathered the hint from Harriet's letter, which was very sentimental about her own loneliness and lack of opportunity, in contrast with Aurelia, who was seeing the world. That elegant beau, Sir Amyas, had just given a sample to tantalise their rusticity, and then had vanished; and here was that oddity, Mr. Arden, more wearisome and pertinacious than ever. So tiresome!

CHAPTER X
THE DARK CHAMBER

Or singst thou rather under force
Of some Divine command,
Commissioned to presage a course
Of happier days at hand?
COWPER.

Aurelia was coming down stairs in the twilight after singing her charges to sleep about three weeks after her arrival, when she saw Jumbo waiting at the bottom of the stairs.

She had long ceased to be afraid of him. Indeed he had quite amazed her by his good-nature in helping to lift down naughty little Letitia, who was clambering up to the window of his master's chamber to look through the crevices of the shutters. He had given the children a gaily dressed rag doll, and was as delighted as they were when he played his fiddle to them and set them dancing.

Still, the whites of his eyes, his shining teeth, and the gold lace of his livery had a startling effect in the darkness, and Aurelia wished he would move away; but he was evidently waiting for her, and when she came near he addressed her thus, "Mis'r Belamour present compliment, and would Miss Delavie be good enough to honour him with her company for a short visit?"

The girl started, dismayed, alarmed, yet unwilling to be unkind to the poor recluse, while she hoped that decorum and propriety would put the visit out of the question. She replied that she would ask Mrs. Aylward whether she might, and Jumbo followed her to the still-room, saying on the way, "Mas'r heard Miss Delavie sing. He always has the window opened to hear her. It makes him hum the air—be merry. He has not asked to speak with lady since he heard the bad news—long, long, ago."

Then Aurelia felt that nothing short of absolute impropriety ought to make her gratify her shrinking reluctance. Mrs. Aylward seemed to think her doubts uncalled for, and attributed her hesitation to fear of the dark room.

"Oh, no I am not so childish," said the young lady with nervous dignity; "but would it be proper?"

"Bless me, madam, he is as old as your father, and as civil a gentleman as lives. I would come in with you but that I am expecting Mr. Potts with the tallies. You need have no scruples."

There was no excuse nor escape, and Aurelia followed the negro in trepidation. Crossing the hall, he opened for her the door of the lobby corresponding to her own, and saying, "Allow me, ma'am," passed before her, and she heard another door unclosed, and a curtain withdrawn. Beyond she only saw a gulf of darkness, but out of it came a deep manly voice, subdued and melancholy, but gentlemanlike and deferential.

"The young lady is so kind as to come and cheer the old hermit. A thousand thanks, madam. Permit me."

Aurelia's hand was taken by one soft for want of use, and she was led forward on a deep piled carpet, and carefully placed on a chair in the midst of the intense black darkness. There was a little movement and then the voice said, "I am most sensible of your goodness, madam."

"I—I am glad. You are very good, sir," murmured Aurelia, oppressed by the gloom and the peculiar atmosphere, cool—for the windows were open behind the shutters—but strangely fragrant.

"How does my excellent friend, Major Delavie?"

"I thank you, sir, he is well, though his wound troubles him from time to time."

"Commend me to him when you write, if you are good enough to remember it."

"I thank you, sir. He will be rejoiced to hear of you."

"He does me too much honour."

These conventionalities being exhausted, a formidable pause ensued, first broken by Mr. Belamour, "May I ask how my fair visitor likes Bowstead?"

"It is a fine place, sir."

"But somewhat lonely for so youthful a lady?"

"I have the children, sir."

"I often hear their cheerful voices."

"I hope we do not disturb you, sir, I strive to restrain them, but I fear we are all thoughtless."

"Nay, the innocent sounds of mirth ring sweetly on my ears, like the notes of birds. And when I have heard a charming voice singing to the little ones, I have listened with delight. Would it be too presumptuous to beg the air songstress to repeat her song for the old recluse?"

"O, sir, I have only nursery ditties, caught from our old German maid," cried Aurelia, in dismay.

"That might not diminish the charm to me," he said. "In especial there was one song whose notes Jumbo caught as you accompanied yourself on the spinnet."

And Jumbo, who seemed able to see in the dark, played a bar on his violin, while Aurelia trembled with shyness.

"The Nightingale Song," she said. "My dear mother learnt the tune abroad. And I believe that she herself made the English words, when she was asked what the nightingales say."

"May I hear it? Nightingales can sing in the dark." Refusal was impossible, and Jumbo's violin was a far more effective accompaniment than her own very moderate performance on the spinnet; so in a sweet, soft, pure, untrained and trembling voice, she sang—

"O Life and Light are sweet, my dear, O life and Light are sweet;
But sweeter still the hope and cheer
When Love and Life shall meet.
Oh! then it is most sweet, sweet, sweet, sweet, sweet, sweet.

"But Love puts on the yoke, my dear, But Love puts on the yoke;
The dart of Love calls forth the tear,
As though the heart were broke.
The very heart were broke, broke, broke, broke, broke, broke.

"And Love can quench Life's Light, my dear, Drear, dark, and melancholy;
Seek Light and Life and jocund cheer,
And mirth and pleasing folly.
Be thine, light-hearted folly, folly, folly, folly, folly, folly.

"'Nay, nay,' she sang. 'yoke, pain, and tear,

For Love I gladly greet;

Light, Life, and Mirth are nothing here,

Without Love's bitter sweet.

Give me Love's bitter sweet, sweet, sweet, sweet, sweet, sweet.'"

"Accept my fervent thanks, kind songstress. So that is the nightingale's song, and your honoured mother's?"

"Yes, sir. My father often makes us sing it because it reminds him of her."

"Philomel could not have found a better interpreter," said the grave voice, sounding so sad that Aurelia wished she could have sung something less affecting to his spirits.

"I gather from what you said that you are no longer blessed with the presence of the excellent lady, your mother," presently added Mr. Belamour.

"No, sir. We lost her seven years ago."

"And her husband mourns her still. Well he may. She was a rare creature. So she is gone! I have been so long in seclusion that no doubt time has made no small havoc, and my friends have had many griefs to bewail."

Aurelia knew not what answer to make, and was relieved when he collected himself and said: —

"I will trespass no longer on my fair visitor's complaisance, but if she have not found the gloom of this apartment insupportable, it would be a charitable action to brighten it once more with her presence."

"O sir, I will come whenever you are pleased to send for me," she exclaimed, all her doubts, fears, and scruples vanishing at his tone of entreaty. "My father would be so glad. I will practise my best song to sing to you to-morrow."

"My best thanks are yours," and her hand was taken, she was carefully conducted to the door and dismissed with a gentle pressure of her fingers, and a courteous: "Goodnight, madam; *Au revoir*, if I may venture to say so."

By contrast, the hall looked almost light, and Aurelia could see the skip of joy with which Jumbo hurried to fetch a candle. As he gave it to her, he made his teeth flash from ear to ear, as he exclaimed: "Pretty missy bring new life to mas'r!"

Thus did a new element come into Aurelia's life. She carefully prepared Harriet's favourite song, a French *romance*, but Mr. Belamour did not like it equally well with the Nightingale, which he made her repeat, rewarding her by telling her of the charming looks and manners of her mother, so that she positively enjoyed her visit. The next night he made inquiries into her walks at Bowstead, asking after the favourite nooks of his childhood, and directing her to the glades where grew the largest dewberries and sweetest blackberries. This led to her recital of a portion of *Midsummer Night's Dream*, for he drew her on with thanks at every pause: "I have enjoyed no such treat for many years," he said.

"There are other pieces that I can recite another time," said Aurelia timidly.

"You will confer a great favour on me," he answered.

So she refreshed her memory by a mental review of *Paradise Lost* over her embroidery frame, and was ready with Adam's morning hymn, which was much relished. Compliments on her elocution soon were turned by her into the praise of "sister," and as she became more at ease, the strange man in the dark listened with evident delight to her pretty fresh prattle about sister and brother, and father and home. Thus it had become a daily custom that she should spend the time between half past seven and nine in the company of the prisoner of darkness, and she was beginning to look forward to it as the event of the day. She scarcely expected to be sent for on Sunday evening, but Jumbo came as usual with the invitation, and she was far from sorry to quit a worm-eaten Baxter's *Saints' Rest* which she had dutifully borrowed from Mrs. Aylward.

"Well, my fair visitor," said the voice which had acquired a tone of pleased anticipation, "what mental repast has your goodness provided?"

"It is Sunday, sir."

"Ah!" as if it had not occurred to him, and with some disappointment.

"I could say the Psalms by heart, sir, if you would like it, for it is the 20th day of the month."

"Thank you. Your voice can make anything sweet."

Aurelia was shocked, and knew that Betty would be more so, but she was too shy to do anything except to begin: "Praise thou the Lord, O my soul."

It was a fortunate thing that it was a Psalm of such evident beauty, for it fell less familiarly on his ear than her passages from the poets. At the end he said: "Yes, that is true poetry. Praise fits well with happy young lips. You have been to church?"

"No, sir, Mr. Greaves does not come to-day."

"Then how did the gentle saint perform her orisons?"

"Please do not so call me, sir! I tried to read the service, but I could not get the children to be still, so I had to tell them about Joseph, and I found a beautiful Bible full of pictures, like our Dutch one at home."

"You found the old Bible? My mother used to show it to my brother and me—my poor mother!"

He mentioned one or two of the engravings, which he had never forgotten, but the evening was less of a success than usual, and Aurelia doubted whether we would wish for her that day se'nnight. All her dread of him was gone; she knew she had brought a ray of brightness into his solitary broken life, and her mind was much occupied with the means of affording him pleasure. Indeed she might have wearied of the lack of all companionship save that of the young children; and converse with a clever highly cultivated mind was stimulating and expanding all her faculties. When the stores or her memory were becoming exhausted, Jumbo was bidden to open a case of books which had lain untouched since they were sent sown from Mr. Belamour's chambers at the Temple, and they were placed at her disposal. Here was Mr. Alexander Pope's translation of the *Iliad* of Homer, which had appeared shortly before the fatal duel, and Aurelia eagerly learnt whole pages of it by heart for the evening's amusement, enjoying extremely the elucidations and criticisms of her auditor, who would dwell on a passage all day, beg to have it repeated a second time in the evening, and then tell her what his memory or his reflection had suggested about it. Moreover, having heard some inexplicable report, through Jumbo, of the Porteous mob, Mr. Belamour became curious to learn the truth, and this led to his causing the newspapers to be sent weekly to be read and reported to him by Aurelia. It seemed incredible that a man of much ability should have been content to spend all these years in the negro's sole society, but no doubt the injury done to the brain had been aggravated by grief and remorse, so that he had long lain, with suspended faculties, in a species of living death; whence he had only gradually, and as it were unconsciously, advanced to his present condition. Perhaps Mr. Wayland's endeavours to rouse him had come too soon, or in a less simple and attractive form, for they had been reluctantly received and had proved entirely unsuccessful; while the child-like efforts of the girl, following his lead instead of leading him, were certainly awakening him, and renewing his spirits and interest in the world at large in an unlooked-for manner.

CHAPTER XI
A VOICE FROM THE GRAVE

He hath a word for thee to speak.
KEBLE.

No difference was made to Aurelia's visits to Mr. Belamour on Sunday evenings, but he respected her scruples against indulgence in profane literature, and encouraged her to repeat passages of Scripture, beginning to taste the beauty of the grand cadences falling from her soft measured voice. Thus had she come to the Sermon on the Mount, and found herself repeating the expansion of the Sixth Commandment ending with, "And thou be cast into prison. Verily I say unto thee, thou shalt not come out thence until thou hast paid the uttermost farthing."

A groan startled her. Then came the passage and the unhappy man's history with a sudden stab. A horror of the darkness fell on her. She felt as if he were in the prison and she reproaching him, and cried out—"O sir, forgive me. I forgot; I did not say it on purpose."

"No, my child, it was Mary speaking by your voice. No, Mary, I shall never come out. It will never be paid."

She shook with fright as Jumbo touched her, saying, "Missee, go; mas'r bear no more;" but, as she rose to go away, a sweet impulse made her pause and say, "It is paid, *He* paid. You know Who did—in his own Blood."

Jumbo drew her away almost by force, and when outside, exclaimed, "Missee never speak of blood or kill to mas'r—he not bear it. Head turn again—see shapes as bad as ever."

The poor child cried bitterly, calling herself cruel, thoughtless, presumptuous; and for the next few days Jumbo's eyes glared at her as he reported his master to be very ill; but, on the third day, he came for her as usual. She thought Mr. Belamour's tones unwontedly low and depressed, but no reference was made to the Sunday, and she was glad enough to plunge into the council of Olympus.

A day or two later, Dame Wheatfield sent her husband with an urgent invitation to Miss Amoret with her sisters and cousin to be present at her harvest home. Mrs. Aylward, with a certain tone of contempt, gave her sanction to their going with Molly, by the help of the little pony cart used about the gardens. Aurelia, in high glee, told Mr. Belamour, who encouraged her to describe all her small adventures, and was her oracle in all the difficult questions that Fidelia's childish wisdom was wont to start.

"To Wheatfield's farm, did you say? That is in Sedhurst. There are but three fields between it and the church."

Presently he added: "I am tempted to ask a great kindness, though I know not whether it will be possible to you."

"Indeed, sir, I will do my utmost."

"There are two graves in Sedhurst Church, I have never dared to inquire about them. Would it be asking too much from my gentle friend to beg of her to visit them, and let me hear of them."

"I will, I will, sir, with all my heart."

By eight o'clock the next evening she was again with him, apologizing for being late.

"I scarcely expected this pleasure to-night. These rural festivities are often protracted."

"O sir, I was heartily glad to escape and to get the children away. The people were becoming so rude and riotous that I was frightened. I never would have gone, had I known what it would be like, but at home the people are fond of asking us to their harvest feasts, and they always behave well whilst we are there."

"No doubt they hold your father in respect."

"Yes," said Aurelia, unwilling to tell him how much alarmed and offended she had been, though quite unintentionally. Dame Wheatfield only intended hospitality; but in her eyes "Miss" was merely a poor governess, and that to the little Waylands—mere interlopers in the eyes of the Belamour tenantry. So the good woman had no idea that the rough gallantry of the young farmer guests was inappropriate, viewing it as the natural tribute to her guest's beauty, and mistaking genuine offence for mere coyness, until, finding it was real earnest, considerable affront was taken at "young madam's fine airs, and she only a poor kinswoman of my Lady's!" Quite as ill was it received that the young lady had remonstrated against the indigestible cakes and strange beverages administered to all her charges, and above all to Amoret. She had made her escape on the plea of early hours for the children, leaving Molly behind her, just as the boisterous song was beginning in which Jack kisses Bet, Joe kisses Sue, Tom kisses

Nan, &c. down to poor Dorothy Draggletail, who is left in the lurch. The farewell had been huffy. "A good evening to you, madam; I am sorry our entertainment was not more to your taste." She had felt guilty and miserable at the accusation of pride, and she could not imagine how Mrs. Aylward could have let her go without a warning; the truth being that Mrs. Aylward despised her taste, but thought she knew what a harvest supper was like.

All this was passed over in silence by Aurelia's pride and delicacy. She only described the scene when the last waggon came in with its load, the horses decked with flowers and ribbons, and the farmer's youngest girl enthroned on the top of the shocks, upholding the harvest doll. This was a little sheaf, curiously constructed and bound with straw plaits and ribbons. The farmer, on the arrival in the yard, stood on the horse-block, and held it high over the heads of all the harvesters, and the chorus was raised:

"*A knack, a knack, a knack,*
Well cut, well bound,
Well shocked, well saved from the ground,
Whoop! whoop! whoop!"

After which the harvest doll displaced her last year's predecessor over the hearth, where she was to hang till next year.

All this Aurelia described, comparing the customs with those of her own county, her heart beating all the time under the doubt how to venture on describing the fulfilment of her commission. At last Mr. Belamour said,

"In such a scene of gaiety, no doubt the recollection of sorrow had no place."

"O sir, you could not think I should forget."

"I thought I might have asked more than was possible to you."

"It was the only part of the day that I enjoyed. I took little Fay with me, for no one seemed to care for her, while Amy was queening it with all the Wheatfields, and Letty was equally happy with her foster mother. I could see the church spire, so I needed not to ask the way, and we crossed the stubble fields, while the sun sent a beautiful slanting light through the tall elm trees that closed in the churchyard, but let one window glitter between them like a great diamond. It looked so peaceful after all the noise we left behind, even little Fay felt it, and said she loved the quiet walk along the green baulks [An unplowed strip of land—D.L.]. The churchyard has a wooden rail with steps to cross it on either side, and close under the church wall is a tomb, a great square simple block, surmounted by an urn."

"Yes, let me hear," said the voice, eager, though stifled.

"I thought it might be what you wished me to see and went up to read the names."

"Do not spare. Never fear. Let me hear the very words."

"On one face of the block there was a name—

'WILLIAM SEDHURST,

AGED 27,

DIED MAY 13, 1729.'

On the other side was this inscription:—

'MARY,

ONLY DAUGHTER OF GEORGE SEDHURST, ESQUIRE,

AGED 19,

DIED AUGUST 1st, 1729.

Love is strong as Death.

Sorrow not as others that have no Hope.'

In smaller letters down below, 'This epitaph is at her own special request.'

"Sir," continued Aurelia, "it was very curious. I should not have observed those words if it had not been that a large beautiful butterfly, with rainbow eyes on its wings, sat sunning itself on the white marble, and Fay called me to look at it."

"Her message! May I ask you to repeat it again?"

"The texts? 'Love is strong as death. Sorrow not as others that have no hope.'"

"Did you call them Scripture texts?"

"Yes, sir; I know the last is in one of the Epistles, and I will look for the other."

"It matters not. She intended them for a message to me who lay in utter darkness and imbecility well befitting her destroyer."

"Nay, they have come to you at last," said Aurelia gently. "You really never knew of them before?"

"No, I durst not ask, nor did any one dare to speak to me. My brother, who alone would have done so, died, I scarcely know when; but ere the very consciousness of my own wretched existence had come back to me. Once again repeat the words, gentle messenger of mercy."

She obeyed, but this time he mournfully murmured, "Hope! What hope for their destroyer?"

"They are God's words, as well as hers," the girl answered, with diffident earnestness, but in reply she only heard tightened breaths, which made her say, "You cannot bear more, sir. Let me call Jumbo, and bid you good night."

Jumbo came at the mention of his name. Somehow he was so unlike other human beings, and so wholly devoted to his master, that it never seemed to be a greater shock to find that he had been present than if he had been a faithful dog.

A few days later he told Aurelia that Mas'r was not well enough to see her. He had set forth as soon as the moon had set, and walked with his trusty servant to Sedhurst, where he had traced with his finger the whole inscription, lingering so long that the sun was above the horizon before he could get home; and he was still lying on the bed where he had thrown himself on first coming in, having neither spoken nor eaten since. Jumbo could not but grumble out that Mas'r was better left to himself.

Yet when Aurelia on the third evening was recalled, there was a ring of refreshment in the voice. It was still melancholy, but the dejection was lessened, and though it was only of Achilles and Patroclus that they talked, she was convinced that the pressure of the heavy burthen of grief and remorse was in some degree lightened.

CHAPTER XII
THE SHAFTS OF PHOEBE

Her golden bow she bends,
Her deadly arrows sending forth.
Greek Hymn (KEIGHTLEY).

On coming in from a walk, Aurelia was surprised by the tidings that Mistress Phoebe Treforth had come to call on her, and had left a billet. The said billet was secured with floss silk sealed down in the antiquated fashion, and was written on full-sized quarto paper. These were the contents:—

"Madam,

> "*My Sister and Myself are desirous of the Honour of your*
> *Acquaintance, and shall be happy if you will do use the*
> *Pleasure of coming to partake of Dinner at Three o'Clock*
> *on Tuesday, the 13th instant.*

> "*I remain,*
> "*Yours to command,*
> "*DELIA TREFORTH."*

Aurelia carried the invitation to her oracle.

"My cousins are willing to make your acquaintance?" said he. "That is well. Jumbo shall escort you home in the evening."

"Thank you, sir, but must I accept the invitation?"

"It could not be declined without incivility. Moreover, the Mistresses Treforth are highly respected, and your father and sister will certainly think it well for you to have female friends."

"Do you think those ladies could ever be my friends, sir?" she asked, with an intonation that made him reply, with a sound of amusement.

"I am no judge in such matters, but they are ladies connected and esteemed, who might befriend and counsel you in case of need, and at any rate, it is much more suitable that you should be on terms of friendly intercourse with them. I am heartily glad they have shown you this attention."

"I do not mean to be ungrateful, sir."

"And I think you have disproved that

Crabbed age and youth
Cannot live together."

"If they were only like you, sir!"

"What would they say to that?" he said with the slight laugh that had begun to enliven his voice. "I suppose your charges are not included in the invitation?"

"No; but Molly can take care of them, if my Lady will not object to my leaving them."

"She cannot reasonably do so."

"And, sir, shall I be permitted to come home in time for you to receive me?"

"I fear I must forego that pleasure. The ladies will insist on cards and supper. Jumbo shall come for you at nine o'clock."

Aurelia submitted, and tripped down arrayed in the dress that recalled the fete at Carminster, except that only a little powder was sprinkled on her temples. The little girls jumped round her in admiring ecstasy, and, under Molly's charge, escorted her to the garden gate, and hovered outside to see her admitted, while she knocked timidly at the door, in the bashful alarm of making her first independent visit.

The loutish man ushered her into a small close room, containing a cat, a little spaniel, a green parrot, a spinning-wheel, and an embroidery frame. There were also the two old ladies, dressed with old-fashioned richness, a little faded, and a third, in a crimson, gold-laced joseph [A long riding coat with a small cape, worn by women in the 18th century.—D.L.], stout, rubicund, and hearty, to whom Aurelia was introduced thus—

"Mrs. Hunter, allow me to present to you Miss Delavie, a relative of my Lady Belamour. Miss Delavie, Mrs. Hunter of Brentford."

"I am most happy to make your acquaintance, Miss," said the lady, in a jovial voice, and Aurelia made her curtsey, but at that moment the man announced that dinner was served, whereupon Mrs. Delia handed Mrs. Hunter in, and Mrs. Phoebe took the younger guest.

The ladies' faces both bore token of their recent attention to the preparation of the meal, and the curious dishes would have been highly interesting to Betty, but there was no large quantity of any, and a single chicken was the *piece de resistance*, whence very tiny helps were dealt out, and there was much unnecessary pressing to take a little more, both of that and of the brace of partridges which succeeded it. As to conversation, there was room for none, except hospitable invitations from the hostesses to take the morsels that they cut for their guests, praises of the viands from Mrs. Hunter, and endeavours to fish at the recipes, which the owners guarded jealously as precious secrets. Aurelia sat perfectly silent, as was then reckoned as proper in a young lady of her age, except when addressed. A good deal of time was also expended in directing John Stiggins, the ladies' own man, and George Brown, who had ridden with Mrs. Hunter from Brentford, in the disposal of the dishes, and the handing of the plates. George Brown was the more skilled waiter, and as the man who was at home did not brook interference, their disputes were rude and audible, and kept the ladies in agonies lest they should result in ruin to the best china.

At last, however, the cloth was removed, walnuts, apples, pears, and biscuits were placed on the table, a glass of wine poured out for each lady, and the quartette, with the cat and dog, drew near the sunny window, where there was a little warmth. It was a chilly day, but no one ever lighted a fire before the 5th of November, Old Style.

Then began one of those catechisms which fortunately are less unpleasant to youth and simplicity than they are to persons of an age to resent inquiry, and who have more resources of conversation. In truth, Aurelia was in the eyes of the Treforth sisters, descendants of a former Sir Jovian, only my Lady's poor kinswoman sent down to act *gouvernante* to the Wayland brats, who had been impertinently quartered in the Belamour household. She would have received no further notice, had it not been reported through the servants that "young Miss" spent the evenings with their own cousin, from whom they had been excluded ever since his illness.

The subject was approached through interrogations on Miss Delavie's home and breeding, how she had travelled, and what were her accomplishments, also whether she were quite sure that none of the triad was either imbecile nor deformed. Mrs. Hunter seemed to have heard wonderful rumours about the poor children.

"Has their lady mother seen them?"

"Yes, madam. She had been there with them shortly before my arrival."

"Only once in their lives!" There was a groan of censure such as would have fired the loyal Major in defence.

"No wonder, Sister Phoebe, my Lady Belamour does not lead the life of a tender mother."

"She has the little boy, Archer, with her in London," Aurelia ventured to say.

"And a perfect puppet she makes of the poor child," said Mrs. Hunter. "My sister Chetwynd saw him with his mother at a masquerade, my Lady Belamour flaunting as Venus, and he, when he ought to have been in his bed, dressed in rose-colour and silver, with a bow and arrows, and gauze wings on his shoulders!"

"What will that child come to?"

"Remember, Sister Delia, he is no kin of ours. He is only a Wayland!" returned Mrs. Phoebe, in an accent as if the Waylands were the most contemptible of vermin.

"I hope," added Mrs. Delia, "that these children are never permitted to incommode our unfortunate cousin, Mr. Belamour."

"I trust not, madam," said Aurelia. "Their rooms are at a distance from his; they are good children, and he says he likes to hear young voices in the gardens."

"You have, then, seen Mr. Belamour?"

"I cannot say that I have seen him," said Aurelia, modestly; "but I have conversed with him."

"Indeed! Alone with him?"

"Jumbo was there."

The two old ladies drew themselves up, while Mrs. Hunter chuckled and giggled. "Indeed!" said Mrs. Phoebe; "we should never see a gentleman in private without each other's company, or that of some female companion."

"I consulted Mrs. Aylward," returned Aurelia, "and she said he was old enough to be my father."

"Mrs. Aylward may be a respectable housekeeper, though far too lavish of butcher's meat, but I should never have recourse to her on a matter of decorum," said Mrs. Phoebe.

Aurelia's cheeks burnt, but she still defended herself. "I have heard from my father and my sister," she said, "and they make no objection."

"Hoity-toity! What means this heat, miss?" exclaimed Mrs. Phoebe; "I am only telling you, as a kindness, what we should have thought becoming with regard even to a blood relation of our own."

"Thank you, ma'am," said Aurelia; "but, you see, you are so much nearer his age, that the cases are not alike."

She said it in all simplicity, and did not perceive, at first, why the two sisters drew themselves up in so much offence, or why Mrs. Hunter cried, "Oh, fie, for shame, you saucy chit! Bless me!" she continued, more good-naturedly, "Cousin Phoebe, times are changed since we were young, and poor Sir Jovian and his brother were the county beaux. The child is right enough when one comes to think of it; and for my part, I should be glad that poor Mr. Amyas had some one young and cheerful about him. It is only a pity his nephew, the young baronet, never comes down to see him."

"Like mother like son," said Mrs. Phoebe; "I grieve to think what the old place will come to."

"Well," said Mrs. Hunter, "I do not hear the young gentleman ill spoken of; though, more's the pity, he is in a bad school with Colonel Mar for his commanding officer, the fine gallant who is making his mother the talk of the town!"

The gossip and scandal then waxed fast and furious on the authority of Mrs. Hunter's sister, but no one paid any more attention to Aurelia, except that when there was an adjournment to the next room, she was treated with such double stiffness and ceremony as to make her feel that she had given great offence, and was highly disapproved of by all but Mrs. Hunter. And Aurelia could not like her, for her gossip had been far broader and coarser than that of the Mistresses Treforth, who, though more bitter were more of gentlewomen. Happily much of what passed was perfectly unintelligible to Betty's carefully shielded pupil, who sat all the time with the cat on her lap, listening to its purring music, but feeling much more inclined to believe nothing against my Lady, after her father's example, than to agree with those who were so evidently prejudiced. Tea was brought in delicate porcelain cups, then followed cards, which made the time pass less drearily till supper. This consisted of dishes still tinier than those at dinner, and it was scarcely ended when it was announced that Jumbo had come for Miss Delavie.

Gladly she departed, after an exchange of curtsies, happily not hearing the words behind her:—

"An artful young minx."

"And imagine the impudence of securing Jumbo's attendance, forsooth!"

"Nay," said Mrs. Hunter, "she seemed to me a pretty modest young gentlewoman enough."

"Pretty! Yes, she comes of my Lady's own stock, and will be just such another."

"Yes; it is quite plain that it is true that my Lady sent her here because she had been spreading the white apron for the young baronet."

"And now she is trying her arts on poor cousin Amyas Belamour. You heard how she would take no advice, and replied with impertinence."

"Shall you give my Lady a hint?"

"Not I. I have been treated with too much insolence by Lady Belamour to interfere with her again," said Mrs. Phoebe, drawing herself up; "I shall let things take their course unless I can remonstrate with my own kinsman."

CHAPTER XIII
THE FLUTTER OF HIS WINGS

Then is Love's hour to stray!
Oh, how he flies away! — T. MOORE.

Meanwhile Aurelia, mounted on a pair of pattens brought by the negro to keep her above the dew, was crossing the park by the light of a fine hunter's moon, Jumbo marching at a respectful distance in the rear. He kept on chuckling to himself with glee, and when she looked round at him, he informed her with great exultation that "Mas'r had not been alone. His honour had been to see him. Mas'r so glad."

"Sir Amyas!" exclaimed Aurelia: "Is he there still?"

"No, missie. He went away before supper."

"Did he see the young ladies?"

"Oh, yes, missie. He came before mas'r up, quite promiskius," said Jumbo, who loved a long word. "I tell him, wait till mas'r be dress, and took him to summer parlour. He see little missies out in garden; ask what chil'ren it was. His Hounour's sisters, Miss Fay, Missie Letty, Missie Amy, I say! His Honour wonder. 'My sisters,' he say, 'my sisters here,' and out he goes like a flash of lightning and was in among them."

Aurelia's first thought was "Oh, I hope they were clean and neat, and that they behaved themselves. I wish I had been at home." Wherewith followed the recollection that Sir Amyas had been called her beau, and her cheeks burnt; but the recent disagreeable lecture on etiquette showed her that it would only have led to embarrassment and vexation to have had any question of an interview with a young gentleman by so little her elder. Nor would she have known what to say to him. Old Mr. Belamour in the dark was a very different matter, and she had probably had an escape from much awkwardness.

Molly received her with her favourite exclamation: "Lawk, miss, and who do you think have been here?"

"Jumbo told me, Molly."

"Ain't he a perfect pictur of a man? And such a gentleman! He gave me a whole goolden guinea for my good care of his little sisters, and says he: 'Their father shall hear of them, and what little ladies they be.'"

"I am glad they behaved themselves prettily."

"Yes, that they did, ma'am. It was good luck that they had not been grubbing in their gardens as you lets 'em do, ma'am, but they was all as clean as a whistle, a picking up horse-chestnuts under the big tree at the corner of the bowling green, when out on the steps we sees him, looking more like an angel than a man, in his red coat, and the goold things on his shoulders, and out he comes! Miss Amy, she was afeard at first: 'Be the soldiers a coming?' says she, and runs to me; but Miss Letty, she holds out her arms, and says "It's my papa," and Miss Fay, she stood looking without a word. Then when his Honour was in among them: "My little sisters, my dear little sisters," says he, "don't you know me?" and down he goes on one knee in the grass, never heeding his beautiful white small-clothes, if you'll believe me, miss, and holds out his arms, and gets Miss Fay into one arm, and Miss Letty into t'other, and then Miss Amy runs up, and he kisses them all. Then miss Letty says again 'Are you my papa from foreign parts?' and he laughs and says: 'No, little one, I'm your brother. Did you never hear of your brother Amyas?' and Miss Fay stood off a little and clapped her little hands, and says: 'O brother Amyas, how beautiful you are!'"

Aurelia could not help longing to know whether she had been mentioned, but she did not like to inquire, and she was obliged to rest satisfied with the assurance that her little girls had comported themselves like jewels, like lambs, like darling lumps of sugar, or whatever metaphors were suggested by the imagination of Molly, who had, apparently, usurped the entire credit of their good manners. It was impossible to help feeling a little aggrieved, or, maugre [in spite of—D.L.] all inconvenient properties to avoid wishing to have been under the horse-chestnut tree, even though she might have shown herself just such a bashful little speechless fool as she had been when Sir Amyas had danced with her at Carminster.

She was destined to hear a good deal more of the visitor the next day. The children met her with the cry of "Cousin Aura, our brother"—"our big beautiful brother—Brother Amyas."—They were with difficulty calmed into saying their prayers, and Amoret startled the little congregation by adding to "bless by father, my mother, my brothers and sisters," "and pray bless big brother Amyas best of all, for I love him very much indeed!"

All day little facts about "brother Amyas" kept breaking out. Brother Amyas had beautiful gold lace, brother Amyas had a red and white feather; brother Amyas had given Fay and Letty each a ride on his shoulder, but

Amy was afraid; brother Amyas said their papa would love them very much. He had given them each a new silver shilling, and Amoret had in return presented him with her doll's beautiful pink back-string that Cousin Aura had made for her. This wonderful brother had asked who had taught them to be such pretty little gentlewomen, and at this Aurelia's heart beat a little, but provoking Fidelia replied: "I told him my Mammy Rolfe taught me to be genteel," and Letty added: "And he said Fay was a conceited little pussy cat."

A strange indefinable feeling between self-respect and shyness made Aurelia shrink from the point-blank question whether the ungrateful little things had acknowledged their obligations to her. She was always hoping they would say something of their own accord, and always disappointed.

Evening came, and she eagerly repaired to the dark room, wondering, yet half dreading to enter on the subject, and beginning by an apology for having by no means perfected herself in Priam's visit to Achilles.

"If you have been making visits," said Mr. Belamour: "I too have had a visitor."

"The children told me so," she answered.

"He was greatly delighted with them," said Mr. Belamour.

"While they, poor little things, never were more happy in their lives. He must have been very kind to them, yet he did not know that they were here."

"His mother is not communicative respecting them. Ladies who love power seek to preserve it by making little mysteries."

"It was to see you, sir, that he came."

"Yes. He ingenuously avowed that he had always been urged to do so by his stepfather, but his mother has always put obstacles in the way, and assured him that he would not gain admission. I have certainly refused to see her, but this is a very different matter—my brother's only child, my godson, and my ward!"

"I am very glad he has come to see you, sir, and I am sure it has given you pleasure."

"Pleasure in seeing that he is a lad of parts, and of an ingenuous, affectionate, honest nature, but regret in perceiving how I failed in the confidence that his father reposed in me."

"But, sir, you could not help it!"

"Once I could not. It was, I know not how long, before I knew that my brother was no more; and thinking myself dead to the world and the world to me, I took no heed to what, it now seems to me, I was told of guardianship to the boy. I was incapable of fulfilling any such charge, and I shunned the pain of hearing of it," he continued, rather as if talking to himself than to his auditor. "When I could, I gave them my name and they asked no more. Yet what did they tell me of a sealed letter from my brother, addressed to me? True, I heard of it more than once, but I could ask no one to read it to me, and I closed my ears. In Wayland's hands I knew the youth was well cared for, and only now do I feel that I have ill requited my brother's confidence."

"Indeed, sir, I cannot see how you could have done otherwise," said Aurelia, who could not bear to hear his tone of self-reproach.

"My amiable visitor!" he exclaimed, as though recalled to a sense of her presence. "Excuse the absence of mind which has inflicted on you the selfish murmurs of the old recluse. Tell me how you prospered with my cousins, whom I remember as sprightly maidens. Phoebe had somewhat of the prude, Delia of the coquette."

"I could imagine what you say of Mistress Phoebe, sir, better than of Mistress Delia."

"Had they any guests to meet you?"

"A Mrs. Hunter, sir, from Brentford, a doctor's wife I suppose."

"You are right. She was a cousin of theirs on the other side of the house, a loud-voiced buxom lass, who was thought to have married beneath here when she took Dr. Hunter; but apparently they have forgiven her."

Mr. Belamour was evidently much interested and amused by Aurelia's small experiences and observations, such as they were. In spite of the sense of past omission which had been aroused by his nephew's visit, it had evidently raised his spirits, for he laughed when Aurelia spiced her descriptions with a little playful archness, and his voice became more cheery.

So, too, it was on the ensuing evening when Aurelia, to compensate for the last day's neglect, came primed with three or four pages of the conversation between Priam and Achilles, which she rehearsed with great feeling, thinking, like Pelides himself, of her own father and home. It was requited with a murmured "Bravo," and Mr. Belamour then begged of her, if she were not weary, to favour him with the Nightingale Song, Jumbo as usual accompanying her with his violin. At the close there was again a "Bravo! Truly exquisite!" in a tone as if the hermit were really finding youth and life again. Once more at his request, she sang, and was applauded with even more fervour, with a certain tremulous eagerness in the voice. Yet there was probably a dread of the excitement being too much, for this was followed by "Thank you, kind songstress, I could listen for ever, but it is becoming late, and I must not detain you longer."

She found herself handed out of the room, with somewhat curtailed good nights, although nine o'clock, her usual signal, had not yet struck. When she came into the lamplit hall, Jumbo was grinning and nodding like a maniac, and when she asked what was the matter, he only rolled his eyes, and said, "Missie good! Mas'r like music!"

The repressed excitability she had detected made her vaguely nervous (not that she would have so called herself), and as the next day was the blank Sunday, she appeased and worked off her restlessness by walking with the children to Sedhurst church. It was the sixteenth Sunday after Trinity, and the preacher, who had caught somewhat of the fire of Wesley and Whitfield, preached a sermon which arrested her attention, and filled her with new thoughts. Taking the Epistle and Gospel in connection, he showed the death-in-life of indifference, and the quickening touch of the Divine Love, awakening the dead spirit into true life. On that life, with its glow of love, hope, and joy, the preacher dwelt with enthusiasm such as Aurelia had never heard, and which carried her quite out of herself. Tears of emotion trembled in her eyes, and she felt a longing desire to walk on in that path of love to her Maker, whom she seemed to have never known before.

She talked with a new fervour to the children of the birds and flowers, and all the fair things they loved, as the gifts of their Father in Heaven; and when she gathered them round the large pictured Bible, it was to the Gospel that she turned as she strove to draw their souls to the appreciation of the Redeeming Love there shown. She saw in Fay's deep eyes and thoughtful brow that the child was taking it in, though differently from Amy, who wanted to kiss the picture, while Letty asked those babyish material questions about Heaven that puzzle wiser heads than Aurelia's to answer.

So full was she of the thought, that she forgot her sense of something strange and unaccountable in Mr. Belamour's manner before the evening, nor was there anything to remind her of it afresh, for he was as calmly grave and kindly courteous as ever; and he soon led her to pour forth all her impressions of the day. Indeed she repeated to him great part of the sermon, with a voice quivering with earnestness and emotion. He was not stirred in the same way as she had been, saying in his pensive meditative way, "The preacher is right. Love is life. The misfortune is when we stake our all on one love alone, and that melts from us. Then indeed there is death—living death!"

"But there is never-failing love, and new life that never dies!" cried Aurelia, almost transported out of herself.

"May you ever keep hold of both unobscured, my sweet child," he returned, with a sadness that repressed and drove her back into herself again, feeling far too childish and unworthy to help him to that new life and love; though her young heart yearned over him in his desolation, and her soul was full of supplication for him.

CHAPTER XIV
THE CANON OF WINDSOR

Turn, gentle hermit of the dale. — GOLDSMITH.

"My child, will you do me a favour?" said Mr. Belamour the next evening, in a tone no longer formal, but paternal. "Take this packet" (he put one into the girl's hand) "to the light and inform me what is the superscription."

It was a thick letter, with a large red wax seal, bearing the well known arms of Belamour and Delavie, and the address was

To *AMYAS BELAMOUR, ESQ., K.C.,*

OF THE INNER TEMPLE, LONDON.
To be opened after my death.]

JOVIAN BELAMOUR.
Dec. 14th, 1727.

"I thought so," said Mr. Belamour, when she returned to him with intelligence. "Little did my poor brother guess how long it would be unopened! Will my gentle friend confer another obligation on me?"

Aurelia made her ready assent, hoping to be asked to read the letter, when he continued, "I cannot read this myself. Even could I bear the light, the attempt to fix my eyes sends darts shooting through my brain, which would take away my very power of comprehension. But," he continued, "there are only two men living to whom I could entrust my brother's last words to me. One, your own good father, is out of reach; the other has frequently proffered his good offices and has been rejected. Would you add to your kindness that of writing to entreat my old friend, Dr. Godfrey, to favour with a visit one who has too often and ungratefully refused him admission."

Feminine curiosity felt balked, but Aurelia was ashamed of the sensation, and undertook the task. Instructions were given her that she was to write —

"*If Amyas Belamour's old Schoolfellow and Friend can overlook*
and pardon the undeserved Rebuffs to His Constancy and

Solicitude for a lonely and sullen Wretch, and will once more come and spend a Night at Bowstead, he will confer an inestimable Favour upon one who is more sensible of his Goodness than when it has been previously offered."

This letter, written in Aurelia's best Italian hand, on a large sheet of paper, she brought with her the next evening. She was bidden to fold down the exact place for the signature, which Mr. Belamour proceeded to affix, and she was then to carry it to the candles in the lobby, and there fold, seal, and address it to the Reverend Edward Godfrey, D.D., Canon of Windsor, Windsor. She found the A. Belamour very fairly written except that it was not horizontal, and she performed the rest of the task with ladylike dexterity, sealing it with a ring that had been supplied for the purpose. It did not, as she expected, bear the Belamour sheaf of arrows, but was a gem, representing a sleeping Cupid with folded wings, so beautiful that she asked leave to take another impression for Harriet, who collected seals, after the fashion of the day.

"You are welcome," Mr. Belamour replied. "I doubt its great antiquity, since the story of Cupid and Psyche cannot be traced beyond Apuleius. I used it because Dr. Godfrey will remember it. He was with me at Rome when I purchased it."

The ring was of the size for a lady's finger, and Aurelia durst ask no more.

How the letter was sent she knew not, but Mrs. Aylward was summoned to Mr. Belamour's room, and desired to have a room ready at any time for his friend.

Three days later, towards sunset, a substantial-looking clergyman, attended by two servants, rode up to the door; and was immediately appropriated by Jumbo, disappearing into the mysterious apartments; Aurelia expected no summons that night, but at the usual hour, the negro brought a special request for the honour of her society; and as she entered the dark room, Mr. Belamour said, "My fair and charitable visitor will permit me to present to her my old and valued friend, Dr. Godfrey." He laid the hand he had taken on one that returned a little gentlemanly acknowledgment, while a kind fatherly voice said, "The lady must pardon me if I do not venture to hand her to her chair."

"Thank you, sir, I am close to my seat."

"Your visitors acquire blind eyes, Belamour," said Dr. Godfrey, cheerfully.

"More truly they become eyes to the blind," was the answer. "I feel myself a man of the world again, since this amiable young lady has conned the papers on my behalf, and given herself the trouble of learning the choicest passages of the poets to repeat to me."

"You are very good, sir," returned Aurelia; "it is my great pleasure."

"That I can well believe," said Dr. Godfrey. "Have these agreeable recitations made you acquainted with the new poem on the *Seasons* by Mr. James Thomson?"

"No," replied Mr. Belamour, "my acquaintance with the *belles letters* ceased nine years ago."

"The descriptions have been thought extremely effective. Those of autumn were recalled to my mind on my way."

Dr. Godfrey proceeded to recite some twenty lines of blank verse, for in those days people had more patience and fewer books, and exercised their memories much more than their descendants do. Listening was far from being thought tedious.

> *"'But see the fading many-coloured roads,*
> *Shade deepening over shade, the country round*
> *Imbrown; a crowded umbrage, dusk and dim,*
> *Of every hue, from wan, declining green,*
> *To sooty dark.'"*

The lines had a strange charm to one who had lived in darkness through so many revolving years. Mr. Belamour eagerly thanked his friend, and on the offer to lend him the book, begged that it might be ordered for him, and that any other new and interesting work might be sent to him that was suitable to the fair lips on which he was dependent.

"You are secure with Mr. Thomson," said the Doctor. "Hear the conclusion of his final hymn."

> *"'When even at last the solemn hour shall come,*
> *And wing my mystic flight to future worlds,*
> *I cheerful will obey; there with new powers*
> *Will rising wonders sing. I cannot go*
> *Where Universal Love not smiles around,*
> *Sustaining all yon orbs, and all their suns,*
> *From seeming evil still educing good,*
> *And better thence again, and better still,*

In infinite progression. But I lose
Myself in Him, in Light ineffable;
Come then expressive Silence, mine the praise.'"

"'Universal Love!'" repeated Mr. Belamour; "the poet sings as you do, my amiable friend! I can conceive the idea better than I could a few months ago."

"'*From seeming evil, still educing good,'*"

quoted Dr. Godfrey earnestly, as if feeling his way.

"More of this another time," said Mr. Belamour hastily. "What say the critics respecting this new aspirant?"

The ensuing conversation much interested Aurelia, as it was on the men of letters whose names had long been familiar to her, and whom the two gentlemen had personally known. She heard of Pope, still living at Twickenham, and of his bickerings with Lady Mary Wortley Montagu; of young Horace Walpole, who would never rival his father as a politician, but who was beginning his course as a *dilettante*, and actually pretending to prefer the barbarous Gothic to the classic Italian. However, his taste might be improved, since he was going to make the grand tour in company with Mr. Gray, a rising young poet, in whom Dr. Godfrey took interest, as an Etonian and a Cantab.

At nine o'clock Mr. Belamour requested Miss Delavie to let him depute to her the doing the honours of the supper table to his friend, who would return to him when she retired for the night.

Then it was that she first saw the guest, a fine, dignified clergyman, in a large grey wig, with a benignant countenance, reminding her of the Dean of Carminster. When she was little, the Dean had bestowed on her comfits and kisses; but since she had outgrown these attentions, he was wont to notice her only by a condescending nod, and she would no more have thought of conversing with him at table than in his stall in the cathedral. Thus it was surprising to find herself talked to, as Betty might have been, by this reverend personage, who kindly satisfied her curiosity about the King, Queen, and Princesses, but with a discretion which did not diminish that blind loyalty which saw no defects in "our good king," though he was George II. She likewise answered a few questions about Mr. Belamour's tastes and habits, put in a very different manner from those of the Mistress Treforth, and as soon as supper was over she rose and retired.

She did not see Dr. Godfrey again until he was ready for a late breakfast, having been up nearly the whole night with his friend. His horses were ordered immediately after the meal, as he had an appointment in London, and he presently looked up, and said,

"Madam, you must excuse me, I was silent from thinking how I can adequately express my respect and gratitude for you."

"I beg your pardon, sir," exclaimed Aurelia, thinking her ears mistaken.

"My gratitude," he repeated, "for the inestimable blessing you have been to my dear and much valued friend, in rousing him from that wretched state of despondency in which no one could approach him."

"You are too good, sir," returned Aurelia. "It was he who sent for me."

"I know you did it in all simplicity, my dear child—forgive the epithet, I have daughters of my own, and thankful should I be if one of them could have produced such effects. I tell you, madam, my dear friend, one of the most estimable and brilliant men of his day, was an utter wreck, both in mind and body, through the cruel machinations of an unprincipled woman. How much was to the actual injury from his wound, how much to grief and remorse, Heaven only knows, but the death of his brother, who alone had authority with him, left him thus to cut himself off entirely in this utter darkness and despair. I called at first monthly, then yearly, after the melancholy catastrophe, and held many consultations with good Mr. Wayland, but all in vain. It was reserved for your sweet notes to awaken and recall him to what I trust is indeed new life."

Tears filled Aurelia's eyes, and she could only murmur something about being very glad.

"Yes," pursued Dr. Godfrey, "it is as if I saw him rising from his living tomb in all senses of the word. I find that your artless Sunday evening conversations have even penetrated the inner hopeless gloom, still more grievous than the outer darkness in which he lived."

"Indeed, sir, I never meant to be presumptuous."

"God's blessing on such presumption, my good child! If you had been fully aware of his state of mind, you might never have ventured nor have touched the sealed heart, as you have done, as I perceive, in your ignorance, out of your obedient reverence to the Lord's day. Am I not right?"

"Yes, sir, I thought one *could* not repeat plays and poems on Sunday, and I was frightened when I found those other things were strange to him; but he bade me go on."

"For the sake of the music of your voice, as he tells me, at first; but afterwards because you became the messenger of hope to one who had long lain in the shadow of death, thinking pardon and mercy too much out of reach to be sought for. You have awakened prayer within him once more."

She could not speak, and Dr. Godfrey continued, "You will be glad to hear that I am to see the curate on my way through Brentford, and arrange with him at times to read prayers in the outer room. What is it?" he added; "you look somewhat doubtful."

"Only, sir, perhaps I ought not to say so, but I cannot think Mr. Belamour well ever care for poor Mr. Greaves. If he could only hear that gentleman who comes to Sedhurst! I never knew how much fire could be put into the service itself, and yet I have often been at Carminster Cathedral."

"True, my dear young lady. These enthusiasts seem to be kindling a new fire in the Church, but I am not yet so convinced of their orthodoxy and wisdom as to trust them unreservedly; and zeal pushed too far might offend our poor recluse, and alienate him more than ever. He is likely to profit more by the direct words of the Church herself, read without personal meaning, than by the individual exhortations of some devout stranger."

"Yes, sir. Thank you, I never meant to question your judgment. Indeed I did not."

The horses were here announced, and Dr. Godfrey said,

"Then I leave him to you with a grateful heart. I am beginning to hope that there is much hypochondriacism in his condition, and that this may pass away with his despondency. I hope before many weeks are over to come and visit him again, before I go to my parish in Dorsetshire."

Then, with a fatherly blessing, the Canon took his leave.

He was scarcely gone before there was a great rustling in the hall, and Mrs. Phoebe and Mrs. Delia Treforth were announced. Aurelia was surprised, for she had been decidedly sensible of their disapproval when she made her visit of ceremony after her entertainment by them. She, however, had underrated the force of the magnet of curiosity. They had come to inquire about the visitor, who had actually spent a night at the Park. They knew who he was, for "Ned Godfrey" had been a frequent guest at Bowstead in the youth of all parties, and they were annoyed that he had not paid his respects to them.

"It would have been only fitting to have sent for us, as relations of the family, to assist in entertaining him," said Mrs. Phoebe. "Pray, miss, did my eccentric cousin place you in the position of hostess?"

"It fell to me, madam," said Aurelia.

"You could have asked for *our* support," said Mrs. Phoebe, severely. "It would have become you better, above all then Sir Amyas Belamour himself was here."

"He has only been here while I was with you, madam, and was gone before my return."

"*That* is true," but Mrs. Phoebe looked at the girl so inquisitively that her colour rose in anger, and exclaimed, "Madam, I know not what you mean!"

"There, sister," said Mrs. Delia, more kindly. "She is but a child, and Bet Batley is a gossip. She would not know his Honour in the dark from the blackamoor going down to visit his sweetheart."

Very glad was Aurelia when the ladies curtsied themselves out of her summer parlour, declaring they wished to speak to Mrs. Aylward, who she knew could assure them of the absurdity of these implied suspicions.

And Mrs. Aylward, who detested the two ladies, and repelled their meddling, stiffly assured them both of Miss Delavie's discretion and her own vigilance, which placed visits from the young baronet beyond the bounds of possibility. Supposing his Honour should again visit his uncle, she should take care to be present at any interview with the young lady. She trusted that she knew her duty, and so did Miss Delavie.

CHAPTER XV
THE QUEEN OF BEAUTY

O bright regina, who made thee so faire,
Who made thy colour vermeilie and white?
Now marveile I nothing that ye do hight
The quene of love. —CHAUCER.

Only a week had elapsed before the quiet of Bowstead was again disturbed by the arrival of two grooms, with orders that everything should be made ready the next day for the arrival of my Lady, who was on her way to Carminster for a few weeks, and afterwards to Bath. Forthwith Mrs. Aylward and her subordinates fell into a frenzy of opening shutters, lighting fires, laying down carpets and uncovering furniture. Scrubbing was the daily task for the maids, and there was nothing extra possible in that line, but there was hurry enough to exacerbate the temper, and when Aurelia offered her services she was tartly told that she could solely be useful by keeping the children out of the way; for in spite of all rebuffs, they persisted in haunting the footsteps of the housekeeper and maids, Fay gazing with delight at the splendours that were revealed, Amy proffering undesired aid, Letty dancing in the most inconvenient places, romancing about her mamma and little brother, and making sure that her big beautiful brother was also coming.

The were very unwilling to let Aurelia call them away to practise them in bridling, curtseying, and saying "Yes, madam," according to the laws of good breeding so carefully inculcated by sister at home. So anxious was she that she tried them over and over again till they were wearied out, and became so cross and naughty that nothing restored good-homour except gathering blackberries to feast brother Archer.

The intelligence produced less apparent excitement in the dark chamber. When Aurelia, in an eager, awe-stricken voice began, "O sir, have you heard that my Lady is coming?" He calmly replied,

"The sounds in the house have amply heralded her, to say nothing of Jumbo."

"I wonder what she will do!"

"You will not long have known her, my fair friend, without discovering that she is one of the most inscrutable of her sex. The mere endeavour to guess at her plans only produces harassing surmises and alarms."

"Do you think, sir, she can mean to take me away?"

"I suppose that would be emancipation to you, my poor child."

"I should dance to find myself going home," said Aurelia, "yet how could I bear to leave my little girls, or you, sir. Oh! if you could only live at the Great House, at home, I should be quite happy."

"Then you would not willingly abandon the recluse?"

"Indeed," she said with a quivering in her voice, "I cannot endure the notion. You have been so kind and good to me, sir, and I do so enjoy coming to you. And you would be all alone again with Jumbo! Oh sir, could you not drive down if all the coach windows were close shut up? You would have my papa to talk to!"

"And what would your papa say to having a miserable old hermit inflicted on him?"

"He would be only too glad."

"No, no, my gentle friend, there are other reasons. I could not make my abode in Lady Belamour's house, while in that of my nephew, my natural home, I have a right to drag out what remains of the existence of mine. Nay, are you weeping, my sweet child? That must not be; your young life must take no darkness from mine. Even should Lady Belamour's arbitrary caprice bear you off without another meeting, remember that you have given me many more happy hours than I ever supposed to be in store for me, and have opened doors which shall not be closed again."

"You will get some one to recite to you?" entreated Aurelia, her voice most unsteady.

"Godfrey shall seek out some poor scholar or exhausted poetaster, with a proviso that he never inflicts his own pieces on me," said Mr. Belamour, in a tone more as if he wished to console her than as it were a pleasing prospect. "Never fear, gentle monitress, I will not sink into the stagnation from which your voice awoke me. Neither Godfrey nor my nephew would allow it. Come, let us put it from our minds. It has always been my experience, that whatever I expected from my much admired sister-in-law, that was the exact reverse of what she actually did. Therefore let us attend to topics, though I wager that you have no fresh acquisitions for me to-day."

"I am ashamed, sir, but I could not fix my mind even to a most frightful description of wolves in Mr. Thomson's 'Winter.'"

"That were scarcely a soothing subject; but we might find calm in something less agitating and more familiar. Perhaps you can recall something too firmly imprinted on your memory to be disturbed by these emotions."

Aurelia bethought herself that she must not disappoint her friend on what might prove their last evening; she began very unsteadily:—

"'Hence, loathed Melancholy.'"

However by the time "Jonson's learned sock" was on, her mechanical repetition had become animated, and she had restored herself to equanimity. When the clock struck nine, her auditor added his thanks, "In case we should not meet again thus, let me beg of my kind visitor to wear this ring in memory of one to whom she has brought a breath indeed from L'Allegro itself. It will not be too large. It was made for a lady."

And amid her tearful thanks she felt a light kiss on her fingers, revealing to her that the hermit must possess a beard, a fact, which in the close-shaven Hanoverian days, conveyed a sense of squalor and neglect almost amounting to horror.

In her own room she dropped many a tear over the ring, which was of course the Cupid intaglio, and she spent the night in strange mixed dreams and yearnings, divided between her father, Betty, and Eugene on the one hand, and Mr. Belamour and the children on the other. Home-sick as she sometimes felt, dull as Bowstead was, she should be sadly grieved to leave those to whom she felt herself almost necessary, though her choice must needs be for her home.

Early the next day arrived an old roomy berlin loaded heavily with luggage, and so stuffed with men and maids that four stout horses had much ado to bring it up to the door. The servants, grumbling heartily, declared that my Lady was only going to lie here for a single night, and that Sir Amyas was not with her.

Late in the afternoon, a couple of outriders appeared to say that the great lady was close at hand, and Aurelia, in her best blue sacque, and India muslin cap, edged with Flanders lace, had her three little charges, all in white with red shoes, red sashes, and red ribbons in their caps, drawn up in the hall to welcome their mother.

Up swept the coach with six horses, Mr. Dove behind—runners in fact, who at times rested themselves by an upright swing on the foot-board.

The door of the gorgeous machine was thrown open, and forth sprang a pretty little boy. Next descended the friendly form of Mrs. Dove, then a smart person, who was my Lady's own woman, and finally something dazzlingly grand and beautiful in feathers, light blue, and silver.

Aurelia made her reverence, and so did the little triad; the great lady bent her head, and gave a light kiss to the brow of each child, and the boy sprang forward, crying: "You are my sisters. You must play with me, and do whatever I choose." Amoret and he began kissing on the spot, but Fidelia, regarding *must* as a forbidden word, looked up at Aurelia with an inquiring protest in her eyes; but it was not heeded, in the doubt whether to follow Lady Belamour, who, with a stately greeting to Mrs. Aylward, had sailed into the withdrawing-room. The question was decided by Mrs. Aylward standing back to make room, and motioning her forward, so she entered, Letty preceding her and Fay clinging to her.

By the hearth stood the magnificent figure, holding out a long, beautiful, beringed hand, which Aurelia shyly kissed, bending as before a queen, while her forehead received the same slight salute as had been given to the little girls. "My cousin Delavie's own daughter," said the lady: "You have the family likeness."

"So I have been told, madam."

"Your father is well, I hope."

"He was pretty well, I thank you Ladyship, when I heard from my sister ten days ago."

"I shall see him in a week's time, and shall report well of his little daughter," said Lady Belamour kindly. "I am under obligations to you, my dear. You seem to have tamed my little savages."

Aurelia was amazed, for the universal awe of my Lady had made her expect a harsh and sever Semiramis style of woman, whereas she certainly saw a majestic beauty, but with none of the terrors that she had anticipated. The voice was musical and perfectly modulated, the manner more caressing than imperious towards herself, and studiously polite to the house keeper. While orders were being given as to arrangements, Aurelia took in the full details of the person of whom she had heard so much. It seemed incredible that Lady Belamour could have been mother to contemporaries of Betty, for she looked younger than Betty herself. Her symmetry and carriage were admirable, and well shown by the light blue habit laced richly and embroidered with silver. A small round hat with a cluster of white ostrich feathers was placed among the slightly frizzed and powdered masses of mouse-coloured hair, surmounting a long ivory neck, whose graceful turn, the theme of many a sonnet, was not concealed by the masculine collar of the habit. The exquisite oval contour of the cheek, the delicate ear, and Grecian profile were as perfect in moulding as when she had been Sir Jovian's bride, and so were the porcelain blue of the eyes, the pencilled arches of eyebrow, and the curve of the lips, while even her complexion retained its smooth texture, and tints of the lily and rose. Often as Aurelia had heard of her beauty, its splendour dazzled and astonished her, even in this travelling dress.

Archer, who was about a year older than his sisters, was more like Amoret than the other two, with azure eyes, golden curls, and a plump rosy face, full of fun and mischief. Tired of the confinement of the coach, he was rushing round the house with Amoret, opening the doors and looking into the rooms. The other little sisters remained beside Aurelia till their mother said, pointing to Fay: "That child seems to mean to eat me with her eyes. Let all the children be with Nurse Dove, Mrs. Aylward. Miss Delavie will do me the pleasure of supping with me at seven. Present my compliments to Mr. Belamour, and let him know that I will be with him at eight o'clock on particular business." Then turning to the two children, she asked their names, and was answered by each distinctly, with the orthodox "madam" at the end.

"You are improved, little ones," she said: "Did Cousin Aurelia teach you?"

"And Mammy Rolfe," said constant Fay.

"She must teach you next not to stare," said Lady Belamour. "I intend to take one to be a companion to my boy, in the country. When I saw them before, they were rustic little monsters; but they are less unpresentable now. Call your sister, children." And, as the two left the room, she continued: "Which do you recommend, cousin?"

"Fidelia is the most reasonable, madam," said Aurelia.

"But not the prettiest, I trust. She is too like her father, with those dark brows, and her eyes have a look deep enough to frighten one. They will frighten away the men, if she do not grow out of it."

Here the door burst open, and, without any preliminary bow, Master Archer flew in, crying out "Mamma, mamma, we *must* stay here. The galleries are so long, and it is such a place for whoop-hide!"

His sisters were following his bad example, and rushing in with equal want of ceremony, but though their mother held the boy unchecked on her knee, Aurelia saw how she could frown. "You forget yourselves," she said.

Amoret looked ready to cry, but at a sign from their young instructress, they backed and curtsied, and their mother reviewed them; Letitia was the most like the Delavies, but also the smallest, while Amoret was on the largest scale and would pair best with her brother, who besides loudly proclaimed his preference for her, and she was therefore elected to the honour of being taken home. Aurelia was requested as a favour to bid the children's woman have the child's clothes ready repaired to her own room.

The little wardrobe could only be prepared by much assistance from Aurelia herself, and she could attend to nothing else; while the children were all devoted to Archer, and she only heard their voices in the distance, till—as she was dressing for her *tete-a-tete* supper—Fay came to her crying, "Archer is a naughty boy—he said wicked words—he called her ugly, and had cuffed and pinched her!"

Poor child! she was tired out, and disappointed, and Aurelia could only comfort her by hearing her little prayers, undressing her, and giving her the highly-esteemed treat of sleeping in Cousin Aura's bed; while the others were staying up as long as it pleased Master Archer. This actually was the cause of my Lady being kept waiting, and an apology was needful. "Fidelia was tired out, and was crying."

"A peevish child! I am glad I did not choose her."

"She is usually very good, madam," said Aurelia, eagerly.

"Is she your favourite?"

"I try not to make favourites, madam."

"Ah! there spoke the true Manor House tone," said her Ladyship, rather mockingly. "Maybe she will be a wit, for she will never be a beauty, but the other little one will come on in due time after Amoret."

"Your Ladyship will find Amoret a dear, good, affectionate child," said Aurelia. "Only—-"

"Reserve that for nurse, so please you, my good girl. It is enough for me to see the brats on their good manners now and then. You have had other recreations—shall I call them, or cares? I never supposed, when I sent you here to attend on the children, that the hermit of Bowstead would summon you! I assure you it is an extraordinary honour."

"I so esteem it, madam," said Aurelia, blushing.

"More honour than pleasure, eh?"

"A great pleasure, madam."

"Say you so?" and the glittering blue eyes were keenly scanning the modest face. "I should have thought a young maid like you would have had the dismals at the mere notion of going near his dark chamber. I promise you it gives me the megrim [migraine—D.L.] to look forward to it."

"I was affrighted at first, madam," said Aurelia; "but Mr. Belamour is so good and kind to me that I exceedingly enjoy the hours I spend with him."

"La, child, you speak with warmth! We shall have you enamoured of a voice like the youth they make sonnets about—what's his name?"

"Narcissus, madam," said Aurelia, put out of countenance by the banter.

"Oh, you are learned. Is Mr. Belamour your tutor, pray? And—oh fie! I have seen that ring before!"

"He gave it to me yesterday," faltered Aurelia, "in case you should intend to take me away, and I should not see him again. I hope I was not wrong in accepting it, madam."

"Wrong, little fool, assuredly not," said my Lady, laughing. "It is an ensign of victory. Why, child, you have made a conquest worthy of—let me see. You, or the wits, could tell me who it was that stormed the very den of Cocytus and bore off the spoil!"

Aurelia liked the tone too little to supply the names; yet she felt flattered; but she said quietly, "I am happy to have been the means of cheering him."

The grave artlessness of the manner acted as a kind of check, and Lady Belamour said in a different tone, "Seriously, child, the family are truly obliged for your share in rousing the poor creature from his melancholy. My good man made the attempt, but all in vain. What do you to divert him?"

In inquires of this kind the supper hour passed, and Lady Belamour was then to keep her appointment with her brother-in-law. She showed so much alarm and dread that Aurelia could not but utter assurances and encouragements, which again awoke that arch manner, partly bantering, partly flattering, which exercised a sort of pleasant perplexing fascination on the simple girl.

After being dismissed, Aurelia went in search of Mrs. Dove, whom she found with Molly, taking stock of Amoret's little wardrobe. The good woman rose joyfully. "Oh, my dear missie! I am right thankful to see you looking so purely. I don't know how I could have held up my head to Miss Delavie if I had not seen you!"

"Ah! you will see my sister and all of them," cried Aurelia, a sudden rush of home-sickness bringing tears to her eyes, in oblivion alike of her recluse and her pupils. "Oh! if I were but going with you! But what folly am I talking? You must not let them think I am not happy, for indeed I am. Will you kindly come to my room, dear nurse, and I will give you a packet for them?"

Mrs. Dove willingly availed herself of the opportunity of explaining how guiltless she had been of the sudden separation at Knightsbridge four months back. She had been in such haste to ride after and overtake the coach, that she had even made Dove swear at her for wanting to give the horses no time to rest, and she had ridden off on her own particular pillion long before the rest. She had been surprised that she never succeeded in catching up the carriage, but never suspected the truth till she had dismounted in Hanover Square and asked whether "Miss" were with my Lady. Nobody knew anything about Miss Delavie, nor expected her; and the good woman's alarm was great until she had had an interview with her Ladyship, when she was told not to concern herself about the young lady, who was safely bestowed in the country with the Miss Wayland. "But that it was here, if you'll believe me, missie, I was as innocent as the babe unborn, and so was his Honour, Sir Amyas. Indeed, my Lady gave him to understand that she had put you to boarding-school with his little sisters."

"Oh! nurse, that is impossible!"

"Lawk-a-day, missie, there's nothing my Lady wouldn't say to put him off the scent. Bless you, 'tis not for us servants to talk, or I could tell you tales! But there, mum's the word, as my Dove says, or he wouldn't ha' sat on his box these twenty year!"

"My Lady is very kind to me," said Aurelia, with a little assumption of her father's repressive manner.

"I'm right glad to hear it, Miss Aureely. A sweet lady she can be when she is in the mood, though nothing like so sweet as his Honour. 'Tis ingrain with him down to the bone, as I may say—and I should know, having had him from the day he was weaned. To see him come up to the nussery, and toss about his little brother, would do your very heart good; and then he sits him down, without a bit of pride, and will have me tell him all about our journey up to Lunnon, and the fair, and the play and all; and the same with Dove in the stables. He would have the whole story, and how we was parted at Knightsbridge, I never so much as guessing where you was—you that your sister had given into my care! At last, one day when I was sitting a darning of stockings in the window at the back, where I can see out over to the green fields, up his Honour comes, and says he, with his finger to his lips, 'Set your heart at rest, nurse, I've found her!' Then he told me how he went down to see his old uncle. Mr. Wayland had been urging him on one side that 'twas no more than his duty; and her Ladyship, on the other, would have it that Mr. Belamour was right down melancholy mad, and would go into a raving fit if his nevvy did but go near the place."

"She did not say that!"

"Oh yes, she did, miss, I'll take my oath of it, for I was in the coach with Master Wayland on my knee, when she was telling a lady how hard it was they could have no use of Bowstead, because of Sir Jovian's brother being there, who had got the black melancholics, and could not be removed. The lady says how good she was to suffer it, and she answers, that there was no being harsh with poor Sir Jovian's brother, though he had a strange spleen at her and her son, and always grew worse when they did but go near the house; but that some measures must be taken when her son came of age or was married."

"But he came at last!"

"He said he wanted to see for himself, and thought he could at least find out from the servants whether his uncle was in the state they reported. And there he found his three little sisters, and that you was their tutoress, and they couldn't say enough about you, nor the poor gentleman neither. 'I didn't see her, nurse,' says he, 'but there's a bit of her own sweet fingers' work.' And sure enough, I knew it, for it was a knot of the very ribbon you had in your hair the day I came to talk to your sister about the journey."

"That was what Amy told me she gave him."

"Nothing loth would he be to take it, miss! Though says he, 'Don't you let my mother know I have tracked her, nurse,' says he. 'It is plain enough why she gives out that I am not to go near my uncle, and if she guessed where I had been, she would have some of her fancies.' 'Now your Honour, my dear,' says I, 'you'll excuse your old nurse, but her sister put her in my charge, and though I bless Heaven that you are no young rake, yet you will be bringing trouble untold on her and hers if you go down there a courting of her unbeknownst.' 'No danger of that, nurse,' says he; 'why there's a she-dragon down there (meaning Mrs. Aylward) that was ready to drive me out of my own house when I did but speak of waiting to see her.'"

"No, I am glad he will not come again. Yet it makes his uncle happy to see him. I will keep out of the way if he does."

"Right too, miss. A young lady never loses by discretion."

"Oh, do not speak in—in that way," said Aurelia, blushing at the implication. "Besides, he is going home with my Lady to dear Carminster."

"No, no, he remains with his regiment in town, unless he rides down later when he can have his leave of absence, and my Lady is at the Bath. He will not if he can help it, for he is dead set against the young lady they want to marry him to, and she is to be there. What! you have not heard? It is my Lady Arabella, sister to that there Colonel as is more about our house than I could wish. She is not by the same mother as him and my Lord Aresfield. Her father married a great heiress for his second wife, whose father had made a great fortune by victualling the army in the war time. Not that this Dowager Countess, as they call her, is a bit like the real quality, so that it is a marvel how my Lady can put up with her; only money-bags will make anything go down, more's the pity, and my Lady is pressed, you see, with her losses at play. It was about this match that Sir Amyas was sent down to Battlefield, the Countess's place in Monmouthshire, when he came to Carminster last summer, and his body servant, Mr. Grey, that has been about him from a child, told me all about it. This Lady Belle, as they call her, is only about fourteen, and such a spoilt little vixen, that they say nobody has been able to teach her so much as to read, for her mother, the Dowager, never would have her crossed in anything, and now she has got too headstrong for any of 'em. Mr. Grey said dressing for supper, they heard the most horrid screams, and thought some one must be killed at least. Sir Amyas was for running out, but at the door they met a wench who only said, 'Bless you! that's nought. It's only my young lady in her tantrums!' So in the servants' hall, Grey heard it was all because her mamma wouldn't let her put on two suits of pearls and di'monds both together. She lies on her back, and rolls and kicks till she gets her own way; and by what the servants say, the Dowager heerself ain't much better to her servants. Her woman had got a black eye she had given her with her fan. She has never had no breeding, you see, and there are uglier stories about her than I like to tell you, Miss Aureely; and as to the young lady, Sir Amyas saw her with his own eyes slap the lackey's face for bringing her brown sugar instead of white. She is a little dwarfish thing that puts her finger in her mouth and sulks when she is not flying out into a rage; but Colonel Mar is going to have her up to a boarding-school to mend her manners, and he and my lady are as much bent on marrying his Honour to her as if she was a perfect angel."

"They never can!"

"Well, miss, they do most things they have a mind to; and they mean to do this before my Lady's husband comes home."

"But Mr. Belamour is his nephew's guardian."

"That's what my Lady is come down here for. Either she will get his consent out of him, or she will make the poor gentleman out to be *non compos*, and do without him."

"Oh, nurse, he is the wisest, cleverest gentleman I ever saw, except my papa."

"Do you say do, miss? But you are young, you see. A gentleman to shut himself up in the dark like that must needs be astray in his wits."

"That is because of his eyes, and his wound. Nobody could talk to him and doubt his reason."

"Well, missie, I hope you are in the right; but what my Lady's interest is, that she is apt to carry out, one way or t'other! Bless me, if that be not Master Archer screaming. I thought he was fast off to sleep. There never was a child for hating the dark. Yes, yes, I'm coming, my dearie! Lack a daisy, if his mamma heard!"

CHAPTER XVI
AUGURIES

Venus, thy eternal sway
All the race of man obey.
EURIPIDES *(Anstice).*

Aurelia sat up late to finish her despatches to the beloved ones at home, and pack the little works she had been able to do for each, though my Lady's embroidery took up most of her sedentary hours. Mrs. Dove undertook the care of the guinea's worth of presents to the little sisters from Sir Amyas, which the prudent nurse advised her to withhold till after Master Archer was gone, as he would certainly break everything to pieces. He was up betimes, careering about the garden with all his sisters after him, imperiously ordering them about, but nevertheless bewitching them all, so that Amoretta was in ecstasies at her own preferment, scarcely realising that it would divide her from the others; while Letty made sure that she should soon follow, and Fidelia gravely said, "I shall always know you are loving me still, Amy, as Nurse Rolfe does."

Lady Belamour breakfasted in her own room at about ten o'clock. Her woman, Mrs. Loveday, a small trim active person, with the worn and sharpened remains of considerable prettiness of the miniature brunette style, was sent to summon Miss Delavie to her apartment and inspect the embroidery she had been desired to execute for my Lady. Three or four bouquets had been finished, and the maid went into such raptures over them as somewhat to disgust their worker, who knew that they were not half so well done as they would have been under Betty's direction. However, Mrs. Loveday bore the frame to her Ladyship's room, following Aurelia, who was there received with the same stately caressing manner as before.

"Good morning, child. Your roses bloom well in the forenoon! Pity they should be wasted in darkness. Not but that you are duly appreciated there. Ah! I can deepen them by what our unhappy recluse said of you. I shall make glad hearts at Carminster by his good opinion, and who knows what preferment may come of it—eh? What is that, Loveday?"

"It is work your Ladyship wished me to execute," said Aurelia.

"Handsome—yes; but is that all? I thought the notable Mistress Betty brought you up after her own sort?"

"I am sorry, madam, but I could not do it quickly at first without my sister's advice, and I have not very much time between my care of the children and preparing repetitions for Mr. Belamour."

"Ha! ha! I understand. There are greater attractions! Go on, child. Mayhap it may be your own wedding gown you are working at, if you finish it in time! Heavens! what great wondering eyes the child has! All in good time, my dear. I must talk to your father."

It was so much the custom to talk to young maidens about their marriage that this did not greatly startle Aurelia, and Lady Belamour continued: "There, child, you have done your duty well by those little plagues of mine, and it is Mr. Wayland's desire to make you a recompense. You may need it in any change of circumstances."

So saying, she placed in Aurelia's hand five guineas, the largest sum that the girl had ever owned; and as visions arose of Christmas gifts to be bestowed, the thanks were so warm, the curtsey so expressively graceful, the smile so bright, the soft eyes so sparkling, that the great lady was touched at the sight of such simple-hearted joy, and said, "There, there, child, that will do. I could envy one whom a little makes so happy. Now you will be able to make yourself fine when my son brings home his bride; or—who knows?—you may be a bride yourself first!"

That sounds, thought Aurelia, as if Mr. Belamour had made her relinquish the plan of that cruel marriage, for I am sure I have not yet seen the man I am to marry.

And with a lighter heart the young tutoress stood between Fay and Letty on the steps to see the departure, her cheeks still feeling Amoret's last fond kisses, and a swelling in her throat bringing tears to her eyes at the thought how soon that carriage would be at Carminster. Yet there were sweet chains in the little hands that held her gown, and in the thought of the lonely old man who depended on her for enlivenment.

The day was long, for Amoret was missed; and the two children were unusually fretful and quarrelsome without her, disputing over the new toys which Brother Amyas's guinea had furnished in demoralising profusion. It was strange too see the difference made by the loss of the child who would give up anything rather than meet a look of vexation, and would coax the others into immediate good humour. There was reaction, too, after the excitement, for which the inexperienced Aurelia did not allow. At the twentieth bickering as to which doll should ride on the spotted hobby-horse, the face of Letty's painted wooden baby received a scar, and Fay's lost a leg, whereupon Aurelia's endurance entirely gave way, and she pronounced them both naughty children, and sent them to bed before supper.

Then her heart smote her for unkindness, and she sat in the firelight listless and sad, though she hardly knew why, longing to go up and pet and comfort her charges, but withheld by the remembrance of Betty's assurances that leniency, in a like case, would be the ruin of Eugene.

At last Jumbo came to summon her, and hastily recalling a cheerful air, she entered the room with "Good evening, sir; you see I am still here to trouble you."

"I continue to profit by my gentle friend's banishment. Tell me, was my Lady in a gracious mood?"

"O sir, how beautiful she is, and how kind! I know now why my father was so devoted to her, and no one can ever gainsay her!"

"The enchantress knows how to cast her spells. She was then friendly?"

"She gave me five guineas!" said Aurelia exultingly. "She said Mr. Wayland wished to recompense me."

"Did he so? If it came from him I should have expected a more liberal sum."

"But, oh!" in a tone of infinite surprise and content, "this is more than I ever thought of. Indeed I never dreamt of her giving me anything. Sir, may I write to your bookseller, Mr. Tonson, and order a book of Mr. James Thomson's *Seasons* to give to my sister Harriet, who is delighted with the extracts I have copied for her?"

"Will not that consume a large proportion of the five guineas, my generous friend?"

"I have enough left. There is a new gown which I never have worn, which will serve for the new clothes my Lady spoke of to receive her son's bride."

"She entered on that subject then?"

"Only for a moment as she took leave. Oh, sir, is it possible that she can know all about this young lady?"

"What have you heard of her?"

"Sir, they say she is a dreadful little vixen."

"Who say? Is she known at Carminster?"

"No, sir," said Aurelia, disconcerted. "It was from Nurse Dove that I heard what Sir Amyas's man said when he came back from Battlefield. I know my sister would chide me for listening to servants."

"Nevertheless I should be glad to hear. Was the servant old Grey? Then he is to be depended on. What did he say?"

Aurelia needed little persuasion to tell all that she had heard from Mrs. Dove, and he answered, "Thank you, my child, it tallies precisely with what the poor boy himself told me."

"Then he has told his mother? Will she not believe him?"

"It does not suit her to do so, and it is easy to say the girl will be altered by going to a good school. In fact, there are many reasons more powerful with her than the virtue and happiness of her son," he added bitterly. "There's the connection, forsooth. As if Lady Aresfield were fit to bring up an honest man's wife; and there's the fortune to fill up the void she has made in the Delavie estates."

"Can no one hinder it, sir? Cannot you?"

"As a last resource the poor youth came hither to see whether the guardian whose wardship has hitherto been a dead letter, were indeed so utterly obdurate and helpless as had been represented."

"And you have the power?"

"So far as his father's will and the injunctions of his final letter to me can give it, I have full power. My consent is necessary to his marriage while still a minor, and I have told my Lady I will never give it to his wedding a Mar."

"I was sure of it; and it is not true that they will be able to do without it?

"Without it! Have you heard any more? You pause. I see—she wishes to declare me of unsound mind. Is that what you mean?"

"So Nurse Dove said, sir," faltered Aurelia; "but it seemed too wicked, too monstrous, to be possible."

"I understand," he said. "I thought there was an implied threat in my sweet sister-in-law's soft voice when she spoke of my determined misanthropy. Well, I think we can guard against that expedient. After all, it is only till my nephew comes of age, or till his stepfather returns, that we must keep the enchantress at bay. Then the poor lad will be safe, providing always that she and her Colonel have not made a rake of him by that time. Alas, what a wretch am I not to be able to do more for him! Child, you have seen him?"

"I danced with him, sir, but I was too much terrified to look in his face. And I saw his cocked hat over the thorn hedge."

"Fancy free," muttered Mr. Belamour. "Fair exile for a cocked hat and diamond shoe-buckles! You would not recognise him again, nor his voice?"

"No, sir. He scarcely spoke, and I was attending to my steps."

Mr. Belamour laughed, and then asked Aurelia for the passage in the *Iliad* where Venus carries off Paris in a cloud. He thanked her somewhat absently, and then said,

"Dr. Godfrey said something of coming hither before he goes to his living in Dorsetshire. May I ask of you the favour of writing and begging him to fix a day not far off, mentioning likewise that my sister-in-law has been here."

To this invitation Dr. Godfrey replied that he would deviate from the slow progress of his family coach, and ride to Bowstead, spending two nights there the next week; and to Aurelia's greater amazement, she was next requested to write a billet to the Mistresses Treforth in Mr. Belamour's name, asking them to bestow their company on him for the second evening of Dr. Godfrey's visit.

"You, my kind friend, will do the honours," he said, "and we will ask Mrs. Aylward to provide the entertainment."

"They will be quite propitiated by being asked to meet Dr. Godfrey," said Aurelia. "Shall you admit them, sir?"

"Certainly. You do not seem to find them very engaging company, but they can scarce be worse than I should find in such an asylum as my charming sister-in-law seems to have in preparation for me."

"Oh! I wish I had said nothing about that. It is too shocking!"

"Forewarned, forearmed, as the proverb says. Do you not see, my amiable friend, that we are providing a body of witnesses to the sanity of the recluse, even though he may 'in dark Cimmerian desert ever dwell'?"

The visit took place; Dr. Godfrey greeted Miss Delavie as an old friend, and the next day pronounced Mr. Belamour to be so wonderfully invigorated and animated, that he thought my Lady's malignant plan was really likely to prove the best possible stimulus and cure.

Then the Canon gratified the two old ladies by a morning call, dined with Aurelia and her pupils, who behaved very well, and with whom he afterwards played for a whole hour so kindly that they placed him second in esteem to their big and beautiful brother. Mrs. Phoebe and Mrs. Delia came dressed in the faded splendours of the Louis XIV. period, just at twilight, and were regaled with coffee and pound cake. They were a good deal subdued, though as Aurelia listened to the conversation, it was plain enough what Mr. Belamour meant when he said that his cousin Delia was something of the coquette.

Still they asked with evident awe if it were true that their unfortunate cousin really intended to admit them, and they evidently became more and more nervous while waiting for Jumbo's summons. Dr. Godfrey gave his arm to Mrs. Phoebe, and Mrs. Delia gripped hold of Aurelia's, trembling all over, declaring she felt ready to swoon, and marvelling how Miss Delavie could ever have ventured, all alone too!

After all, things had been made much less formidable than at Aurelia's first introduction. The sitting-room was arranged as it was when Mr. Greaves read prayers, with a very faint light from a shrouded lamp behind the window curtain. To new comers it seemed pitchy darkness, but to Aurelia and Dr. Godfrey it was a welcome change, allowing them at least to perceive the forms of one another, and of the furniture. From a blacker gulf, being the doorway to the inner room, came Mr. Belamour's courteous voice of greeting to his kinswomen, who were led up by their respective guides to take his hand; after which he begged them to excuse the darkness, since the least light was painful to him still. If they would be seated he would remain where he was, and enjoy the society he was again beginning to be able to appreciate. He was, in fact, sitting within his own room, with eyes covered from even the feeble glimmer in the outer room.

It was some minutes before they recovered their self-possession, but Dr. Godfrey and Mr. Belamour began the conversation, and they gradually joined in. It was chiefly full of reminiscences of the lively days when Dr. Godfrey had been a young Cantab visiting his two friends at Bowstead, and Phoebe and Delia were the belles of the village. Aurelia scarcely opened her lips, but she was astonished to find how different the two sisters could be from the censorious, contemptuous beings they had seemed to her. The conversation lasted till supper-time, and Mr. Belamour, as they took their leave, made them promise to come and see him again. Then they were conducted back to the supper-room, Mrs. Phoebe mysteriously asking "Is he always like this?"

The experiment had been a great success, and Aurelia completed it by asking Mrs. Phoebe to take the head of the supper-table.

CHAPTER XVII
THE VICTIM DEMANDED

And if thou sparest now to do this thing,
I will destroy thee and thy land also. —MORRIS.

"Well, sir, have you seen my Lady?"

"Not a year older than when I saw her last," returned Major Delavie, who had just dismounted from his trusty pony at his garden gate, and accepted Betty's arm; "and what think you?" he added, pausing that Corporal Palmer might hear his news. "She has been at Bowstead, and brings fresh tidings of our Aura. The darling is as fair and sprightly as a May morning, and beloved by all who come near her—bless her!"

Palmer echoed a fervent "Amen!" and Betty asked, "Is this my Lady's report?"

"Suspicious Betty! You will soon be satisfied," said the Major in high glee. "Did not Dove meet me at the front door, and Mrs. Dove waylay me in the hall to tell me that the child looked blooming and joyous, and in favour with all, gentle and simple? Come her, Eugene, ay, and Harriet and Arden too. Let us hear what my little maid says for herself. For look here!" and he held aloft Aurelia's packet, at sight of which Eugene capered high, and all followed into the parlour.

Mr. Arden was constantly about the house. There was no doubt that he would soon be preferred to a Chapter living in Buckinghamshire, and he had thus been emboldened to speak out his wishes. It would have been quite beneath the dignity of a young lady of Miss Harriet's sensibility to have consented, and she was in the full swing of her game at coyness and reluctance, daily vowing that nothing should induce her to resign her liberty, and that she should be frightened out of her life by Mr. Arden's experiments; while her father had cordially received the minor Canon's proposals, and already treated him as one of the family. Simpering had been such a fattening process that Harriet was beginning to resume more of her good looks than had ever been brought back by Maydew.

"Open the letter, Betty. Thanks, Arden," as the minor Canon began to pull off his boots, "only take care of my knee. My Lady has brought down her little boy, and one of Aurelia's pupils; I declare they are a perfect pair of Loves. What are you fumbling at, Betty?"

"The seal, sir, it is a pity to break it," said Betty, producing her scissors from one of her capacious pockets. "It is an antique, is it not, Mr. Arden?"

"A very beautiful gem, a sleeping Cupid," he answered.

"How could the child have obtained it?" said Harriet.

"I can tell you," said the Major. "From old Belamour. My Lady was laughing about it. The little puss has revived the embers of gallantry in our poor recluse. Says she, 'He has actually presented her with a ring, nay, a ring bearing Love himself.'"

Somehow the speech, even at second hand, jarred upon Betty, but her father was delighted with my Lady's description of his favourite, and the letters were full of contentment. When the two sisters, arrayed in their stiffest silks, went up to pay their respects to my Lady the next afternoon, their reception was equally warm. My Lady was more caressing to her old acquaintance, Betty, than that discreet personage quite liked, while she complimented and congratulated Harriet on her lover, laughing at her bashful disclaimers in such a charmingly teasing fashion as quite to win the damsel's heart, and convince her that all censure of Lady Belamour was vile slander. The children were sent for, and Amoret was called on to show how Cousin Aurelia had taught her to dance, sing and recite. The tiny minuet performed by her and Archer was an exceedingly pretty exhibition as far as it went, but the boy had no patience to conclude, and jumped off into an extempory *pas seul*, which was still prettier, and as Amoret was sole exhibitor of the repetition of Hay's "Hare and many friends," he became turbulent after the first four lines, and put a stop to the whole.

Then came in a tall, large, handsome, dashing-looking man, with the air of a "*beau sabreur*," whom Lady Belamour presented to her cousins as "Colonel Mar, my son's commandant, you know who has been kind enough to take Carminster on his way, so as to escort me to the Bath. I am such a sad coward about highwaymen. And we are to meet dear Lady Aresfield there to talk over a little matter of business."

Colonel Mar made a magnificent bow, carelessly, not to say impertinently, scanned the two ladies, and having evidently decided they had neither beauty nor fashion to attract him, caught up little Amy in his arms, and began to play a half teasing, half caressing game with the children. Betty thought it high time to be gone, and as she took leave, was requested to send up her little brother to play with his cousins. This did not prove a success, for Eugene constituted himself champion to Amoret, of whom Archer was very jealous, though she was his devoted and submissive slave. Master Delavie's rustic ways were in consequence pronounced to be too rude and rough for the dainty little town-bred boy, the fine ladies' pet.

The Major dined at the Great House, but came home so much dismayed and disgusted that he could hardly mention even to Betty what he had seen and heard. He only groaned out at intervals, "This is what the service is coming to! That fop to be that poor lad's commanding officer! That rake to be always hovering about my cousin!"

Others spoke out more plainly. Stories were afloat or orgies ending in the gallant Colonel being under the supper table, a thing only too common, but not in the house of a solitary lady who had only lately quitted the carousers. Half the dependants on the estate were complaining of the guest's swaggering overbearing treatment of themselves, or of his insolence to their wives or daughters; and Betty lived in a dreadful unnamed terror lest he should offer some impertinence to her father which the veteran's honour might not brook. However, there was something in the old soldier's dignity and long service that kept the arrogance of the younger man in check, and repressed all bluster towards him.

Demands for money were, as usual, made, but the settlement of accounts was deferred till the arrival of Hargrave, the family man of business, who came by coach to Bath, and then rode across to Carminster. The Major dined that day at the Great House, and came home early, with something so strange and startled about his looks that Betty feared that her worst misgivings were realised. It was a relief to hear him say, "Come hither, Betty, I want a word with you." At least it was no duel!

"What is it, dear sir?" she asked, as she shut his study door. "Is it come at last? Must we quit this place?"

"No, I could bear that better, but what do you think she asks of me now?—to give my little Aurelia, my beautiful darling, to that madman in the dark!"

"Oh!" exclaimed Betty, in a strange tone of discovery. "May I inquire what you said?"

"I said—I scarce know what I said. I declared it monstrous, and not to be thought of for a moment; and then she went on in her fashion that would wile a bird off a bush, declaring that no doubt the proposal was a shock, but if I would turn the matter over, I should see it was for the dear child's advantage. Belamour dotes on her, and after being an old man's darling for a few years, she may be free in her prime, with an honourable name and fortune."

"I dare say. As if one could not see through the entire design. My Lady would call her sister-in-law to prevent her being daughter-in-law!"

"That fancy has had no aliment, and must long ago have died out."

"Listen to Nurse Dove on that matter."

"Women love to foster notions of that sort."

"Nay, sir, you believe, as I do, that the poor child was conveyed to Bowstead in order that the youth might lose sight of her, and since he proves refractory to the match intended for him, this further device is found for destroying any possible hope on his part."

"I cannot say what may actuate my Lady, but if Amyas Belamour be the man I knew, and as the child's own letters paint him, he is not like to lend himself to any such arrangement."

"Comes the offer from him, or is it only a scheme of my Lady's?"

"He never writes more than a signature, but Hargrave is empowered to make proposals to me, very handsome proposals too, were not the bare idea intolerable."

"Aurelia is not aware of it, I am sure," said Betty, to whom Hargrave had brought another packet of cheerful innocent despatches, of which, as usual, the unseen friend in the dark was the hero.

"Certainly not, and I hope she never may be. I declared the notion was not to be entertained for a moment; but Urania never, in her life, would take no for an answer, and she talked me nearly out of my senses, then bade me go home, think it over, and discuss it with my excellent and prudent daughter; as if all the thinking and talking in the world could make it anything but more intolerable."

His prudent daughter understood in the adjective applied to her a hint which the wily lady would not have dared to make direct to the high-spirited old soldier, namely, that the continuance of his livelihood might depend on his consent. Betty knew likewise enough of the terrible world of the early eighteenth century to be aware that even such wedlock as this was not the worst to which a woman like Lady Belamour might compel the poor girl, who was entirely in her power, and out of reach of all protection; unless—An idea broke in on her—"If we could but go to Bowstead, sir," she said, "then we could judge whether the notion be as repugnant to Aurelia as it is to us, and whether Mr. Belamour be truly rational and fit to be trusted with her."

"I tell you, Betty, it is a mere absurdity to think of it. I believe the child is fond of, and grateful to, the poor man, but if she supposed she loved him, it would be mere playing on her ignorance."

"Then we could take her safely home and bear the consequences together, without leaving her alone exposed to any fresh machination of my Lady."

"You are right, Betty. You have all your sainted mother's good sense. I will tell my cousin that this is not a matter to be done blindly, and that I withhold my reply till I have seen and spoken with her and this most preposterous of suitors."

"Yes, it is the only way," said Betty. "We can then judge whether it be a cruel sacrifice, or whether the child have affection and confidence enough in him to be reasonably happy with him. What is his age, father?"

"Let me see. Poor Sir Jovian was much older than Urania, but he died at forty years old. His brother was some three years his junior. He cannot be above forty-six or seven. That is not the objection, but the moody melancholy—Think of our gay sprightly child!"

"We will see, sir."

"We! Mistress Betty? The cost will be severe without you!"

"Nay, sir, I cannot rest without going too; you might be taken ill."

"You cannot trust a couple of old campaigners like Palmer and me? What did we do without you?"

"Got lamed for life," said Betty, saucily. "No, I go on a pillion behind Palmer, and my grandfather's diamond ring shall pay expenses."

"Sir Archibald's ring that he put on two baby fingers of yours when he went off to Scotland."

"Better part with that then resign my Aurelia in the dark, uncertain whether it be for her good."

CHAPTER XVIII
THE PROPOSAL

Love sweetest lies concealed in night. —*T. MOORE.*

The Major rode up to the Great House to announce that he would only give his answer after having conferred with both his daughter and the suitor.

With tears in her beautiful blue eyes, Lady Belamour demanded why her dear cousin Harry could not trust the Urania he had known all her life to decide what was for the happiness of the sweet child whom she loved like her own.

She made him actually feel as if it were a cruel and unmerited suspicion, but she did not over come him. "Madam," he said, "it would be against my orders, as father of a family, to give my child away without doing my poor best for her."

There, in spite of all obstacles suggested and all displeasure manifested, he stuck fast, until, without choosing to wait till a shower of sleet and rain was over. Vexation and perplexity always overset his health, and the chill, added to them, rendered him so ill the next morning that Betty knew there was no chance of his leaving his room for the next month or six weeks; and she therefore sent a polite and formal note to the Great House explaining that he could not attend to business.

This brought upon her the honour of a visit from the great lady herself. Down came the coach-and-four, and forth from it came Lady Belamour in a magnificent hoop, the first seen in those parts, managing it with a grace that made her an overwhelming spectacle, in contrast with Betty, in her close-fitting dark-grey homespun, plain white muslin apron, cap, kerchief, and ruggles, scrupulously neat and fresh, but unadorned. The visit was graciously designed for "good cousin Harry," but his daughter was obliged, not unwillingly, though quite truly, to declare him far too suffering with pain and fever.

"La, you there, then," said the lady, "that comes of the dear man's heat of temper. I would have kept him till the storm was over but he was far too much displeased with his poor cousin to listen to me. Come, cousin Betty, I know you are in all his counsels. You will bring him to hear reason."

"The whole affair must wait, madam, till he is able to move."

"And if this illness be the consequence of one wet ride, how can he be in a condition to take the journey?"

"You best know, madam whether a father can be expected to bestow his daughter in so strange a manner without direct communication either with her or with the other party."

"I grant you the idea is at first sight startling, but surely he might trust to me; and he knows Amyas Belamour, poor man, to be the very soul of honour; yes, and with all his eccentricity to have made no small impression on our fair Aurelia. Depend upon it, my dear Betty, romance carried the day; and the damsel is more enamoured of the mysterious voice in the dark, than she would be of any lusty swain in the ordinary light of day."

"All that may be, madam, but she is scarce yet sixteen, and it is our duty to be assured of her inclinations and of the gentleman's condition."

"You will not trust me, who have watched them both," said Lady Belamour, with her most engaging manner. "Now look here, my dear, since we are two women together, safe out of the hearing of the men, I will be round with you. I freely own myself imprudent in sending your sister to Bowstead to take charge of my poor little girls, but if you had seen the little savages they were, you would not wonder that I could not take them home at once, nor that I should wish to see them acquire the good manners that I remembered in the children of this house; I never dreamt of Mr. Belamour heeding the little nursery. He has always been an obstinate melancholic lunatic, confined to his chamber by day, and wandering like a ghost by night, refusing all admission. Moreover my good Aylward had appeared hitherto a paragon of a duenna for discretion, only over starched in her precision. Little did I expect to find my young lady spending all her evenings alone with him, and the solitary hermit transformed into a gay and gallant bachelor like the Friar of Orders Gray in the song. And since matters have gone to such a length, I, as a woman who has seen more of the world than you have, my dear good Betty, think it expedient that the Friar and his charmer should be made one without loss of time. We know her to be innocence itself, and him for a very Sidney for honour, but the world—"

"It is your doing, madam," exclaimed Betty, passionately, completely overset by the insinuation; "you bid us trust you, and then confess that you have exposed my sweet sister to be vilely slandered! Oh my Aurelia, why did I let you out of my sight?" she cried, while hot tears stood in her eyes.

"I know your warmth, my dear," said Lady Belamour with perfect command of temper; "I tell you I blame myself for not having recollected that a lovely maiden can tame even a savage brute, or that even in the sweet rural country walls have ears and trees have tongues. Not that any harm is done so far, nor ever will be; above all if your good father do not carry his romantic sentiments so far as to be his ruin a second time. Credit me, Betty, they will not serve in any world save the imaginary one that crazed Don Quixote. What advantage can the pretty creature gain? She is only sixteen, quite untouched by true passion. She will obtain a name and fortune, and become an old man's idol for a few years, after which she will probably be at liberty by the time she is of an age to enjoy life."

"He is but five-and-forty!" said Betty.

"Well, if she arouse him to a second spring, there will be few women who will not envy her."

"You may colour it over, madam," said Betty, drawing herself up, "but nothing can conceal the fact that you confess yourself to have exposed my innocent helpless sister to malignant slander; and that you assure me that the only course left is to marry the poor child to a wretched melancholic who has never so much as seen her face."

"You are outspoken, Miss Delavie," said Lady Belamour, softly, but with a dangerous glitter in her blue eyes. "I pardon your heat for your father's sake, and because I ascribe it to the exalted fantastic notions in which you have been bred; but remember that there are bounds to my forbearance, and that an agent in his state of health, and with his stubborn ideas, only remains on sufferance."

"My father has made up his mind to sacrifice anything rather than his child," cried Betty.

"My dear girl, I will hear you no more. You are doing him no service," said Lady Belamour kindly. "You had better be convinced that it is a sacrifice, or an unwilling one, before you treat me to any more heroics."

Betty successfully avoided a parting kiss, and remained pacing up and down the room to work off her indignation before returning to her father. She was quite as angry with herself, as with my Lady, for having lost her temper, and so given her enemy an advantage, more especially as when her distress became less agitating, her natural shrewdness began to guess that the hint about scandal was the pure fruit of Lady Belamour's invention, as an expedient for obtaining her consent. Yet the mere breath of such a possibility of evil speaking was horror to her, and she even revolved the question of going herself to Bowstead to rescue her sister. But even if the journey had been more possible, her father was in no condition to be left to

Harriet's care, and there was nothing to be done except to wait till he could again attend to the matter, calm herself as best she could, so as not to alarm him, and intercept all dangerous messages.

Several days had passed, and though the Major had not left his bed, he had asked whether more had been heard from my Lady, and discussed the subject with his daughter, when a letter arrived in due course of post. It was written in a large bold hand, and the signature, across a crease in the paper, was in the irregular characters that the Major recognised as those of Mr. Belamour.

"DEAR AND HONOURED SIR,

"*Proposals have been made to you on my Behalf for the Hand of your fair and amiable Daughter, Miss Aurelia Delavie. I am well aware how preposterous and even shocking they may well appear to you; yet, let me assure you, on the Faith of a Man of Honour that if you will entrust her to me, wretched Recluse though I be, and will permit her to bear my Name, I will answer for her Happiness and Welfare. Situated as I am, I cannot enter into further explanations; but we are old Acquaintance, though we have not met for many Years, and therefore I venture to beg of you to believe me when I say that if you will repose Confidence in me, and exercise Patience, I can promise your admirable Daughter such Preferment as she is far from expecting. She has been the Blessing of my darkened Life, but I would never have presumed to ask further were it not that I have no other Means of protecting her, nor of shielding her from Evils that may threaten her, and that might prove far worse than bearing the Name of*

"*Your obedient Servant to command,*

"*AMYAS BELAMOUR.*

"Bowstead Park, Dec. 3rd, 1737."

"Enigmatical!" said Betty.

"It could hardly be otherwise if he had to employ a secretary" said her father. "Who can have written for him?"

"His friend, Dr. Godfrey, most probably," said Betty. "It is well spelt as well as indited, and has not the air of being drawn up by a lawyer."

"No, it is not Hargrave's hand. It is strange that he says nothing of the settlements."

"Here is a postscript, adding, 'Should you consent, Hargrave will give you ample satisfaction as to the property which I can settle on your daughter.'"

"Of that I have no doubt," said the Major. "Well, Betty, on reflection, if I were only secure that no force was put on the child's will, and if I could exchange a few words face to face with Amyas Belamour, I should not be so utterly averse as I was at first sight. She is a good child, and if she like him, and find it not hard to do her duty by him, she might be as happy as another. And since she is out of our reach it might save her from worse. What say you, child?"

"That last is the strongest plea with me," said Betty, with set lips.

They took another evening for deliberation, but there was something in the tone of the letter that wrought on them, and it ended in a cautious consent being given, on the condition of the father being fully satisfied of his daughter's free and voluntary acquiescence.

"After all," he said to Betty, "I shall be able to go up to Bowstead for the wedding, and if I find that her inclinations have been forced, I can take her away at all risks."

CHAPTER XIX
WOOING IN THE DARK

You may put out my eyes with a ballad-maker's pen, and hang me
up for the sign of blind Cupid. —Much Ado About Nothing.

Aurelia had been walking in the park with her two remaining charges, when a bespattered messenger was seen riding up to the door, and Letitia dropped her hoop in her curiosity and excitement.

Lady Belamour, on obtaining the Major's partial acquiescence, had felt herself no longer obliged to vegetate at Carminster, but had started for Bath, while the roads were still practicable; and had at the same time sent off a courier with letters to Bowstead. Kind Mrs. Dove had sent a little packet to each of the children, but they found Cousin Aura's sympathy grievously and unwontedly lacking, and she at last replied to their repeated calls to here to share their delight, that they must run away, and display their treasures to Molly and Jumbo. She must read her letters alone.

The first she had opened was Betty's, telling her of her father's illness, which was attributed in great part to the distress and perplexity caused by Lady Belamour's proposal. Had it not been for this indisposition, both father and sister would have come to judge for themselves before entertaining it for a moment; but since the journey was impossible, he could only desire Betty to assure her sister that no constraint should be put on her, and that if she felt the least repugnance to the match, she need not consider her obliged to submit. More followed about the religious duty of full consideration and prayer before deciding on what would fix her destiny for life, but all was so confusing to the girl, entirely unprepared as she was, that after hastily glancing on in search of an explanation which she failed to find, she laid it aside, and opened the other letter. It began imperially

"MY COUSIN,

"No doubt you are already informed of the Honour that has been
done you by the Proposal that Mr. Amyas Belamour has made to
your Father

for your Hand. It is no slight Compliment to a young Maid like you, from one of the most noted Wits about Town in the last Reign; and you will no doubt shew the Good Sense to esteem yourself fortunate beyond all reasonable Expectations or Deserts of your own, as well as to act for the Advantage of your Family. Be assured that I shall permit no foolish Flightiness nor Reluctance to interfere with you true Welfare. I say this, because, as you well know, your Father's Affection is strong and blind, and you might easily draw him into a Resistance which could but damage both his Health and his Prospects. On receiving the tidings of your Marriage, I promise to settle on him the Manor House with an Annuity of Three hundred Pounds; but if he should support you in any foolish Refusal, I shall be obliged to inform him that I can dispense with his Services; therefore you will do wisely to abstain from any childish expressions of Distaste.

"On your Marriage, you will of course have the enjoyment of the Pin Money with which Mr. Belamour will liberally endow you, and be treated in all Respects as a Married Lady. My Daughters shall be sent to School, unless you wish to make them your Companions a little longer. Expecting to hear from you that you are fully sensible to the good Fortune and the Obligations you are under to me,

"*I remain*

"*Yours &c.*

"*URANIA BELAMOUR.*"

It was with a gasp of relief that Aurelia discovered what was required of her. "Marry Mr. Belamour? Is that all? Then why should they all think I should so much dislike it, my Lady, and my papa, and sister and all? Nobody ever was so good to me, and maybe I could make him a little happier, though it is not what I expected of him, to forget his Mary! Oh, no, I am not afraid; I might have been afraid six months ago, but now it is a different thing. I am not so foolish! And my dear papa will have the Manor House for ever! And Eugene will be able to go to a good school and have a pair of colours in good time! A fortunate girl! Yes, of course I am! Then Mrs. Phoebe and Mrs. Delia will not flout me any more, even if young Sir Amyas should come here! Ah! here are the little girls returning! Keep them here? Of course I will. What toys and books I will get for them!"

Yet, when the time for her summons drew nigh, a great dread and shyness overcame her, lest Mr. Belamour should begin on the subject; and she only nerved herself by recollecting that he could have had no one to read to him her father's letter of reply, and that he was scarcely likely to speak without knowing the contents. Still, it was only shyness and embarrassment that made her advance timidly, but in one moment a new sensation, a strange tremor came over her, as instead of merely her fingertips, her whole hand was grasped and fervently pressed, and in the silence that ensued the throbbing of her heart and the panting of her breath seemed to find an echo. However, the well-known voice began, "My fair visitor is very good in honouring me to-night."

Was it coming? Her heart gave such a throb that she could only murmur something inarticulate, while there was a hasty repressed movement near her.

"You have heard from your father?" said Mr. Belamour.

"My father is ill, sir," she faltered.

"Ah, yes, so I was sorry to understand. Has he not sent a message to you through your sister?"

"He has, sir," Aurelia continued, with difficulty, to utter.

There was another silence, another space of tightened breath and beating heart, absolutely audible, and again a hushed, restless movement heralded Mr. Belamour's next words, "Did I no tell you truly that my Lady devises most unexpected expedients?"

"Then would you not have it so, sir?" asked Aurelia, in a bewildered voice of perplexity. "Oh!" as again one of those echoes startled her, "tell me what it all means."

"Hush! listen to me," said Mr. Belamour, in a voice that added to her undefined alarm by what seemed to her imperious displeasure as uncalled for as it was unusual; but the usual fatherly gentleness immediately prevailed, "My child, I should never have entertained the thought for a moment but for—but for Lady Belamour. This sounds like no compliment," he added, catching himself up, and manifesting a certain embarrassment and confusion very unlike his usual calm dignity of demeanour, and thus adding to the strange fright that was growing upon Aurelia. "But you must understand that I would not—even in semblance—have dreamt of your being apparently linked to age, sorrow, and infirmity, save that—strange as it may seem—Lady Belamour has herself put into my hands the best means of protecting you, and finally, as I trust, securing your happiness."

"You are very good, sir," she continued to breathe out, amid the flutterings of her heart, and the reply produced a wonderful outburst of ardour in a low but fervent voice. "You will! You will! You sweetest of angels, you will be mine!"

There was something so irresistibly winning in the sound, that it drew forth an answer from the maiden's very heart. "Oh! yes, indeed—" and before she could utter another word she was snatched into a sudden, warm, vehement embrace, from which she was only partly released, as—near, but still not so near as she would have expected—this extraordinary suitor seemed to remonstrate with his ardent self, saying, "Now! now! that will do! So be it then, my child," he continued. "Great will be the need of faith, patience, trust, ay, and of self-restraint, but let these be practised for a little space, and all will be well."

She scarcely heard the latter words. The sense of something irrevocable and unfathomable was overpowering her. The mystery of these sudden alterations of voice, now near, now far off, was intolerable. Here were hands claiming her, fervent, eager breathings close upon her, and that serious, pensive voice going on all that time. The darkness grew dreadful to her, dizziness came over her; she dashed aside the hands, started up with a scream, and amid the strange noises and flashes of a swoon, knew no more till she heard Mrs. Aylward's voice over her, found the horrid smell of burnt feathers under her nose, and water trickling down her face, dim candlelight was round her, and she perceived that she was on a low settee in the lobby.

"There, she is coming round. You may tell your master, Jumbo, 'twas nothing but the mince pies."

"Oh, no—" began Aurelia, but her own voice seemed to come from somewhere else, and being inexperienced in fainting, she was frightened.

"That is right, you are better. Now, a drop of strong waters."

Aurelia choked, and put them aside, but was made to swallow the draught, and revived enough to ask, "How came I here?"

"Jumbo must have carried you out, ma'am, and laid you here before ever he called any one," said Mrs. Aylward. "Dear, dear, to think of your being taken like that. But the tins of those mince-pies are over large! You must halve one next time."

Aurelia was sensible enough to the reproof of greediness to begin to protest against the mince-pie theory, but she recollected that she could not account for her swoon, and thereupon became as red as she had been pale, thus confirming the housekeeper's opinion. A sound of footsteps made her start up and cry, "What's that?" in nervous fright; but Mrs. Aylward declared it was fancy, and as she was by this time able to walk, she was conducted to her own room. There she was examined on her recent diet, and was compelled to allow the housekeeper to ascribe her illness to neglect of autumnal blood-letting and medicine; and she only stave off the send for the barber and his lancet the next morning by promising to swallow a dose compounded of all that was horrible.

She was altogether much shaken, she dreamed strange dreams by night, was capable of little by day, was declared by the children to be cross, and was much inclined to plead indisposition as an excuse for not visiting that alarming room in the evening. Indeed for the greater part of the day she felt as if she must avail herself of the pretext, and as if she neither could nor would encounter that strange double creature in the dark; but somehow she had been as much fascinated as terrified, and, in spite of her resolve, she found herself mechanically following Jumbo, shuddering all over and as cold as ice.

The dark chambers were warmed by German stoves, so that the atmosphere was always equable, and it seemed to revive her, while a kind, warm hand led her as usual to her seat, and it was the usual gentle, courteous, paternal tone that addressed her, "How chill and trembling you are! My poor child, you were sadly alarmed last night."

Aurelia murmured some excuse about being very foolish.

"It was not you who was foolish," was the reply; and though her hand was retained it was evidently for the sake of warming it, and comforting her, not of caressing it in the startling mode of yesterday. There was a pause, during which her composure began to be restored, and some inquiries whether she were quite recovered; to which she replied with eager affirmatives, feeling indeed quite herself again, now that all was in its familiar state around her. Then this strange suitor spoke again. "It is a hard and cruel fate that my Lady has sought to impose on you."

"Oh, do not say so, sir I—-"

"No," he interrupted somewhat hastily, "do not try to deny it, my child; I know better than you can what it would amount to. Believe me, I only lend myself to her arrangement because I know no better means of guarding you and preserving you for better days."

"I know how kind you are, sir."

"And you trust me?"

"Indeed I do."

"That is all I ask. I shall never be a husband to you more than in name, Aurelia, nor ask of you more than you give me now, namely, your sweet presence for a few hours in the evening, without seeing me. Can you bear thus to devote your young life, for a time at least?"

"You know, sir, how glad I always am to be with you," said Aurelia, relieved yet half regretting that strange fervour. "I will do my very best to please you."

"Ah! sweet child," he began, with a thrill of deep feeling in his voice; but checking himself he continued, "All I ask is patience and trust for a time—for a time—you promise it!"

"With all my heart," said Aurelia.

"I will use my best endeavours to requite that trust, my child," he said. "Is not the Christian watchword faith, not sight? It must be yours likewise."

"I hope so," she said, scarcely understanding.

He then interrogated her somewhat closely as to the letters which had prepared her for the proposal; and as Aurelia was far too simple to conceal anything under cross-examination, Mr. Belamour soon found out what her Ladyship's threats and promises had been.

"The Manor House?" he said. "That is the original nucleus of the property which had hitherto gone to the heir male?"

"So my sister told me," said Aurelia.

"That letter, which Dr. Godfrey read to me, spoke of my poor brother's discomfort in holding it. It is well if thus tardily she refund it, though not as your price, my poor child. It should have been as matter of justice, if not by her husband's dying wish. So this is the alternative set before you! Has it been set before your father likewise?"

"Almost certainly she will have threatened to dismiss him if he do not consent. It was that which made my sister decide on sending me here, or what would become of him and Eugene? But I should think my Lady knew my father better than to seem to offer any kind of price, as you call it, for me."

"Precisely. You have heard from this maternal sister of yours? Does he then give his consent?"

"They say they will not have my inclinations forced, and that they had rather undergo anything than that I should be driven to—to—"

"To be as much a sacrifice as Iphigenia," he concluded the sentence.

"Indeed, sir," said Aurelia, quite restored, "I cannot see why they should imagine me to have such objections, or want me to be so cautious and considerate. I shall write to my papa that it is not at all repugnant to me, for that you are very, very good to me; and if I can make your time pass ever so little more pleasantly, it is a delight to me. I am sure I shall like you better than if—-"

"Stay, stay, child," he said, half laughing; "remember, it is as a father that I ask you to love and trust the old recluse."

She thought she had been forward, crimsoned in the dark, and retired into her shell for the rest of the evening. She was glad when with his usual tact, Mr. Belamour begged for the recitation he knew she could make with the least effort of memory.

At the end, however, she ventured to ask—"Sir, shall I be permitted ever to see my father and sister?"

"Certainly, my child. In due time I hope you will enjoy full liberty, though you may have to wait for it."

Aurelia durst not ask what was in her mind, whether they would not come to the wedding, but that one great hope began to outweigh all the strange future. She began to say something about being too young, ignorant, and foolish for him, but this was kindly set aside, she hardly knew how. Mr. Belamour himself suggested the formula in which she might send her consent to Lady Belamour, begging at the same time to retain the company of the little Misses Wayland. To her father she wrote such a letter as might satisfy all doubts as to the absence of all repugnance to the match, and though the Major had sacrificed all to love and honour himself, *mariages de convenance* were still so much the rule, and wives, bestowed in all passiveness with unawakened hearts, so often proved loving and happy matrons, that it would have been held unreasonable to demand more than absence of dislike on the part of the bride.

Therewith things returned to their usual course, and she was beginning to feel as if all had been a dream, when one evening, about a week later, her suitor appeared to have one of those embarrassing fits of youthful ardour; her hand was passionately seized, caressed, toyed with by a warm strong hand, and kissed by lips that left a burning impression and that were no longer hairy. Surely he had been shaving! Was the time for which he bade her wait, his full recovery, and the resumption of the youthfulness that seemed to come on him in fits and starts, and then to ebb away, and leave him the grave courteous old man she had first known? And why was it always in a whisper that he spoke forth all those endearments which thrilled her with such strange emotions?

When she came into the light, she found her fourth finger encircled with an exquisite emerald ring, which seemed to bind her to her fate, and make her situation tangible. Another time she was entreated to give a lock of her hair, and she of course did so, though it was strange that it should confer any pleasure on her suitor in the dark.

CHAPTER XX
THE MUFFLED BRIDEGROOM

This old fantastical Duke of dark corners. —
Measure for Measure.

There was some coming and going of Mr. Hargrave in the ensuing weeks; and it began to be known that Miss Delavie was to become the wife of the recluse. Mrs. Aylward evidently knew it, but said nothing; Molly preferred a petition to be her waiting maid; Jumbo grinned as if overpowered with inward mirth; the old ladies in the pew looked more sour and haughty than ever to discourage "the artful minx," and the little girls asked all manner of absurd and puzzling questions.

My Lady was still at Bath, and Aurelia supposed that the marriage would take place on her return; and that the Major and Betty would perhaps accompany her. The former was quite in his usual health again, and had himself written to give her his blessing as a good dutiful maiden, and declare that he hoped to be with her for her wedding, and to give himself to his honoured friend.

She was the more amazed and startled when, one Sunday evening in spring, Mr. Hargrave came to her as she sat in her own parlour, saying, "Madam, you will be amazed, but under the circumstances, the parson and myself being both here, Mr. Belamour trusts you will not object to the immediate performance of the ceremony."

Aurelia took some moments to realise what the ceremony was; and then she cried, "Oh! but my father meant to have been here."

"Mr. Belamour thinks it better not to trouble Major Delavie to come up," said Mr. Hargrave; and as Aurelia stood in great distress and disappointment at this disregard of her wishes, he added, "I think Miss Delavie cannot fail to understand Mr. Belamour's wishes to anticipate my Lady's arrival, so that he may be as little harassed as possible with display and publicity. You may rely both on his honour and my vigilance that all is done securely and legally."

"Oh! I know that," said Aurelia, blushing; "but it is so sudden! And I was thinking of my father—-"

"Your honoured father has given full consent in writing," said the steward. "Your doubts and scruples are most natural, my dear madam, but under the circumstances they must give way, for it would be impossible to Mr. Belamour to go through a public wedding."

That Aurelia well knew, though she had expected nothing so sudden or so private; but she began to feel that she must allow all to be as he chose; and she remembered that she had never pressed on him her longing for her father's presence, having taken it as a matter of course, and besides, having been far too shy to enter on the subject of her wedding. So she rose up as in a dream, saying, "Shall I go as I am?"

"I fear a fuller toilet would be lost upon the bridegroom," said the lawyer with some commiseration, as he looked at the beautiful young creature about to be bound to the heart-broken old hermit. "You will have to do me the honour of accepting my services in the part of father."

He was a man much attached to the family, and especially to Mr. Belamour, his first patron, and was ready to do anything at his bidding or for his pleasure. Such private weddings were by no uncommon up to the middle of the last century. The State Law was so easy as to render Gretna Green unnecessary, when the presence of any clergyman anywhere, while the parties plighted their troth before witnesses, was sufficient to legalise the union; nor did any shame or sense of wrong necessarily attach to such marriages. Indeed they were often the resource of persons too bashful or too refined to endure the display and boisterous merriment by which a public wedding was sure to be attended. Every one knew of excellent and respectable couples who had not been known to be married till the knot had been tied for several days or weeks—so that there was nothing in this to shock the bride. And as usual she did as she was told, and let Mr. Hargrave lead her by her finger-tips towards Mr. Belamour's apartments. Mrs. Aylward was waiting in the lobby, with a fixed impassive countenance, intended to imply that though obedient to the summons to serve as a witness, it was no concern of hers. On the stairs behind her the maids were leaning over the balusters, stuffing their aprons into their mouths lest their tittering should betray them.

The sitting-room was nearly, but not quite, dark, for a lamp, closely shaded, cast a dim light on a Prayer-book, placed on a small table, behind which stood poor Mr. Greaves—a black spectre, whose white bands were just discernible below a face whose nervous, disturbed expression was lost in the general gloom. He carefully avoided looking at the bride, fearing perhaps some appeal on her part such as would make his situation perplexing. Contempt and poverty had brought his stamp of clergymen very low, and rendered them abject. He had been taken by surprise, and though assured that this was according to my Lady's will, and with the consent of the maiden's father, he was in an agony of fright, shifting awkwardly from leg to leg, and ruffling the leaves of the book, as a door opened and the bridegroom appeared, followed by Jumbo.

Aurelia looked up with bashful eagerness, and saw in the imperfect light a tall figure entirely covered by a long dark dressing-gown, a grey, tight curled lawyer's wig on the head, and the upper part of the face sheltered from the scanty rays of the lamp by a large green shade.

Taking his place opposite to her as Mr. Hargrave arranged them, he bowed in silence to the clergyman, who, in a trembling voice, began the rite which was to unite Amyas Belamour to Aurelia Delavie. He intended to shorten the service, but his nervous terror and the obscurity of the room made him stumble in finding the essential passages, and blunder in dictating the vows, thus increasing the confusion and bewilderment of poor little Aurelia. Somehow her one comfort was in the touch of the hand that either clasped hers, or held the ring on her finger—a strong, warm, tender, trustworthy hand, neither as white nor as soft as she would have expected, but giving her a comfortable sense both of present support and affection, and of identity with that eager one which had sought to fondle and caress her. There was a certain tremor about both, but hers was from bashful fright, his, from scarcely suppressed eagerness.

The steward had a form of certificate ready for signature. When it was presented to the bridegroom he put up his hand for a moment as if to push back the shade, but, in dread of admitting even a feeble ray of light, gave up the attempt, took the pen and wrote Amyas Belamour where the clergyman pointed. Aurelia could hardly see what she was doing, and knew she had written very badly. The lawyer and housekeeper followed as witnesses; and the bridegroom, laying a fee of ten guineas on the desk, took his bride by the hand and led her within the door whence he had issued. It was instantly closed, and at the same moment she was enfolded in a pair of rapturous arms, and held to a breast whose throbs wakened response in her own, while passionate kisses rained on her face, mingled with ecstatic whispers and murmurs of "Mine! mine! my own!"

On a knock at the door she was hastily released, and Mr. Hargrave said, "Here are the certificates, sir." — Mr. Belamour put one into her hand, saying "Keep it always about you; never part with it. And now, my child, after all the excitement you have gone through, you shall be subjected to no more to-night. Fare you well, and blessings attend your dreams."

Strange that while he was uttering this almost peremptory dismissal, she should feel herself in a clinging grasp, most unwilling to let her go! What did it all mean? Could she indeed be a wife, when here she was alone treading the long dark stair, in looks, in habits, in externals, still only the little governess of my Lady's children! However, she had hardly reached her room, before there was a knock at the door, and the giggling, blushing entrance of Molly with "Please, ma'am, Madam Belamour, I wishes you joy with all my heart. Please can't I do nothing for you? Shall I help you undress, or brush your hair?"

Perhaps she expected a largesse in honour of the occasion, but Aurelia had spent all her money on Christmas gifts, and had nothing to bestow. However, she found on the breakfast-table a parcel addressed to Madam Belamour, containing a purse with a startling amount of golden guineas in it. She was rather surprised at the title, which was one generally conferred on dignified matrons whose husbands were below the rank of knighthood, such as the wives of country squires and of the higher clergy. The calling her mother Madam Delavie had been treated as an offence by Lady Belamour; and when the day had gone by, with nothing else to mark it from others, Aurelia, finding her recluse in what she mentally called his quiet rational mood, ventured, after thanking him, modestly to inquire whether that was what she was to be called.

"It is better thus," hes said. "You have every right to the title."

She recollected that he was a baronet's younger son, a distinction in those days; and that she had been told that his patent of knighthood had been made out, though he had never been able to appear at court to receive the accolade, and had never assumed the title; so she only said "Very well, sir, I merely thought whether my Lady would think it presuming."

He laughed a little. "My Lady will soon understand it," he said. "Her husband will be at home in a few weeks. And now, my dear Madam Belamour," he add playfully, "tell me whether there is any wish that I can gratify."

"You are very kind, sir—-"

"What does that pause mean, my fair friend?"

"I fear it is too much to ask, sir, but since you inquire what would please me most, it would be if you could spare me to go to my sister Harriet's wedding?"

"My child," he said, with evident regret, "I fear that cannot be. It will not be prudent to make any move until Mr. Wayland's return; but after that I can assure you of more liberty. Meantime, let us consider what wedding present you would like to send her."

Aurelia had felt her request so audacious that she subsided easily; and modestly suggested a tea-service. She thought of porcelain, but Mr. Belamour's views were of silver, and it ended in the lady giving the cups and saucers, and the gentleman the urn and the tea and coffee pots and other plate; but it was a drawback to the pleasure of this munificence that the execution of the order had to be entrusted to Mr. Hargrave. The daring hope Aurelia had entertained of shopping for a day, with Mrs. Aylward as an escort, and choosing the last fashions to send to her sisters was quashed by the grave reply that it was better not for the present. What was the meaning of all this mystery, and when was it to end? She felt that it would be ungrateful to murmur, for Mr. Belamour evidently was full of sorrow whenever he was obliged to disappoint her, and much was done for her pleasure. A charming little saddle-horse, two riding-habits, with a groom, and a horse for him, were sent down from London for her benefit; gifts showered upon her; and whenever she found her husband in one of those perplexing accesses of tenderness she was sure to carry away some wonderful present, a beautiful jewelled watch, an *etui* case, a fan, a scent-bottle, or patch-box with a charming enamel of a butterfly. The little girls were always looking for something pretty that she would show them in the morning, and thought it must be a fine thing to have a husband who gave such charming things. Those caressing evenings, however, always frightened Aurelia, and sent her away vaguely uneasy, often to lie awake full of a vague yearning and alarm; and several days of restlessness would pass before she could return to her ordinary enjoyment of her days with the children and her evenings with Mr. Belamour. Yet when there was any long intermission of those fits of tender affection, she missed them sorely, and began to fear she had given offence, especially as this strangely capricious man seemed sometimes to repel those modest, timid advances which at other times would fill him with ill-suppressed transport. Then came longings to see and satisfy herself as to what was indeed the aspect of him whom she was learning to love.

No wonder there was something unsettled and distressed about her, overthrowing much of that gentle duteous ness which she had brought from home. She wrote but briefly and scantily to her sister, not feeling as if she could give full confidence; she drifted away from some of the good habits enjoined on her, feeling that, as a married woman, she was less under authority. She was less thorough in her religious ways, less scrupulous in attending to the children's lessons; and the general fret of her uncertainties told upon her temper with them. They loved her heartily still, and she returned their affection, but she was not so uniformly patient and good-humoured. Indeed since Amoret's departure some element of harmony was missing, and it could not now be said that a whine, a quarrel, or a cry was a rare event. Even the giving up my lady's wearisome piece of embroidery had scarcely a happy effect, for Aurelia missed the bracing of the task-work and the attention it required, and the unoccupied time was spent in idle fretting. A little self-consequence too began to set in, longing for further recognition of the dignities of Madam Belamour.

The marriage had been notified to Lady Belamour and to Major Delavie, and letters had been received from each. My Lady travelled to London early in April in company with Lady Aresfield, and, to the relief of the inmates of Bowstead, made no deviation thither. No one else was officially told that the wedding had taken place, but all the village knew it; and Mrs. Phoebe and Mrs. Delia so resented it that they abandoned the state pew to Madam Belamour and the children, made their curtsies more perpendicularly than ever, and, when formally invited to supper, sent a pointed and ceremonious refusal, so that Aurelia felt hurt and angered.

CHAPTER XXI ·
THE SISTERS' MEETING

By all hope thou hast to see again
Our aged father and to soothe his pain,
I charge thee, tell me, hast thou seen the thing
Thou callst thine husband? —MORRIS.

After numerous delays Mr. Arden had at length been presented to the living of Rundell Canonicorum, and in one of the last days of April Harriet Delavie had become his wife. After a fortnight of festivities amongst their old Carminster friends, the happy couple were to ride, pillion-wise, to take possession of tier new home, passing through London, and there spending time enough with some relations of the bridegroom to show Harriet the wonders of the City.

Thence Mrs. Arden sent an urgent invitation from her hospitable hostess to Mrs. Belamour, to come and spend some days in Gracechurch Street and share with her sister the pleasures of the first sight of London.

"I assure you," wrote Harriet, "that though they be Woolstaplers, it is all in the Wholesale Line; and they are very genteel, and well-bred Persons, who have everything handsome about them. Indeed it is upon the Cards that the Alderman may, ere many years be passed, be my Lord Mayor; but yet he and his good Wife have a proper Appreciation of Family, and know how to esteem me as one of the Delavies. They would hold themselves infinitely honoured by your Visit; and if you were here, we might even be invited to Lady Belamour's, and get Tickets for Ranelagh. I called at my Lady's Door, but she was not within, nor has she returned my Visit, though I went in the Alderman's own Coach; but if you were with me she would have no Colour for Neglect, you being now her Sister-in-law, though it makes me laugh to think of it. But as we poor married Ladies are compelled to obey our Lords and Masters; and as Mr. Belamour may chance to be too high in his Notions to permit you to be a Guest in this House (as I told our good Cousin Arden was very like), we intend to lie a Night at Brentford, and remain there for a Day, trusting that your Husband will not be so cruel as to prevent a Meeting, either by your coming to see us, or our coming to see you in your present Abode, which I long to do. It is a Year since we parted, and I cannot tell you how I long to clasp my beloved Sister in my Arms."

Harriet could not long more for such a meeting than did Aurelia, and there was, it must be owned, a little relief, that it was Harriet, and not the severer judge, Betty, who thus awaited her. She could hardly brook the delay until the evening, and even wondered whether it were not a wife's privilege to anticipate the hour; but she did not venture, and only hovered about impatient for Jumbo's summons. She came in with a rapid movement that led Mr. Belamour to say, "Ha, my fair visitor, I perceive that you have some tidings to bring to-day."

Everything was rapidly poured out, and she anxiously awaited the decision. She had little hope of being allowed to go to Gracechurch Street, and did not press for it; but she could not refrain from showing her earnest desire for the sight of her sister, so that it was plain that it would have been a cruel disappointment to her, if she had been prevented from meeting the newly-married couple. She detected a certain sound of annoyance or perplexity in the tones that replied, and her accents became almost plaintively imploring as she concluded, "Pray, pray, sir, do not deny me."

"No, my child, I could not be cruel enough for a refusal," he answered; "I was but considering how most safely the thing may be contrived. I know it would be your wish, and that it would seem more befitting that you should act as hostess for your sister, but I fear that must be for another time. This is not my house, and there are other reasons for which it would be wiser for you to receive no one here."

"It will be quite enough for me if I may only go to Brentford to meet my dear, dear Harriet."

"Then be it so, my child. Present my compliments to Mrs. Arden, and entreat her to excuse the seeming inhospitality of the invalid."

Aurelia was overflowing with joy at the anticipated meeting, wrote a delighted letter to make the appointment, and skipped about the dark stairs and passages more like the butterfly she was than like Madam Belamour; while Fay and Letty found her a more delightful playfellow than ever, recovering all the animation she had lost during the last weeks. Her only drawback to the pleasure was that each intervening evening convinced her more strongly that Mr. Belamour was uneasy and dissatisfied about the meeting, which he could not prohibit. On the previous night he asked many questions about her sister, in especial whether she were of an inquisitive disposition.

"That rather depends on how much she has to say about herself," returned Aurelia, after some reflection. "She likes to hear about other people's affairs, but she had much rather talk of her own."

This made Mr. Belamour laugh. "Considering," he said, "how recently she has undergone the greatest event of a woman's life, let us hope that her imagination and her tongue may be fully occupied by it during the few hours that you are to pass together. It seems hard to put any restraint on your ingenuous confidence, my sweet friend; but I trust to your discretion to say as little as you can contrive of your strange position here, and of the infirmities and caprices of him whose name you have deigned to bear."

"Sir, do you think I could?"

"It is not for my own sake, but for yours, that I would recommend caution," he continued. "The situation is unusual, and such disclosures might impel persons to interfere for what they thought your interest; but you have promised me your implicit trust, and you will, I hope, prove it. You can understand how painful would be such well-meaning interference, though you cannot understand how fatally mischievous it would be."

"I had better say I can tell her nothing," said Aurelia, startled.

"Nay, that would excite still greater suspicion. Reply briefly and carefully, making no mysteries to excite curiosity, and avert the conversation from yourself as much as possible."

Man of the world and brilliant talker as he had been, he had no notion of the difficulty of the task he had imposed on the simple open-hearted girl, accustomed to share all her thoughts with her sister; and she was too gay and joyous to take full note of all his cautions, only replying sincerely that she hoped that she should say nothing amiss, and that she would do her best to be heedful of his wishes.

In spite of all such cautions, she was too happy to take in the notion of anxiety. She rose early in the morning, caring for the first time to array herself in the insignia of her new rank. Knowing that the bridle-path lay through parks, woodlands and heaths, so that there was no fear of dust, she put on a dainty habit of white cloth, trimmed and faced with blue velvet, and a low-crowned hat with a white feather. On her pretty grey horse, the young Madam Belamour was a fair and gracious sight, as she rode into the yard of the Red Lion at Brentford. Harriet was at the window watching for her, and Mr. Arden received her as she sprang off her steed, then led her up to the parlour, where breakfast was spread awaiting her.

"Aurelia, what a sweet figure you make," cried Harriet, as the sisters unwound their arms after the first ecstasy of embracing one another again. "Where did you get that exquisite habit?"

"It came down from London with another, a dark blue," said Aurelia. "I suppose Mr. Belamour ordered them, for they came with my horse. It is the first time I have worn it."

"Ah! fine things are of little account when there is no one to see them," said Mrs. Arden, shaking her head in commiseration.

She was attired in a grey riding-dress with a little silver lace about it, and looked wonderfully plump and well, full of importance and complacency, and with such a return of comeliness that Aurelia would hardly have recognised the lean, haggard, fretful Harriet of the previous year. Her sentiment and romance, her soft melancholy and little affectations had departed, and she was already the notable prosperous wife of a beneficed clergyman, of whose abilities she was very proud, though she patronised with good-humoured contempt his dreamy, unpractical, unworldly ways.

The questions poured forth from Aurelia's heart-hunger about brother, sister and home, were answered kindly and fully over the breakfast-table; but as if Harriet had turned that page in her life, and expected Aurelia to have done the same, every now and then exclaiming: "La! you have not forgotten that! What a memory you have, child!"

She wanted much more to talk of the parsonage and glebe of Rundell Canonicorum, and of how many servants and cows she should keep, and showed herself almost annoyed when Aurelia brought her back to Carminster by asking whether Eugene had finished his Comenius, and if the speckled hen had hatched many chickens, whether Palmer had had his rheumatic attack this spring, or if the Major's letter to Vienna had produced any tidings of Nannerl's relation. Harriet seemed only to be able to reply by an effort of memory, and was far more desirous of expatiating on the luxuries at alderman Arden's, and the deference with which she had been treated, in contrast to the indignity of Lady Belamour's neglect.

It was disappointing to find that her father had heard nothing from my Lady about the settlement of the Manor House.

"Was the promise in writing?" asked Mr. Arden, who had been silent all this time.

"Certainly, in a letter to me."

"I recommend you to keep it carefully until Mr. Wayland's return," said Mr. Arden: "he will see justice done to you."

"Poor Mr. Wayland! When he does return, I pity him; but it is his own fault for leaving his lady to herself. Have you ever seen the gallant colonel, sister?"

"Never."

"Ah! most like he is not much at Bowstead. But do not folk talk there?"

"My dear," said Mr. Arden, "you would do well to imitate your honoured father's discretion on certain points."

"Bless me, Mr. Arden, how you startled me. I thought you were in a brown study." She winked at Aurelia as if to intimate that she meant to continue the subject in his absence, and went on; "I assure you, I had to be on the alert all the way to take care he looked at the sign-posts, or we might have been at York by this time. And in London, what do you think was all my gentleman cared to go and see? Why, he must needs go to some correspondents of his who are Fellows of the Royal Society. I took it for granted they must be friends of his Majesty or of the Prince of Wales at the least, and would have had him wait for his new gown and cassock; but la! it was only a set of old doctors and philosophers, and he wished to know what musty discoveries they had been making. That was one thing he desired in London, and the other was to hear that crazy Parson Wesley preach a sermon hours long!"

"I was well rewarded in both instances," said Mr. Arden gravely.

Aurelia did not take advantage of the opportunity of shining in the eyes of her new brother-in-law by showing her acquaintance with the discussions on electricity which she had studied for Mr. Belamour's benefit, nor did she speak of Dr. Godfrey's views of Wesley and Whitfield. Had she so ventured, her sister would have pitied her, and Mr. Arden himself been somewhat shocked at her being admitted to knowledge unbecoming to a pretty young lady. Intellect in ladies would have been a startling idea, and though very fond of his wife, he never thought of her as a companion, but only as the mistress of his house and guardian of his welfare.

The dinner was ordered at one, and at three Aurelia would ride home, while Mr. and Mrs. Arden went on about twelve miles to the house of a great grazier, brother to the Alderman's wife, where they had been invited to make their next stage, and spend the next day, Sunday, when Harriet reckoned on picking up information about cattle, if she were not actually presented with a cow or a calf. They went out and walked a little about the town, where presently they met Mrs. Hunter. Aurelia met her puzzled stare with a curtsey, and she shouted in her hearty tone "Miss Delavie!—I mean Mrs. Belamour! Who would have thought of seeing you here!"

"I am here to meet my sister—Mrs. Arden. Let me—let me present you," said Aurelia in obedience to an imperious sign from her sister, going through the form for the first time, while Harriet volubly declared her happiness in making Mrs. Hunter's acquaintance, and explained how they were on their way to take possession of Mr. Arden's rectory of Rundell Canonicorum, the words rolling out of her mouth with magnificent emphasis. "I congratulate you, ma'am," said Mrs. Hunter, cordially, "and you too, my dear," she added, turning to Aurelia. "I would have been out long ago to call on you—a sort of relation as you are now, as I may say—but it was kept all so mum, one never knew the time to drink your health; and my Cousins Treforth wouldn't so much as give me a hint. But la! says I, why should you talk about artfulness? I'm right glad poor Mr. Amyas should find a sprightly young lady to cure him of his mopishness. Never mind them, my dear, if they do look sour on you. I'll come over one of these days and talk to them. Now, I must have you come in to take your dinner with us. The Doctor will be right pleased to find you. I'll take no excuse. I thank Heaven I'm always ready whoever may drop in. There's spring chicken and sparrow-grass."

However, on hearing their dinner was ordered at the inn, the good lady was satisfied that to dine with her was impossible; but she insisted on their coming in to partake of wine and cake in her best parlour.

This, however, was a little more than Mr. Arden could endure, he made an excuse about seeing to the horse, and escaped; while Mrs. Hunter led the two sisters to her closely shut-up parlour, wainscoted, and hung with two staring simpering portraits of herself and her husband, clean as soap could make it, but smelling like a long closed box. She went to a cupboard in the wall, and brought out a silver salver, a rich cake, glasses and wine, and pouring out the wine, touched the glass with her lips, as she wished health and happiness to the two brides before her.

"We shall soon have another wedding in the family, if report speaks true," she added. "They say—but you should be the best informed, Madam Belamour—

"We hear nothing of the matter, ma'am," said Aurelia.

"That's odd, since Mr. Belamour is young Sir Amyas's guardian; and they cannot well pass him over now he has begun life again as it were," laughed Mrs. Hunter. "'Tis said that my Lady is resolved the wedding shall be within six weeks."

"There are two words to that question," said Harriet, oracularly; "I know from good authority that young Sir Amyas is determined against the match."

"But is it true, ma'am," cried Mrs. Hunter, eagerly, "that my Lady and the Countess of Aresfield met at Bath, and that my Lady is to have 3,000 pounds down to pay off her debts before her husband comes home, the day her son is married to Lady Arabella?"

"Every word of it is true, ma'am," said Harriet, importantly.

"Well now, that folk should sell their own flesh and blood!"

"How have you heard it, sister Harriet?" asked Aurelia.

"From a sure hand, my love. No other than Mrs. Dove. She is wife to my Lady's coachman," explained Mrs. Arden to her hostess, "and nurse to the two children it is her pleasure to keep with her."

"Dear good Nurse dove!" cried Aurelia, "did she come to see you?"

"Yes, that did she! So I have it from the fountain-head, as I may say, that the poor young gentleman's hand and heart are to be made over without his will, that so his mother may not have such a schedule of debts wherewith to face her husband on his return!"

"Her jewels have been all paste long ago, I know very well," said Mrs. Hunter, not to be outdone; "though, would you believe it, Doctor Hunter is like all the men, and will believe nothing against her! But this beats all the rest! Why, I have it from my maid, who is sister to one of the servants at the boarding-school in Queen Square, whither they have sent the Lady Belle, that she is a regular little shrew. She flew at one of the young ladies like a wild cat, because she did not yield place to her at once, and scratched her cheeks till the blood ran down, and tore out whole handfuls of her hair. She was like one possessed, and they had to call the lackey before they could get her safe tied down in bed, where they kept her on bread and water, trying to get her to make her apology; but not a word could be got out of her, till they had to yield the point lest she should fall sick."

Aurelia mentally applauded her own discretion in not capping this with Mrs. Dove's former tale, and only observing that the marriage could not take place before the young baronet was of age, without the consent of his personal guardian, Mr. Belamour.

"You will excuse me, my dear, in speaking of your husband, but he has so long been incapable of acting, that they say his consent can be dispensed with."

"Aye, poor cousin Amyas Belamour!" said Mrs. Hunter. "He was the only man who ever durst resist my Lady's will before, and you see to what she has brought him!"

"Her son is resisting her now," said Harriet; "and our good Dove says it makes her blood boil to see the way the poor young gentleman is treated. He, who was the darling for whom nothing was good enough a while ago, has now scarce a place in his mother's own house. She is cold and stately with him, and Colonel Mar, the Lady Belle's brother, being his commanding officer, there is no end to the vexations and annoyances they give him, both at home and in his quarters. Mrs. Dove says his own man, Grey, tells her it is a wonder how he stands out against it all! And a truly well-bred young gentleman he is. He came to pay me his call in Gracechurch Street only yesterday, knowing our kindred, and most unfortunate was it that I was stepped out to the office to speak as to our boxes being duly sent by the Buckingham wain; but he left his ticket, and a message with the servant, 'Tell my cousin, Mrs. Arden,' he said, 'that I much regret not having seen her, and I should have done myself the honour of calling sooner to inquire for her good father, if I had known she was in town."

"Well, I have never seen the young gentleman since he was a mere child," said Mrs. Hunter. "His mother has bred him to neglect his own home and relations, but I am sorry for him."

"They say," continued Harriet significantly, "that they are sure there is some cause for his holding out so stiffly—I verily believe My Lady suspected—"

"O hush, Harriet!" cried Aurelia, colouring painfully.

"Well, it is all over now, so you need not be offended," said Harriet, laughing. "Besides, if my Lady had any such notion when she brought about your marriage, she must be disappointed, for the young spark is as resolute as ever."

"And no wonder, if he knows what the lady is like," said Aurelia.

"Ah! he has admitted as much to the King."

"To the King!" cried both auditors.

"Oh yes! you know my Lady is very thick with my Lady Suffolk, and she persuaded the King to speak to him at the levee. '*Comment*', says his majesty in French, 'are you a young rebel, sir, that refuse the good things your mother provides you?' Not a whit was my young gentleman moved. He bowed, and answered that he was acting by the desire of his guardian. Excuse me, sister, but the King answered—'A raving melancholic! That will not serve your turn, sir. Come to your senses, fulfil your mother's bond, and we'll put you on the Duke's staff, where you may see more of service than of home, or belike get into gay quarters, where you may follow any other *fantaisie* if that is making you commit such *betises!*' At that Sir Amyas, who is but an innocent youth, flamed up in his cheeks till they were as red as his coat, and said his honour was engaged; on which his majesty swore at him for an idiot, and turned his back. Every word of this Mrs. Dove heard Colonel Mar tell my Lady—and then they fell to rating the poor youth, and trying to force out who this secret flame may be; but his is of the same stuff as his mother, adamantine and impervious. And now the Colonel keeps him on hard duty continually, and they watch him day and night to find out what places he haunts. But bless me, Mrs. Hunter, is the church clock striking? We must be gone, or my good man will be wondering where we are."

Mrs. Hunter would fain have kept them, and the last words and compliments were of long duration, while Aurelia looked on in some surprise at the transformation of all Harriet's languishing affected airs into the bustling self-importance of Mrs. Arden. She was however much occupied with all she had heard, and was marvelling how her sister began again as soon as they were in the street again. "You are very discreet, Aurelia, as it becomes a young married lady, but have you no notion who this innamorata of the baronet may be?"

"No, indeed, how should I?"

"I thought he might have confided in your husband, since he makes so sure of his support."

"He has only once come to visit Mr. Belamour, and that was many months ago."

"It is strange," mused Harriet; "Mrs. Dove says she would have taken her Bible oath that it was you, and my Lady believed as much, or she would not have been in such haste to have you wedded. Nay, I'll never believe but he made his confidences to Betty when he came to the Manor House the Sunday after you were gone, though not a word could I get from her."

"It must have been all a mistake," said Aurelia, not without a little twinge at the thought of what might have been. "I wish you would not talk of it."

"Well he could have been but a fickle adorer—'tis the way of men, my dear, for he must have found some new flame while his mother and the Colonel were both at the Bath. They have proof positive of his riding out of town at sundown, but whither he goes is unknown, for he takes not so much as a groom with him, and he is always in time for morning parade."

"Poor young man, it is hard to be so beset with spies and watchers," said Aurelia.

"Most true," said Harriet, "but I am monstrous glad you are safe married like me, child, so that no one can accuse us. Such romantic affairs are well enough to furnish a course of letters to the *Tatler*, or the *Gentlewomen's Magazine*, but I am thankful for a comfortable life with my good man."

Therewith they reached their inn, where Harriet, having satisfied herself that the said good man was safe within, and profiting by the unwonted calm to write his inaugural sermon, took Aurelia to her bedroom to prepare for dinner, and to indulge in further confidences.

"So, Aurelia, I can report to my father that you are looking well, and as cheerful as can be expected."

"Nay, I have always told you I am happy as the day is long."

"What, when you have never so much as seen your husband?"

"Only at our wedding, and then he was forced to veil his face from the light."

"Nor has he ever seen you?"

"Not unless he then saw me."

"If he were not then charmed enough to repeat the view, you are the most cruelly wasted and unworthily matched—"

"Hush, sister!" broke out Aurelia in eager indignation.

"What! is a lovely young creature, almost equal to what I was before my cruel malady, to waste her bloom on a wretched old melancholic, who will not so much as look at her!"

"Harriet, I cannot hear this—you know not of what you are talking! What is my poor skin-deep beauty—if beauty it be—compared with the stores of goodness and wisdom I find in him?"

"La! child, what heat is this? One would really think you loved him."

"Of course I do! I love and honour him more than any one I ever met—except my dear father."

"Come, Aura, you are talking by rote out of the marriage service. You may be open with me, you know, it will go no further; and I do long to know whether you can be truly content at heart," said Harriet with real affection.

"Dear sister," said Aurelia, touched, "believe me that indeed I am. Mr. Belamour is kindness itself. He is all he ever promised to be to me, and sometimes more."

"Yet if he loved you, he could never let you live moped up there. Are you never frighted at the dark chamber? I should die of it!"

"The dark does not fright me," said Aurelia.

"You have a courage I have not! Come, now, were you never frighted to talk with a voice in the dark?"

"Scarcely ever!" said aurelia.

"Scarcely—when was that?"

"You will laugh, Harriet, but it is when he is most—most tender and full of warmth. Then I hardly know him for the same."

"What! If he be not always tender to my poor dear child, he must be a wretch indeed."

"O no, no, Harriet! How shall I ever make you understand?" cried Aurelia. "Never for a moment is he other than kind and gentle. It is generally like a father, only more courtly and deferential, but sometimes something seems to come over him, and he is—oh! I cannot tell you—what I should think a lover would be," faltered Aurelia, colouring crimson, and hiding her face on her sister's shoulder, as old habits of confidence, and need of counsel and sympathy were obliterating all the warnings of last night.

"You silly little chit! Why don't you encourage these advances? You ought to be charmed, not frightened."

"They would ch—-I should like it if it were not so like two men in one, the one holding the other back."

Harriet laughed at this fancy, and Aurelia was impelled to defend it. "Indeed, Harriet, it is really so. There will be whispers—oh, such whispers!"—she sunk her voice and hid her face again—"close to my ear, and—endearments—while the grave voice sounds at the other end of the room, and then I long for light. I swooned for fright the first time, but I am much more used to it now."

"This is serious," said Harriet, with unwonted gravity. "Do you really think that there is another person in the room?"

"I do not feel as if it could be otherwise, and yet it is quite impossible."

"I would not bear it," said her sister. "You ought not to bear it. How do you know that it is not some vile stratagem? It might even be the blackamoor!"

"No, no, Harriet! I know better than that. It is quite impossible. Besides, I am sure of this—that the hands that wedded me are the same hands that caress me," she added, with another blushing effort, "strong but delicate hands, rather hard inside, as with the bridle. I noticed it because once I thought his hands soft with doing nothing and being shut up."

"That convinces me the more, then, there is some strange imposition practised upon you," said Harriet, anxiously.

"Oh, no!" said Aurelia, inconsistently; "Mr. Belamour is quite incapable of doing anything wrong by me. I cannot let you have such shocking notions. He told me I must be patient and trust him, though I should meet with much that was strange and inexplicable."

"This is trusting him much too far. They are playing on your inexperience, I am sure. If you were not a mere child, you would see what a shocking situation this is."

"I wish I had not told you," said Aurelia, tears rushing into her eyes. "I ought not! He bade me be cautious how I talked, and you have made me quite forget!"

"Did he so? Then it is evident that he fears disclosure! Something must be done. Why not write to our father?"

"I could not! He would call it a silly fancy."

"And it might embroil him with my Lady," added Harriet. "We must devise another mode."

"You will not—must not tell Mr. Arden," exclaimed Aurelia, peremptorily.

"Never fear! He heeds nothing more sublunary than the course of the planets. But I have it. His device will serve the purpose. Do you remember Eugene confounding him with Friar Bacon because he was said to light a candle without flint or steel? It was true. When he was a bachelor he always lit his own candle and fire, and he always carries the means. I was frighted the first time he showed me, but now I can do it as well as he. See," she said, opening a case, "a drop of this spirit upon this prepared cotton;" and as a bright flame sprang up and made Aurelia start, she laughed and applied a taper to it. "There, one such flash would be quite enough to prove to you whether there be any deception practised on you."

"I could never do it! Light is agony to Mr. Belamour, and what would he think?"

"He would take it for lightning, which I suppose he cannot keep out."

"One flash did come through everything last summer, but I was not looking towards him."

"You will be wiser this time. Here, I can give you this little box, for Mr. Arden compounded a fresh store in town."

"I dare not, sister. He has ever bidden me trust without sight; and you cannot guess how good he is to me, and how noble and generous. I cannot insult him by a doubt."

"Then he should not act as no true woman can endure."

"And it would hurt him."

"Tut, tut, child; if the lightning did not harm him how can this flash? I tell you no man has a right to trifle with you in this manner, and it is your duty to yourself and all of us to find out the truth. Some young rake may have bribed the black, and be personating him; and some day you may find yourself carried off you know not where."

"Harriet, if you only knew either Mr. Belamour or Jumbo, you would know that you are saying things most shocking!"

"Convince me, then! Look here, Aurelia, if you cannot write to me and explain this double-faced or double-voiced husband of yours, I vow to you that I shall speak to Mr. Arden, and write to my father."

"Oh! do not, do not, sister! Remember, it is of no use unless this temper of affection be on him, and I have not heard it this fortnight, no, nor more."

"Promise me, then, that you will make the experiment. See, here is a little chain-stitch pouch—poor Peggy Duckworth's gift to me—with two pockets. Let me fasten it under your dress, and then you will always have it about you."

"If the bottle broke as I rode home!"

"Impossible; it is a scent-bottle of strong glass."

Here Mr. Arden knocked at the door, regretting to interrupt their confidences, but dinner awaited them; and as, immediately after, Mrs. Hunter brought her husband in his best wig to call on Madame Belamour and her relations, the sisters had no more time together, till the horses were at the door, and they went to their room together to put on their hats.

A whole mass of refusals and declarations of perfect confidence were on Aurelia's tongue, but Harriet cut them all short by saying, "Remember, you are bound for your own honour and ours, to clear up this mystery!"

Then they rode off their several ways, Madame Belamour towards Bowstead, Mr. and Mrs. Arden on their sturdy roadster towards Lea Farm.

CHAPTER XXII
A FATAL SPARK

And so it chanced; which in those dark
And fireless halls was quite amazing,
Did we not know how small a spark
Can set the torch of love ablazing.
T. MOORE.

Aurelia rode home in perplexity, much afraid of the combustibles at her girdle, and hating the task her sister had forced on her. She felt as if her heedless avowals had been high treason to her husband; and yet Harriet was her elder, and those assurances that as a true woman she was bound to clear up the mystery, made her cheeks burn with shame, and her heart thrill with the determination to vindicate her husband, while the longing to know the face of one who so loved her was freshly awakened.

She was strongly inclined to tell him all, indeed she knew herself well enough to be aware that half a dozen searching questions would draw out the whole confession of her own communication and Harriet's unworthy suspicions; and humiliating as this would be, she longed for the opportunity. Here, however, she was checked in her meditations by a stumble of her horse, which proved to have lost a shoe. It was necessary to leave the short cut, and make for the nearest forge, and when the mischief was repaired, to ride home by the high road.

She thus came home much later than had been expected; Jumbo, Molly, and the little girls were all watching for her, and greeted her eagerly. The supper was already on the table for her, and she had only just given Fay and Letty the cakes and comfits she had bought at Brentford for them when Jumbo brought the message that his master hoped that madam, if not too much fatigued, would come to him as soon as her supper was finished.

Accordingly, she came without waiting to change her dress, having only taken off her hat and arranged her hair.

She felt guilty, and dreaded the being questioned, yet longed to make her avowal and have all explained. The usual greetings passed, and then Mr. Belamour said, "I heard your horse hoofs come in late. You were detained?"

She explained about the shoe, and a few sentences were passing about her sister when she detected a movement, as if a step were stealing towards her, together with a hesitation in the remark Mr. Belamour was making about Mrs. Hunter's good nature.

Quite irrelevantly came in the whispering voice, "Where is my dearest life?"

"Sir, sir!" she cried, driven at last to bay, "what is this? Are you one or two?"

"One with you, my sweetest life! Your own—your husband!"

Therewith there was a kind of groan further off, and as Aurelia felt a hand on her dress, her fight and distress at the duality were complete. While, in the dark, the hands were still groping for her, she eluded them, and succeeded in carrying out Harriet's manoeuvre so far that a quick bright flame leapt forth, lighting up the whole room, and revealing two—yes, two! But it did not die away! In her haste, and in the darkness, she had poured the whole contents of the bottle on the phosphoric cotton, and dropped both without knowing it on a chintz curtain. A fresh evening breeze was blowing in from the window, open behind the shutters, and in one second the curtain was a flaming, waving sheet. Some one sprang up to tear it down, leaping on a table in the window. The table overbalanced, the heavy iron curtain-rod came out suddenly, and there was a fall, the flaming mass covering the fallen! The glare shone on a strange white face and head as well as on Jumbo's black one, and with a trampling and crushing the fire died down, quenched as suddenly as it began, and all was obscurity again.

"Nephew, dear boy, speak," exclaimed Mr. Belamour; and as there was no answer, "Open the shutters, Jumbo. For Heaven's sake let us see!"

"Oh! what have I done?" cried poor Aurelia, in horror and misery, dropping by him on the ground, while the opened shutters admitted the twilight of a May evening, with a full moon, disclosing a strange scene. A youth in a livery riding coat lay senseless on the ground, partly covered by the black fragments of the curtain, the iron rod clenched in one hand, the other arm doubled under him. A face absolutely white, with long snowy beard and hair hung over him, and an equally white pair of hands tried to lift the head. Jumbo had in a second sprung down, removed the fallen table, and come to his masters help. "Struck head with this," he said, as he tried to unclasp the fingers from the bar, and pointed to a grazed blow close to the temple.

"We must lay him on my bed," said Mr. Belamour. Then, seeing the girl's horror-stricken countenance, "Ah, child, would that you had been patient; but it was overtasking you! Call Aylward, I beg of you. Tell her he is here, badly hurt. What, you do not know him," as her bewildered eyes and half-opened lips implied the question she could not utter, "you do not know him? Sir Amyas—my nephew—your true husband!"

"Oh! and I have killed him!" she cried, with clasped hands.

"Hush, child, no, with God's mercy! Only call the woman and bring a light."

She rushed away, and appeared, a pale terrified figure, with the smell of fire on her hair and white dress, in the room where Mrs. Aylward was reading her evening chapter. She could scarcely utter her message as she stood under the gaze of blank amazement; but Mrs. Aylward understood enough to make her start up without another word, and hurry away, candle in hand.

Aurelia took up the other, and followed, trembling. When she reached the outer room the rush of air almost blew out her light, and pausing, afraid to pass on, she perceived that Mr. Belamour and Jumbo were carrying the insensible form between them into the inner apartment, while a moan or two filled her heart with pangs of self-reproach.

She hung about, in terrible anxiety, but not daring to come forward while the others were engaged about the sufferer, for what seemed a very long time before she heard Mrs. Aylward say, "His arm is broke, sir. We must send for Dr. Hunter. The maids are all in their beds, but I will go and wake one, and send her to the stables to call the groom."

"I had best go," said Mr. Belamour. "You are of more use than I. He sleeps at the stables, you say?" Then, seeing the waiting, watching form of Aurelia, he said, "Come in, my poor child. Perhaps your voice may rouse him." Every one, including himself, seemed to have forgotten Mr. Belamour's horror of the light, for candles were flaring on all the tables, as he led the you girl in, saying, "Speak to him."

At the death-like face in its golden hair, Aurelia's voice choked in her throat, and it was in an unnatural hoarse tone that she tried to say, "Sir—Sir Amyas—"

"I trust he will soon be better," said Mr. Belamour, marking her dismay and grief with his wonted kindness, "but his arm needs the surgeon, and I must be going. Let Lady Belamour sit here, Mrs. Aylward. I trust you with the knowledge. It was my nephew, in disguise, who wedded her, unknown to her. She is entirely blameless. Let Jumbo fetch her a cordial. There, my child, take this chair, so that his eyes may fall on you when he opens them. Bathe his head if you will. I shall return quickly after having sped the groom on his journey."

Gloomy and doubtful were the looks cast on Aurelia by the housekeeper, but all unseen by the wondering, bewildered, remorseful eyes fixed on the white face on the pillow, heedless of its perfect symmetry of feature, and knowing only that this was he who had thrilled her heart with his tender tones, who had loved her so dearly, and dared so much for her sake, but whom her impatience and distrust had so cruelly injured. Had she seen him strong, well, and ardent, as she had so lately heard him, her womanhood would have recoiled indignantly at the deception which had stolen her vows; but the spectacle of the young senseless face and prostrate form filled her with compassion, tenderness, and remorse, for having yielded to her sister's persuasions. With intense anxiety she watched, and assisted in the fomentations, longing for Mr. Belamour's return; but time passed on and still he came not. No words passed, only a few faint sighs, and one of the hands closed tight on Aurelia's.

CHAPTER XXIII
WRATH AND DESOLATION

Straight down she ran
.... and fatally did vow To wreake her on the mayden messenger
Whom she had caused be kept as prisonere.
SPENSER.

Hark! there was the trampling of horses and thundering of wheels at the door! Could the doctor be come already, and in such a fashion?

Jumbo hurried to admit him, and Mrs. Aylward moved to arrange matters, but the clasp that was on Aurelia's hand would not let her go.

Presently there came, not Dr. Hunter's tread, but a crisp, rustling sound, and the tap of high heels, and in the doorway stood, tall, erect, and terrible, Lady Belamour, with a blaze of wrath in her blue eyes, and concentrated rage in her whole form, while in accents low, but coming from between her teeth, she demanded, "Miserable boy, what means this?"

"Oh! madam, take care! he is sadly hurt!" cried Aurelia, with a gesture as if to screen him.

"I ask what this means?" repeated Lady Belamour, advancing, and seeming to fill the room with her majestic figure, in full brocaded dress, with feathers waving in her hair.

"His Honour cannot answer you, my Lady," said Mrs. Aylward. "He has had a bad fall, and Mr. Belamour is gone to send for the doctor."

"This is the housekeeping in my absence!" said Lady Belamour, showing less solicitude as to her son's condition than indignation at the discovery, and her eyes and her diamonds glittering fearfully.

"My Lady," said Mrs. Aylward, with stern respectfulness, "I knew nothing of all this till this lady called me an hour ago telling me Sir Amyas was hurt. I found him as you see. Please your Ladyship, I must go back to him."

"Speak then, you little viper," said Lady Belamour, turning on Aurelia, who had risen, but was held fast by the hand upon hers. "By what arts have you well nigh slain my son? Come here, and tell me."

"None, madam!" gasped Aurelia, trembling, so that she grasped her chair-back with her free hand for support. "I never saw him till to-night."

"Lies will not serve you, false girl. Come here this instant! I *know* that you have been shamelessly receiving my son here, night after night."

"I never knew!"

"Missie Madam never knew," chimed in Jumbo. "All in the dark. She thought it old mas'r."

Lady Belamour looked contemptuously incredulous; but the negro's advocacy gave a kind of courage to Aurelia, and availing herself of a slight relaxation of the fingers she withdrew her hand, and coming forward, said, "Indeed, madam, I know nothing, I was entirely deceived. Only hearing two voices in the dark alarmed me, so that I listened to my sister, and struck a light to discover the truth. Then all caught fire, and blazed up, and—"

"Then you are an incendiary as well as a traitor," said her Ladyship, with cold, triumphant malignity. "This is work for the constable. Here, Loveday," to her own woman, who was waiting in the outer room, "take this person away, and lock her into her own room till morning, when we can give her up to justice."

"Oh, my Lady," cried Aurelia, crouching at her feet and clinging to her dress, "do not be so cruel! Oh! let me go home to my father!"

"Madam!" cried a voice from the bed, "let alone my wife! Come, Aurelia. Oh!"

Then starting up in bed had wrenched his broken arm, and he fell back senseless again, just as Aurelia would have flown back to him, but his mother stood between, spurning her away.

Another defender, if she could so be called, spoke for her. "It is true, please your Ladyship," said Mrs. Aylward, "that Mr. Belamour called her the wife of this poor young gentleman."

Jumbo too exclaimed, "No one knew but Jumbo; His Honour marry pretty missie in mas'r's wig and crimson dressing-gown."

"A new stratagem!" ironically observed the incensed lady. "But your game is played out, miss, for madam I cannot call you. Such a marriage cannot stand for a moment; and if a lawyer like Amyas Belamour pretended it could, either his wits were altogether astray or he grossly deceived you. Or, as I believe, he trafficked with you to entrap this unhappy youth, whose person and house you have, between you, almost destroyed. Remove her, Loveday, and lock her up till we can send for a magistrate to take depositions in the morning. Go quietly, girl I will not have my son disturbed with your outcries."

Poor Aurelia's voice died in her throat. Oh! why did not Mr. Belamour come to her rescue? Ah! he had bidden her trust and be patient; she had transgressed, and he had abandoned her! There was no sign of life or consciousness in the pallid face on the bed, and with a bleeding heart she let the waiting-maid lead her through the outer apartment, still redolent of the burning, reached her own chamber, heard the key turn in the lock, and fell across her bed in a sort of annihilation.

The threat was unspeakably frightful. Those were days of capital punishment for half the offences in the calendar, and of what was to her scarcely less dreadful, of promiscuous imprisonment, fetters, and gaol fever. Poor Aurelia's ignorance could hardly enhance these horrors, and when her perceptions began to clear themselves, her first thought was of flight from a fate equally dreadful to the guilty or not guilty.

Springing from the bed, she tried the other door of her room, which was level with the wainscoting, and not readily observed by a person unfamiliar with the house. It yielded to her hand, and she knew there was a whole suite of empty rooms thus communicating with one another. It was one of those summer nights that are never absolutely dark, and there was a full moon, so that she had light enough to throw off her conspicuous white habit, all scorched and singed as it was, and to put on her dark blue cloth one, with her camlet cloak and hood. She made up a small bundle of clothes, took her purse, which was well filled with guineas and silver, and moved softly to the door. Hide and seek had taught her all the modes of eluding observation, and with her walking shoes in her hand, and her feet slippered, she noiselessly crept through one empty room after another, and descended the stair into her own lobby, where she knew how to open the sash door.

One moment the thought that Mr. Belamour would protect her made her pause, but the white phantom she had seen seemed more unreal than the voice she was accustomed to, and both alike had vanished and abandoned her to her fate. Nay, she had been cheated from the first. Everything had given way with her. My Lady might be coming to send her to prison. Hark, some one was coming! She darted out, down the steps, along the path like a wild bird from a cage.

CHAPTER XXIV
THE WANDERER

Widowed wife and wedded maid,

Betrothed, betrayer, and betrayed.—SCOTT.

Aurelia's first halt was in a moss-grown summer-house at the end of the garden, where she ventured to sit down to put on her stout leather shoes. The children's toys, a ball and a set of ninepins lay on the floor! How many ages ago was it that she had made that sarcastic reply to Letty?—perhaps her last!

A nightingale, close overhead, burst into a peal of song, repeating his one favourite note, which seemed to her to cry out "Although my heart is broke, broke, broke, broke." The tears rushed into her eyes, but at a noise as of opening doors or windows at the house, terror mastered her again, and she hurried on to hide herself from the dawning light, which was beginning to increase, as she crossed the park, on turf dank with Maydew, and plunged deep into the thick woods beyond, causing many a twittering cry of wondering birds.

Day had fully come, and slanting golden beams were shining through the tender green foliage, and illuminating the boles of the trees, ere she was forced by failing strength again to pause and sit on a faggot, while gathering breath and considering where she should go. Home was her first thought. Who could shield her but her father and sister? How she longed for their comfort and guardianship! But how reach them? She had money but could do little for her. England never less resembled those days of Brian Boromhe when the maiden with the gems, rich and rare wandered unscathed form sea to sea in Ireland. Post chaises, though coming into use, had not dawned on the simple country girl's imagination. She knew there was a weekly coach from London to Bath, passing through Brentford, and that place was also a great starting-place for stage waggons, of which one went through Carminster, but her bewildered brain could not recall on what day it started, and there was an additional shock of despair when she remembered that it was Sunday morning. The chill of the morning dew was on her limbs, she was exhausted by her fatigues of the night, a drowsy recollection of the children in the wood came over her, and she sank into a dreamy state that soon became actual sleep. She was wakened by a strong bright sunbeam on her eyes, and found that this was what had warmed her limbs in her sleep. A sound as of singing was also in her ears, and of calling cows to be milked. She did not in the least know where she was, for she had wandered into parts of the wood quite strange to her, but she thought she must be a great way from home, and quite beyond recognition, so she followed the voice, and soon came out on a tiny meadow glade, where a stout girl was milking a great sheeted cow.

She knew now that she was faint with hunger and thirst, and must take food before she could go much farther, so taking out a groat, her smallest coin, she accosted the girl, and offered it for a draught of milk. To her dismay the girl exclaimed "Lawk! It be young Madam! Sarvice, ma'am!"

"I have lost myself in the wood," said Aurelia. "I should be much obliged for a little milk."

"Well to be sure. Think of that! And have ee been out all night? Ye looks whisht!" said the girl, readily filling a wooden cup she had brought with her, for in those days good new milk was a luxury far more easily accessible than in ours. She added a piece of barley bread, her own intended breakfast, and was full of respectful wonder, pity, and curiosity, proposing that young Madam should come and rest in mother's cottage in the wood, and offering to guide her home as soon as the cows were milked and the pigs fed. Aurelia had some difficulty in shaking her off, finding also that she had gone round and round in the labyrinthine paths, and was much nearer the village of Bowstead than she had intended.

Indeed, she was obliged to deceive the kindly girl by walking off in the direction she pointed out, intending to strike afterwards into another path, though where to go she had little idea, so long as it was out of reach of my Lady and her prison.

Oh! if Harriet were only at Brentford, or if it were possible to reach the Lea Farm where she was! Could she ask her way thither, or could she find some shelter near or in Brentford till the coach or the waggon started? This was the most definite idea her brain, refreshed somewhat by the food, could form; but in the meantime she was again getting bewildered in the field paths. It was a part she did not know, lying between the backs of the cottages and their gardens, and the woods belonging to the great house; and the long sloping meadows, spangled with cowslips were much alike. The cowslips seemed to strike her with a pang as she recollected her merry day among them last spring, and how little she then thought of being a homeless wanderer. At last, scarce knowing where she was, she sat down on the step of a stile leading to a little farmyard, leant her head on the top bar and wept bitterly.

Again she startled by hearing a voice saying, "Sister, what is that in the field?" and starting up, she saw Mrs. Delia in high pattens, and her Sunday silk tucked up over her quilted petticoat, with a basket of corn in her hand, surrounded by her poultry, while Mrs. Phoebe was bending over a coop. She had stumbled unawares on their back premises, and with a wild hope, founded on their well-known enmity to Lady Belamour, she sprang over the stile. Mrs. Delia retreated in haste, but Mrs. Phoebe came to the front.

"Oh! Mrs. Phoebe," she cried, "I ask your pardon."

"Mrs. Belamour! Upon my word! To what are we indebted for this visit?"

"Oh! of your kindness listen to me, madam," said Aurelia. "My Lady is come, and there is some dreadful mistake, and she is very angry with me; and if you would only take me in and hide me till the waggon goes and I can get home!"

"So my Lady has found you out, you artful hussy," returned Mrs. Phoebe. "I have long guessed at your tricks! I knew it was no blackamoor that was stealing into the great house."

"I do not know what you mean."

"Oh! it is of no use to try your feigned artlessness on us. I wonder at your assurance, after playing false with uncle and nephew both at once."

"If you would but hear me!"

"I have heard enough of you already. I wonder you dare show your face at a respectable house. Away with you, if you would not have me send the constable after you!"

The threat renewed Aurelia's terror, and again she fled, but this time she fell into a path better known to her, that leading to Sedhurst, and ultimately to Brentford.

The recollection of Dame Wheatfield's genial good nature inspired her with another hope, and she made her way towards the farm. The church bells were ringing, and she saw the farmer and his children going towards the church, but not the mistress, and she might therefore hope to find her at home and alone. As she approached, a great dog began a formidable barking, and his voice brought out the good woman in person. "Down, Bouncer! A won't hurt'ee, my lass. What d'ye lack that you bain't at church?"

"May I speak to you, Mrs. Wheatfield?"

"My stars, if it bain't young Miss—Madam, I mean! Nothing ain't wrong with the child?"

"O no, she is quite well, but—"

"What, ye be late for church? Come in and sit ye down a bit and sup after your walk. We have been and killed Spotty's calf, though 'twas but a staggering Bob, but us couldn't spare the milk no longer. So we've got the l'in on un for dinner, and you're kindly welcome if you ain't too proud. Only I wish you had brought my little missie."

"O Mrs. Wheatfield! Shall I ever see the dear little girl again? Oh! can you help me? Do you know where Lea Farm is? I'd pay anything for a horse and man to take me there, where my sister is staying."

"Well, I don't know as my master would hire a horse out of a Sunday, unless 'twere very particler—illness or suchlike. Lea Farm did you say ma'am? Is it the Lea out by Windmill hill—Master Brown's; or Lea Farm, down by the river—Tom Smith's?"

"No, this is Mr. Meadows's, a grazier."

"Never heard tell on him, ma'am, but the master might, when he comes in. But bless me," she added, after a moment's consideration, "what will your master say? He'll be asking how it comes that a lady like you, with a coach and horses of her own, should be coming after a horse here. You ain't been and got into trouble with my Lady, my dear?"

"Oh! Dame, indeed I have; pray help me!"

It was no wonder that Mrs. Wheatfield failed to gather more than that young Madam had almost burnt the house, and had fallen under grievous displeasure, so as even to fear the constable.

"Bless your poor heart! Think of that now! But I'm afeard we can't do nothing for you. My master would be nigh about killing me if I harboured you and got him into trouble, with the gentry."

"If you could only hide me in some loft or barn till I could meet the coach for Bath! Then I should be almost at home."

"I dare not. The children are routing about everywhere on a Sunday afternoon; and if so be as there's a warrant out after you" (Aurelia shuddered) "my man would be mad with me. He ain't never forgot how his grandfather was hanged up there in that very walnut for changing clothes with a young gentleman in the wars long ago."

"Then I must go! Oh, what will become of me?"

"Stay a bit! It goes to my heart to turn you from the door, and you so white and faint. And they won't be out of church yet a while. You've ate nothing all this time! What was you thinking of doing, my dear?"

"I don't know. If I could only find out the right Lea Farm, and get a man and horse to take me there—but my sister goes on Monday, and I might not find her, and nobody knows where it is. And nobody will take me in or hide my till the coach goes! Oh, what will become of me?"

"It is bitter hard," said the Dame. "I wish to my heart I could take you in, but you see there's the master! I'll tell you what: there's my cousin, Patty Woodman; she might take you in for a night or two. But you'd never find your way to her cot; it lies out beyond the spinneys. I must show you the way. Look you here. Nobody can't touch you in a church, they hain't got no power there, and if you would slip into that there empty place as opens with the little door, as the ringers goes in by, afore morning prayers is over I'll make an excuse to come to evening prayer alone, or only with little Davy, as is lying asleep there. If Patty is there I'll speak, and you can go home with her. If not, I must e'en walk with you out to the spinney. Hern is a poor place, but her's a good sort of body, and won't let you come to no harm; and her goes into Brentford with berries and strawberries to meet the coaches, so may be she'll know the day."

"Oh, thank you, thank you, dear Mrs. Wheatfield! If I can only get safe home!"

"Come, don't be in haste. You'll take a bit of bread and cheese, and just a draught of ale to hearten you up a bit."

Aurelia was too sick at heart for food, and feared to delay, lest she should meet the congregation, but Mrs. Wheatfield forced on her a little basket with some provisions, and she gladly accepted another draught of milk.

No one came out by the little door she was told; all she had to do would be to keep out of sight when the ringers came in before the afternoon service. She knew the way, and was soon close to Mary Sedhurst's grave. "Ah! why was he not constant to her," she thought; "and oh! why has he deserted me in my need?"

The little door easily yielded, and she found herself—after passing the staircase-turret that led by a gallery to the belfry in the centre of the church—in an exceedingly dilapidated transept; once, no doubt, it had been beautiful, before the coloured glass of the floriated window had been knocked out and its place supplied with bricks. The broken effigy of a crusading Sedhurst, devoid of arms, feet, and nose was stowed away in the eastern sepulchre, in company with funeral apparatus, torn books, and moth-eaten cushions. But this would not have shocked her even in calmer moments. She only cared to find a corner where she was entirely sheltered, between a green stained pier and the high wall and curtain of a gigantic pew, where no doubt sweet Mary Sedhurst had once worshipped. The lusty voices of the village choir in some exalted gallery beyond her view were shouting out a familiar tune, and with some of Betty's mild superstition about "the singing psalms," she heard—

> "Since I have placed my trust in God
> A refuge always nigh,
> Why should I, like tim'rous bird
> To distant mountains fly?

> "Behold the wicked bend their bow,
> And ready fix their dart,
> Lurking in ambush to destroy
> The man of upright heart.

> "When once the firm assurance fails
> Which public faith imparts,
> 'Tis time for innocence to flee
> From such deceitful arts.

> "The Lord hath both a temple here
> And righteous throne above,
> Whence He surveys the sons of men,
> And how their counsels move."

Poor timorous bird, whom even the firm assurance of wedded faith had failed, what was left to her but to flee from the darts levelled against her? Yet that last verse brought a sense of protection. Ah! did she deserve it? A prayerless night and prayerless morning had been hers, and no wonder, since she had never gone to bed nor risen with the ordinary forms; but it was with a pang that she recollected that the habit of calling out in her heart for guidance and help had been slipping from her for a long time past, and she had never asked for heavenly aid when her judgment was perplexed by Harriet, no, nor for protection in her flight.

She resolved to say her morning prayers with full attention so soon as the church was empty, and meantime to follow the service with all her powers, though her pulses were still throbbing and her head aching.

In the far distance she heard the Commandments, and near to her the unseen clerk responding, and then followed a gospel of love and comfort. She could not catch every word, but there was a sense of promised peace and comfort, which began to soothe the fluttering heart, for the first time enjoying a respite from the immediate gripe of deadly terror.

The sermon chimed in with these feelings, not that she could have any account of it, nor preserved any connected memory, but it was full of the words, Faith, Love, Sacrifice, so that they were borne in on her ear and thought. Heavenly Love surrounding as with an atmosphere those who had only faith to "taste and see how gracious the Lord is," believing that which cannot be seen, and therefore having it revealed to their inmost sense, and thus living the only real life.

This was the chief thought that penetrated to her mind as she crouched on the straw hassock behind the pew, and shared unseen in the blessing of peace. No one saw her as the hob-nailed shoes trooped out of church, and soon she was entirely alone, kneeling still in her hiding-place, and whispering half-aloud the omitted morning prayer, whose heartfelt signification had, she felt, been neglected for a long, long time.

Since when? Ah! ever since those strange mysterious voices and caresses had come to charm and terrify her, and when her very perplexity should have warned her to cling closer to the aid of her Heavenly Father. Vague yearnings, uplifted feelings, discontents, and little tempers had usurped the place of higher feelings, and blinded her eyes. And through it all, her heart began to ache and long for tidings of him on whose pale features she had gazed so long and who had ventured and suffered so much for her, nay, who had started into a moment's life for her protection! All the tumult of resentment at the deception practised on her fell on the uncle rather than the nephew; and in spite of this long year of tender kindness and consideration from the recluse, there was a certain consideration from the recluse, there was a certain leaping of heart at finding herself bound not to him but to the youth whose endearments returned with a flood of tender remembrance. And she had fled just as he had claimed her as his wife, had fled just as he had claimed her as his wife, unheeding whether he died of the injury she had caused him! All that justified her alarm was forgotten, her heartstrings had wound themselves round him, and began to pull her back.

Then she thought of the danger of directing Lady Belamour's wrath on her father, and leading to his expulsion and destitution. She had been sent from home, and bestowed in marriage to prevent his ruin, and should she now ensure it? Her return to him or even her disappearance would no doubt lead to high words from him, and then he would be cast out to beggary in his old age. No, she could only save him by yielding herself up, exonerating him from all knowledge of her strange marriage, far more of the catastrophe, and let my Lady do her worst! She had, as she knew, not been going on well lately, but she had confessed her faults, and recovered her confidence that her Heavenly Father would guard her as long as she resolutely did her duty. And her duty, as daughter and a wife, if indeed she was one, was surely to return, where her heart was drawing her. It might be very terrible, but still it was going nearer to *him*, and it would save her father.

The door was still open; she wrote a few words of gratitude and explanation to Dame Wheatfield, on a piece of a torn book, wrapped a couple of guineas in it, and laid it in the basket, then kneeling again to implore protection and safety, and if it might be, forgiveness and reconciliation, she set forth. "Love is strong as death," said Mary Sedhurst's tomb. She knew better what that meant than when her childish eyes first fell upon it. A sense of Divine Love was wrapping her round with a feeling of support and trust, while the human love drew her onwards to confront all deadly possibilities in the hope of rejoining her husband, or at least of averting misfortune from her father.

CHAPTER XXV
VANISHED

Where there is no place
For the glow-worm to lie,
Where there is no space
For receipt of a fly,
Where the midge dares not venture
Lest herself fast she lay,
If Love come, he will enter
And find out the way. —*OLD SONG.*

Major Delavie and his eldest daughter were sitting down to supper in the twilight, when a trampling of horses was heard in the lane a carriage was seen at the gate, and up the pathway came a slender youthful figure, in a scarlet coat, with an arm in a sling.

"It is!—yes, it is!" exclaimed Betty: "Sir Amyas himself!"

In spite of his lameness, the Major had opened the door before Palmer could reach it; but his greeting and inquiry were cut short by the young man's breathless question: "Is she here?"

"Who?"

"My wife—my love. Your daughter, sweet Aurelia! Ah! it was my one hope."

"Come in, come in, sir," entreated Betty, seeing how fearfully pale he grew. "What has befallen you, and where is my sister?"

"Would that I knew! I trusted to have found her here; but now, sir, you will come with me and find her!"

"I do not understand you, sir," said the Major severely, "nor how you are concerned in the matter. My daughter is the wife of your uncle, Mr. Belamour, and if, as I fear, you bear the marks of a duel in consequence of any levity towards her, I shall not find it easy to forgive."

"On my word and honour it is no such thing," said the youth, raising a face full of frank innocence: "Your daughter is my wife, my most dear and precious wife, with full consent and knowledge of my uncle. I was married to her in his clothes, in the darkened room, our names being the same!"

"Was this your promise?" Betty exclaimed.

"Miss Delavie, to the best of my ability I have kept my promise. Your sister has never seen me, nor to her knowledge spoken with me."

"These are riddles, young man," said the Major sternly. "If all be not well with my innocent child, I shall know how to demand an account."

"Sir," said the youth: "I swear to you that she is the same innocent maiden as when she left you. Oh!" he added with a gesture of earnest entreaty, "blame me as you will, only trace her."

"Sit down, and let us hear," said Betty kindly, pushing a chair towards him and pouring out a glass of wine. He sank into the first, but waved aside the second, becoming however so pale that the Major sprang to hold the wine to his lips saying: "Drink, boy, I say!"

"Not unless you forgive me," he replied in a hoarse, exhausted voice.

"Forgive! Of course, I forgive, if you have done no wrong by my child. I see, I see, 'tis not wilfully. You have been hurt in her defence."

"Not exactly," he said: "I have much to tell," but the words came slowly, and there was a dazed weariness about his eye that made Betty say, in spite of her anxiety—"You cannot till you have eaten and rested. If only one word to say where she is!"

"Oh! that I could! My hope was to find her here," and he was choked by a great strangling sob, which his youthful manhood sought to restrain.

Betty perceived that he was far from being recovered from the injury he had suffered, and did her best to restrain her own and her father's anxiety till she had persuaded him to swallow some of the excellent coffee which Nannerl always made at sight of a guest. To her father's questions meantime, he had answered that he had broken his arm ten days ago, but he could not wait, he had posted down as soon as he could move.

"You ought to sleep before you tell us farther," said the Major, speaking from a strong sense of the duties of a host; but he was relieved when the youth answered, "You are very good, sir, but I could not sleep till you know all."

"Speak, then," said the Major, "I cannot look at your honest young countenance and think you guilty of more than disobedient folly; but I fear it may have cost my poor child very dear! Is it your mother that you dread?"

"I would be thankful even to know her in my mother's keeping!" he said.

"Is there no mistake?" said the Major; "my daughter, Mrs. Arden, saw her at Brentford, safe and blooming."

"Oh, that was before—before—" said Sir Amyas, "the day before she fled from my mother at Bowstead, and has been seen no more."

He put his hand over his face, and bowed it on the table in such overpowering grief as checked the exclamations of horror and dismay and the wrathful demands that were rising to the lips of his auditors, and they only looked at one another in speechless sorrow. Presently he recovered enough to say, "Have patience with me, and I will try to explain all. My cousin, Miss Delavie, knows that I loved her sweet sister from the moment I saw her, and that I hurried to London in the hope of meeting her at my mother's house. On the contrary, my mother, finding it vain to deny all knowledge of her, led me to believe that she was boarded at a young ladies' school with my little sisters. I lived on the vain hope of the holidays, and meantime every effort was made to drive me into a marriage which my very soul abhorred, the contract being absolutely made by the two ladies, the mothers, without my participation, nay, against my protest. I was to be cajoled or else persecuted into it—sold, in fact, that my mother's debts might be paid before her husband's return! I knew my Uncle Belamour was my sole true personal guardian, though he had never acted further than by affixing his signature when needed. I ought to have gone long before to see him, but as I now understand, obstacles had been purposely placed in my way, while my neglectful reluctance was encouraged. It was in the forlorn hope of finding in him a resource that took me to Bowstead at last, and then it was that I learnt how far my mother could carry deception. There I found my sisters, and learnt that my own sweetest life had been placed there likewise. She was that afternoon visiting some old ladies, but my uncle represented that my meeting her could only cause her trouble and lead to her being removed. I was forced then to yield, having an engagement in London that it would have been fatal to break, but I came again at dark, and having sworn me to silence, he was forced to let me take advantage of the darkness of his chamber to listen to her enchanting voice. He promised to help me, as far as he had the power, in resisting the hateful Aresfield engagement, and he obtained the assistance of an old friend in making himself acquainted with the terms of his guardianship, and likewise of a letter my father had left for him. He has given me leave to show a part of it to you, sir," he added, "you will see that my father expressed a strong opinion that you were wronged in the matter of the estates, and declared that he had hoped to make some compensation by a contract between one of your daughters and my brother who died. He charged my uncle if possible to endeavour to bring about such a match between one of your children and myself. Thus, you see, I was acting in the strictest obedience. You shall see the letter at once, if I may bid my fellow Gray bring my pocket-book from my valise."

"I doubt not of your words, my young friend; your father was a gentleman of a high and scrupulous honour. But why all this hide-and-seek work?—I hate holes and corners!"

"You will see how we were driven, sir. My mother came in her turn to see my uncle, and obtain his sanction to her cherished plan, and when he absolutely refused, on account of Lady Aresfield's notorious character, if for no other, she made him understand that nothing would be easier than to get him declared a lunatic and thus to dispense with his consent. Then, finding how the sweet society of your dear daughter had restored him to new life and spirit, she devised the notable expedient of removing what she suspected to be the chief cause of my contumacy, by marrying the poor child to him. He scouted the idea as a preposterous and cruel sacrifice, but it presently appeared that Colonel Mar was ready to find her a debauched old lieutenant who would gladly marry—what do I say?—it profanes the word—but accept the young lady for a couple of hundred pounds. Then did I implore my uncle to seem to yield, and permit me to personate him at the ceremony. Our names being the same, and all being done in private and in the dark, the whole was quite possible, and it seemed the only means of saving her from a terrible fate."

"He might—or you might, have remembered that she had a father!" said the Major.

"True. But you were at a distance, and my mother's displeasure against you was to be deprecated."

"I had rather she had been offended fifty times than have had such practices with my poor little girl!" said Major Delavie. "No wonder the proposals struck me as strange and ambiguous. Whose writing was it?"

"Mine, at his dictation," said the youth. "He was unwilling, but my importunity was backed by my mother's threats, conveyed through Hargrave, that unless Aurelia became his wife she should be disposed of otherwise, and that his sanity might be inquired into. Hargrave, who is much attached to my uncle, and is in great awe of my Lady, was thoroughly frightened, and implored him to secure himself and the young lady by consenting, thinking, too, that anything that would rouse him would be beneficial."

"It is strange!" mused the Major. "A clear-headed punctilious man like your uncle, to lend himself to a false marriage! His ten years of melancholy must have changed him greatly!"

"Less than you suppose, sir; but you will remember that my mother is esteemed as a terrible power by all concerned with her. Even when she seemed to love me tenderly, I was made to know what it was to cross her will, and alas! she always carries her point."

"It did seem a mode of protection," said Betty, more kindly.

"And" added the youth, "my uncle impressed on me from the first that he only consented on condition the I treated this wedlock as betrothal alone, never met my sweet love save in his dark room, and never revealed myself to her. He said it was a mere expedient for guarding her until I shall come of age, or Mr. Wayland comes home, when I shall woo her openly, and if needful, repeat the ceremony with her full knowledge. Meanwhile I wrote the whole to my stepfather, and am amazed that he has never written nor come home."

"That is the only rational thing I have heard," said the Major. "Though— did your uncle expect your young blood to keep the terms?"

"Indeed, sir, I was frightened enough the first evening that I ventured on any advances, for they startled her enough to make her swoon away. I carried her from her room, and my uncle dragged me back before the colour came back to that lovely face so that the women might come to her. That was the only time I ever saw her save through the chinks of the shutters. Judge of the distraction I lived in!"

Betty looked shocked, but her father chuckled a little, though he maintained his tone of censure "And may I inquire how often these distracting interviews took place?"

"Cruelly seldom for one to whom they were life itself! Mar is, as you know, colonel of my corps, and my liberty has been restrained as much as possible; I believe I have been oftener on guard and on court-martial than any officer of my standing in the service; but about once in a fortnight I could contrive to ride down to a little wayside inn where I kept a fresh horse, also a livery coat and hat. I tied up my horse in a barn on the borders of the park, and put on a black vizard, so as to pass for my uncle's negro in the dark. I could get admittance to my uncle's rooms unknown to any servant save faithful Jumbo—who has been the sole depository of our secret. However, since my mother's return from Bath, where the compact with Lady Aresfield was fully determined, the persecution has been fiercer. I may have aroused suspicion by failing to act my part when she triumphantly announced my uncle's marriage to me, or else by my unabated resistance to the little termagant who is to be forced on me. At any rate, I have been so intolerably watched whenever I was not on duty, that my hours of bliss became rarer than ever. Well, sir, my uncle charges me with indiscretion, and says my ardour aroused unreasonable suspicions. He was constantly anxious, and would baulk me in my happiest and most tantalising moments by making some excuse for breaking up the evening, and then would drive me frantic by asking whether he was to keep up my character for consistency in my absence. However, ten days since, the twelfth of May, after three weeks' unendurable detention in town on one pretext or another, I escaped, and made my way to Bowstead at last. My uncle told me that he had been obliged unwillingly to consent to our precious charge going to meet her sister at Brentford, and that she was but newly come home. Presently she entered, but scarcely had I accosted her before a blaze broke out close to us. The flame caught the dry old curtains, they flamed up like tinder, and as I leaped up on a table to tear them down, it gave way with me, I got a blow on the head, and knew no more. It seems that my uncle, as soon as the fire was out, finding that my arm was broken, set out to send the groom for the doctor—he being used to range the park at night. The stupid fellow, coming home half tipsy from the village, saw his white hair and beard in the moonlight, took him for a ghost, and ran off headlong. Thereupon my uncle, with new energy in the time of need, saddled the horse, changed his dressing-gown with the groom's coat, and rode off to Brentford. Then, finding that Dr. Hunter was not within, he actually went on to London, where Dr. Sandys, who had attended him ever since his would, forced him to go to bed, and to remain there till his own return. Thus my darling had no one to protect her, when, an hour or so after the accident, my mother suddenly appeared. Spies had been set on me by Mar, and so soon as they had brought intelligence of my movements she had hurried off from Ranelagh, in full dress, just as she was, to track and surprise me. My uncle, having gone by the bridle path, had not met her, and I was only beginning to return to my senses. I have a dim recollection of hearing my mother threatening and accusing Aurelia, and striving to interfere, but I was as one bound down, and all after that is blank to me. When my understanding again became clear, I could only learn that my mother had locked her into her own room, whence she had escaped, and"—with a groan—"nothing has been heard of her since!" Again he dropped his head on his hand as one in utter dejection.

"Fled! What has been done to trace her?" cried the Major.

"Nothing could be done till my mother was gone and my uncle returned. The delirium was on me, and whatever I tried to say turned to raving, all the worse if I saw or heard my mother, till Dr. Sandys forbade her coming near me. She was invited to the Queen's Sunday card party moreover, so she fortunately quitted Bowstead just before Mr. Belamour's return."

"Poor gentleman, he could do nothing," said Betty.

"Indeed I should have thought so, but it seems that he only needed a shock to rouse him. His state had become hypochondriacal, and this strong emotion has caused him to exert himself; and when he came into the daylight, he found he could bear it. I could scarce believe my eyes when, on awakening from a sleep, I found him by my bedside, promising me that if I would only remain still, he would use every endeavour to recover the dear one. He went first to Brentford, thinking she might have joined her sister there, but Mr. and Mrs. Arden had left it at the same time as she did. Then he travelled on to their Rectory at Rundell Canonicorum, thinking she might have followed them, but they had only just arrived, and had heard nothing of her; and he next sought her with his friend the Canon of Windsor, but all in vain. Meantime my mother had visited me, and denied all knowledge of her, only carrying away my little sisters, I believe because she found them on either side of my bed, telling me tales of their dear Cousin Aura's kindness. When my uncle returned to Bowstead I could bear inaction no longer, and profited by my sick leave to travel down hither, trusting that she might have found her way to her home, and longing to confess all and implore your pardon, sir,—and, alas! Your aid in seeking her."

With the large tears in his eyes, the youth rose from his chair as he spoke, and knelt on one knee before the Major, who exclaimed, extremely affected—"By all that is sacred, you have it, my dear boy. It is a wretched affair, but you meant to act honourably throughout, and you have suffered heavily. May God bless you both, and give us back my dear child. My Lady must have been very hard with her, to make her thus fly, all alone."

"You do not know, I suppose, any cause for so timid a creature preferring flight to a little restraint?"

"It seems," said Sir Amyas sadly, "that something the dear girl said gave colour to the charge of having caused the fire, and that my mother in her first passion threatened her with the constable!"

"My poor Aurelia! that might well scare her," cried Betty: "but how could it be?"

"They say she spoke of using something her sister had given her to discover what the mystery was that alarmed her."

"Ah! that gunpowder trick of Mr. Arden's—I always hated it!" exclaimed Betty.

"Gunpowder indeed!" growled the old soldier. "Well, if ever there's mischief among the children, Harriet is always at the bottom of it. I hope Mr. Belamour made her confess if she had a hand in it."

"I believe he did," said Sir Amyas.

"Just like her to set the match to the train and then run away," said the Major.

"Still, sir," said Betty, her womanhood roused to defence, "though I am angered and grieved enough that Harriet should have left Aurelia to face the consequences of the act she instigated, I must confess that even by Sir Amyas's own showing, if he will allow me to say so, my sisters were justified in wishing to understand the truth."

"That is what my uncle tells me," said the baronet. "He declares that if I had attended to his stipulations, restrained my fervour, or kept my distance, there would have been neither suspicion nor alarm. As if I had not restrained myself!"

"Ay, I dare say," said the Major, a little amused.

"Well, sir, what could a man do with most bewitching creature in the world, his own wife, too, on the next chair to him?"

There was a simplicity about the stripling—for he was hardly more—which forced them to forgive him; besides, they were touched by his paleness and fatigue. His own man—a respectable elderly servant whom the Major recollected waiting on Sir Jovian—came to beg that his honour would sit up no longer, as he had been travelling since six in the morning, and was quite worn out. Indeed, so it proved; for when the Major and Betty not only promised to come with him on the search the next day, but bade him a kind affectionate good-night, the poor lad, all unused to kindness, fairly burst into tears, which all his dawning manhood could not restrain.

CHAPTER XXVI
THE TRACES

Oh, if I were an eagle to soar into the sky,
I'd gaze around with piercing eye when I my love might spy.

The second-best coach, which resided at Bowstead, the same which had carried Aurelia off from Knightsbridge, had brought Sir Amyas Belamour to Carminster—an effeminate proceeding of which he was rather ashamed, though clearly he could not have ridden, and he had hoped to have brought his bride back in it.

There was plenty of room in it to take back the Major, Betty, and even Eugene, since he could not well have been left without his sister or Palmer, who was indispensable to the Major. He was so enchanted at "riding in a coach," and going perhaps to see London, that he did not trouble himself much about sister Aurelia being lost, and was in such high spirits as to be best disposed of outside, between Palmer and Gray, where he could at his ease contemplate the horses, generally four in number, though at some stages only two could be procured, and then at an extra steep hill a farmer's horse from the hayfield would be hitched on in front. Luckily there was no lack of money; Mr. Belamour and Hargrave had taken care that Sir Amyas should be amply supplied, and thus the journey was as rapid as posting could be in those days of insufficient inns, worse roads, and necessary precautions against highwaymen.

The road was not the same as that which the young baronet had come down by, as it was thought better to take the chance of meeting a different stage waggon, Sir Amyas and his servant having, of course, examined the one they had overtaken in coming down. At every possible resting place on the route was inquiry made, but all in vain; no one had seen such a young gentlewoman as was described, or if some answer inspired hope for a moment, it was dashed again at once. The young gentlewoman once turned out to be the Squire's fat lady, and another time was actually pursued into a troop of strolling players, attiring themselves in a barn, whence she came with cheeks freshly rouged with blood taken from a cat's tail.

The young baronet had meanwhile become very dear to the Major and his daughter. He had inherited his mother's indescribable attractiveness, and he was so frank, so affectionate, so unspoilt, so grateful for the little attentions demanded by his maimed condition, so considerate of the Major, and so regardless of himself, and, above all, so passionately devoted to his dearest life, as he called Aurelia, that it was impossible not to take him into their hearts, and let him be, as he entreated, a son and a brother.

The travellers decided on first repairing to Bowstead, thinking it probable that the truant might have returned thither, or that Mr. Belamour might have found her in some one of the cottages around. Hopes began to rise, and Major Delavie scolded Sir Amyas in quite a paternal manner whenever he began to despond, though the parts were reversed whenever the young people's expectations began to soar beyond his own spirits at the moment.

"Is yonder Hargrave? No, it is almost like my father!" exclaimed Sir Amyas, in amazement, as the coach lumbered slowly up the approach, and a very remarkable figure was before them. The long white beard was gone, the hair was brushed back, tied up, and the ends disposed of in a square black silk bag, hanging down behind; and the dark grey coat, with collar and deep cuffs of black velvet, was such as would be the ordinary wear of an elderly man of good position; but the face, a fine aquiline one, as to feature, was of perfectly absolute whiteness, scarcely relieved by the thin pale lips, or the eyes, which, naturally of a light-grey, had become almost as colourless as the rest of the face, and Betty felt a shock as if she had seen a marble statue clothed and animated, bowing and speaking.

The anxious inquiry and the mournful negative had been mutually exchanged before the carriage door was opened, and all were standing together in the avenue.

"I have, however, found a clue, or what may so prove," said Mr. Belamour, when the greetings had passed. "I have discovered how our fugitive passed the early part of the Sunday;" and he related how he had elicited from the Mistresses Treforth that they had seen her and driven her away with contumely.

Sir Amyas and the Major were not sparing of interjections, and the former hoped that his uncle had told them what they deserved.

"Thereby only incurring the more compassion," said Mr. Belamour, dryly, and going on to say that he had extended his inquires to Sedhurst, and had heard of her visit to Dame Wheatfield; also, that the good woman, going to seek her at the church, had found only the basket with the guineas in the paper. She had regarded this merely as a wrapper, and, being unable to read, had never noticed the writing, but she had fortunately preserved it, and Mr. Belamour thus learnt Aurelia's intention of throwing herself on Lady Belamour's mercy.

"My mother utterly denied all knowledge of her, when I cried out in anguish when she came to see me!" said Sir Amyas.

"So she does to Hargrave, whom she sent off to interrogate Mrs. Arden," said Mr. Belamour.

"Have you any reason to think the child could have reached my Lady?" inquired Betty, seeing that none of the gentlemen regarded my Lady's denials as making any difference to their belief, though not one of them chose to say so.

"Merely negative evidence," said Mr. Belamour. "I find that no one in the house actually beheld the departure of my Lady on that Sunday afternoon. The little girls had been found troublesome, and sent out into the park with Molly, and my nephew was giving full employment to Jumbo and Mrs. Aylward in my room. The groom, who was at the horses' heads, once averred that he saw two women get into the carriage besides her ladyship; but he is such a sodden confused fellow, and so contradicts himself, that I can make nothing of him."

"He would surely know his young mistress," said Sir Amyas.

"Perhaps not in the camlet hood, which Dame Wheatfield says she wore."

"Was good old Dove acting as coachman?" said Betty. "We should learn something from him."

"It was not her own coach," said Mr. Belamour. "All the servants were strangers, the liveries sanguine, and the panels painted with helmets and trophies."

"Mar's," said Sir Amyas, low and bitterly.

"I guessed as much," said his uncle. "It was probably chosen on purpose, if the child has friends in your own household."

"Then I must demand her," said the Major. "She cannot be denied to her father."

"At any rate we must go to town to-morrow," said Mr. Belamour. "We have done all we can here."

"Let us send for horses and go on at once," cried Sir Amyas.

"Not so fast, nephew. I see, by her face, that Miss Delavie does not approve, though our side of the town is safer than Hounslow."

"I was not thinking of highwaymen, sir, but we set forth at five this morning, and Sir Amyas always becomes flushed and feverish if he is over fatigued; nor is my father so strong as he was."

"Ah, ha! young sir, in adopting Betty for a sister you find you have adopted a quartermaster-general, eh?" said the Major; "but she is quite right. We should not get to town before ten or eleven at night, and what good would that do? No, no, let us sup and have a good night's rest, and we will drive into town long enough before fine ladies are astir in the morning, whatever may be the fashionable hour nowadays."

"Yes, nephew, you must content yourself with acting host to your father and sister-in-law in your own house," said his uncle.

"It seems to me more like yours, sir," rejoined the youth; but at the hall door, with all his native grace, he turned and gave his welcome, kissing Betty on the cheek with the grave ceremony of the host, and lamenting, poor fellow, that he stood alone without his bride to receive them.

"Is that Jumbo?" asked Betty. "I must thank him for all his kind service to my dear sister."

Faithful Jumbo fairly wept when—infinite condescension for those days—Major Delavie shook hands with him and thanked him.

"If pretty Missie Madam were but safe and well, Jumbo would wish no more," he sobbed out.

"Poor Jumbo," said Mr. Belamour, "he has never been the same man since pretty Missie Madam has been lost. I hear his violin mourning for her till it is enough to break one's heart!"

However Eugene created a diversion by curious inquiries whether Jumbo would indeed play the fiddle of which he had heard from Archer and Amoret, and he ran off most eagerly after the negro to be introduced to the various curiosities of the place.

Mrs. Aylward attended Miss Delavie to her room, and showed herself much softened. As a good, conscientious woman, she felt that she had acted a selfish part towards the lonely maiden, and Betty's confident belief that she had been a kind friend was a keen reproach.

"Indeed, madam," she said, "I would lief you could truly call me such, but when young Miss came here first I took her for one of that flighty sort that it is wise not to meddle with more than needful. I have kept my place here these thirty years by never making or meddling, and knowing nothing about what don't concern me, and is out of my province. Now, I wish I had let the poor young lady be more friendly with me, for maybe I could have been of use to her in her need.

"You had no suspicion?"

"No, ma'am; though I find there were those who suspected some one came up here disguised as Jumbo; but I was never one to lend an ear to gossip, and by that time I trusted the dear young lady altogether, and knew she would never knowingly do aught that was unbecoming her station, or her religion."

"I am glad the dear child won your good opinion," said Betty.

"Indeed, ma'am, that you may say," returned Mrs. Aylward, whom anxiety had made confidential; "for I own I was prejudiced against her from the first, as, if you'll excuse me, ma'am, all we Bowstead people are apt to be set against whatever comes from my Lady's side. However, one must have been made of the nether millstone not to feel the difference she made in the house. She was the very life of it with her pretty ways, singing and playing with the children, and rousing up the poor gentleman too that had lived just like a mere heathen in a dungeon, and wouldn't so much as hear a godly word in his despair. And now he has a minister once a fortnight to read prayers, and is quite another man—all through that blessed young lady, who has brought him back to light and life." And as Betty's tears flowed at this testimony to her sister, the housekeeper added, "Never you fear, ma'am; she is one of God's innocents and His Hand will be over her."

Meantime, having dismissed the young lover to take, if he could, a much needed night's rest, the Major was listening to Mr. Belamour's confession. "I was the most to blame, in as much as an old fool is worse than a young one; and I would that the penalty fell on me alone."

"If she be in my cousin's hands I cannot believe that she will permit any harm to befall her," said the good Major, still clinging to his faith in Urania—the child he had taught to ride, and with whom he had danced her first minuet.

"What I dread most is her being forced into some low marriage," said Mr. Belamour. "The poor child's faith in the ceremony that passed must have been overthrown, and who can tell what she may be induced to accept?"

"It was that threat which moved you?" said the Major.

"Yes. Hargrave assured me that my Lady had actually offered her to him, with a bribe of a farm on easy terms; and when she found that he had other intentions, there seemed to be some broken-down sycophant of Mar's upon the cards, but of course I was preferable, both because my fair sister-in-law has some lingering respect for the honour of her own blood, and because the bar between Aurelia and my nephew would be perpetual.

I knew likewise that it was my brother's earnest desire that a match should take place between your children and his.

"He did me too much honour. The lad showed me the extract from his letter."

"I could not give him the whole. It was fit for no eyes but mine, who had so long neglected it, and barely understood that it existed. My poor brother's eyes were fully opened to his wife's character, and even while he loved her to distraction, and yielded to her fascinating mastery against his better judgment, he left me the charge of trying in some degree to repair the injustice he believed you to be suffering, and of counteracting evil influences on her son."

"That seems at least to have been done."

"By no efforts of mine; but because the boy was happily permitted to remain with the worthy tutor his father had chosen for him, and because Wayland is an excellent man, wise and prudent in all things save in being bewitched by a fair face. Would that he were returned! When I first consented to act this fool's part, I trusted that he would have been at home soon enough to prevent more than the nominal engagement, and when my Lady's threats rendered it needful to secure the poor child by giving her my name, I still expected him before my young gentleman should utterly betray himself by his warmth."

"He tells me that he has written."

"True. On that I insisted, and I am the more uneasy, for there has been ample time for a reply. It is only too likely, from what my nephew tells me of his venturesome explorations, that he may have fallen into the hands of the Moorish corsairs! Hargrave says it is rumoured; but my Lady will not be checked in her career of pleasure, and if she is fearful of his return, she may precipitate matters with the poor girl!"

"Come, come, sir, I cannot have you give way to despondency. You did your best, and if it did not succeed, it was owing to my foolish daughter Arden. Why, if she was not satisfied about her sister, could she not have come here, and demanded an explanation? That would have been the straightforward way!"

"Would that she had! Or would that I had sooner discovered my own entire recovery, which I owe in very truth to the sweet being who has brought new life alike of body and mind to me, and who must think I have requited her so cruelly."

CHAPTER XXVII
CYTHEREA'S BOWER

There Citherea, goddesse was and quene,
Honourid highly for her majeste,
And eke her sonne, the mighty god I weene,
Cupid the blinde, that for his dignite
A M lovers worshipp on ther kne.
There was I bid on pain of dethe to pere,
By Mercury, the winged messengre.—CHAUCER.

By twelve o'clock on the ensuing day Mr. Belamour, with Eugene and Jumbo, was set down at a hotel near Whitehall, to secure apartments, while the Major went on to demand his daughter from Lady Belamour, taking with him Betty, whom he allowed to be a much better match for my Lady than he could be. Very little faith in his cousin Urania remained to him in the abstract, yet even now he could not be sure that she would not talk him over and hoodwink him in any actual encounter. Sir Amyas likewise accompanied him, both to gratify his own anxiety and to secure admission. The young man still looked pale and worn with restless anxiety; but he had, in spite of remonstrances, that morning discarded his sling, saying that he should return to his quarters. Let his Colonel do his worst then; he had still more liberty than if compelled to return to his mother's house.

Lady Belamour had, on her second marriage, forsaken her own old hereditary mansion in the Strand, where Sir Jovian had died, and which, she said, gave her the vapours. Mr. Wayland, whose wealth far exceeded her own, had purchased one of the new houses in Hanover Square, the fashionable quarter and very much admired; but the Major regretted the gloomy dignity of the separate enclosure and walled court of Delavie House, whereas the new one, in modern fashion, had only an area and steps between the front and the pavement.

The hall door stood wide open, with a stately porter within, and lackeys planted about at intervals. Grey descended from the box, and after some inquiry, brought word that "her Ladyship was at breakfast," then, at a sign from his master, opened the carriage door. Sir Amyas, taking Betty by the tips of her fingers, led her forward, receiving by the way greetings and inquiries from the servants, whose countenances showed him to be a welcome arrival.

"Is it a reception day, Maine?" he asked of a kind of major-domo whom he met on the top of the broad stairs.

"No, your honour."

"Is company with her ladyship?"

"No, not company, sir," with a certain hesitation, which damped Betty's satisfaction in the first assurance.

What did she see as Maine opened the door? It was a very spacious bedroom, the bed in an alcove hung with rose-coloured satin embroidered with myrtles and white roses, looped up with lace and muslin. Like draperies hung round the window, fluted silk lined the room, and beautiful japanned and inlaid cabinets and *etageres* adorned the walls, bearing all varieties and devices of new and old porcelain from Chins, Sevres, Dresden, or Worcester, tokens of Mr. Wayland's travels. There was a toilette table before one window covered with lacquer ware, silver and ivory boxes, and other apparatus, and an exquisite Venetian mirror with the borders of frosted silver work.

Not far off, but sideways to it, sat Lady Belamour in a loose sacque of some rich striped silk, in crimson and blue stripes shot with gold threads. Slippers, embroidered with gold, showed off her dainty feet, and a French hairdresser stood behind her chair putting the finishing touches to the imposing fabric of powder, flower, and feather upon her head. A little hand-mirror, framed in carved ivory inlaid with coral, and a fan, lay on a tiny spindle-legged table close in front of her, together with a buff-coloured cup of chocolate. At a somewhat larger table Mrs. Loveday, her woman, was dispensing the chocolate, whilst a little negro boy, in a fantastic Oriental costume, waited to carry the cups about.

On a sofa near at hand, in an easy attitude, reclined Colonel Mar, holding out to Lady Belamour a snuff-box of tortoiseshell and gold, and a lady sat near on one of the tall black-and-gold chairs drinking chocolate, while all were giving their opinions on the laces, feathers, ribbons, and trinkets which another Frenchman was displaying from a basket-box placed on the floor, trying to keep aloof a little Maltese lion-dog, which had been roused from its cushion, and had come to inspect his wares. A little further off, Archer, in a blue velvet coat, white satin waistcoat, and breeches and silk stockings, and Amoret, white-frocked, blue-sashed, and bare-headed (an innovation of fashion), were admiring the nodding mandarins, grinning nondescript monsters, and green lions of extraordinary form which an emissary from a curiosity-shop was unpacking. Near the door, in an attitude weary yet obsequious, stood, paper in hand, a dejected figure in shabby plum-colour— *i.e.* a poor author—waiting in hopes that his sonnet in praise of Cytherea's triumphant charms would win his the guinea he so sorely needed, as

> To quench the blushes of ingenuous shame,
>
> And heap the shrine of luxury and pride
>
> With incense kindled at the Muses' flame.

The scene was completed by a blue and yellow macaw at one window chained to his perch, and a green monkey tethered in like manner at the other.

Of course Elizabeth Delavie did not perceive all these details at once. Her first sensation was the shock to the decorum of a modest English lady at intruding into a bed-room; but her foreign recollections coming to her aid, she accepted the fashion with one momentary feminine review of her own appearance, and relief that she had changed her travelling gear for her Sunday silks, and made her father put on his full uniform. All this passed while Sir Amyas was leading her into the room, steering her carefully out of the monkey's reach. Then he went a step or two forward and bent before his mother, almost touching the ground with one knee, as he kissed her hand, and rising, acknowledged the lady with a circular sweep of his hat, and his Colonel with a military salute, all rapidly, but with perfect ease and gracefulness. "Ah! my truant, my runaway invalid!" said Lady Belamour, "you are come to surrender."

"I am come," he said gravely, holding out his stronger hand to his little brother and sister, who sprang to him, "to bring my father-and sister-in-law, Major and Miss Delavie."

"Ah! my good cousin, my excellent Mrs. Betty, excuse me that my tyrant *friseur* prevents my rising to welcome you. It is so good and friendly in you to come in this informal way to cheer me under this terrible anxiety. Let me present you to my kind friend, the Countess of Aresfield, who has been so good as to come in to-day to sustain my spirits. Colonel Mar you know already. Pray be seated. Amyas—Archer—chairs. Let Syphax give you a cup of chocolate."

"Madam," said the Major, disregarding all this and standing as if on parade, "can I see you alone? My business is urgent."

"No evil news, I trust! I have undergone such frightful shocks of late, my constitution is well nigh ruined."

"It is I that have to ask news of you madam."

She saw that, if she trifled with him, something would break out that she would not wish to have said publicly. "My time is so little my own," she said, "I am under command to be at the Palace by two o'clock, but in a few minutes I shall be able to dismiss my tormentor, and then, till my woman comes to dress me, I shall be at your service. Sit down, I entreat, and take some chocolate. I know Mrs. Betty is an excellent housekeeper, and I want her opinion. My dear Lady Aresfield, suffer me to introduce my estimable cousin, Mrs. Betty Delavie."

The Countess looking in her feathers and powder like a beetroot in white sauce, favoured Betty with a broad stare. Vulgarity was very vulgar in those days, especially when it had purchased rank, and thought manners might be dispensed with. Betty sat down, and Amoret climbed on her lap, while a diversion was made by Archer's imperious entreaty that his mamma would purchase a mandarin who not only nodded, but waved his hands and protruded his tongue.

Then ensued what seemed, to the sickening suspense of the two Delavies, a senseless Babel of tongues on all sides; but it ended in the *friseur* putting up his implements, the trades-folk leaving the selected goods unpaid for, and the poor poet bowing himself within reach of the monkey, who made a clutch at his MS., chattered over it, and tore it into fragments. There was a peal of mirth—loudest from Lady Aresfield—but Sir Amyas sprang forward with gentlemanly regrets, apologies, and excuses, finally opening the door and following the poor man out of the room to administer the guinea from his own pocket, while Colonel Mar exclaimed, "Here, Archer, boy, run after him with this. The poor devil has won it by producing a smile from those divine lips—such as his jungle might never have done—-"

"Fie! fie! Mar," said the Lady, shaking her fan at him, "the child will repeat it to him."

"The better sport if he do," said Colonel Mar, carelessly; "he may term himself a very Orpheus charming the beasts, so that they snatch his poems from him!"

Then, as Sir Amyas returned, Lady Belamour entreated her dear Countess to allow him to conduct her to the withdrawing room, and there endeavour to entertain her. The Colonel could not but follow, and the Major and Betty found themselves at length alone with her Ladyship.

"I trust you have come to relieve my mind as to our poor runaway," she began.

"Would to Heaven I could!" said the Major.

"Good Heavens! Then she has never reached you!"

"Certainly not.

"Nor her sister? Oh, surely she is with her sister!"

"No, madam, her sisters knows nothing of her. Cousin, you have children of your own! I entreat of you to tell me what you have done with her."

"How should I have done anything with her? I who have been feeding all this time on the assurance that she had returned to you."

"How could a child like her do so?"

"We know she had money," said Lady Belamour.

"And we know," said Betty, fixing her eyes on the lady, "that though she escaped, on the first alarm, as far as Sedhurst, and was there seen, she had decided on returning to Bowstead and giving herself up to you Ladyship."

"Indeed? At what time was that?" exclaimed my Lady.

"Some time in the afternoon of Sunday!"

"Ah! then I must have left Bowstead. I was pledged to her Majesty's card-table, and royal commands cannot be disregarded, so I had to go away in grievous anxiety for my poor boy. She meant to return to Bowstead, did she? Ah. Does not an idea strike you that old Amyas Belamour may know more than he confesses! He has been playing a double game throughout."

"He is as anxious to find the dear girl as we are madam."

"So he may seem to you and to my poor infatuated boy, but you see those crazed persons are full of strange devices and secrets, as indeed we have already experienced. I see what you would say; he may appear sane and plausible enough to a stranger, but to those who have known him ever since his misfortunes, the truth is but too plain. He was harmless enough as long as he was content to remain secluded in his dark chamber, but now that I hear he has broken loose, Heaven knows what mischief he may do. My dear cousin Delavie, you are the prop left to me in these troubles, with my poor good man in the hands of those cruel pirates, who may be making him work in chains for all I know," and the tears came into her beautiful eyes.

"They will not do that," said Major Delavie, eager to reassure her; "I have heard enough of their tricks to know that they keep such game as he most carefully till they can get a ransom."

"Your are sure of that!"

"Perfectly. I met an Italian fellow at Vienna who told me how it was all managed by the Genoese bankers."

"Ah! I was just thinking that you would be the only person who could be of use—you who know foreign languages and all their ways. If you could go abroad, and arrange it for me!"

"If my daughter were restored—-" began the Major.

"I see what you would say, and I am convinced that the first step towards the discovery would be to put Mr. Belamour under restraint, and separate his black from him. Then one or other of them would speak, and we might know how she has been played upon."

"What does your Ladyship suppose then?" asked the Major.

"This is what I imagine. The poor silly maid repents herself and comes back in search of me. Would that she had found me, her best friend! But instead of that, she falls in with old Belamour, and he, having by this time perceived the danger of the perilous masquerade in which he had involved my unlucky boy, a minor, has mewed her up somewhere, till the cry should be over."

"That would be the part of a villain, but scarcely of a madman," said Betty dryly.

"My dear cousin Betty, there are lunatics endowed with a marvellous shrewdness to commit senseless villanies, and to put on a specious seeming. Depend upon it, my unfortunate brother-in-law's wanderings at night were not solely spent in communings with the trees and brooks. Who knows what might be discovered if he were under proper restraint? And it is to you, the only relation I have, that I must turn for assistance in my most unhappy circumstances," she added, wit a glance so full of sweet helplessness that no man could withstand it. "I am so glad you are here. You will be acting for me as well as for yourself in endeavouring to find your poor lovely child, and the first thing I would have done would be to separate Belamour and his black, put them under restraint, and interrogate them separately. You could easily get an order from a magistrate. But ah, here comes my woman. No more now. You will come to me this evening, and we can talk further on this matter. I shall have some company, and it will not be a regular rout, only a few card-tables, and a little dancing for the young people."

"Your ladyship must excuse me," said Betty, "I have no dress to appear in, even if I had spirits for the company."

"Ah! my dear cousin, how do you think it is with my spirits? Yet I think it my duty not to allow myself to be moped, but to exert myself for the interest of my son. While as to dress, my woman can direct you to the milliner who would equip you in the last mode. What, still obstinate? Nay, then, Harry, I can take no excuse from you, and I may have been able to collect some intelligence from the servants."

Nothing remained but to take leave and walk home, the Major observing—

"Well, what think you of that, Betty?"

"Think, sir?—I think it is not for my lady to talk of villains."

"She is in absolute error respecting Belamour; but then she has not seen him since his recovery. Women are prone to those fancies, and in her unprotected state, poor thing, no wonder she takes alarms."

"I should have thought her rather over-protected."

"Now, Betty, you need not take a leaf out of Mrs. Duckworth's book, and begin to be censorious. You saw how relieved she was to have me, her own blood relation, to turn to, instead of that empty braggart of a fellow. Besides, a man does not bring his step-mother when there's anything amiss."

There was something in this argument, and Betty held her peace, knowing that to censure my Lady only incited her father to defend her.

For her own part her consternation was great, and she walked on in silence, only speaking again to acquiesce in her father's observation that they must say nothing to Mr. Belamour of my Lady's plans for his seclusion.

They found Mr. Belamour in the square parlour of the Royal York, having sent Eugene out for a walk with Jumbo. The boy's return in the most eager state of excitement at the shops, the horses, sedans, and other wonders, did something, together with dinner, to wile away the weary time till, about three hours after the Major and his daughter had returned, they were joined by the young baronet, who came running up the stairs with a good deal more impetuosity than he would have permitted himself at home.

"At last I have escaped," he said. "I fear you have waited long for me?"

"I have been hoping you had discovered some indications," said the Major.

"Alas, no! I should imagine my Lady as ignorant as we are, save for one thing."

"And that was—-?"

"The pains that were taken to prevent my speaking with any of the servants. I was forced to attend on that harridan, Lady Aresfield, till my mother sent for me; and then she made Mar absolutely watch me off the premises. Then I had to go and report myself at head-quarters, and see the surgeon, so that there may be no colour of irregularity for the Colonel to take advantage of."

"Right, right!" said the Major; "do not let him get a handle against you, though I should not call you fit for duty yet, even for holiday-work like yours."

"You still suspect that your mother knows where our Aurelia is?" said Betty. "When I think of her demeanour, I can hardly believe it! But did you hear nothing of your little sisters?"

"I did not ask. In truth I was confounded by a proposal that was made to me. If I will immediately marry my mother's darling, Lady Belle, I may have leave of absence from her and my regiment, both at once, and go to meet Mr. Wayland if I like, or at any rate make the grand tour, while they try to break in my charming bride for me. Of course I said that, being a married man, nothing should induce me to break the law, nor to put any lady in such a position; and equally, of course, I was shown a lawyer's opinion that the transaction was invalid."

"As I always believed," said his uncle. "The ceremony must be repeated when we find her: though even if you were willing, the other parties are very ill-advised to press for a marriage without judgment first being delivered, how far the present is binding. So she wants to send you off on your travels, does she?"

"She wishes me to go and arrange for her husband's ransom," said the Major. "I would be ready enough were my child only found, but I believe government would take it up, he being on his Majesty's service."

"It is a mere device for disposing of you—yes, and of my nephew too," said Mr. Belamour. "As for me, we know already her kind plans for putting me out of reach of interference. I see, she communicated them to you. Did she ask your cooperation, Major? Ah! certainly, an ingenious plan for disuniting us. I am the more convinced that she is well aware of where the poor child is, and that she wishes to be speedy in her measures."

There is no need to describe the half-frantic vehemence of the young lover, nor the way in which the father and sister tried to moderate his transports, though no less wretched themselves.

CHAPTER XXVIII
THE ROUT

Great troups of people travelled thitherward
Both day and night, of each degree and place. —*SPENSER.*

Much against their will, Major Delavie and his *soi-disant* son-in-law
set forth for Lady Belamour's entertainment, thinking no opportunity of
collecting intelligence was to be despised; while she probably wished to
obviate all reports of a misunderstanding as well as to keep them under her
own eye.

The reception rooms were less adorned than the lady's private
apartment. There were pictures on the walls, and long ranks of chairs
ranged round, and card-tables were set out in order. The ladies sat in rows,
and the gentlemen stood in knots and talked, all in full dress, resplendent
figures in brilliant velvet, gold lace, and embroidery, with swords by their
sides, cocked hats, edged with gold or silver lace, under their arms, and
gemmed shoe buckles. The order of creation was not yet reversed; the male
creature was quite as gorgeous in colour and ornament as the female, who
sat in her brocade, powder and patches, fan in hand, to receive the homage
of his snuff-box.

Sir Amyas went the round, giving and returning greetings, which
were bestowed on him with an ardour sufficient to prove that he was a
general favourite. His mother, exquisitely dressed in a rich rose-coloured
velvet train, over a creamy satin petticoat, both exquisitely embroidered,
sailed up with a cordial greeting to her good cousin, and wanted to set
him down to loo or ombre; but the veteran knew too well what the play
in her house was, and saw, moreover, Lady Aresfield sitting like a harpy
before the green baize field of her spoils. While he was refusing, Sir Amyas
returned to him, saying, "Sir, here is a gentleman whom I think you must
have known in Flanders;" and the Major found himself shaking hands with
an old comrade. Save for his heavy heart, he would been extremely happy
in the ensuing conversation.

In the meantime Lady Belamour, turning towards a stout, clumsy, short
girl, her intensely red cheeks and huge black eyes staring out of her powder,

while the extreme costliness of her crimson satin dress, and profusion of her rubies were ridiculous on the unformed person of a creature scarcely fifteen. If she had been any one else she would have been a hideous spectacle in the eyes of the exquisitely tasteful Lady Belamour, who, detecting the expression in her son's eye, whispered behind her fan, "We will soon set all that right;" then aloud, "My son cannot recover from his surprise. He did not imagine that we could steal you for an evening from Queen's Square to procure him this delight." Then as Sir Amyas bowed, "The Yellow Room is cleared for dancing. Lady Belle will favour you, Amyas."

"You must excuse me, madam," he said; "I have not yet the free use of my arm, and could not acquit myself properly in a minuet."

"I hate minuets," returned Lady Belle; "the very notion gives me the spleen."

"Ah, pretty heretic!" said my Lady, making a playful gesture with her fan at the peony-coloured cheek. "I meant this wounded knight to have converted you, but he must amuse you otherwise. What, my Lord I thought you knew I never meant to dance again. Cannot you open the dance without me? I, who have no spirits!"

The rest was lost as she sailed away on the arm of a gentleman in a turquoise-coloured coat, and waistcoat embroidered with gillyflowers; leaving the Lady Arabella on the hands of her son, who, neither as host nor gentleman, could escape, until the young lady had found some other companion. He stiffly and wearily addressed to her the inquiry how she liked London.

"I should like it monstrously if I were not moped up in school," she answered. "So you have come back. How did you hurt your arm?" she said, in the most provincial of dialects.

"In the fire, madam."

"What? In snatching your innamorata from the flames?"

"Not precisely," he said.

"Come, now, tell me; did she set the room a-fire?" demanded the young lady. "Oh, you need not think to deceive me. My brother Mar's coachman told my mamma's woman all about it, and how she was locked up and ran away; but they have her fast enough now, after all her tricks!"

"Who have? For pity's sake tell me, Lady Belle!"

Loving to tease, she exclaimed: "There, now, what a work to make about a white-faced little rustic!"

"Your ladyship has not seen her."

"Have I not, though? I don't admire your taste."

"Is she in Queen's Square?"

"Do not you wish me to tell you where you can find your old faded doll, with a waist just like a wasp, and an old blue sacque—not a bit of powder in her hair?"

"Lady Belle, if you would have me for ever beholden to you—-"

"The cap fits," she cried, clapping her hands. "Not a word to say for her! I would not have such a beau for the world."

"When I have found her it will be time to defend her beauty! If your ladyship would only tell me where she is, you know not what gratitude I should feel!"

"I dare say, but that's my secret. My mamma and yours would be ready to kill me with rage if they knew I had let out even so much."

"They would forgive you. Come, Lady Belle, think of her brave old father, and give some clue to finding her. Where is she?"

"Ah! where you will never get at her!"

"Is she at Queen's Square?"

"What would you do if you thought she was? Get a constable and come and search? Oh, what a rage Madam would be in! Goodness me, what sport!" and she fell back in a violent giggling fit; but the two matrons were so delighted to see the young people talking to one another, that there was no attempt to repress her. Sir Amyas made another attempt to elicit whether Aurelia were really at the school in Queen's Square, but Lady Arabella still refused to answer directly. Then he tried the expedient of declaring that she was only trying to tease him, and had not really seen the lady. He pretended not to believe her, but when she insisted, "Hair just the colour of Lady Belamour's," his incredulity vanished; but on his next entreaty, she put on a sly look imitated from the evil world in which she lived, and declared she should not encourage naughty doings. The youth, who though four years older, was by far the more simple and innocent of the two, replied with great gravity, "It is the Lady Belamour, my own wife, that I am seeking."

"That's just the nonsense she talks!"

"For Heaven's sake, what did she say?"

But Belle was tired of her game, and threw herself boisterously on a young lady who had the "sweetest enamel necklace in the world," and whose ornaments she began to handle and admire in true spoilt-child fashion.

Sir Amyas then betook himself to the Major, who saw at once by his eye and step that something was gained. They took leave together, Lady Belamour making a hurried lamentation that she had seen so little of her dear cousin, but accepting her son's excuse that he must return to his quarters; and they walked away together escorted by Palmer and Grey, as well as by two link-boys, summer night though it was.

Sir Amyas repaired first to the hotel, where Mr. Belamour and Betty were still sitting, for even the fashionable world kept comparatively early hours, and it was not yet eleven o'clock. The parlor where they sat was nearly dark, one candle out and the other shaded so as to produce the dimness which Mr. Belamour still preferred, and they were sitting on either side of the open window, Betty listening to her companion's reminiscences of the evenings enlivened by poor Aurelia, and of the many traits of her goodness, sweet temper, and intelligence which he had stored up in his mind. He had, he said, already learned through her to know Miss Delavie, and he declared that the voices of the sisters were so much alike that he could have believed himself at Bowstead with the gentle visitor who had brought him new life.

The tidings of Lady Arabella's secret were eagerly listened to, and the token of the mouse-coloured hair was accepted; Sir Amyas comparing, to every one's satisfaction, a certain lock that he bore on a chain next his heart, and a little knot, surrounded with diamonds, in a ring, which he had been still wearing from force of habit, though he declared he should never endure to do so again.

It was evident that Lady Belle had really seen Aurelia; and where could that have been save at the famous boarding-school in Queen's Square, where the daughters of "the great" were trained in the accomplishments of the day? The Major, with rising hopes, declared that he had always maintained that his cousin meant no ill by his daughter, and though it had been cruel, not to say worse, in her, to deny all knowledge of the fugitive, yet women would have their strange ways.

"That is very hard on us women, sir," said Betty.

"Ah! my dear, poor Urania never had such a mother as you, and she has lived in the great world besides, and that's a bad school. You will not take our Aurelia much into it, my dear boy," he added, turning wistfully to Sir Amyas.

"I would not let a breath blow on her that could touch the bloom of her charming frank innocence," cried the lad. "But think you she can be in health? Lady Belle spoke of her being pale!"

"Look at my young lady herself!" said the Major, which made them all laugh. They were full of hope. The Major and his daughter would go themselves the next day, and a father's claim could not be refused even though not enforced according to Lady Arabella's desire.

Their coach—for so Sir Amyas insisted on their going—was at the door at the earliest possible moment that a school for young ladies could be supposed to be astir; long before Mr. Belamour was up, for he retained his old habits so much that it was only on great occasions the he rose before noon; and while Eugene, under the care of Jumbo and Grey, was going off in great felicity to see the morning parade in St. James's Park.

One of the expedients of well-born Huguenot refugees had been tuition, and Madame d'Elmar had made here boarding-school so popular and fashionable that a second generation still maintained its fame, and damsels of the highest rank were sent there to learn French, to play the spinnet, to embroider, to dance, and to get into a carriage with grace. It was only countrified misses, bred by old-fashioned scholars, who attempted to go any farther, such as that *lusus naturae*, Miss Elizabeth Carter, who knew seven languages, or the Bishop of Oxford's niece, Catherine Talbot, who even painted natural flowers and wrote meditations! The education Aurelia Delavie had received over her Homer and Racine would be smiled at as quite superfluous.

There was no difficulty about admission. The coach with its Belamour trappings was a warrant of admittance. The father and daughter were shown into a parlour with a print of Marshal Schomberg over the mantelpiece, and wonderful performances in tapestry work and embroidery on every available chair, as well as framed upon the wainscoted walls.

A little lady, more French than English, moving like a perfectly wound up piece of mechanism, all but her bright little eyes, appeared at their request to see Madame. It had been agreed before-hand that the Major should betray neither doubt nor difficulty, but simply say that he had come up from the country and wished to see his daughter.

Madame, in perfectly good English, excused herself, but begged to hear the name again.

There must be some error, no young lady of the name of Delavie was there.

They looked at one another, then Betty asked, "Has not a young lady been placed here by Lady Belamour?"

"No, madam, Lady Belamour once requested me to receive her twin daughters, but they were mere infants; I receive none under twelve year old."

"My good lady," cried the Major, "if you are denying my daughter to me, pray consider what you are doing. I am her own father, and whatever Lady Belamour may tell you, I can enforce my claim."

"I am not in the habit of having my word doubted, sir," and the little lady drew herself up like a true Gascon baroness, as she was.

"Madam, forgive me, I am in terrible perplexity and distress. My poor child, who was under Lady Belamour's charge, has been lost to us these three weeks or more, and we have been told that she has been seen here."

"Thus," said Betty, seeing that the lady still needed to be appeased, "we thought Lady Belamour might have deceived you as well as others."

"May I ask who said the young lady had been seen here?" asked the mistress coldly.

"It was Lady Arabella Mar," said Betty, "and, justly speaking, I believe she did not say it was here that my poor sister was seen, but that she had seen her, and we drew the conclusion that it was here."

"My Lady Arabella Mar is too often taken out by my Lady Countess," said Madame d'Elmar.

"Could I see her? Perhaps she would tell me where she saw my dear sister?" said Betty.

"She went to a rout last evening and has not returned," was the reply. "Indeed my lady, her mother, spoke as if she might never come back, her marriage being on the *tapis*. Indeed, sir, indeed, madam, I should most gladly assist you," she said as a gesture of bitter grief and disappointment passed between father and daughter, both of whom were evidently persons of condition. "If it will be any satisfaction to the lady to see all my pupils, I will conduct her through my establishment."

Betty caught at this, though there was no doubt that the mistress was speaking in good faith. She was led to a large empty room, where a dozen young ladies were drawn up awaiting the dancing master—girls from fourteen to seventeen, the elder ones in mob caps, those with more pretensions to fashion, with loose hair. Their twelve curtsies were made, their twenty-four eyes peeped more or less through their lashes at the visitor, but no such soft brown eyes as Aurelia's were among them.

"Madame," said Betty, "may I be permitted to ask the ladies a question?" She spoke it low, and in French, and her excellent accent won Madame's heart at once. Only Madame trusted to Mademoiselle's discretion not to put mysteries into their minds, or they would be all *tete montee.*

So, as discretely as the occasion would permit, Betty asked whether any one had seen or heard Lady Belle speak of having seen any one—a young lady?

Half-a-dozen tongues broke out, "We thought it all Lady Belle's whimsical secrets," and as many stories were beginning, but Madame's awful little hand waved silence, as she said, "Speak then, Miss Staunton."

"I know none of Lady Belle's secrets, ma'am—ask Miss Howard."

Miss Howard looked sulky; and a little eager, black-eyed thing cried, "She said it was an odious girl whom Lady Belamour keeps shut up in a great dungeon of an old house, and is going to send beyond seas, because she married two men at once in disguise."

"Fie, Miss Crawford, you know nothing about it."

"You told me so, yourself, Miss Howard."

"I never said anything so foolish."

"Hush, young ladies," said Madame. "Miss Howard, if you know anything, I request you to speak."

"It would be a great kindness," said Betty. "Might I ask the favour of seeing Miss Howard in private?"

Madame consented, and Miss Howard followed Betty out of hearing, muttering that Belle would fly at her for betraying her.

"I do not like asking you to betray your friend's confidence," said Betty.

"Oh, as to that, I'm not her friend, and I believe she has talked to a half-a-dozen more."

"I am this poor young lady's sister," said Betty. "We are afraid she has fallen into unkind hands; and I should be very thankful if you could help me to find her. Where do you think Lady Belle saw her?"

"I thought it was in some old house in Hertfordshire," said Miss Howard, more readily, "but I am not sure; for it was last Sunday, which she spent with her mamma. She came back and made it a great secret that she had seen the girl that had taken in Sir Amyas Belamour, who was contracted to herself, to marry him and his uncle both at once in disguise, and then had set the house a-fire. Belle had got some one to let her see the girl, and then she went on about her being not pretty."

"What did she say about sending her beyond seas?"

"Oh! that Miss Crawford made up. She told me that they were going to find a husband for her such as a low creature like that deserved. And she protests she is to be married to Sir Amyas very soon, and come back here while he makes the grand tour. I hope she won't. She will have more spiteful ways than ever."

This was all that Betty could extract. She saw Miss Crawford alone, but her tiding melted into the vaguest second-hand hearsay. The inquiry had only produced a fresh anxiety.

CHAPTER XXIX
A BLACK BLONDEL

And to the castle gate approached in quiet wise,
Whereat soft knocking, entrance he desired.
SPENSER.

"Nephew, is Delavie House inhabited?" inquired Mr. Belamour, as the baffled seekers sat together that evening.

"No, sir," replied Sir Amyas. "My Lady will only lease it to persons of quality, on such high terms that she cannot obtain them for a house in so antiquated a neighbourhood. Oh, you do not think it possible that my dearest life can be in captivity so near us! An old house! On my soul, so it must be; I will go thither instantly."

"And be taken for a Mohock! No, no, sit down, rash youth, and tell me who keeps the house."

"One Madge, an old woman as sour as vinegar, who snarled at me like a toothless cur when I once went there to find an old fowling-piece of my father's."

"Then you ar the last person who should show yourself there, since there are sure to be strict charges against admitting you, and you would only put the garrison on the alert. You had better let the reconnoitring party consist of Jumbo and myself."

The ensuing day was Sunday. Something was said of St. Paul's, then in bloom of youth and the wonder of England; but Betty declared that she could not run about to see fine churches till her mind was at ease about her poor sister. Might she only go to the nearest and quietest church? So she, with her father and Eugene, repaired to St. Clement Danes, where their landlord possessed a solid oak pew, and they heard a sermon on the wickedness and presumption of inoculating for the small-pox.

It was not a genteel neighbourhood, and the congregation was therefore large, for the substantial tradesfolk who had poured into the Strand since it had been rebuilt were far more religiously disposed than the fashionable world, retaining either the Puritan zeal, or the High Church fervour, which were alike discouraged in the godless court. The Major and his son and daughter were solitary units in the midst of the groups of portly citizens, with soberly handsome wives, and gay sons and daughters, who were exchanging greetings; and on their return to their hotel, the Major betook himself to a pipe in the bar, and Eugene was allowed to go for a walk in the park with Palmer, while Betty sat in her own room with her Bible, striving to strengthen her assurance that the innocent would never be forsaken. Indeed Mr. Belamour had much strengthened her grounds of hope and comfort by his testimony to poor Aurelia's perfect guilelessness and simplicity throughout the affair. Yet the echo of that girl's chatter about Lady Belle's rival being sent beyond the sea would return upon her ominously, although it might be mere exaggeration and misapprehension, like so much besides.

A great clock, chiming one, warned her to repair to the sitting-room, where she met Eugene, full of the unedifying spectacle of a fight between two street lads. There had been a regular ring, and the boy had been so much excited that Palmer had had much ado to bring him away. Betty had scarcely hushed his eager communications and repaired his toilette for dinner before Sir Amyas came in, having hurried away as soon as possible after attending his men to and from church.

"Sister," he said, for so he insisted on calling Betty, "I really think my uncle's surmise may be right. I went home past Delavie House last night, just to look at it, and there was—there really was, a light in one of the windows on the first floor, which always used to be as black as Erebus. I had much ado to keep myself from thundering at the gate. I would have done so before now but for my uncle's warning. Where can he be?"

The Major and Mr. Belamour here came in together, and the same torrent was beginning to be poured forth, when the latter cut it short with, "They are about to lay the cloth. Restrain yourself, my dear boy, or—" and as at that moment the waiter entered, he went on with the utmost readiness—"or, as it seems, the Queen of Hungary will never make good her claims. Pray, sir," turning to Major Delavie, "have you ever seen these young Archduchesses whose pretensions seem likely to convulse the continent to its centre?"

The Major, with an effort to gather his attention, replied that he could not remember; but Betty, with greater presence of mind, described how she had admired the two sisters of Austria as little girls walking on the Prater. Indeed she and Mr. Belamour contrived to keep up the ball till the Major was roused into giving an opinion of Prussian discipline, and to tell stories of Leopold of Dessau, Eugene, and Marlborough with sufficient zest to drive the young baronet almost frantic, especially as Jumbo, behind his master's chair, was on the broad grin all the time, and almost dancing in his shoes. Once he contrived to give an absolute wink with one of his big black eyes; not, however, undetected, for Mr. Belamour in a grave tone of reprimand ordered him off to fetch an ivory toothpick-case.

Not till the cloth had been remove, and dishes of early strawberries and of biscuits, accompanied by bottles of port and claret, placed on the table, and the servants had withdrawn, did Mr. Belamour observe, "I have penetrated the outworks."

There was an outburst of inquiry and explanation, but he was not to be prevented from telling the story in his own way. "I know the house well, for my brother lived there the first years of his marriage, before you came on the stage, young sir. Perhaps you do not know how to open the door from without?"

"Oh, sir, tell me the trick!"

Mr. Belamour held up a small pass-key. There was a certain tone of banter about him which almost drove his nephew wild, but greatly reassured Miss Delavie.

"Why—why keep me in torments, instead of taking me with you?" cried the youth.

"Because I wished my expedition to be no failure. I could not tell whether my key, which I found with my watch and seals, would still serve me. Ah! you look on fire; but remember the outworks are not the citadel."

"For Heaven's sake, sir, torture me not thus!"

"I knew that to make my summons at the out gate would lead to a summary denial by the sour porteress, so I experimented on the lock of the little door into the lane, and admitted myself and Jumbo into the court; but the great hall-door stood before me jealously closed, and the lower windows were shut with shutters, so that all I could do was to cause Jumbo to awake the echoes with a lusty peal on the knocker, which he repeated at intervals, until there hobbled forth to open it a crone as wrinkled and crabbed as one of Macbeth's witches. I demanded whether my Lady Belamour lived there. She croaked forth a negative sound, and had nearly shut the door in my face, but I kept her in parley by protesting that I had often visited my Lady there, and offering a crown-piece if she would direct me to her."

"A crown! a kingdom, if she would bring us to the right one!" cried Sir Amyas.

"Of course she directed me to Hanover Square, and then, evidently supposing there was something amiss with the great gates, she insisted on coming to let me out, and securing them after me."

The youth gave a great groan, saying, "Excuse me, sir, but what are we the better of that?"

"Endure a little while, impatient swain, and you shall hear. I fancy she recognised the Belamour Livery on Jumbo, for she hobbled by my side maundering apologies about its being against orders to admit gentle or simple, beast or body into the court, and that a poor woman could not lose her place and the roof over her head. But mark me, while this was passing, Jumbo, who had kept nearer the house whistling 'The Nightingale' just above his breath, heard his name called, and presently saw two little faces at an up-stairs window."

"My little sisters!" cried Sir Amyas.

"Even so; and he believes he heard one of them call out, 'Cousin, cousin Aura, come and see Jumbo;' but as the window was high up, I scarce dare credit his ears rather than his imagination, and we were instantly hustled away by the old woman, whose evident alarm is a further presumption that the captive is there, since Faith and Hope scarce have reached the years of being princesses immured in towers."

"It must be so," said Betty; "it would explain Lady Belle's having had access to her! And now?"

"Is it impossible to effect an entrance from the court and carry her away?" asked Sir Amyas.

"Entirely so," said his uncle. "The only door into the court is fit to stand a siege, and all the lower windows are barred and fastened with shutters. The servants' entrance is at the back towards the river, but no doubt it is also guarded, and my key will not serve for it."

"I could get some sprightly fellow of ours to come disguised as Mohocks, and break in," proceeded the youth, eagerly. "Once in the court, trust me for forcing my way to her."

"And getting lodged in Newgate for your pains, or tried by court-martial," said the Major. "No, when right is on our side, do not let us make it wrong. Hush, Sir Amyas, it is I who must here act. Whether you are her husband I do not know, I know that I am her father, and to-morrow morning, as soon as a magistrate can be spoken with, I shall go and demand a search warrant for the body of my daughter, Aurelia Delavie."

"The body! Good Heavens, sir," cried Betty.

"Not without the sweet soul, my dear Miss Delavie," said Mr. Belamour. "Your excellent father has arrived at the only right and safe decision, and provided no farther alarm is given, I think he may succeed. It is scarcely probable that my Lady is in constant communication with her stern porteress, and my person was evidently unknown. For her own sake, as well as that of the small fee I dropped into her hand, she is unlikely to report my reconnoissance."

Sir Amyas was frantic to go with his father-in-law, but both the elder men justly thought that his ambiguous claims would but complicate the matter. The landlord was consulted as to the acting magistrates of the time, and gave two or three addresses.

Another night of prayer, suspense, and hope for Betty's sick heart. Then, immediately after breakfast, the Major set forth, attended by Palmer, long before Mr. Belamour had left his room, or the young baronet could escape from his military duties. Being outside the City, the Strand was under the jurisdiction of justices of the peace for Middlesex, and they had so much more than they could do properly, that some of them did it as little as possible. The first magistrate would not see him, because it was too early to attend to business; the second never heard matters at his private house, and referred him to the office in Bow Street. In fact he would have been wiser to have gone thither at first, but he had hoped to have saved time. He had to wait sitting on a greasy chair when he could no longer stand, till case after case was gone through, and when he finally had a hearing and applied for a warrant to search for his daughter in Delavie House, there was much surprise and reluctance to put such an insult on a lady of quality in favour at Court. On his giving his reasons on oath for believing the young lady to be there, the grounds of his belief seemed to shrink away, so that the three magistrates held consultation whether the warrant could be granted. Finally, after eying him all over, and asking him where he had served, one of them, who had the air of having been in the army, told him that in consideration of his being a gentleman of high respectability who had served his country, they granted what he asked, being assured that he would not make the accusation lightly. The reforms made by Fielding had not yet begun, everybody had too much work, and the poor Major had still some time to wait before an officer—tipstaff, as he was called—could accompany him, so that it was past noon when, off in the Bowstead carriage again, they went along the Strand, to a high-walled court belonging to one of the old houses of the nobility, most of which had perished in the fire of London. There was a double-doored gateway, and after much thundering in vain, at which the tipstaff, a red-nosed old soldier, waxed very irate, the old woman came out in curtseying, crying, frightened humility, declaring that they would find no one there—they might look if they would.

So they drove over the paved road, crossing the pitched pebbles, the door was unbarred, but no Aurelia sprang into her father's arms. Only a little terrier came barking out into the dismal paved hall. Into every room they looked, the old woman asseverating denials that it was of no use, they might see for themselves, that no one had been there for years past. Full of emptiness, indeed, with faded grimy family portraits on the walls, moth-eaten carpets and cushions, high-backed chairs with worm-holes; and yet, somehow, there was one room that did look as if it had recently been sat in. Two little stools were drawn up close to a chair; the terrier poked and smelt about uneasily as though in search of some one, and dragged out from under a couch a child's ball which he began to worry. On the carpet, too, were some fragments of bright fresh embroidery silk, which the practiced eye of the constable noticed. "This here was not left ten or a dozen years ago," said he; and, extracting the ball from the fangs of the dog, "No, and this ball ain't ten year old, neither. Come, Mother What's'-name, it's no good deceiving an officer of the law; whose is this here ball?"

"It's the little misses. They've a bin here with their maid, but their nurse have been and fetched 'em away this morning, and a good riddance too."

"Who was the maid?—on your oath!"

"One Deborah Davis, a deaf woman, and pretty nigh a dumb one. She be gone too."

Nor could the old woman tell where she was to be found. "My Lady's woman sent her in," she said, "and she was glad enough to be rid of her."

"Come, now, my good woman, speak out, and it will be better for you," said the Major. "I know my daughter was here yesterday."

"And what do I know of where she be gone? She went off in a sedan-chair this morning before seven o'clock, and if you was to put me to the rack I couldn't say no more."

As to which way or with whom she had gone, the old woman was, apparently, really ignorant.

The poor Major had to return home baffled and despairing, still taking the tipstaff with him, in case, on consultation with Mr. Belamour, it should be deemed expedient to storm Hanover Square itself, and examine Lady Belamour and her servants upon oath.

Behold, the parlour was empty. Even Betty and Eugene were absent. The Major hastened to knock at Mr. Belamour's door. There was no answer; and when he knocked louder it was still in vain. He tried the door and found it locked. Then he retreated to the sitting-room, rang, and made inquiries of the waiter who answered the bell.

Mr. Belamour had received a note at about ten o'clock, and had gone out with him "in great disorder," said the waiter.

At the same moment there was a knock at the door, and a billet was brought in from Lady Belamour. The Major tore it open and read:—

"*MY DEAR COUSIN,*

"*I grieve for you, but my Suspicions were correct. We have all been completely hoodwinked by that old Villain, my Brother-in-law. I can give him no other Name, for his partial Aberration of Mind has only sharpened his natural Cunning. Would you believe it? He had obtained access to Delavie House, and had there hidden the unfortunate Object of your Search, while he pretended to be assisting you, and this Morning he carried her off in a Sedan. I have sent the good Doves to Bowstead in case he should have the Assurance to return to his old Quarters, but I suspect that they are on the Way to Dover. You had better consult with Hargrave on the means of confirming the strange Marriage Ceremony that has passed between them, since that affords the best Security for your Daughter's Maintenance and Reputation. Believe me, I share in your Distress. Indeed I have so frightful a Megrim that I can scarcely tell what I write, and I dare not admit you to-day.*

"*I remain,*

"*Your loving and much-grieved Cousin,*

"*URANIA BELAMOUR.*"

Poor Major! His horror, perplexity, and despair were indescribable. He had one only hope—that Sir Amyas and Betty might be on the track.

CHAPTER XXX
THE FIRST TASK

After all these there marcht a most faire dame,
Led of two gryslie villains, th' one Despight,
The other cleped Crueltie by name.
SPENSER.

The traces of occupation had not deceived Major Delavie; Aurelia had been recently in Delavie House, and we must go back some way in our narrative to her arrival there.

She had, on her return from Sedhurst on that Sunday, reached Bowstead, and entered by the lobby door just as Lady Belamour was coming down the stairs only attended by her woman, and ready to get into the carriage which waited at the hall door.

Sinking on her knees before her with clasped hands, Aurelia exclaimed, "O madam, I ought not to have come away. Here I am, do what you will with me, but spare my father. He knew nothing of it. Only, for pity's sake, do not put me among the poor wicked creatures in gaol."

"Get into that carriage immediately, and you shall know by decision," said Lady Belamour, with icy frigidness, but not the same fierceness as before; and Aurelia submissively obeyed, silenced by an imperious gesture when she would have asked, "How is it with *him*?" whom she durst not name.

Lady Belamour waited a minute or two while sending Loveday on a last message to the sick room, then entered the large deep carriage, signing to her captive to take a corner where she could hardly be seen if any one looked through the window. Loveday followed, the door was shut by a strange servant, as it was in fact Lady Aresfield's carriage, borrowed both for the sake of speed, and of secrecy towards her own household.

A few words passed by which Aurelia gathered something reassuring as to the state of the patient, and then Lady Belamour turned on her, demanding, "So, young miss, you tried to escape me! Where have you been?"

"Only as far as Sedhurst Church, madam. I would have gone home, but I feared to bring trouble on my father, and I came back to implore you to forgive."

There was no softening of the terrible, beautiful face before her, and she durst put no objective case to her verb. However, the answer was somewhat less dreadful than she had anticipated.

"I have been shamefully duped," said Lady Belamour, "but it is well that it is no worse; nor shall I visit our offences on your father if you show your penitence by absolute submission. The absurd ceremony you went through was a mere mockery, and the old fool, Belamour, showed himself crazed for consenting to such an improper frolic on the part of my son. Whether your innocence be feigned or not, however, I cannot permit you to go out of my custody until the foolish youth or yourself be properly bestowed in marriage elsewhere. Meantime, you will remain where I place you, and exactly fulfil my commands. Remember that any attempt to communicate with any person outside the house will be followed by your Father's immediate dismissal."

"May I not let him know that I am safe?"

"Certainly not; I will see to your father."

It was a period when great ladies did not scruple to scold at the top of their voices, and sometimes proceed to blows, but Lady Belamour never raised her low silvery tones, and thus increased the awfulness of her wrath and the impressiveness of her determination. Face to face with her, there were few who did not cower under her displeasure; and poor Aurelia, resolute to endure for her father's sake, could only promise implicit obedience.

She only guessed when the entered London by the louder rumbling, and for one moment the coach paused as a horse was reined up near it, and with plumed hat in hand the rider bent forward to the window, exclaiming, "Successful, by all that is lovely! Captured, by Jove!"

"You shall hear all another time," said lady Belamour. "Let us go on now."

They did so, but the horseman continued to flash across the windows, and when the coach, after considerable delay, had entered the walled court, rumbled over the pavement, and stopped before a closed door, he was still there. When, after much thundering, the door was opened, Aurelia had a moment's glimpse of a splendid figure in gold and scarlet handing out Lady Belamour, who stood talking with him on the steps of the house for some moments. Then, shrugging his shoulders, he remounted, and cantered off, after which my Lady signed to Aurelia to alight, and followed her into the hall.

"Madge," said Lady Belamour to the witch-like old woman who had admitted her, "this young lady is to remain here. You will open a bedroom and sitting-room for her at the back of the house. Let her be properly cared for, and go out in the court behind, but on no account approach the front gates. Let no one know she is here."

Madge muttered some demands about supplies and payments, and Lady Belamour waved her to settle them with Mrs. Loveday, turning meantime to the prisoner and saying, "There, child, you are to remain here on your good behaviour. Do your best to merit my good will, so that I may overlook what is past. Recollect, the least attempt to escape, or to hold intercourse with the young, or the old, fool, and it shall be the worse with them and with your father."

Therewith she departed, followed by Loveday, leaving Aurelia standing in the middle of the hall, the old hag gazing on her with a malignant leer. "Ho! ho'! So that's the way! He has begun that work early, has he? What's your name, my lass? Oh, you need give yourself airs! I cry you mercy," and she made a derisive curtsey.

Poor Aurelia, pride had less to do with her silence than absolute uncertainty what to call herself. The wedding ring was on her finger, and she would not deny her marriage by calling herself Delavie, but Belamour might be dangerous, and the prefix was likewise a difficulty, so faltered, "You may call me Madam Aurelia."

"Madam Really. That's a queer name, but it will serve while you are here."

"Pray let me go to my room," entreated the poor prisoner, who felt as ineffable disgust at her jailor, and was becoming sensible to extreme fatigue.

"Your room, hey? D'ye think I keep rooms and beds as though this were an inn, single-handed as I am? You must wait, unless you be too fine to lend a hand."

"Anything will do," said Aurelia, "if I may only rest. I would help, but I am so much tired that I can hardly stand."

"My Lady has given it to you well, Mistress Really or Mistress Falsely, which ever you may be," mumbled Madge, perhaps in soliloquy, fumbling at the lock of a room which at last she opened. It smelt very close and fusty, and most of the furniture was heaped together under a cloth in the midst, dimly visible by the light of a heart-shaped aperture in the shutters. Unclosing one of the leaves, the old woman admitted enough daylight to guide Aurelia to a couch against the wall, saying, "You can wait there till I see to your bed. And you'll be wanting supper too!" she added in a tone of infinite disgust.

"O never mind supper, if I can only go to bed," sighed Aurelia, sinking on the couch as the old woman hobbled off. Lassitude and exhaustion had brought her to a state like annihilation—unable to think or guess, hope or fear, with shoes hurting her footsore feet, a stiff dress cramping her too much for sleep, and her weary aching eyes gathering a few impressions in a passive way. On the walls hung dimly seen portraits strangely familiar to her. The man in a green dressing gown with floating hair had a face she knew; so had the lady in the yellow ruff. And was that not the old crest, the Delavie butterfly, with the motto, *Ma Vie et ma Mie*, carved on the mantelpiece? Thus she knew that she must be in Delavie House, and felt somewhat less desolate as she recognised several portraits as duplicates of those at the Great House at Carminster, and thought they looked at her in pity with their eyes like her father's. The youngest son in the great family group was, as she knew, an Amyas, and he put her in mind of her own. Oh, was he her own, when she could not tell whether those great soft, dark-grey eyes that looked so kindly on her had descended to the young baronet? She hoped not, for Harriet and she had often agreed that they presaged the fate of that gallant youth, who had been killed by Sir Bevil Grenville's side. He must have looked just as Sir Amyas did, lying senseless after the hurt she had caused.

No more definite nor useful thought passed through the brain of the overwearied maiden as she rest on the couch, how long she knew not; but it was growing dark by the time Madge returned with a guttering candle, a cracked plate and wedge of greasy-looking pie, a piece of dry bread, a pewter cup of small beer, and an impaired repulsive steel knife with a rounded end, and fork with broken prong. The fact of this being steel was not distressing to one who had never seen a silver fork, but the condition of both made her shudder, and added to the sick sense of exhaustion that destroyed her appetite. She took a little of the bread, and, being parched with thirst, drank some of the beer before Madge came back again. "Oh ho, you're nice I see, my fine Dame Really!"

"Thank you, indeed I can't eat, I am so much tired," said Aurelia apologetically.

"You'll have to put up with what serves your betters, I can tell you," was all the reply she received. "Well be ye coming to your bed?"

So up the creaking stairs she was guided to a room, very unlike that fresh white bower at Bowstead, large, eerie, ghostly-looking, bare save for a dark oak chest, and a bed of the same material, the posts apparently absolute trees, squared and richly carved, and supporting a solid wooden canopy with an immense boss as big as a cabbage, and carved something like one, depending from the centre, as if to endanger the head of the unwary, who should start up in bed. No means of ablution were provided, and Aurelia felt so grimed and dusty that she ventured to beg for an ewer and basin; but her amiable hostess snarled out that she had enough to do without humouring fiddle-faddle whimsies, and that she might wash at the pump if nothing else would serve her.

Aurelia wished she had known this before going up stairs, and, worn out as she was, the sense implanted by her mother that it was wicked to go to sleep dirty, actually made her drag herself down to a grim little scullery, where she was permitted to borrow a wooden bowl, since she was too *nice* forsooth to wash down stairs. She carried it up with a considerable trouble more than half full, and a bit of yellow soap and clean towel were likewise vouchsafed to her. The wash—perhaps because of the infinite trouble it cost her—did her great good,—it gave her energy to recollect her prayers and bring good angels about her. If this had been her first plunge from home, when Jumbo's violin had so scared her, such a place as this would have almost killed her; but the peace that had come to her in Sedhurst Church lingered still round her, and as she climbed up into the lofty bed the verse sang in her ears "Love is strong as death." Whether Love Divine or human she did not ask herself, but with the sense of soothing upon her, she slept— and slept as a seventeen-years'-old frame will sleep after having been thirty-six hours awake and afoot.

When she awoke it was with the sense of some one being in the room. "O gemini!" she heard, and starting up, only just avoiding the knob, she saw Mrs. Loveday's well-preserved brunette face gazing at her.

"Your servant, ma'am," she said. "You'll excuse me if I speak with you here, for I must be back by the time my Lady's bell rings."

"Is it very late?" said Aurelia, taking from under her pillow her watch, which had stopped long ago.

"Nigh upon ten o'clock," said Loveday. "I must not stay, but it is my Lady's wish that you should have all that is comfortable, and you'll let me know how Madge behaves herself."

"Is there any news from Bowstead?" was all Aurelia could at first demand.

"Not yet; but bless you, my dear young lady, you had best put all that matter out of your head for ever and a day. I know what these young gentlemen are. They are not to be hearkened to one moment, not the best of them. Let them be ever so much in earnest at the time, their parents and guardians have the mastery of them sooner or later, and the farther it has gone, the worse it is. I saw you lying asleep here looking so innocent that it went to my heart, and I heard you mutter in your sleep 'Love is strong as death,' but that's only a bit of some play-book, and don't you trust to it, for I never saw love that was stronger than a spider's web."

"Oh, hush, Mrs. Loveday. It is in the Bible!"

"You don't say so, ma'am," the woman said awestruck.

"I would show it you, only all my things are away. God is love, you know," said Aurelia, sitting up with clasped hands, "and He gives it, so it must be strong."

"Well, all the love I've ever seen was more the devil's," said Loveday truly enough; "and you'll find it so if you mean to trust to these fine young beaux and what they say."

Aurelia shook her head a little as she sat up in bed with her clasped hands; and there was a look on her face that Mrs. Loveday did not understand, as she went on with her advice.

"So, my dear young lady, you see all that is left for you is to frame your mind to keep close here, and conform to my Lady's will till all is blown over one way or another."

"I know that," said Aurelia.

"Don't' you do anything to anger her," added the waiting-woman, "for there's no one who can stand against her; and I'll speak up for you when I can, for I know how to come round my Lady, if any one does. Tell me what you want, and I'll get it for you; but don't try to get out, and don't send Madge, for she is not to be trusted with money. If I were you, I'd not let her see that watch, and I'd lock my door at night. You're too innocent, whatever my Lady may say. Here's half a pound of tea and sugar, which you had best keep to yourself, and I've seen to there being things decent down stairs. Tell me, my dear, is there anything you want? Your clothes, did you say? Oh, yes, you shall have them—yes, and your books. Here's some warm water," as a growling was heard at the door; "I must not wait till you are dressed, but there's a box of shells down in your room that Mr. Wayland sent home for my Lady to line a grotto with, and she wants them all sorted out. 'Tell her she must make herself of use if she wants to be forgiven,' says my Lady, for she is in a mighty hurry for them now she has heard of the Duchess of

Portland's grotto; though she has let them lie here unpacked for this half year and more. So if they are all done by night, maybe may Lady will be pleased to let you have a bit more liberty."

Mrs. Loveday departed, having certainly cheered the captive, and Aurelia rose, weary-limbed and sad-hearted, with a patient trust in her soul that Love Divine would not fail her, and that earthly love would do its best.

She found matters improved in the down-stairs room, the furniture was in order, a clean cloth on the table, a white roll, butter, and above all clean bright implements, showing Mrs. Loveday's influence. She ate and drank like a hungry girl, washed up for herself rather than let Madge touch anything she could help, and looked from the window into a dull court of dreary, blighted-looking turf divided by flagged walks, radiating from a statue in the middle, representing a Triton blowing a conch—no doubt intended to spout water, for there was a stone trough round him, but he had long forgotten his functions, and held a sparrow's nest with streaming straws in his hand. This must be the prison-yard, where alone she might walk, since it lay at the back of the house; and with a sense of depression she turned to the task that awaited her.

A very large foreign-looking case had been partly opened, and when she looked in she was appalled at the task to be accomplished in one day. It was crammed with shells of every size and description, from the large helmet-conch and Triton's trumpet, down to the tiny pink cowry and rice-volute, all stuffed together without arrangement or packing, forming a mass in which the unbroken shells reposed in a kind of sand, of *debris* ground together out of the victims; and when she took up a tolerably-sized univalve, quantities of little ones came tumbling out of its inner folds. She took up a handful, and presently picked out one perfect valve like a rose petal, three fairy cups of limpets, four ribbed cowries, and a thing like a green pea. Of course she knew no names, but a kind of interest was awakened by the beauty and variety before her. A pile of papers had been provided, and the housewife [a pocket-size container for small articles (as thread)—D.L.] which Betty made her always carry in her pocket furnished wherewithal to make up a number of bags for the lesser sorts; and she went to work, her troubles somewhat beguiled by the novel beauties of each delicate creature she disinterred, but remembering with a pang how, if she could have described them to Mr. Belamour, he would have discoursed upon the Order of Nature.

London noises were not the continuous roar of vehicles of the present day, but there was sound enough to remind the country girl where she was, and the street cries "Old Clothes!" "Sprats, oh!" "Sweep!" were heard over the wall, sometimes with tumultuous voices that seemed to enhance her loneliness, as she sat on the floor, hour after hour, sifting out the entire shells, and feeling a languid pleasure in joining the two halves of a bivalve, especially those lovely sunset shells that have rosy rays diverging from their crimson hinge over their polished surface, white, or just tinted with the hues of a daffodil sky. She never clasped a pair together without a little half-uttered ejaculation, "Oh, bring me and my dear young love thus together again!" And when she found a couple making a perfect heart, and holding together through all, she kissed it tenderly in the hope that thus it might be with her and with him whose hand and whose voice returned on her, calling her his dearest life!

She durst only quit the shells to eat the dinner which Madge served at one o'clock—a tolerable meal of slices of cold beef from a cook's-shop, but seasoned with sour looks and a murmur at ladies' fancies. The weariness and languor of the former day's exertions made her for the present disinclined to explore the house, even had she had time, and when twilight came there could have been little but fragments at the bottom of the case, though she could see no more to sort them.

And what were these noises around her making her start? Rats! Yes, here they were, venturing out from all the corners. They knew there had been food in the room. This was why Madge had those to gaunt, weird-looking cats in her kitchen! Aurelia went and sat on the step into the court to be out of their way, but Madge hunted her in that the door might be shut and barred; and when she returned trembling to the sitting room, she heard such a scampering and a scrambling that she durst not enter, and betook herself to her chamber and to bed.

Alas! that was no refuge. She had been too much tired to hear anything the night before, but to-night there was scratching, nibbling, careering, fighting, squeaking, recoil and rally, charge and rout, as the grey Hanover rat fought his successful battle with his black English cousin all over the floors and stairs—nay, once or twice came rushing up and over the bed—frightening its occupant almost out of her senses, as she cowered under the bed-clothes, not at all sure that they would not proceed to eating her. Happily daylight came early. Aurelia, at its first ray, darted across the room, starting in horror when she touched a soft thing with her bare foot, opened the shutter, and threw open the casement. Light drove the enemy back to their holes, and she had a few hours' sleep, but when Mrs. Loveday came to the room when she was nearly dressed, she exclaimed, "Why, miss, you look paler than you did yesterday."

"The rats!" said Aurelia under her breath.

"Ah! the rats! Of course they are bad enough in an old desolate place like this. But you've done the shells right beautiful, that I will say; and you may leave this house this very day if you will only give your consent to what my Lady asks. You shall be sent down this very day to Carminster, if so be you'll give up that ring of yours, and sign a paper giving up all claim to be married to his Honour. See, here it is, all ready, in my Lady's letter."

"I cannot," said Aurelia, with her hands behind her.

"You can read my Lady's letter," said Loveday; "that can do you no harm."

Aurelia felt she must do that at least.

"CHILD,

"*I will overlook your Transgression on the One Condition, that you sign this Paper and send it with your so-called Wedding Ring back to me immediately. Otherwise you must take the Consequences, and remain*

where you are till after my Son's Marriage.

"*URANIA BELAMOUR.*"

The paper was a formal renunciation of all rights or claims from the fictitious marriage by which she had been deceived, and an absolute pledge never to renew any contract with Sir Amyas Belamour, Knight Baronet, who had grossly played on her.

"No, I cannot," said Aurelia, pushing it from her.

"Indeed, miss, I would not persuade you to it if it were not for your own good; but you may be sure it is no use holding out against her Ladyship. If you sign it now, and give it up honourable, she will send Mr. Dove home with you, and there you'll be as if nothing had been amiss, no one knowing nothing about it; but if you persist it will not make the marriage a bit more true, and you will only be kept moped up in this dismal place till his Honour is married, and there's no saying what worse my Lady may do to you."

Another night of rats came up before Aurelia's imagination in contrast with the tender welcome at home; but the white face and the tones that had exclaimed, "Madam, what are you doing to my wife?" arose and forbade her. She would not fail him. So she said firmly once more, "No, Mrs. Loveday, I cannot. I do not know what lawyers may say, but I feel myself bound to Sir Amyas, and I will not break my vow—God helping me," she added under breath.

"You must write it to her ladyship then. She will never take such a message through me. Here is paper and pen that I brought, in hopes that you would be wise and submit for your honoured father's sake."

"My father cannot be persecuted for what he has nothing to do with," said Aurelia, with the gentle dignity that had grown on her since her troubles. And taking the pen, she wrote her simple refusal, signing it Aurelia Belamour.

"As you please, ma'am," said Mrs. Loveday, "but I have my Lady's orders to bring this paper every day till you sign it, and it would be better for you if you would do it at once."

Aurelia only shook her head, and asked if Mrs. Loveday had seen that she had finished sorting the shells. Yes; and as she was now dressed they went down together to the sitting-room. The shutters were still closed, Madge would not put a hand to the room except on the compulsion, and Aurelia's enemies had left evidence of their work; not only was the odour of the room like that of a barn, but the paper bags had in some cases been bitten through, and the shells scattered about, and of the loaf and butter which Aurelia had left on a high shelf in the cupboard nothing remained but a few fragments.

Loveday was very much shocked, all the more when Aurelia quietly said she should not mind it so much if the rats would only stay down stairs, and not run over her in bed.

"Yet you will not sign the paper."

"I cannot," again said Aurelia.

"My stars, I never could abear rats! Why they fly at one's throat sometimes!"

"I hope God will take care of me," said Aurelia, in a trembling voice. "He did last night."

Loveday began a formal leave-taking curtsey, but presently turned back. "There now," she said, "I cannot do it, I couldn't sleep a wink for thinking of you among the rats! Look here, I shall send a porter to bring away those shells if you'll make up their bags again that the nasty vermin have eaten, and there's a little terrier dog about the place that no one will miss, he shall bring it down, and depend upon it, the rats won't venture near it."

"Oh! thank you, Mrs. Loveday, how good you are!"

"Ah, don't then! If you could say that my dear!"

Mrs. Loveday hurried away, and after breakfasting, Aurelia repaired the ravages of the rats, and made a last sorting of the residuum of shell dust, discovering numerous minute beauties, which awoke in her the happy thought of the Creator's individual love.

She had not yet finished before Madge's voice was heard in querulous anger, and a heavy tread came along with her. A big man, who could have carried ten times the weight of the box of shells, came in with a little white dog with black ears, under his arm.

"There," said the amiable guardian of the house, "that smart madam says that it's her ladyship's pleasure you should have that little beast to keep down the rats. As if my cats was not enough! But mind you, Madam Really, if so be he meddles with my cats, it will be the worse for him."

The porter took up the box, and departed, and Aurelia was left with her new companion sniffing all round the room, much excited by the neighbourhood of his natural enemies. However, he obeyed her call, and let her make friends, and read the name on the brass plate upon his collar. When she read "Sir A. Belamour, Bart.," she took the little dog in her arms and kissed it's white head.

Being fairly rested, and having no task to accomplish, she felt the day much longer, though less solitary, in the companionship of the dog, to whom she whispered many fond compliments, and vain questions as to his name. With him at her heels and Madge and her cats safely shut into the kitchen, she took courage to wander about the dull court, and then to explore the mansion and try to get a view from the higher windows, in case they were not shuttered up like the lower ones. The emptiness of Bowstead was nothing to this, and she smiled to herself at having thought herself a prisoner there.

Most of the rooms were completely dismantled, or had only ghastly rags of torn leather or tapestry hanging to their walls. The upper windows, however, were merely obscured by dust and cobwebs. Her own bedroom windows only showed the tall front of an opposite house, but climbing to the higher storey, she could see at the back over the garden wall the broad sheet of the Thames, covered with boats and wherries, and the banks provided with steps and stairs, at the opening of every street on the opposite side, where she beheld a confused mass of trees, churches, and houses. Nearer, the view to the westward was closed in by a stately edifice which she did not know to be Somerset House; and from another window on the east side of the house she saw, over numerous tiled roofs, a gateway which she guessed to be Temple Bar, and a crowded thoroughfare, where the people looked like ants, toiling towards the great dome that rose in the misty distance. Was this the way she was to see London?

Coming down with a lagging step, she met Madge's face peering up. "Humph! there you be, my fine miss! No gaping after sweethearts from the window, or it will be the worse for you."

The terrier growled, as having already adopted his young lady's defence, and Aurelia, dreading a perilous explosion of his zeal in her cause, hurried him into her parlour.

CHAPTER XXXI
THE SECOND TASK

Hope no more,

Since thou art furnished with hidden lore,

To 'scape thy due reward if any day

Without some task accomplished passed away.

MOORE.

The little dog's presence was a comfort, but his night of combat and scuffling was not a restful one and the poor prisoner's sickness of heart and nervous terrors grew upon her every hour, with misgivings lest she should be clinging to a shadow, and sacrificing her return to Betty's arms for a phantom. There were moments when her anguish of vague terror and utter loneliness impelled her to long to sign her renunciation that moment; and when she thought of recurring hours and weeks of such days and such nights her spirit quailed within her, and Loveday might have found her less calmly steadfast had she come in the morning.

She did not come, and this in itself was a disappointment, for at least she brought a human voice and a pitying countenance which, temptress though she might be, had helped to bear Aurelia through the first days. Oh! could she but find anything to do! She had dusted her two rooms as well as she could consistently with care for the dress she could not change. She blamed herself extremely for having forgotten her Bible and Prayer-book when hastily making up her bundle of necessaries, and though there was little chance that Madge should possess either, or be able to read, she nerved herself to ask. "Bible! what should ye want of a Bible, unless to play the hypocrite? I hain't got none!" was the reply.

So Aurelia could only walk up and down the court trying to repeat the Psalms, and afterwards the poetry she had learnt for Mr. Belamour's benefit, sometimes deriving comfort from the promises, but oftener wondering whether he had indeed deserted her in anger at her distrustful curiosity. She tried to scrape the mossgrown Triton, she crept up stairs to the window that looked towards the City, and cleared off some of the dimness, and she got a needle and thread and tried to darn the holes in the curtains and cushions, but the rotten stuff crumbled under her fingers, and would not hold the stitches. At last she found in a dusty corner a boardless book with neither beginning nor end, being Defoe's *Plague of London*. She read and read with a horrid fascination, believing every word of it, wondering whether this house could have been infected, and at length feeling for the plague spot!

A great church-clock enabled her to count the hours! Oh, how many there were of them! How many more would there be? This was only her second day, and deliverance could not come for weeks, were her young husband—if husband he were—ever so faithful. How should she find patience in this dreariness, interspersed with fits of alarm lest he should be dangerously ill and suffering? She fell on her knees and prayed for him and for herself!

Here it was getting dark again, and Madge would hunt her in presently and shut the shutters. Hark! what was that? A bell echoing over the house! Madge came after her. "Where are you, my fine mistress! Go you into the parlour, I say," and she turned the key upon the prisoner, whose heart beat like a bird fluttering in a cage. Suddenly her door was opened, and in darted Fidelia and Lettice, who flung themselves upon her with ecstatic shrieks of "Cousin Aura, dear cousin Aura!" Loveday was behind, directing the bringing in of trunks from a hackney coach. All she said was, "My Lady's daughters are to be with you for the night, madam; I must not say more, for her ladyship is waiting for me."

She was gone, while the three were still in the glad tangle of an embrace beginning again and again, with all sorts of little exclamations from the children, into which Aurelia broke with the inquiry for their brother. "He is much better," said Fay. "He is to get up to-morrow, and then he will come and find you."

"Have you seen him?"

"Oh, yes, and he says it is Sister Aura, and not Cousin Aura—"

"My dear, dear little sisters—" and she hugged them again.

"I was sitting upon his bed," said Letty, "and we were all talking about you when my Lady mamma came. Are mothers kinder than Lady mammas?"

"Was she angry?" asked Aurelia.

"Oh! she frightened me," said Fay. "She said we were pert, forward misses, and we must hold our tongues, for we should be whipped if we ever said you name, Cousin—Sister Aura, again; and she would not let us go to wish Brother Amyas good-bye this morning."

Aurelia's heart could not but leap with joy that her tyrant should have failed in carrying to Bowstead the renunciation of the marriage. Whether Lady Belamour meant it or not, she had made resistance much easier by the company of Faith and Hope, if only for a single night. She gathered from their prattle that their mother, having found that their talk with their brother was all of the one object of his thoughts, had carried them off summarily, and had been since driving about London in search of a school at which to leave them; but they were too young for Queen's Square, and there was no room at another house at which Lady Belamour had applied. She would not take them home, being, of course, afraid of their tongues, and in her perplexity had been reduced to letting them share Aurelia's captivity at least for the night.

What joy it was! They said it was an ugly dark house, but Aurelia's presence was perfect content to them, and theirs was to her comparative felicity, assuring her as they did, through their childish talk, of Sir Amyas's unbroken love and of Mr. Belamour's endeavours to find her. What mattered it that Madge was more offended than ever, and refused to make the slightest exertion for "the Wayland brats at that time of night" without warning. They had enough for supper, and if Aurelia had not, their company was worth much more to her than a full meal. The terrier's rushes after rats were only diversion now, and when all three nestled together in the big bed, the fun was more delightful than ever. Between those soft caressing creatures Aurelia heard no rats, and could well bear some kicks at night, and being drummed awake at some strange hour in the morning.

Mrs. Loveday arrive soon after the little party had gone down stairs. She said the children were to remain until her ladyship had decided where to send them; and she confirmed their report that his Honour was recovering quickly. As soon as he was sufficiently well to leave Bowstead he was to be brought to London, and married to Lady Arabella before going abroad to make the grand tour; and as a true well-wisher, Mrs. Loveday begged Miss Delavie not to hold out when it was of no use, for her Ladyship declared that her contumacy would be the worse for her. Aurelia's garrison was, however, too well reinforced for any vague alarms to shake even her out works, and she only smiled her refusal, as in truth Mrs. Loveday must have expected, for it appeared that she had secured a maid to attend on the prisoners; an extremely deaf woman, who only spoke in the broken imperfect mode of those who have never heard their own voice, deficiencies that made it possible that Madge would keep the peace with her.

Lady Belamour had also found another piece of work for Aurelia. A dark cupboard was opened, revealing shelves piled with bundle of old letters and papers. There was a family tradition that one of the ladies of the Delavie family had been an attendant of Mary of Scotland for a short time, and had received from her a recipe for preserving the complexion and texture of the skin, devised by the French Court perfumer. Nobody had ever seen this precious prescription; but it was presumed to be in the archives of the family, and her ladyship sent word that if Miss Delavie wished to deserve her favour she would put her French to some account and discover it.

A severe undertaking it was. Piles of yellow letters, files of dusty accounts, multitudes of receipts, more than one old will had to be conned it was possible to be certain they were not the nostrum. In the utter solitude, even this occupation would have been valuable, but with the little girls about her, and her own and their property, she had alternative employments enough to make it an effort to apply herself to this.

Why should she? she asked herself more than once; but then came the recollection that if she showed herself willing to obey and gratify my Lady, it might gain her good will, and if Sir Amyas should indeed hold out till Mr. Wayland came home—Her heart beat wildly at the vision of hope.

She worked principally at the letters, after the children had gone to bed, taking a packet up stairs with her, and sitting in the bedroom, deciphering them as best she might by the light of the candles that Loveday had brought her.

Every morning Loveday appeared with supplies, and messages from her Ladyship, that it was time Miss submitted; but she was not at all substantially unkind, and showed increasing interest in her captive, though always impressing on her that her obstinacy was all in vain. My Lady was angered enough at his Honour having got up from his sick bed and gone off to Carminster, and if Miss did not wish to bring her father into trouble she must yield. No, this gladdened rather than startled Aurelia, though her heart sank within her when she was warned that Mr. Wayland had been taken by the corsairs, so that my Lady would have the ball at her own foot now. The term of waiting seemed indefinitely prolonged.

The confinement to the dingy house and courtyard was trying to all three, who had been used to run about in the green park and breezy fields; but Aurelia did her best to keep her little companions happy and busy, and the sense of the insecurity of her tenure of their company aided her the more to meet with good temper and sweetness the various rubs incidental to their captivity in this close warm house in the hottest of summer weather. The pang she had felt at her own fretfulness, when she thought she had lost them, made her guard the more against giving way to impatience if they were troublesome or hard to please. Indeed, she was much more gentle and equable now, in the strength of her resolution, than she had been when uplifted by her position, yet doubtful of its mysteries.

Sundays were the most trying time. The lack of occupation in the small space was wearisome, and Aurelia's heart often echoed the old strains of Tate and Brady,

> *I sigh whene'er my musing thoughts*
> *Those happy days present,*
> *When I with troops of pious friends*
> *Thy temple did frequent.*

She and her charges climbed up to the window above, which happily had a broken pane, tried to identify the chimes of the church bells by the notable nursery rhyme,

> *Oranges and lemons,*
> *Say the bells of St. Clements, &c.,*

watched the church-goers as far as they could see them, and then came down to such reading of the service and other Sunday occupations as Aurelia could devise. On the Sunday of her durance it was such a broiling day that, unable to bear the heat of her parlour, she established herself and her charges in a nook of the court, close under the window, but shaded by the wall, which was covered with an immense bush of overhanging ivy, and by the elm tree in the court. Here she made Fay and Letty say their catechism, and the Psalm she had been teaching them in the week, and then rewarded them with a Bible story, that of Daniel in the den of lions. Once or twice the terrier (whose name she had learnt was Bob) had pricked his ears, and the children had thought there was a noise, but the sparrows in the ivy might be accountable for a great deal, and the little ones were to much wrapped in her tale to be attentive to anything else.

"Then it came true!" said Letty. "His God Whom he trusted did deliver him out of the den of lions?"

"God always does deliver people when they trust Him," said Fay, with gleaming eyes.

"Yes, one way or the other," said Aurelia.

"How do you think He will deliver us?" asked Letty; "for I am sure this is a den, though there are no lions."

"I do not know how," said Aurelia, "but I know He will bear us through it as long as we trust Him and do nothing wrong," and she looked up at the bright sky with hope and strength in her face.

"Hark! what's that?" cried Letty, and Bob leapt up and barked as a great sob became plainly audible, and within the room appeared Mrs. Loveday, her face all over tears, which she was fast wiping away as she rose up from crouching with her head against the window-sill.

"I beg your pardon, ma'am," said she, her voice still broken when she rejoined them, "but I would not interrupt you, so I waited within; and oh, it was so like my poor old mother at home, it quite overcame me! I did not think there was anything so near the angels left on earth."

"Nay, Loveday," said Fay, apprehending the words in a different sense, "the angels are just as near us as ever they were to Daniel, only we cannot see them. Are they not, Cousin Aura?"

"Indeed they are, and we may be as sure that they will shut the lions' mouths," said Aurelia.

"Ah! may they," sighed Loveday, who had by this time mastered her agitation, and remembered that she must discharge herself of her messages, and return hastily to my Lady's toilette.

"I have found the recipe," said Aurelia. "Here it is." And she put into Loveday's hand a yellow letter, bearing the title in scribbled writing, "*Poure Embellire et blanchire la Pel, de part de Maistre Raoul, Parfumeur de la Royne Catherine.*"

CHAPTER XXXII
LIONS

The helmet of darkness Pallas donned,
To hide her presence from the sight of man.
Derby's HOMER.

The next morning Loveday returned with orders from Lady Belamour that Miss Delavie should translate the French recipe, and make a fair copy of it. It was not an easy task, for the MS. was difficult and the French old; whereas Aurelia lived on the modern side of the *Acadamie*, her French was that of Fenelon and Racine.

However, she went to work as best she could in her cool corner, guessing at many of the words by lights derived from *Comenius*, and had just made out that the chief ingredients were pounded pearls and rubies, mixed with white of eggs laid by pullets under a year old, during the waxing of the April moon, when she heard voices chattering in the hall, and a girlish figure appeared in a light cloak and calash, whom Loveday seemed to be guiding, and yet keeping as much repressed as she could.

"Gracious Heavens!" were the first words to be distinguished; "what a frightful old place; enough to make one die of the dismals! I won't live here when I'm married, I promise Sir Amyas! Bless me, is this the wench?"

"Your Ladyship promised to be careful," entreated Loveday, while Aurelia rose, with a graceful gesture of acknowledgment, which, however remained unnoticed, the lady apparently considering herself unseen.

"Who are these little girls?" asked she, in a giggling whisper. "Little Waylands? Then it is true," she cried, with a peal of shrill laughter. "There are three of them, only Lady Belamour shuts them up like kittens—I wonder she did not. Oh, what sport! Won't I tease her now that I know her secret!"

"Your ladyship!" intreated Loveday in distress in an audible aside, "you will undo me." Then coming forward, she said, "You did not expect me at this hour, madam; but if your French copy be finished, my Lady would like to have it at once."

"I have written it out once as well as I could," said Aurelia, "but I have not translated it; I will find the copy."

She rose and found the stranger full before her in the doorway, gazing at her with an enormous pair of sloe-black eyes, under heavy inky brows, set in a hard, red-complexioned face. She burst into a loud, hoydenish laugh as Loveday tried to stammer something about a friend of her own.

"Never mind, the murder's out, good Mrs. Abigail," she cried, "it is me. I was determined to see the wench that has made such a fool of young Belamour. I vow I can't guess what he means by it. Why, you are a poor pale tallow-candle, without a bit of colour in your face. Look at me! Shall you ever have such a complexion as mine, with ever so much rouge?"

"I think not," said Aurelia, with one look at the peony face.

"Do you know who I am, miss? I am the Lady Bella Mar. The Countess of Aresfield is my mamma. I shall have Battlefield when she dies, and twenty thousand pounds on my wedding day. The Earl of Aresfield and Colonel Mar are my brothers, and a wretched little country girl like you is not to come between me and what my mamma has fixed for me; so you must give it up at once, for you see he belongs to me."

"Not yet, madam," said Aurelia.

"What do you say? Do you pretend that your masquerade was worth a button?"

"That is not my part to decide," said Aurelia. "I am bound by it, and have no power to break it."

"You mean the lawyers! Bless you, they will never give it to you against me! You'd best give it up at once, and if you want a husband, my mamma has one ready for you."

"I thank her ladyship," said Aurelia, with simple dignity, "but I will not give her the trouble."

She glanced at her wedding ring, and so did Lady Belle, who screamed, "You've the impudence to wear that! Give it to me."

"I cannot," repeated Aurelia.

"You cannot, you insolent, vulgar, low" —

"Hush! hush, my lady," entreated Loveday. "Come away, I beg of your ladyship!"

"Not till I have made that impudent hussy give me that ring," cried Belle, stamping violently. "What's that you say?"

"That your ladyship asks what is impossible," said Aurelia, firmly.

"Take that then, insolent minx!" cried the girl, flying forward and violently slapping Aurelia's soft cheeks, and making a snatch at her hair.

Loveday screamed, Letty cried, but Fidelia and Bob both rushed forward to Aurelia's defence, one with her little fists clenched, beating Lady Belle back, the other tearing at her skirts with his teeth. At that moment a man's step was heard, and a tall, powerful officer was among them, uttering a fierce imprecation. "You little vixen, at your tricks again," he said, taking Belle by the waist, while she kicked and screamed in vain. She was like an angry cat in his arms. "Be quiet, Belle," he said, backing into the sitting-room. "Let Loveday compose your dress. Recover your senses and I shall take you home: I wish it was to the whipping you deserve."

He thrust her in, waved aside Loveday's excuses about her ladyship not being denied, and stood with his back to the door as she bounced shrieking against it from within.

"I fear this little devil has hurt you, madam," he said.

"Not at all, I thank you, sire." said Aurelia, though one side of her face still tingled.

"She made at you like a little game-cock," he said. "I am glad I was in time. I followed when I found she had slipped away from Lady Belamour's, knowing that her curiosity is only equalled by her spite. By Jove, it is well that her nails did not touch that angel face!"

Aurelia could only curtsey and thank him, hoping within herself that Lady Belle would soon recover, and wondering how he had let himself in. There was something in his manner of examining her with his eyes that made her supremely uncomfortable. He uttered fashionable expletives of admiration under his breath, and she turned aside in displeasure, bending down to Fidelia. He went on, "You must be devilishly moped in this dungeon of a place! Cannot we contrive something better?"

"Thank you, sir, I have no complaint to make. Permit me to see whether the Lady Arabella is better."

"I advise you not. Those orbs are too soft and sparkling to be exposed to her talons. 'Pon my honour, I pity young Belamour. But there is no help for it, and such charms ought not to be wasted in solitude on his account. These young lads are as fickle as the weather-cock, and have half-a-dozen fancies in as many weeks. Come now, make me your friend, and we will hit on some device for delivering the enchanted princess from her durance vile."

"Thank you, sir, I promised Lady Belamour to make no attempt to escape."

At that moment out burst Lady Belle, shouting with laughter: "Ho! ho! Have I caught you, brother, gallanting away with Miss? What will my lady say? Pretty doings!"

She had no time for more. Her brother fiercely laid hold of her, and bore her away with a peremptory violence that she could not resist, and only turning at the hall door to make one magnificent bow.

Loveday was obliged to follow, and the children were left clinging to Aurelia and declaring that the dreadful young lady was as bad as the lions; while Aurelia, glowing with shame and resentment at what she felt as insults, had a misgiving that her protector had been the worse lion of the two.

She had no explanation of the invasion till the next morning, when Loveday appeared full of excuses and apologies. From the fact of Lady Aresfield's carriage having been used on Aurelia's arrival, her imprisonment was known, and Lady Belle, spending a holiday at Lady Belamour's, had besieged Loveday with entreaties to take her to see her rival. As the waiting-woman said, for fear of the young lady's violent temper, but more probably in consideration of her bribes, she had yielded, hoping that Lady Belle would be satisfied with a view from the window, herself unseen. However, from that moment all had been taken out of the hands of Loveday, and she verily believed the Colonel had made following his sister an excuse for catching a sight of Miss Delavie, for he had been monstrously smitten even with the glimpse he had had of her in the carriage. And now, as his sister had cut short what he had to say, he had written her a billet. And Loveday held out a perfumed letter.

Aurelia's eyes flashed, and she drew herself up: "You forget, Loveday, I promised to receive no letters!"

"Bless me, ma'am, they, that are treated as my lady treats you, are not bound to be so particular as that."

"O fie, Loveday," said Aurelia earnestly, "you have been so kind, that I thought you would be faithful. This is not being faithful to your lady, nor to me."

"It is only from my wish to serve you, ma'am," said Loveday in her fawning voice. "How can I bear to see a beautiful young lady like you, that ought to be the star of all the court, mewed up here for the sake of a young giddy pate like his Honour, when there's one of the first gentlemen in the land ready to be at your feet?"

"For shame! for shame!" exclaimed Aurelia, crimson already. "You know I am married."

"And you will not take the letter, nor see what the poor gentleman means? May be he wants to reconcile you with my lady, and he has power with her."

Aurelia took the letter, and, strong paper though it was, tore it across and across till it was all in fragments, no bigger than daisy flowers. "There," she said, "you may tell him what I have done to his letter."

Loveday stared for a minute, then exclaimed, "You are in the right, my dear lady. Oh, I am a wretch—a wretch—" and she went away sobbing.

Aurelia hoped the matter was ended. It had given her a terrible feeling of insecurity, but she found to her relief that Madge was really more trustworthy than Loveday. She overheard from the court a conversation at the back door in which Madge was strenuously refusing admission to some one who was both threatening and bribing her, all in vain; but she was only beginning to breathe freely when Loveday brought, not another letter, but what was less easy to stop, a personal message from "that poor gentleman."

"Loveday, after what you said yesterday, how can you be so—wicked?" said Aurelia.

"Indeed, miss, 'tis only as your true well-wisher."

Aurelia turned away to leave the room.

"Yes, it is, ma'am! On my bended knees I will swear it," cried Loveday, throwing herself on them and catching her dress. "It is because I know my lady has worse in store for you!"

"Nothing can be worse than wrong-doing," said Aurelia.

"Ah! you don't know. Now, listen, one moment. I would not—indeed I would not—if I did not know that he meant true and honourable—as he does, indeed he does. He is madder after you then ever he was for my lady, for he says you have all her beauty, and freshness and simplicity besides. He is raving. And you should never leave me, indeed you should not, miss, if you slipped out after me in Deb's muffler—and we'd go to the Fleet. I have got a cousin there, poor fellow—he is always in trouble, but he is a real true parson notwithstanding, and I'd never leave your side till the knot was tied fast. Then you would laugh at my lady, and be one of the first ladies in the land, for my Lord Aresfield is half a fool, and can't live long, and when you are a countess you will remember your poor Loveday."

"Let me go. You have said too much to a married woman," said Aurelia, and as the maid began the old demonstrations of the invalidity of the marriage, and the folly of adhering to it when nobody knew where his honour was gone, she said resolutely, "I shall write to Lady Belamour to send me a more trustworthy messenger."

On this Loveday fairly fell on the floor, grovelling in her wild entreaty that my Lady might hear nothing of this, declaring that it was not so much for the sake of the consequences to herself as to the young lady, for there was no guessing what my lady might not be capable of if she guessed at Colonel Mar's admiration of her prisoner. Aurelia, frightened at her violence, finally promised not to appeal to her ladyship as long as Loveday abstained from transmitting his messages, but on the least attempt on her part to refer to him, a complaint should certainly be made to my lady.

"Very well, madam," said Loveday, wiping her eyes. "I only hope it will not be the worse for you in the end, and that you will not wish you had listened to poor Loveday's advice."

"I can never wish to have done what I know to be a great sin," said Aurelia gravely.

"Ah! you little know!" said Loveday, shaking her head sadly and ominously.

Something brought to Aurelia's lips what she had been teaching the children last Sunday, and she answered,

"My God, in Whom I have trusted, is able to deliver me out of the mouth of lions, and He will deliver me out of thy hand."

"Oh! if ever there were one whom He should deliver!" broke out Loveday, and again she went away weeping bitterly.

Aurelia could not guess what the danger the woman threatened could be; so many had been mentioned as possible. A forcible marriage, incarceration in some lonely country place, a vague threat of being taken beyond seas to the plantation—all these had been mentioned; but she was far more afraid of Colonel Mar forcing his way in and carrying her off, and this kept her constantly in a state of nervous watchfulness, always listening by day and hardly able to sleep by night.

Once she had a terrible alarm, on a Sunday. Letty came rushing to her, declaring that Jumbo, dear Jumbo, and a gentleman were in the front court. Was it really Jumbo? Come and see! No, she durst not, and Fay almost instantly declared that Madge had shut them out. The children both insisted that Jumbo it was, but Aurelia would not believe that it could be anything but an attempt of her enemies. She interrogated Madge, who had grown into a certain liking for one so submissive and inoffensive. Madge shook her head, could not guess how such folks had got into the court, was sure they were after no good, and declared that my Lady should hear of all the strange doings, and the letters that had been left with her. Oh, no, she knew better than to give them, but my Lady should see them.

CHAPTER XXXIII
THE COSMETIC

But one more task I charge thee with to-day,
For unto Proserpine then take thy way,
And give this golden casket to her hands.
MORRIS.

Late on that Sunday afternoon, a muffled and masked figure came through the house into the court behind, and after the first shock Aurelia was relieved to see that it was too tall, and moved too gracefully, to belong to Loveday.

"Why, child, what a colour you have!" said Lady Belamour, taking off her mask. "You need no aids to nature at your happy age. That is right, children," as they curtsied and kissed her hand. "Go into the house, I wish to speak with your cousin."

Lady Belamour's unfailing self-command gave her such dignity that she seemed truly a grand and majestic dame dispensing justice, and the gentle, shrinking Aurelia like a culprit on trial before her.

"You have been here a month, Aurelia Delavie. Have you come to your senses, and are you ready to sign this paper?"

"No, madam, I cannot."

"Silly fly; you are as bent as ever on remaining in the web in which a madman and a foolish boy have involved you?"

"I cannot help it, madam."

"Oh! I thought," and her voice became harshly clear, though so low, "that you might have other schemes, and be spreading your toils at higher game."

"Certainly not, madam."

"Your colour shows that you understand, in spite of all your pretences."

"I have never used any pretences, my lady," said Aurelia, looking up in her face with clear innocent eyes.

"You have had no visitors? None!"

"None, madam, except once when the Lady Arabella Mar forced her way in, out of curiosity, I believe, and her brother followed to take her away."

"Her brother? You saw him?" Each word came out edged like a knife from between her nearly closed lips.

"Yes, madam."

"How often?"

"That once."

"That has not hindered a traffic in letters."

"Not on my side, madam. I tore to fragments unread the only one that I received. He had no right to send it!"

"Certainly not. You judge discreetly, Miss Delavie. In fact you are too transcendent a paragon to be retained here." Then, biting her lip, as if the bitter phrase had escaped unawares, she smiled blandly and said, "My good girl, you have merited to be returned to your friends. You may pack your mails and those of the children!"

Aurelia shuddered with gladness, but Lady Belamour checked her thanks by continuing, "One service you must first do for me. My perfumer is at a loss to understand your translation of the recipe for Queen Mary's wash. I wish you to read and explain it to her."

"Certainly, madam."

"She lives near Greenwich Park," continued Lady Belamour, "and as I would not have the secret get abroad, I shall send a wherry to take you to the place early to-morrow morning. Can you be ready by eight o'clock?"

Aurelia readily promised, her heart bounding at the notion of a voyage down the river after her long imprisonment and at the promise of liberty! She thought her husband must still be true to her, since my lady would have been the first to inform her of his defection, and as long as she had her ring and her certificate, she could feel little doubt that her father would be able to establish her claims. And oh! to be with him and Betty once more!

She was ready in good time, and had spent her leisure in packing. When Loveday appeared, she was greeted with a petition that the two little girls might accompany her; but this was refused at once, and the waiting-maid added in her caressing, consoling tone that Mrs. Dove was coming with their little brother and sister to take them a drive into the country. They skipped about with glee, following Aurelia to the door of the court, and promising her posies of honeysuckles and roses, and she left her dear love with them for Amoret and Nurse Dove.

At the door was a sedan chair, in which Aurelia was carried to some broad stone stairs, beside which lay a smartly-painted, trim-looking boat with four stout oarsmen. She was handed into the stern, Loveday sitting opposite to her. The woman was unusually silent, and could hardly be roused to reply to Aurelia's eager questions as she passed the gardens of Lincoln's Inn, saw St. Paul's rise above her, shot beneath the arch of London Bridge, and beheld the massive walls of the Tower with its low-browed arches opening above their steps. Whenever a scarlet uniform came in view, how the girl's eyes strained after it, thinking of one impossible, improbable chance of a recognition! Once or twice she thought of a far more terrible chance, and wondered whether Lady Belamour knew how little confidence could be placed in Loveday; but she was sure that their expedition was my lady's own device, and the fresh air and motion, with all the new scenes, were so delightful to her that she could not dwell on any alarms.

On, on, Redriffe, as the watermen named Rotherhithe, was on one bank, the marshes of the Isle of Dogs were gay with white cotton-grass and red rattle on the other. Then came the wharves and building yards of Deptford, and beyond them rose the trees of Greenwich Park, while the river below exhibited a forest of masts. The boat stopped at a landing-place to a little garden, with a sanded path, between herbs and flowers. "This is Mistress Darke's," said Loveday, and as a little dwarfish lad came to the gate, she said, "We would speak with your mistress."

"On your own part?'

"From the great lady in Hanover Square."

The lad came down to assist in their landing, and took them up the path to a little cupboard of a room, scented with a compound of every imaginable perfume. Bottles of every sort of essence, pomade, and cosmetic were ranged on shelves, or within glass doors, interspersed with masks, boxes for patches, bunches of false hair, powder puffs, curling-irons, and rare feathers. An alembic [a device used in distillation—D.L.] was in the fireplace, and pen and ink, in a strangely-shaped standish, were on the table. Altogether there was something uncanny about the look and air of the room which made Aurelia tremble, especially as she perceived that Loveday was both frightened and distressed.

The mistress of the establishment speedily appeared. She had been a splendid Jewish beauty, and still in middle age, had great owl-like eyes, and a complexion that did her credit to her arts; but there was something indescribably repulsive in her fawning, deferential curtsey, as she said, in a flattering tone, with a slightly foreign accent, "The pretty lady is come, as our noble dame promised, to explain to the poor Cora Darke the great queen's secret! Ah! how good it is to have learning. What would not my clients give for such a skin as hers! And I have many more, and greater than you would think, come to poor Cora's cottage. There was a countess here but yesterday to ask how to blanch the complexion of miladi her daughter, who is about to wed a young baronet, beautiful as Love. Bah! I might as well try to whiten a clove gillyflower! Yet what has not nature done for this lovely miss?"

"Shall I read you the paper?" said Aurelia, longing to end this part of the affair.

"Be seated, fair and gracious lady."

Aurelia tried to wave aside a chair, but Mrs. Darke, on the plea of looking over the words as she read, got her down upon a low couch, putting her own stout person and hooked face in unpleasant proximity, while she asked questions, and Aurelia mentioned her own conjectures on the obsolete French of the recipe, while she perceived, to her alarm, that the woman understood the technical terms much better than she did, and that her ignorance could have been only an excuse.

At last it was finished, and she rose, saying it was time to return to the boat.

"Nay, madam, that cannot be yet," said Loveday; "the watermen are gone to rest and dine, and we must wait for the tide to shoot the bridge."

"Then pray let us go out and walk in Greenwich Park," exclaimed Aurelia, longing to escape from this den.

"The sweet young lady will take something in the meantime?" said Mrs. Darke.

"I thank you, I have breakfasted," said Aurelia.

"My Lady intended us to eat here," said Loveday in an undertone to her young lady, as their hostess bustled out. "She will make it good to Mrs. Darke."

"I had rather go to the inn—I have money—or sit in the park," she added as Loveday looked as if going to the inn were an improper proposal. "Could we not buy a loaf and eat in the park? I should like it so much better."

"One cup of coffee," said Mrs. Darke, entering; "the excellent Mocha that I get from the Turkey captains."

She set down on a small table a wonderful cup of Eastern porcelain, and some little sugared cakes, and Aurelia, not to be utterly ungracious, tasted one, and began on the coffee, which was so hot that it had to be taken slowly. As she sipped a soothing drowsiness came over her, which at first was accounted for by the warm room after her row on the river; but it gained upon her, and instead of setting out for her walk she fell sound asleep in the corner of the couch.

"It has worked. It is well," said Mrs. Darke, lifting the girl's feet on the couch, and producing a large pair of scissors.

Loveday could not repress a little shriek.

"Hush!" as the woman untied the black silk hood, drew it gently off, and then undid the ribbon that confined the victim's abundant tresses. "Bah! it will be grown by the time she arrives, and if not so long as present, what will they know of it? It will be the more agreeable surprise! Here, put yonder cloth under her head while I hold it up."

"I cannot," sobbed Loveday. "This is too much. I never would have entered my Lady's service if I had known I was to be set to such as this."

"Come, come, Grace Loveday, I know too much of you for you to come the Presician over me."

"Such a sweet innocent! So tender-hearted and civil too."

"Bless you, woman, you don't know what's good for her! She will be a very queen over the black slaves on the Indies. Captain Karen will tell you how the wenches thank him for having brought 'em out. They could never do any good here, you know, poor lasses; but out there, where white women are scarce, they are ready to worship the very ground they tread upon."

"I tell you she ain't one of that sort. She is a young lady of birth, a cousin of my Lady's own, as innocent as a babe, and there are two gentlemen, if not ⁓ three, a dying for her."

"I lay you anything not one of 'em is worth old Mr. Van Draagen, who turns his thousands every month. 'Send me out a lady lass,' says he, 'one that will do me credit with the governor's lady.' Why she will have an estate as big as from here to Dover, and slaves to wait on her, so as she need never stoop to pick up her glove. He has been married twice before, and his last used to send orders for the best brocades in London. He stuck at no expense. The Queen has not finer gowns!"

"But to think of the poor child's waking up out at sea."

"Oh! Mrs. Karen will let her know she may think herself well off. I never let 'em go unless there's a married woman aboard to take charge of them, and that's why I kept your lady waiting till the *Red Cloud* was ready to sail. You may tell her Ladyship she could not have a better berth, and she'll want for nothing. I know what is due to the real quality, and I've put aboard all the toilette, and linen, and dresses as was bespoke for the last Mrs. Van Draagen, and there's a civil spoken wench aboard, what will wait on her for a consideration."

"Nay, but mistress," said Loveday, whispering: "I know those that would give more than you will ever get from my Lady if they found her safe here."

"Of course there are, or she would not be here now," said Mrs. Darke, with a horrid grin; "but that won't do, my lass. A lady that's afraid of exposure will pay you, if she pawns her last diamond, but a gentleman— why, he gets sick of his fancy, and snaps his fingers at them that helped him!" Then, looking keenly at Loveday, "You've not been playing me false, eh?"

"O no, no," hastily exclaimed Loveday, cowering at the malignant look.

"If so be you have, Grace Loveday, two can play at that game," said Mrs. Darke composedly. "There, I have left her enough to turn back. What hair it is! Feel the weight of it! There's not another head of the mouse-colour to match your Lady's in the kingdom," she added, smoothing out the severed tresses with the satisfaction of a connoisseur. "No wonder madame could not let this be wasted on the plantations, when you and I and M. le Griseur know her own hair is getting thinner than she would wish a certain Colonel to guess. There! the pretty dear, what a baby she looks! I will tie her on a cowl, lest she should take cold on the river. See these rings. Did you Lady give no charge about them?"

"I had forgot!" said the waiting-woman, confused; "she charged me to bring them back, old family jewels, she said, that must not be carried off to foreign parts; but I cannot, cannot do it. To rob that pretty creature in her sleep."

"Never fear. She'll soon have a store much finer than these! You fool, I tell you she will not wake these six or eight hours. Afraid? There, I'll do it! Ho! A ruby? A love-token, I wager; and what's this? A carved Cupid. I could turn a pretty penny by that, when your lady finds it convenient, and her luck at play goes against her. Eh! is this a wedding-ring? Best take that off; Mr. Van Draagen might not understand it, you see. Here they are. Have you a patch-box handy for them in your pocket? Why what ails the woman? You may thank your stars there's some one here with her wits about her! None of your whimpering, I say, her comes Captain Karen."

Two seafaring men here came up the garden path, the foremost small and dapper, with a ready address and astute countenance. "All right, Mother Darkness, is our consignment ready? Aye, aye! And the freight?"

"This lady has it," said Mrs. Darke, pointing to Loveday; "I have been telling her she need have no fears for her young kinswoman in your hands, Captain."

He swore a round oath to that effect, and looking at the sleeping maiden, again swore that she was the choicest piece of goods ever confided to him, and that he knew better than let such an article arrive damaged. Mr. Van Draagen ought to come down handsomely for such an extra fine sample; but in the meantime he accepted the rouleau of guineas that Loveday handed to him, the proceeds, as she told Mrs. Darke, of my Lady's winnings last night at loo.

All was ready. Poor Aurelia was swathed from head to foot in a large mantle, like the chrysalis whose name she bore, the two sailors took her up between them, carried her to their boat, and laid her along in the stern. Then they pushed off and rowed down the river. Loveday looked up and looked down, then sank on the steps, convulsed with grief, sobbing bitterly. "She said He could deliver her from the mouth of lions! And He has not," she murmured under her breath, in utter misery and hopelessness.

CHAPTER XXXIV
DOWN THE RIVER

The lioness, ye may move her
To give o'er her prey,
But ye'll ne'er stop a lover,
He will find out the way.

Elizabeth Delavie and her little brother were standing in the bay window of their hotel, gazing eagerly along the street in hopes of seeing the Major return, when Sir Amyas was seen riding hastily up on his charger, in full accoutrements, with a soldier following. In another moment he had dashed up stairs, and saying, "Sister, read that!" put into Betty's hand a slip of paper on which was written in pencil—

"If Sir A. B. would not have his true love kidnapped to the plantations, he had best keep watch on the river gate of Mistress Darke's garden at Greenwich. No time to lose."

"Who brought you this?" demanded Betty, as well as she could speak for horror.

"My mother's little negro boy, Syphax. He says Mrs. Loveday, her waiting-woman, gave it to him privately on the stairs, as she was about to get into a sedan, telling him I would give him a crown if he gave it me as I came off parade."

"Noon! Is there time?"

"Barely, but there shall be time. There is no time to seek your father."

"No, but I must come with you."

"The water is the quickest way. There are stairs near. I'll send my fellow to secure a boat."

"I will be ready instantly, while you tell your uncle. It might be better if he came."

Sir Amyas flew to his uncle's door, but found him gone out, and, in too great haste to inquire further, came down again to find Betty in cloak and hood. He gave her his arm, and, Eugene trotting after them, they hurried to the nearest stairs, remembering in dire confirmation what Betty had heard from the school-girl. Both had heard reports that young women were sometimes thus deported to become wives to the planters in the southern colonies or the West Indies, but that such a destiny should be intended for their own Aurelia, and by Lady Belamour, was scarcely credible. Doubts rushed over Betty, but she remembered what the school-girl had said of the captive being sent beyond seas; and at any rate, she must risk the expedition being futile when such issues hung upon it. And if they failed to meet her father, she felt that her presence might prevail when the undefined rights of so mere a lad as her companion might be disregarded.

His soldier servant had secured a boat, and they rapidly descended to the river; Sir Amyas silent between suspense, dismay and shame for his mother, and Betty trying to keep Eugene quiet by hurried answers to his eager questions about all he saw. They had to get out at London Bridge, and take a fresh boat on the other side, a much larger one, with two oarsmen, and a grizzled old coxswain, with a pleasant honest countenance, who presently relieved Betty of all necessity of attending to, or answering, Eugene's chatter.

"Do you know where this garden is?" said she, leaning across to Sir Amyas, who had engaged the boat to go to Greenwich.

He started as if it were a new and sudden thought, and turning to the steersman demanded whether he knew Mrs. Darke's garden.

The old man gave a kind of grunt, and eyed the trio interrogatively, the young officer with his fresh, innocent, boyish face and brilliant undisguised uniform, the handsome child, the lady neither young, gay, nor beautiful, but unmistakeably a decorous gentlewoman.

"Do you know Mrs. Darke's?" repeated Sir Amyas.

"Aye, do I? Mayhap I know more about the place than you do."

There was that about his face that moved Betty and the young man to look at one another, and the former said, "She has had to do with—evil doings?"

"You may say that, ma'am."

"Then," they cried in one breath, "you will help us!" And in a very few words Betty explained their fears for her young sister, and asked whether he thought the warning possible.

"I've heard tell of such things!" said the old man between his teeth, "and Mother Darkness is one to do 'em. Help you to bring back the poor young lass? That we will, if we have to break down the door with our fists. And who is this young spark? Her brother or her sweetheart?"

"Her husband!" said Sir Amyas. "Her husband from whom she has been cruelly spirited away. Aid me to bring her back, my good fellow, and nothing would be too much to reward you."

"Aye, aye, captain, Jem Green's not the man to see an English girl handed over to they slave-driving, outlandish chaps. But I say, I wish you'd got a cloak or summat to put over that scarlet and gold of yourn. It's a regular flag to put the old witch on her guard."

On that summer's day, however, no cloak was at hand. They went down the river very rapidly, for the tide was running out and at length Jem Green pointed out the neat little garden. On the step sat a woman, apparently weeping bitterly. Could it be the object of their search? No, but as they came nearer, and she was roused so as to catch sight of the scarlet coat, she beckoned and gesticulated with all her might; and as they approached Sir Amyas recognised her as his mother's maid.

"You will be in time yet," she cried breathlessly. "Oh! take me in, or you won't know the ship!"

So eager and terrified was she, that but for the old steersman's peremptory steadiness, her own life and theirs would have been in much peril, but she was safely seated at last, gasping out, "The *Red Cloud*, Captain Karen. They've been gone these ten minutes."

"Aye, aye," gruffly responded Green, and the oars moved rapidly, while Loveday with another sob cried, "Oh! sir, I thought you would never come!"

"You sent the warning?"

Yes, sir, I knew nothing till the morning, when my Lady called me up. I lie in her room, you know. She had given orders, and I was to take the sweet lady and go down the river with her to Mrs. Darke, the perfuming woman my Lady has dealings with about here hair and complexion. There I was to stay with her till—till this same sea-captain was to come and carry her off where she would give no more trouble. Oh, sir, it was too much—and my Lady knew it, for she had tied my hands so that I had but a moment to scribble down that scrip, and bid Syphax take it to you. The dear lady! she said, 'her God could deliver her out of the mouth of the lion,' and I could not believe it! I thought it too late!"

"How can we thank you," began Betty; but she was choked by intense anxiety, and Jem Green broke in with an inquiry where the ship was bound for. Loveday only had a general impression of the West Indies, and believed that the poor lady's destined spouse was a tobacconist, and as the boat was soon among a forest of shipping where it could not proceed so fast, Green had to inquire of neighbouring mariners where the *Red Cloud* was lying.

"The *Red Cloud*, Karen, weighs anchor for Carolina at flood tide to-night. Shipper just going aboard," they were told.

Their speed had been so rapid that they were in time to see the boat alongside, and preparations being made to draw up some one or something on board. "Oh! that is she!" cried Loveday in great agitation. "They've drugged her. No harm done. She don't know it. But it is she!"

Sir Amyas, with a voice of thunder, called out, "Halt, villain," at the same moment as Green shouted "Avast there, mate!" And their boat came dashing up alongside.

"Yield me up that lady instantly, fellow!" cried Sir Amyas, with his sword half drawn.

"And who are you, I should like to know," returned Karen, coolly, "swaggering at an honest man taking his freight and passengers aboard?"

"I'll soon show you!"

"Hush, sir," said Green, who had caught sight of pistols and cutlasses, "let me speak a moment. Look you here, skipper, this young gentleman and lady have right on their side. This is her sister, and he is her husband. They are people of condition, as you see."

"All's one to me on the broad seas."

"That may be," said Green, "but you see you can't weigh anchor these three hours or more; and what's to hinder the young captain here from swearing against you before a magistrate, and getting your vessel searched, eh?"

"I've no objection to hear reason if I'm spoke to reasonable," said Karen, sulkily; "but I'll not be bullied like a highwayman, when I've my consignment regularly made out, and the freight down in hand, square."

"You may keep your accursed passage-money and welcome," cried Sir Amyas, "so you'll only give me my wife!"

"Show him the certificate," whispered Betty.

Sir Amyas had it ready, and he read it loud enough for all on the Thames to hear. Karen gave a sneering little laugh. "What's that to me? My passenger here has her berth taken in the name of Ann Davis."

"Like enough," said Loveday, "but you remember me, captain, and I swear that this poor young lady is what his Honour Sir Amyas say. He is a generous young gentleman, and will make it up to you if you are at any loss in the matter."

"A hundred times over!" exclaimed Amyas hotly.

"Hardly that," said Karen. "Van Draagen might have been good for a round hundred if he'd been pleased with the commission."

"I'll give you and order—" began Sir Amyas.

"What have you got about you, sir?" interrupted Karen. "I fancy hard cash better than your orders."

The youth pulled out his purse. There was only a guinea or two and some silver. "One does not go out to parade with much money about one," he said, with a trembling endeavour for a smile, "but if you would send up to my quarters in Whitehall Barracks—-"

"Never mind, sir," said Karen, graciously. "I see you are in earnest, and I'll put up with the loss rather than stand in the light of a couple of true lovers. Here, Jack, lend a hand, and we'll hoist the young woman over. She's quiet enough, thanks to Mother Darkness."

The sudden change in tone might perhaps be owing to the skipper's attention having been called by a sign from one of his men to a boat coming up from Woolwich, rowed by men of the Royal navy, who were certain to take part with an officer; but Sir Amyas and Betty were only intent on receiving the inanimate form wrapped up in its mantle. What a meeting it was for Betty, and yet what joy to have her at all! They laid her with her head in her sister's lap, and Sir Amyas hung over her, clasping one of the limp gloved hands, while Eugene called "Aura, Aura," and would have impetuously kissed her awake, but Loveday caught hold of him. "Do not, do not, for pity's sake, little master," she said; "the potion will do her no harm if you let her sleep it off, but she may not know you if you waken her before the time."

"Wretch, what have you given her?" cried Sir Amyas.

"It was not me, sir, it was Mrs. Darke, in a cup of coffee. She vowed it would do no hurt if only she was let to sleep six or eight hours. And see what a misery it has saved her from!"

"That is true," said Betty. "Indeed I believe this is a healthy sleep. See how gently she breathes, how soft and natural her colour is, how cool and fresh her cheek is. I cannot believe there is serious harm done."

"How soon can we reach a physician?" asked Sir Amyas, still anxiously, of the coxswain.

"I can't rightly say, sir," replied he; "but never you fear. They wouldn't do aught to damage such as she."

Patience must perforce be exercised as, now against the tide and the stream, the wherry worked its way back. Once there was a little stir; Sir Amyas instantly hovered over Aurelia, and clasped her hand with a cry of "My dearest life!" The long dark eyelashes slowly rose, the eyes looked up for one moment from his face to her sister's, and then to her brother's, but the lids sank as if weighed down, and with a murmur, "Oh, don't wake me," she turned her face around on Betty's lap and slept again.

"Poor darling, she thinks it a dream," said Betty. "Eugene, do not. Sir, I entreat! Brother, yes I *will* call you so if you will only let her alone! See how happy and peaceful her dear face is! Do not rouse her into terror and bewilderment."

"If I only were sure she was safe," he sighed, hanging over, with an intensity of affection and anxiety that brought a dew even to the old steersman's eyes; and he kindly engrossed Eugene by telling about the places they passed, and setting him to watch the smart crew of the boat from the Royal Arsenal at Woolwich, which was gaining on them.

Meanwhile the others interrogated Loveday, who told them of the pretext on which Lady Belamour had sent her captive down to Mrs. Darke's. No one save herself had, in my Lady's household, she said, an idea of where the young lady was, Lady Belamour having employed only hired porters except on that night when Lady Aresfield's carriage brought her. This had led to the captivity being know to Lady Belle and her brother, and Loveday had no doubt that it was the discovery of their being aware of it, as well as Jumbo's appearance in the court, that had made her mistress finally decide on this frightful mode of ridding herself of the poor girl. The maid was as adroit a dissembler as her mistress, and she held her peace as to her own part in forwarding Colonel Mar's suit, whether her lady guessed it or not, but she owned with floods of tears how the sight of the young lady's meek and dutiful submission, her quiet trust, and her sweet, simple teaching of the children, had wakened into life again a conscience long dead to all good, and made it impossible to her to carry out this last wicked commission without an attempt to save the creature whom she had learnt to reverence as a saint. Most likely her scruples had been suspected by her mistress, for there had been an endeavour to put it out of her power to give any warning to the victim. Yet after all, the waiting-maid had been too adroit for the lady, or, as she fully owned, Aurelia's firm trust had not been baulked, and deliverance from the lions had come.

CHAPTER XXXV
THE RETURN

And now the glorious artist, ere he yet
Had reached the Lemnian Isle, limping, returned;
With aching heart he sought his home.
Odyssey—COWPER.

How were they to get the slumbering maiden home? That was the next question. Loveday advised carrying her direct to her old prison, where she would wake without alarm; but Sir Amyas shuddered at the notion, and Betty said she *could* not take her again into a house of Lady Belamour's.

The watermen, who were enthusiastic in the cause, which they understood as that of one young sweetheart rescued by the other, declared that they would carry the sweet lady between them on the cushions of their boat, laid on stretchers; and as they knew of a land-place near the *Royal York*, with no need of crossing any great thoroughfare, Betty thought this the best chance of taking her sister home without a shock.

The boat from Woolwich had shot London Bridge immediately after them, and stopped at the stairs nearest that where they landed; and just as Sir Amyas, with an exclamation of annoyance at his unserviceable arm, had resigned Aurelia to be lifted on to her temporary litter, a hand was laid on his shoulder, a voice said "Amyas, what means this?" and he found himself face to face with a small, keen-visaged, pale man, with thick grizzled brows overhanging searching dark grey eyes, shaded by a great Spanish hat.

"Sir! oh sir, is it you?" he cried, breathlessly; "now all will be well!"

"I am very glad you think so, Amyas," was the grave answer; "for all this has a strange appearance."

"It is my dearest wife, sir, my wife, whom I have just recovered after—Oh, say, sir, if you think all is well with her, and it is only a harmless sleeping potion. Sister—Betty—this is my good father, Mr. Wayland. He is as good as a physician. Let him see my sweetest life."

Mr. Wayland bent over the slumbering figure still in the bottom of the boat, heard what could be told of the draught by Loveday, whom he recognized as his wife's attendant, and feeling Aurelia's pulse, said, "I should not think there was need for fear. To the outward eye she is a model of sleeping innocence." "Well you may say so," and "She is indeed," broke from the baronet and the waiting-maid at the same instant; but Mr. Wayland heeded them little as he impatiently asked, "Where and how is your mother, Amyas?"

"In health sir, at home, I suppose," said Sir Amyas; "but oh, sir, hear me, before you see her."

"I must, if you walk with me," said Mr. Wayland, turning for a moment to bid his servant reward and dismiss the boat's crew, and see to the transport of his luggage; and in the meantime Aurelia was lifted by her bearers.

Sir Amyas again uttered a rejoicing, "We feared you were in the hands of the pirates, sir."

"So I was; but the governor of Gibraltar obtained my release, and was good enough to send me home direct in a vessel on the king's service," said Mr. Wayland, taking the arm his stepson offered to assist his lameness. "Now for your explanation, Amyas; only let me hear first that my babes are well."

"Yes, sir, all well. You had my letter?"

"Telling of that strange disguised wedding? I had, the very day I was captured."

By the time they had come to the place where their ways parted, Mr. Wayland had heard enough to be so perplexed and distressed that he knew not that he had been drawn out of the way to Hanover Square, till at the entrance of the *Royal York*, they found Betty asseverating to the landlady that she was bringing no case of small pox into the house; and showing, as a passport of admittance, two little dents on the white wrist and temple.

At that instant the sound brought Major Delavie hurrying from his sitting-room at his best speed. There was a look of horror on his face as he saw his daughter's senseless condition, but Betty sprang to his side to prevent his wakening her, and Aurelia was safely carried up stairs and laid upon her sister's bed, still sleeping, while Betty and Loveday unloosed her clothes. Her bearers were sent for refreshment to the bar, and the gentlemen stood looking on one another in the sitting-room, Mr. Wayland utterly shocked, incredulous of the little he did understand, and yet unable to go home until he should hear more; and the Major hardly less horrified, in the midst of his relief. "But where's Belamour!" he cried, "Your uncle, I mean."

"Where?" said Sir Amyas. "They said he was gone out."

"So they told me! And see here!"

Major Delavie produced Lady Belamour's note.

"A blind!" cried Sir Amyas, turning away under a strange stroke of pain and sham. "Oh! mother, mother!" and he dashed out of the room.

Poor Mr. Wayland sat down as one who could stand no longer. "Of what do they suspect her?" he said hoarsely.

"Sir," said the good Major, "I grieve sincerely for and with you. Opposition to this match with my poor child seems to have transported my poor cousin to strange and frantic lengths, but you may trust me to shield and guard her from exposure as far as may be."

Her husband only answered by a groan, and wrung Major Delavie's hand, but their words were interrupted by Sir Amyas's return. He had been to his uncle's chamber, and had found on the table a note addressed to the Major. Within was a inclosure directed to A. Belamour, Esq.

> "If you have found the way to the poor captive, for pity's sake
> come to her rescue. Be in the court with your faithful black
> by ten o'clock, and you may yet save on who loves and looks to
> you."

On the outer sheet was written—

> "I distrust this handwriting, and suspect a ruse. In case I do
> not return, send for Hargrave, Sandys, Godfrey, as witnesses to
> my sanity, and storm the fair one's fortress in person. A. B."

"It is not my Aurelia's writing," said the Major. "Bravest of friends, what has he not dared on her account!"

"This is too much!" cried Mr. Wayland, striving in horror against his convictions. "I cannot hear my beloved wife loaded with monstrous suspicions in her absence!"

"I am sorry to say this is no new threat ever since poor Belamour has crossed her path," said the Major.

"What have you done, sir!" asked Sir Amyas.

"I fear I have but wasted time," said the Major. "I have been to Hanover Square, and getting no admittance there, I came back in the hope you might be on the track with Betty—as, thank God, you were! The first thing to be done now is to find what she has done with Belamour," he added, rising up.

"That must fall to my share," said Mr. Wayland, pale and resolute. "Come with me, Amyas, your young limbs will easily return before the effect of the narcotic has passed, and I need fuller explanation."

Stillness than came on the Delavie party. The Major went up stairs, and sat by Aurelia's bed gazing with eyes dazzled with tears at the child he had so longed to see, and whom he found again in this strange trance. A doctor came, and quite confirmed Mr. Wayland's opinion, that the drug would not prove deleterious, provided the sleep was not disturbed, and Betty continued her watch, after hearing what her father knew of Mr. Belamour. She was greatly struck with the self-devotion that had gone with open eyes into so dreadful a snare as a madhouse of those days rather than miss the least chance of saving Aurelia.

"If we go by perils dared, the uncle is the true knight-errant," said she to her father. "I wonder which our child truly loves the best!"

"Betty!" said her father, scandalised.

"Ay, I know, Sir Amyas is a charming boy, but what a boy he is! And she has barely spoken with him or seen him, whereas Mr. Belamour has been kind to her for a whole twelvemonth. I know what I should do if I were in her place. I would declare that I intended to be married to the uncle, and would keep it!"

"He would think it base to put the question."

"He would; but indeed, dear sir, I think it would be but right and due to the dear child herself that she should have here free choice, and not be bound for ever by a deception! Yes, I know the poor boy's despair would be dreadful, but it would be better for them both than such a mistake."

"Hush! I hear him knocking at the door, you cruel woman."

The bedroom opened into the parlour the party had hired, so that both could come out and meet Sir Amyas with the door ajar, without relaxing their watch upon the sleeper. The poor young man looked pale, shocked, and sorrowful. "Well," said he, after having read in their looks that there was no change, "he knows the worst." Then on a further token of interrogation, "It may have been my fault; I took him, unannounced, through the whole suite of rooms, and in the closet at the end, with all the doors open, she was having an altercation with Mar. He was insisting on knowing what she had done with"—(he signed towards the other room) "she, upbraiding him with faithlessness. They were deaf to an approach, till Mr. Wayland, in a loud voice, ordered me back, saying 'it was no scene for a son.'"

"I trust it will not end in a challenge?" asked the Major, gravely.

"No, my father's infirmity renders him no fighting man, and I—I may not challenge my superior officer."

"But your uncle?" said Betty, much fearing that such a scene might have led to his being forgotten.

"I should have told you. We had not made many steps from hence before we met poor Jumbo wandering like a dog that had lost his master. Mr. Belamour had taken the precaution of giving Jumbo the pass-key, and not taking him into that house (some day I will pull every brick of it down), so he watched till by and by he saw a coach come out with all the windows closed, and as his master had bidden him in such a case, he kept along on the pavement near, and never lost sight of it till he had tracked it right across the City to a house with iron-barred windows inside a high wall. There it went in, and he could not follow, but he asked the people what place it was, and though they jeered at him, he made out that it was as we feared. Nay, do not be alarmed, sister, he will soon be with us. My poor father shut me out, and I know not what passed with my mother, but just as I could wait no longer to return to my dearest, he came out and told me that he had found out that my uncle was in a house at Moorfields, and he is gone himself to liberate him. He is himself a justice of the peace, and he will call for Dr. Sandys by the way, that there may be no difficulty. He is gone in the coach-and-four, with Jumbo on the box, so that matters will soon be righted."

"And a heroic champion set free," said Betty moving to return to her sister, when the others would not be denied having another look at the sweet slumberer, on whose face there was now a smile as if her dreams were marvellously lovely; or, as Betty thought, as if she knew their voices even in her sleep.

Sir Amyas had not seen his mother again. He only knew that Mr. Wayland had come out with a face as of one stricken to the heart, a sad contrast to that which had greeted him an hour before, and while the carriage was coming round, had simply said, "I did wrong to leave her."

It would not bear being talked over, and both son and kinsman took refuge in silence. Two hours more of this long day had passed, and then a coach stopped at the door. Sir Amyas hurried down in his eager anxiety, and came back with his uncle, holding him by the hand like a child, in his gladness, and Betty came out to meet them in the outer room with a face of grateful welcome and outstretched hands.

"Sir! sir! you have done more than all of us."

"Yet you and your young champion here were the victors," said Mr. Belamour.

"Ah, we dared and suffered nothing like you."

"I hope you did not suffer much," said the major, looking at the calm face and neatly-tied white hair, which seemed to have suffered no disarrangement.

"No," said Mr. Belamour, smiling, "my little friend Eugene, ay, and my nephew himself, are hoping to hear I was released from fetters and a heap of straw, but I took care to give them no opportunity. I merely told them they were under a mistake, and had better take care. I gave them a reference or two, but I saw plainly that was of no use, though they promised to send, and then I did exactly as they bade me, so as to deprive them of all excuse for meddling with me, letting them know that I could pay for decent treatment so long as I was in their hands."

"Did you receive it?"

"I was told in a mild manner, adapted to my intelligence, that if I behaved well, I might eat at the master's table, and have a room with only one inmate. Of the former I have not an engaging experience, either as to the fare, the hostess, or the company. Of the latter, happily I know little, as I only know that my comrade was to be a harmless gibbering idiot; of good birth, poor fellow. However, the sounds I heard, and the court I looked into, convinced me that my privileges were worth paying for."

He spoke very quietly, but he shuddered involuntarily, and Betty, unable to restrain her tears, retreated to her sister's side.

CHAPTER XXXVI
WAKING

So Love was still the Lord of all. — SCOTT.

The summer sun was sinking and a red glow was on the wall above Aurelia's head when she moved again, upon the shutting of the door, while supper was being taken by the gentlemen in the outer room.

Presently her lips moved, and she said, "Sister," not in surprise, but as if she thought herself at home, and as Betty gently answered, "Yes, my darling child," the same voice added, "I have had such a dream; I thought I was a chrysalis, and that I could not break my shell nor spread my wings."

"You can now, my sweet," said Betty, venturing to kiss her.

Recollection came. "Sister Betty, is it you indeed?" and she threw her arms round Betty's neck, clinging tight to her in delicious silence, till she raised her head and said: "No, this is not home. Oh, is it all true?"

"True that I have you again, my dear, dearest, sweetest child," said Betty. "Oh, thank God for it."

"Thank God," repeated Aurelia. "Now I have you nothing will be dreadful. But where am I? I thought once I was in a boat with you and Eugene, and some one else. Was it a dream? I can't remember anything since that terrible old woman made me drink the coffee. You have not come there, have you?"

"No, dear child, it was no dream that you were in a boat. We had been searching everywhere for you, and we were bringing you back sound, sound asleep," said Betty, in her tenderness speaking as it to a little child.

"I knew you would," said Aurelia; "I knew God would save me. Love is strong as death, you know," she added dreamily: "I think I felt it all round me in that sleep."

"That was what you murmured once or twice in your sleep," said Betty.

"And now, oh! it is so sweet to lie here and know it is you. And wasn't *he* there too?"

"Sir Amyas? Yes, my dear. He came for you. He and my father and the others are in the other room waiting for you to wake."

"I hear their voices," cried Aurelia, with a start, sitting up. "Oh! that's my papa's voice! Oh! how good it is to hear it!"

"I will call him as soon as I have set you a little in order. Are you sure you are well, my dearest? No headache?"

"Quite, quite well! Why, sister, I have not been ill; and if I had, I should skip to see you and hear their voices, only I wish they would speak louder! That's Eugene! Oh! they are hushing him. Let me make haste," and she moved with an alacrity that was most reassuring. "But I can't understand. Is it morning or evening?"

"Evening, my dear. They are at supper. Are not you hungry?"

"Oh, yes, I believe I am;" but as she was about to wash her hands: "My rings, my wedding-ring? Look in my glove!"

"No, they are not there my dear, they must have robbed you! And oh! Aurelia, what have you done to your hair?"

"My hair? It was all there this morning. Sister, it was that woman, I remember now, I was not quite sound asleep, but I had no power to move or cry out, and the woman was snipping and Loveday crying."

"Vile creature!" burst out Betty.

"My hair will grow!" said Aurelia; "but I had so guarded my wedding-ring—and what will he, Sir Amyas, think?"

Their voices were at this moment heard, and in another second Aurelia was held against her father's breast, as in broken words he sobbed out thanks for her restoration, and implored her pardon for having trusted her out of his care.

"Oh! sir, do not speak so! Dear papa, I have tried hard to do you no harm, and to behave well. Please, sir, give me your blessing."

"God bless you indeed, my child. He has blessed you in guarding you as your innocence deserved, though I did not. Ah! others are impatient. The poor old father comes second now."

After a few minutes spent in repairing the disorder of her dress, and her hands in those of her father and little brother, she was led to the outer room where in the twilight there was a rapturous rush, an embrace, a fondling of the hand in the manner more familiar to her than the figure from before whom it proceeded. She only said in her gentle plaintive tone, "Oh, sir, it was not my fault. They took away your rings."

"Nay," said a voice, new to her, "here are your rings, Lady Belamour. I must trust to your Christian charity to pardon her who caused you to be stripped of them."

The name of Lady Belamour made her start as that of her enemy, but a truly familiar tone said, "You need not fear, my kind friend. This is Mr. Wayland, who, to our great joy, has returned, and has come to restore your jewels."

"Indeed I am very glad yours is not lost," said Aurelia, not a little bewildered.

Mr. Wayland said a few words of explanation that his wife's agent at Greenwich had brought them back to her.

"Pray let me have them," entreated Sir Amyas; "I must put them on again!"

"Stay," said Major Delavie; "I can have such things done only under true colours and in the full light of day. The child is scarcely awake yet, and does not know one from the other! Why neither of you so much as know the colour of the eyes of the other! Can you tell me sir?"

"Heavenly," exclaimed the youth, in an ecstatic tone of self-defence, which set the Major laughing and saying, "My silly maid knows as little which gentleman put on the ring."

"I do, sir," said Aurelia indignantly; "I know his voice and hand quite well," and in the impulse she quitted her father's arm and put both hands into those of her young adorer, saying, "Pray sir, pardon me, I never thought to hurt you so cruelly."

There was a cry of, "My own, my dearest life," and she was clasped as she had been immediately after her strange wedding.

However, the sound of a servant's step made them separate instantly, and Betty begged that the supper might not be removed, since it was many hours since her sister had tasted food.

Sir Amyas and Betty hovered about her, giving her whatever she could need, in the partial light, while the others stood apart, exchanging such explanations as they could. Mr. Wayland said he must report himself to Government on the morrow; but intended afterwards to take his wife to Bowstead, whither she had sent all her children with Mrs. Dove. There was a great tenderness in his tone as he spoke of her, and when he took leave Mr. Belamour shrugged his shoulders saying, "She will come round him again!"

"It is true enough that he ought not to have left her to herself," said the Major.

"You making excuses for her after the diabolical plot of to-day?" said Mr. Belamour; "I could forgive her all but that letter to you."

"My Lady loves her will," quoted the Major; "it amounts to insanity in some women, I believe."

"So I might say does men's infatuation towards women like her," muttered Mr. Belamour.

By this time Aurelia had finished her meal, and Betty was anxious to carry her off without any more excitement, for she was still drowsy and confused. She bade her father good night, asking his blessing as of old, but when Mr. Belamour kissed her hand and repeated the good night, she said, "Sir, I ought to have trusted you; I am so sorry."

"It is all well now, my child," he said, soothingly, understanding Betty's wish; "Sleep, and we will talk it over."

So the happy sisters once more slept in each other's arms, till in the early summer morning Betty heard the whole story from Aurelia, now fully herself, though she slumbered again after all was poured into her sister's bosom.

Betty had sympathised step by step, and felt even more strongly than Harriet that the situation had been intolerable for womanhood, and that only Aurelia's childishness could have endured it so long. Only the eldest sister held that it would have been right and honourable to have spoken before flashing out the flame; but when, with many tears of contrition, Aurelia owned that she had long thought so, and longed to confess it, what could the motherly sister do but kiss the tears away, and rejoice that the penance was over which had been borne with such constancy and self-devotion.

Then Betty rose quietly, and after giving thanks on her knees that the gentle spirit had passed through all unscathed, untainted with even the perception of evil, she applied herself to the adaptation of one of her morning caps to her poor shorn lamb's head. Nor did Aurelia wake again till her father came to the door to make sure that all was well with his recovered treasure, and to say that Loveday would recover for her the box of clothes, which old Madge had hidden.

Loveday had gone back to her mistress, who either had not discovered her betrayal, or, as things had turned out, could not resent it.

So, fresh and blooming, Aurelia came out into the sitting-room, whence her father held out his arms to her. He would have her all to himself for a little while, since even Eugene was gone to his daily delight, the seeing the changing of the guard.

"And now, my child, tell me," he said, when he had heard a little of her feelings through these adventures, "what would you have me do? Remember, such a wedding as yours goes for nothing, and you are still free to choose either or neither of your swains."

"Oh, papa!" in a remonstrating tone.

"You were willing to wed your old hermit?"

"I was content *then*. He was very kind to me."

"Content then, eh? Suppose you were told he was your real husband?"

"Sir, he is not!" cried Aurelia, frightened.

"If he were?"

"I would try to do my duty," she said, in a choked voice.

"Silly child, don't cry. And how, if after these fool's tricks it turns out that the other young spark is bound to that red-faced little spitfire and cannot have you?"

"Papa, don't!" she cried. "You know he is my husband in my heart, and always will be, and if he cannot come back to me take me home, and I will try to be a good daughter to you," and she hid her face on his shoulder.

"Poor child, it is a shame to tease her," said her father, raising up her face; "I only wanted to know which of them you would wish to put on the ring again. I see. You need not be afraid, you shall have the ruby one. But as for the little gold one, wait for that till it is put on in church, my dear. Ah! and there's the flutter of his wings, or rather the rattle of his spurs. Now then, young people, you shall not be hindered from a full view of each others lineaments. It is the first time you ever had a real sight of each other, neither of you being in a swoon, is it not? I trust you do not repent upon further acquaintance. Aurelia got as far as the shoe-buckles once, I believe."

"She will get no farther this time, sir, if you annihilate her with your pleasantry," said Betty, fully convinced by this time.

"Ah! young Love has made himself more dazzling than ever," continued the Major, too delighted to be stopped. "The fullest dress uniform, I declare; M. le Capitaine is bent on doing honour to the occasion."

"Would that it were on for no other reason, sir," said Sir Amyas; "but the King and Queen have taken it into their heads to go off to Kew and here am I under orders to command the escort. I verily believe it is all spite on the Colonel's part, for Russell would have exchanged the turn with me, but he sent down special orders for me. I have but half an hour to spend here, and when I shall be able to get back again Heaven only knows."

However, he and Aurelia were permitted to improve that half hour to the utmost in their own way, while the Major and Betty were reading a long and characteristic letter from Mrs. Arden, inquiring certainly for her sister's fate, but showing far more solicitude in proving that she (Harriet Arden) had acted a wise, prudent, and sisterly part, and that it was most unreasonable and cruel to treat her as accountable for her sister's disappearance. It was really making her quite ill, and Mr. Arden was like a man—so disagreeable about it.

Betty was very glad this epistle had not come till it was possible to laugh at it. She would have sat down to reply to it at once, had not a billet been brought in from the widow of one of her father's old brother officers who had heard of his being in town, and begged him to bring his daughter to see her, excusing herself for not waiting on Miss Delavie, as she was very feeble and infirm.

It was a request that could not be refused, but Aurelia was not equipped for such a visit, and shrank timidly from showing herself. So when Mr. Belamour came down it was agreed that she should remain at home under his protection, in which she could be very happy, though his person was as strange to her as his voice was familiar. Indeed she felt as if a burden was on her mind till she could tell him of her shame at having failed in the trust and silence that he had enjoined on her.

"My child," he said, "we have carried it too far. It was more than we ought to have required of you, and I knew it. I had made up my mind, and told my nephew that the first time you really asked I should tell the whole truth, and trust to your discretion, while of course he wished for nothing more."

"As my sister said, it was my fault."

"Nay, I think you had good cause to stand on your defence, and I cannot have you grieve over it. You have shown an unshaken steadiness under trial since, such as ought indeed to be compensation."

"I deserved it all," said Aurelia; "and I do hope that I am a little wiser and less foolish for it all; a little more of a woman," she added, blushing.

"A soul trained by love and suffering, as in the old legend," said Mr. Belamour thoughtfully.

Thoroughly pleasant was here *tete-a-tete* with him, especially when she artlessly asked him whether her dear sister were not all she had told him, and he fervently answered that indeed she was "a perfect lesson to all so-called beauties of what true loveliness of a countenance can be."

"Oh, I am so glad," cried Aurelia. "I never saw a face—a woman's I mean—that I like as well as my dear sister's!"

She was sorry when they were interrupted by a call from Mr. Wayland, who had reported himself at the Secretary of War, but could do no more that day, and had come to inquire for her. He and Mr. Belamour drew apart into a window, and conversed in a low voice, and then they came to her, and Mr. Wayland desired to know from where she found the recipe for the cosmetic which had nearly cost her so dearly.

"It was in a shelf in the wainscoting, in a sort of little study at that house," said Aurelia.

"Among other papers?"

"Quantities of other papers."

"Of what kind?"

"Letters, and bills, and wills, and parchments! Oh, so dusty! Some were on paper tumbling to pieces, and some on tiny slips of parchment."

"And you read them all?"

"I had to read them to see what they were, as well as I could make out, and sorted them and tied them up in bundles."

"Can you tell me whether they were Delavie wills?"

"I should think they were. I know that the oldest of all were Latin, and I could make nothing out in them but something about *Manoriem* and Carminster, and what looked like the names of some of the fields at home."

"Do you think you could show me those slips?"

"I do not suppose any one has touched them."

"Then, my dear young lady, you would confer a great favour on me if you would allow Mr. Belamour and myself to escort you to Delavie and show us these papers. I fear it may be alarming and distressing."

"Oh no, sir, I know no harm can happen to me where Mr. Belamour is," she said, smiling.

"It may be very important," he said, and she went to put on her hood.

"Surely," said Mr. Wayland, "the title-deeds cannot have been left there?"

"No. The title-deeds to the main body of the property are at Hargrave's. I have seen them, at the time of my brother's marriage; but still this may be what was wanting."

"Yet the sending this child to search is presumption that no such document existed."

"Of course no one supposed it did," said Mr. Wayland, on the defence again.

Aurelia was quickly ready in her little hood and kerchief, and trim high-heeled shoes. She was greatly surprised to find how near she had been to her friends during these last few days of her captivity, and when Madge obeyed the summons to the door, the old woman absolutely smiled to see her safe, and the little terrier danced about her in such transports that she begged to take him back with her.

She opened the door of the little empty book room, where nothing stood except the old bureau. That, she said, had been full of letters, but all the oldest things had been within a door opening in the wainscot, which she should never have found had not Bob pushed it open in his search for rats, and then she found a tin case full of papers and parchments, much older, she thought, than the letters. She had tied them up together, and easily produced them.

Mr. Wayland handed them to Mr. Belamour, whose legal eye was better accustomed to crabbed old documents. A conversation that had begun on the way about Fay and Letty was resumed, and interested both their father and Aurelia so much that they forgot to be impatient, until Mr. Belamour looked up from his examination, saying, "This is what was wanting. Here is a grant in the 12th year of Henry III. to Guglielmus ab Vita and the heirs male of his body to the Manor, lying without the city of Carminster, and here are three wills of successive lords of Delavie expressly mentioning heirs male. Now the deeds that I have seen do not go beyond 1539, when Henry Delavie had a grant of the Grange and lands belonging to Carminster Abbey—the place, in fact, where the Great House stands, and there is in that no exclusion of female heirs. But the Manor house can certainly be proved to be entailed in the male line alone, according to what was, I believe, the tradition of the family."

"There is no large amount of property involved, I fear," said Mr. Wayland.

"There is an old house, much out of repair, and a few farms worth, may be, 200 pounds a year, a loss that will not be material to you, sir, I hope."

"Do you mean—?" said Aurelia, not daring to ask farther.

"I mean, my dear young lady," said Mr. Wayland, "that your researches have brought to light the means of doing tardy justice to your good father."

"His right to the Manor House is here established," explained Mr. Belamour. "It will not be a matter of favour of my Lady's, but, as my brother supposed, he ought to have been put in possession on the old Lord's death."

"And Eugene will be a gentleman of estate," cried Aurelia, joyously. "Nor will any one be able to drive out my dear father! Oh! how happy I am."

Both she and Mr. Belamour spared Mr. Wayland the knowledge of my Lady's many broken promises, and indeed she was anxious to get back to the *Royal York*, lest her father and sister should have returned, and think her again vanished.

They all met at the door, and much amazed were the Major and Betty to encounter her with her two squires. Mr. Wayland took the Major to show him the parchments. Betty had her explanation from her sister and Mr. Belamour.

"You actually ventured back to that dreadful house," she said, looking at them gratefully.

"You see what protectors I had," said Aurelia, with a happy smile.

"Yes," said Betty, "I have been longing to say—only I cannot," for she was almost choked by a great sob, "how very much we owe to you, sir. I could say it better if I did not feel it so much." And she held out her hand.

"You cannot owe to me a tithe of what I owe to your sister," said Mr. Belamour, "and through her to you, madam. Much as nature had done for her, never would she have been to the miserable recluse the life and light-bringing creature she was, save for the 'sister' she taught me to know and love, even before I saw her."

A wonderful revelation here burst on Aurelia, the at least half-married woman, and she fled precipitately, smiling to herself in ecstasy, behind her great fan.

Betty, never dreaming of the drift of the words, so utterly out of the reach of love did she suppose herself, replied, composedly, "Our Aurelia is a dear good girl, and I am thankful that through all her trials she has so proved herself. I am glad she has been a comfort to you, sir. She—"

"And will not you complete the cure, and render the benefit lasting?" said Mr. Belamour, who had never let go the hand she had given him in gratitude, and now gave it a pressure that conveyed, for the first time, his meaning.

"Oh!" she cried, trying to take it away, "your kindness and gratitude are leading you too far, sir. A hideous old fright like me, instead of a lovely young thing like her! It is an absurdity."

"Stay, Miss Delavie. Remember that your Aurelia's roses and lilies were utterly wasted on me; I never thought whether she was beautiful save when others raved about her. I never saw her till yesterday; but the voice, the goodness, the amiability, in fact all that I did truly esteem and prize in her I had already found matured and mellowed together with that beauty of countenance which is independent of mere skin-deep complexion and feature. You know my history, and how far I am from being able to offer you a fresh untouched young heart, such as my nephew brings to the fair Aurelia; but the devotion of my life will be yours if you will accept it."

"Sir, I cannot listen to you. You are very good, but I can never leave my father. Oh, let me go away!"

CHAPTER XXXVII
MAKING THE BEST OF IT

At last the Queen said, "Girl, I bid thee rise,
For now thou hast found favour in mine eyes,
And I repent me of the misery
That in this place thou hast endured me,
Altho' because of it the Joy indeed
Shall now be mine, that pleasure is thy meed."
MORRIS.

Those were evil times, and the court examples were most corrupting, so that a splendid and imperious woman like Urania, Lady Belamour, had found little aid from public opinion when left to herself by the absence of her second husband. Selfish, unscrupulous, and pleasure-loving she was by nature, but during Sir Jovian Belamour's lifetime she had been kept within bounds. Then came a brief widowhood, when debt and difficulty hurried her into accepting Mr. Wayland, a thoughtful scientific man, whose wealth had accumulated without much volition of his own to an extent that made her covet his alliance. Enthralled by her charm of manner, he had not awakened to the perception of what she really was during the few years that had elapsed before he was sent abroad, and she refused to accompany him.

Then it was that wealth larger than she had before commanded, and a court appointment, involved her in more dangerous habits. Her debts, both of extravagance and of the gaming table, were enormous, trenching hard on the Delavie property, and making severe inroads on Mr. Wayland's means; but the Belamour estates being safely tied up, she had only been able to borrow on her dower. She had sinned with a high hand, after the fashion of the time, and then, in terror at the approaching return of her husband, had endeavoured to conceal the ravages of her extravagance by her bargain for her son's hand.

The youth, bred up at a distance, and then the companion of his step-father, had on his return found his home painfully altered in his two years' absence, and had been galled and grieved by the state of things, so that even apart from the clearing of his prospects, the relief was great. The quarrel with Colonel Mar that Mr. Wayland had interrupted was not made up. There was no opportunity, for Mr. Wayland at once removed his family to Bowstead, there to remain while he transacted his business in London.

Moreover Mr. Belamour and Mr. Wayland agreed in selling the young baronet's commission. The Major allowed that it was impossible that he should remain under the command of his present Colonel, but regretted that he should not continue in the service, declaring it the best school for a young man, and that he did not want to see his son-in-law a muddle-brained sporting country squire. He would have had Sir Amyas exchange into the line, and see a little service before settling down, but Maria Theresa had not as yet set Europe in a blaze, and in the absence of a promising war Sir Amyas did more incline to his uncle's representations of duties to tenants and to his county, and was even ready to prepare himself for them when he should be of sufficient age to undertake them. However, in the midst of the debates a new scheme was made. Mr. Belamour had been called upon and welcomed by his old friends, who, being men of rank and influence, had risen in life while he was immured at Bowstead. One of these had just received a diplomatic appointment at Vienna, and in spite of insular ignorance of foreign manners was at a loss for a capable suite. Mr. Belamour suggested Major Delavie, as from his long service in Austria likely to be very useful. The Envoy caught at the idea, and the thought of once more seeing his old comrades enchanted the Major, whose only regret was that his hero, Prince Eugene, had been dead three years; but to visit his grave would be something. Appointments ran in families, so that nothing could be easier than to obtain one for the young baronet; and though Mr. Belamour did not depend on his own health enough to accept anything, he was quite willing to join the party, and to spend a little time abroad, while his nephew was growing somewhat older, making an essay of his talents, and at any rate putting off the commencement of stagnation. Thus matters settled themselves, the only disappointed member of the family being Mrs. Arden, who thought it very hard that she could not stir any one up to request an appointment of her husband as chaplain—not even himself!

Mr. Wayland was at once called upon to go out to America to superintend the defences of the Canadian frontier, and he resolved on taking his family out, obtaining land, and settling there permanently. He would pay all my Lady's debts, but she should never again appear in London society, and cruel exile as it must seem to her, he trusted that his affection and tenderness would in time reconcile her to the new way of life, knowing as she did that he had forgiven much that had made him look like a crushed and sorrowful man in the midst of all the successes and the honours he received from his country.

She remained quietly at Bowstead, and none of them saw her except her son and the Major, to the latter of whom her husband brought a message that she would esteem it a favour if he would come and visit her there, the day before he returned to Carminster. Very much affected, the good Major complied with her request, went down with Mr. Wayland and spent a night at Bowstead.

He found that she had accepted her fate with the good grace of a woman whose first instinct was not to make herself disagreeable. She was rather pale, and not "made up" in any way, but exquisitely though more simply dressed, and more beautiful than ever, her cousin thought, as he always did whenever he came into her presence. She was one of those people whose beauty is always a fresh surprise, and she was far more self-possessed than he was.

"So, Cousin Harry, where am I to begin my congratulations! I did you and unwitting service when I sent your daughter to search among those musty old parchments. I knew my father believed in the existence of some such document, but I thought all those hoards in Delavie House were devoid of all legal importance, and had been sifted again and again. Besides, I always meant to settle that old house upon you."

"I have always heard so, cousin," he answered.

"But it was such a mere trifle," she added, "that it never seemed worth while to set the lawyers to work about that alone, so I waited for other work to be in hand."

"There is a homely Scottish proverb, my Lady, which declares that the scrapings of the muckle pot are worth the wee pot fu'. A mere trifle to you is affluence to us."

"I am sincerely rejoiced at it, Harry" (no doubt she thought she was), "you will keep up the old name, while my scrupulous lord and master gives up my poor patrimony to the extortionate creditors for years to come. It is well that the young lovers have other prospects. So Harry, you see after all, I kept my word, and your daughter is provided for," she continued with an arch smile. "Pretty creature, I find my son bears me more malice than she does for the robbery that was perpetrated on her. It was too tempting, Harry. Nature will repair her loss, but at out time of life we must beg, borrow, or steal."

"That was the least matter," said the Major gravely.

"This is the reason why I wished to see you," said my Lady, laying her white hand on his, "I wanted to explain."

"Cousin, cousin, had not you better leave it alone?" said Major Delavie. "You know you can always talk a poor man out of his senses at the moment."

"Yet listen, Harry, and understand my troubles. Here I was pledged, absolutely pledged, to give my son to Lady Aresfield's daughter. I do not know whether she may not yet sue me for breach of contract, though Wayland has repaid her the loans she advanced me; and on the other hand, in spite of all my precautions, Mar had obtained a sight of your poor daughter, and I knew him well enough to be aware that to put her entirely and secretly out of his reach was the only chance preserving her from his pursuit. I had excellent accounts of the worthy man to whom I meant her to be consigned, and I knew that when she wrote to you as a West Indian queen you would be able to forgive your poor cousin. I see what you would say, but sending her to you was impossible, since I had to secure her both from Amyas and from Mar. It would only have involved you in perplexities innumerable, and might have led even to bloodshed! I may not have acted wisely, but weak women in difficulties know not which path to choose."

"There is always the straight one," said he.

"Ah! you strong men can easily says so, but for us poor much-tried women! However," she said suddenly changing her tone, "Love has check-mated us, and I rejoice. Your daughter will support the credit of the name! I am glad the new Lady Belamour will not be that little termagant milkmaid Belle, whom circumstances compelled me to inflict upon my poor boy! The title will be your daughter's alone. I have promised my husband that in the New World I will sink into plain Mrs. Wayland." Then with a burst of genuine feeling she exclaimed, "He *is* a good man, Harry."

"He is indeed, Urania, I believe you will yet be happier than you have ever been."

"What, among barbarians who never saw a loo-table, and get the modes three months too late! And you are laughing at me, but see I am a poor frivolous being, not sufficient to myself like your daughters! They say

Aurelia was as sprightly as a spring butterfly all the time she was shut up at Bowstead with no company save the children and old Belamour!"

"They are lovely children, madam, Aurelia dotes on them, and you will soon find them all you need."

"Their father is never weary of telling me so. He is never so happy as when they hang about him and tell him of Cousin Aura, or Sister Aura as they love to call her."

"It was charming to see them dance round her when he brought them to spend the day with her. Mr. Wayland brought his good kinswoman, who will take charge of them on the voyage, and Aurelia was a little consoled at the parting by seeing how tender and kind she is with them."

"Aye! If I do not hate that woman it will be well, for she is as much a duenna for me as governess for the children! Heigh-ho! what do not our follies bring on us? We poor creatures should never be left to the great world."

The pretty air of repentance was almost irresistible, well as the Major knew it for the mood of the moment, assumed as what would best satisfy him.

"I rejoice," she went on, "in spite of my lovely daughter-in-law's discretion, she will be well surrounded with guardians. Has the excellent Betty consented?"

"At last, madam. My persuasions were vain till she found that Mr. Belamour would gladly come with us to Austria, and that she should be enabled to watch over both her young sister and me."

"There, again, I give myself credit, Harry. Would the sacred flame ever have awakened in yonder misanthrope had I not sent your daughter to restore him to life?" She spoke playfully, but the Major could not help thinking she had persuaded herself that all his present felicity was owing to her benevolence, and that she would persuade him of it too, if she went on much longer looking at him so sweetly. He *would* not tax her with the wicked note she had written to account for Mr. Belamour's disappearance, and which she had forgotten; he felt that he could not impel one, whom he could not but still regard with tenderness, to utter any more untruths and excuses.

"By the by," she added, "does your daughter take my waiting-maid after all? I would have forgiven her, for she is an admirable hairdresser, but Wayland says he cannot have so ingenious person in his house; though after all I do not see that she is a bit worse than others of her condition, and she herself insists on trying to become Aurelia's attendant, vowing that the sight of her is as good as any Methodist sermon!"

"Precisely, madam. We were all averse to taking her with us, but Aurelia said she owed her much gratitude; and she declared so earnestly that the sight of my dear child brought back all the virtuous and pious thoughts she had forgotten, that even Betty's heart was touched, and she is to go with us, on trial."

"Oh! she is as honest as regards money and jewels as ever I knew a waiting-maid, but for the rest!" Lady Belamour shrugged her shoulders. "However, one is as good as another, and at least she will never let her lady go a fright! See here, Harry. These are the Delavie jewels: I shall never need them more: carry them to your daughters."

"Nay, your own daughters, Urania."

"Never mind the little wretches. Their father will provide for them, and they will marry American settlers in the forests. What should they do with court jewels? It is his desire. See here, this suit of pearls is what I wore at my wedding with Amyas's father, I should like Aurelia to be married in them. Farewell, Harry, you did better for yourself than if you had taken me. Yet maybe I might been a better woman—-" She stopped short as she looked at his honest face, and eyes full of tears.

"No, Urania," he said, "man's love could not have done for you what only another Love can do. May you yet find that and true Life."

The sisters were not married at the same time. Neither Mr. Belamour nor his Elizabeth could endure to make part of the public pageant that it was thought well should mark the *real* wedding at Bowstead. So their banns were put up at St. Clement Danes, and one quiet morning they slipped out, with no witnesses but the Major, Aurelia, and Eugene, and were wedded there in the most unobtrusive manner.

As to the great marriage, a month later at Bowstead, there was a certain bookseller named Richardson, who by favour of Hargrave got a view of it, and who is thought there to have obtained some ideas for the culminating wedding of his great novel.

A little later, the following letter was written from the excellent Mrs. Montagu to her correspondent Mrs. Elizabeth Carter. "There was yesterday presented, preparatory to leaving England for Vienna, the young Lady Belamour, incomparably the greatest beauty who has this year appeared at

Court. Every one is running after her, but she appears perfectly unconscious of the *furore* she has excited, and is said to have been bred up in all simplicity in the country, and to be as good as she is fair. Her young husband, Sir Amyas Belamour, is a youth of much promise, and they seem absolutely devoted, with eyes only for each other. They are said to have gone through a series of adventures as curious as they are romantic; and indeed, when they made their appearance, there was a general whisper, begun by young Mr. Horace Walpole, of

"CUPID AND PSYCHE."